I0564093

This novel is dedicated to both the historical characters involved and the ones I have known in some four plus decades in the North: from the hardscrabble miners in the Fortymile country and the Klond-ike who still moil for gold, to the Native peoples both along the Yukon River and across the North, to the lost loves of Klondike Kate Rockwell and Alexander Pantages, Swiftwater Bill Gates and Gussie Lamore, the modern goodtime girls of the last great gold rush that was painted with oil, and the four women whose ashes grace Mt. Susitna, the Sleeping Lady, and the one whose ashes lie above Eagle River Alaska.

With grateful acknowledgement to Charlie Franco, editor and world traveler at Montag, Mara Renee Briana Hodges, my book editor who is always a pleasure to work with, Rick Febre who worked with me on the cover, and Amanda Ashton at Blush Book Design who formatted and finally got this project finished.

BRUCE LEE BOND

TREASURES *of* THE NIGHT

MONTAG

Montag Press
ISBN: 978-1-940233-24-6
Cover art © 2015 Rick Febre
Cover, layout, & e-book © 2015 Blush Book Design

Montag Press Team:
Project Editor – Mara Hodges
Managing Director – Charlie Franco

A Montag Press Book
www.montagpress.com
Montag Press
1066 47th Ave. Unit #9
Oakland CA 94601 USA

Montag Press, the burning book with the hatchet cover, the skewed word mark and the portrayal of the long-suffering fireman mascot are trademarks of Montag Press.

Printed & Digitally Originated in the United States of America
10 9 8 7 6 5 4 3 2 1

ALSO BY AUTHOR

The Broken Coast, a novel, published by Montag Press Collective in the Lorelei series.

Honor Thy Father, published by Sirens Call Publications in the Slaughterhouse, Vol. #2, Serial Killer Edition.

Girls' Day Out, published by Fox Spirit Books in the Girl at the End of the World Anthology in the United Kingdom and Commonwealth countries.

Midnight Lunch (a Lorelei story in modern Alaska) coming out in the Night to Dawn Anthology by Night to Dawn Magazine & Books LLC.

The Well of Souls, published in Bones, Vol. #2 by James Ward Kirk.

BRUCE LEE BOND

TREASURES *of* THE NIGHT

Contents

PART ONE
The Gilded Promise

Contents

PART TWO
The Golden Gift

PART ONE
The Gilded Promise

I.

ALICE MARY BLEW A RED GLOB FROM HER NOSE AND STAGGERED INTO A little shack on Fourth Avenue clutching a poke of gold.

Honey Bee shrieked and plunked Alice Mary down in a squeaky chair. She scanned the muddy street and slammed the door before pressing a towel to her best friend's swollen cheeks as she glared out the tiny window at the back of a man astride a wheeled sled pulled by dogs.

Alice Mary's green eyes widened at a vision of Fred's grinning face and the flash of a gold tooth. She trembled as something rose in her gorge. Fred saw the tiny blonde from Virginia as nothing more than a rag to leave his spilled seed in: a slave who was born to grovel on the floor of her crib at his pleasure. His laughter echoed in her head and awoke her at odd times from dreams of her own cousin who had come to her bed when she was much too young as their faces merged. Fred had made a habit of terrorizing girls on the Line, and the damn Mounties wouldn't do a thing until he'd actually hurt one so badly they had to. Alice Mary gazed at the bruises on Honey Bee's forearm he'd left the night before and ground her teeth. Fred was everything she hated, and he stank. She'd give anything to see him die.

Honey Bee lifted Alice's quaking chin and gently dabbed at the corners of her mouth. "Dammit, stay *still*, girl!" They hugged, and Honey wiped a tear from her lover's cheek.

Alice Mary gulped air and ground her teeth. "Goddamn it! Ah forgot my goddamn knife!"

———

Two blocks away in the Empire Hotel, Lorelei shook off the girls' travails and opened her eyes. She had her own business to attend to, and there were many men like Fred Dodge in Dawson City this fall. Still, it would be a pleasure to take Fred on a little trip into the hills. She detached herself from the girls' travails, rolled off the bed, and walked to the window.

Dawn spread its coral vault over hills golden with birch too small to cut for firewood scattered amongst the dark stumps of spruce. Dry fireweed shed a million downy flecks over the Yukon's silt-brown water to be sent dancing in the smoke of riverboats. A long line of men bent under packs marched down a ramp onto a quay, overwhelming four young women in heavy pea coats who were newly arrived in this northern Eldorado.

She drew the drapes, brushed raven hair from a white face, and turned blue-green eyes upon Jack, who sat in a chair of polished walnut leaning against the red and gold wallpaper. His oiled hair had made a spot on the shiny embossed fleur-de-lis and smudged the snout of a crimson lion. Jack winked as his habitual Celtic grin became a yawn.

"I don't know, Jack." A barely perceptible ripple started at bare white shoulders and traveled all the way to her toes. It held his gaze, which was quite against his will, as he was trying to put her into a position in which she would have no other choice, but with Lorelei he couldn't help himself as her dimpled smile lit the room. "I'm fine where I am."

"Come on, Lorelei! You can have the whole damn place to do as ya please. None of the girls in this town can hold a candle to ya, and don't tell me ya don't know it. Sweet Jesus, you and I are perfect partners for a resort. I'll hold the fort and move the whiskey, and you just soften up the fools' 'eads a bit and perhaps do a wee bit'a dancin'. Let me show ya the big ol' safe I've got in the basement to keep your loot in. It took a bloody month for ten men to dig it in this damn frozen ground. It's got stone walls and a floor nobody can tunnel into. I got it—"

"Off the Captain of the Columbian. He bought it in St. Michael from an Arab trader who got it from an English steamer off Nome that was repairing its boilers. I believe it belonged to a Lord Chumleigh, who was rather strapped for cash after a night of gambling."

The chair's legs dropped to the floor, and Jack ran a hand sheathed in gold nugget rings across his face. "Damn," Jack's sandy eyebrows furrowed over pale blue eyes, "and which one o' me girls been tellin' ya what's about in me digs, might I ask?"

"Why don't you just say you want me to help you fleece anyone with enough gold, keep the other women in line, and keep you happy in a bed, Jack?"

Jackk leaned back with hands behind his head and chewed at his mustache. It was drooping this morning, as he had failed to wax it after a night with Lorelei. He studied her in the half-light of dawn coming from behind the curtains. She seemed to be moving even when standing still, and her remarkable eyes that were both blue and green and shot with the strangest flecks of red simply mesmerized him. Most goodtime girls were as easy for him as choosing a decent cigar, but Lorelei was anything but. He shook a head swimming with the remnants of whiskey and cocaine, and rubbed his reddened eyes. "I surely do love your ways, lass. Tell me, was it Otto?"

"No, Jack."

"Somebody's been tellin' ya the doin's at me resort."

"Actually no. Now, will you do something for me?"

He ran palms down corduroy pants legs and exhaled. "Name it, lovely."

"I want the room with a bath upstairs at the back of your place, with heavy shutters installed."

"It faces the slope already lass, and will be dark as pitch come winter. If you're worried about security I'll put up bars, but shutters—"

"That is my wish. And if I have another lover you shall remember that our relationship is based upon profit alone, and not possession of me." Her eyes seemed to grow larger. "I can kill you Jack."

An opaque tide of forgetting washed over him as her words passed the portal of rational thought, sinking where she aimed them even as his conscious mind lost their meaning. Jack righted the chair, rubbed his forehead, and wiped his hands. "Then... you're ready to move in?"

"Yes, and I shall require privacy beginning today. You may continue to have access to me at times, but it shall be on my schedule, not yours. Now, you should have breakfast at the Golden North as you'll meet someone there who might be useful to the both of us."

"What in 'ell—"

"Do we have an agreement?"

Jack stood up, scooped up his nugget encrusted pocket watch on its golden fob, and slipped his arms into the shoulder holster in which he carried a short-barreled Webley revolver. The North West Mounted Police had banned pistols in Dawson, but Jack (like many others) managed to hide one under his clothes. He put his coat on, tugged the sleeves down, and rotated his hands, examining his cuffs to ascertain whether they were of equal length. Jack took a cigar from his pocket, put it in his mouth, put his derby hat on his head, and winked.

She grinned. The clothes Jack had spent so much on were worthless outside of town. The miners, trappers, and Indians would look at him in mirth and amazement should he venture beyond the confines of Dawson, the riverboats, or the saloons of Grand Forks. Yet in his establishment he was King of the Klondike—at least in his own mind. "And don't forget to have a good breakfast."

"You're a charming and considerate woman, my dear." He tipped his hat. "I'll have Otto come for your things within the hour. If you should like the loan of a firearm I have a wall full in my study, and more in—"

"That won't be necessary."

"You're a spirited girl. I don't know how I'd do as a comely lady in these parts, truly I don't."

"We have our ways."

"That ya do lass." Jack produced a match to light his cigar.

Lorelei raised a slim white hand, and Jack's fingers froze in place refusing to strike the match on the underside of the table. "Not in here, and I don't want my things moved until dark. Otto's sleeping off his whiskey anyway." She yawned, "See you tonight." She brushed soft lips across his cheek, guided him across the room, and shut the door behind him.

Jack stood in the hall flexing his fingers and examining scarred knuckles above the fat gold rings used both as show and in fights. With a shake of his head, he struck the match on the alder wainscoting and puffed the cigar into a burn. It was impossible to get a well-humidified one this far north, but some miner would give him five dollars in dust for the thing, just like any other luxury during a gold rush.

He stepped onto the wooden sidewalk along Queen Street and shaded his eyes from a rising sun in the southeast. The smell of fried potatoes came to him on the bite of fall air, and his stomach growled in response. Lorelei had been quite right about his needing to eat. He was damn hungry.

The welcome scent of breakfast mixed with a faint moldy smell, as if someone had left wet socks under the trees. During his first autumn in the Klondike, Jack had found the scent of leaves decomposing before being locked in the vise of winter most unpleasant. Now, it was familiar, like an old friend. Fall brought winter, and winter brought prospectors with a summer's wash-up who would spend all their loot in town if they hadn't caught the last sternwheeler to White Horse, or downriver for the strikes at Nome. It was the smell of money.

As he crossed Second toward Front, two goodtime girls he'd swindled a dozen newcomer *Cheechakos* with sashayed out of the Bank of British North America and waved. He nodded slightly, not ready for a show of recognition, as a yellowleg Mountie in his red coat and tan hat who he didn't know was standing nearby and eying them.

The log edifice of the Golden North still had the adjoining tent up with its wooden floor, and smoke was rising from stoves that hadn't been hauled in for the winter yet. Jack stepped smartly into the tent. He loved showing off his fine clothes along the waterfront and checking arrivals from the riverboats. Both newly rich miners and hopeful Cheechakos were often taken in by the first thing they saw and wouldn't wander into a place like Jack's up Harper Street without some urging, like the offer of a free drink, a card game, a cigar, or the golden implication of a tryst with a woman. Or, a black ball of opium. Or a tiny green vial, filled with cocaine. Or, if they became a problem, a wee dose of chloral hydrate in their cups, with the blessing and good graces of Mickey Finn. Whatever it took, Jack Finley was ready to provide it.

He walked to a corner where he could scan the crowd with his back to the canvas wall and sat at a table.

The Chinese girl Tzu Bai everyone called Suzy showed up in the blink of an eye and swiped at the already clean tabletop with a green rag. "Good morning Mista Jackie!" She curtsied, "You likey blekfast?"

"You bet Suzy, what's good?"

"Plenty fresh caribou, but I know you like poak."

"That I do lass."

"Special sausage we have from German man's pigs across river, very fresh, very nice."

"Excellent, and eggs?"

"Yes, yes, very fresh from chicken man in West Dawson, not old off boat. Fresh bake bread, blueberry jam with much sugar—"

"All of it, and coffee, plenty coffee."

"Right now, Mista Jackie." Suzy hurried to the kitchen, where she let out a stream of Cantonese to her father Chan, who was cooking.

"With cream and sugar lass!" Jack examined her slim backside under the calico dress and apron. Suzy was a pretty piece and one of the very few girls of such an age and figure who wasn't working the saloons, theaters, or the new Segregated District along Fourth Avenue where the Mounties had moved the whores from Paradise Alley after last April's fire. It was a damn shame to waste such an obvious asset, but her father wouldn't dream of letting a white man touch her, and the restaurant was doing well. A speculator had offered Chan twenty thousand in gold just for the property it was on for a warehouse and dock. Of course, even though Chan had been grandfathered in by his relations with some of the early arrivals, including Joe Ladue himself, if they *were* thrown out of the Territory to join the other Chinese kept out of the Klondike by the Head Tax and the general deportment of the Mounties, someone would have to take the property in a hurry. Jack grinned at the thought.

Suzy placed a steaming mug of coffee, a can of evaporated milk, and a hard brown cone of sugar in a bowl before him, and Jack twisted the remaining wax on his moustache, stirred his coffee, and took a sip. He should have a conversation with Judge McKenna. He owed Jack four hundred dollars from losing at his tables Friday night. Getting a lot on Front in addition to his place up Harper would be something: a great location for a resort with a dock to boot, and he could always sell it for a tidy profit without lifting a finger.

His mind drifted to getting Suzy to himself one night, perhaps with a couple shots of good whiskey or some of that Chinese brandy, *sam shu,* spiked with a wee drop of Uncle Mickey. *Good God, she must be a virgin,* and the one and only Chink piece in Dawson to boot. It would add a good dose of the exotic to his joint if he could get her working for him.

There was a shriek, and Chan burst from the kitchen swinging a cleaver. "Get out! You get out now!"

A bearded miner stood for a moment, mouth agape, with the offending hand still outstretched toward Suzy's rear end that had elicited her yelp. The big man snatched his wolf fur hat from the peg by the door and stumbled into the street, with Chan's blade parting cigar smoke behind him as he let out a stream of curses in Cantonese.

Jack roared with laughter. "Whack the bloody lug! There ya go Chan!"

The tent erupted in applause as Chan returned to his kitchen.

Jack chuckled and let his thoughts return to Lorelei. What a magnificent specimen she was. It was almost absurd she'd traipse up here to spend the winter above any saloon, let alone his. One of the big showhouses like Swiftwater Bill Gates' Monte Carlo on Front Street, or Nigger Jim Daugherty's Pavilion would hardly do her justice. She was clearly cut of better cloth and could have anything she put her mind to in the great cities of the world: Paris, London, San Francisco… all would fall at her feet. Lorelei wasn't one of these third-class strumpets who found men slavering at their beck and call in the rarified world of the north. She had class and a way to her that bespoke breeding. She had the look of the Black Irish about her with the complexion and eyes to match, and her use of words seemed almost too good for a woman outside of nobility. Jack had trouble following her conversation at times.

He hummed as he trimmed the end off another cigar. Perhaps she *was* nobility, with a family displaced by the Potato Famine or running from some dark scandal in her past. She had her own money, which made it all the harder to forge the kind of deal he'd hoped for, yet now she was moving into his digs nonetheless. Jack imagined his hardscrabble kin in County Cork seeing him with such a prize, and his broad grin painted the canvas ceiling.

A goodtime girl across the tent sawing at a moose steak noticed him and waved. Jack nodded back and struck a match to light his smoke. Lorelei wasn't soft and bosomy like Lulu, who was obviously recovering from another night of servicing who knew how many men. Neither did she have the wide backside amply displayed by women like Babe Wallace or Diamond Tooth Lil. She was like one of those Greek statues, with breasts like ripe fruit over a stomach as flat as a washboard. Her marvelous eyes had more colors than he'd thought possible, and her skin was pure ivory with just the occasional flush of pink, and from closest inspection flawless. Funny thing was he couldn't remember many moments of actually having her. Of course he knew he had, and that it had been wonderful, but he couldn't seem to pierce a cloud veiling his previous night's sojourns. Probably that brandy. Somebody must have spiked it with something along the way. He'd been somewhat in the nether realm from the cocaine anyway.

Whatever. He now had the most beautiful woman in at least two thousand miles moving into his digs, someone to give Gussie Lamore, Diamond Tooth Gertie, who unlike her namesake Lil was leggy and slim, and Klondike Kate a run for their money even if she wasn't on a stage.

Lorelei parted the curtains one last time. The risen sun flashed like a blade off the river bringing tears to her eyes. She gripped the windowsill until the wood groaned in protest and inhaled the cool air as sunlight burned into the pores of her skin. When she could tolerate no more, she shut away the day.

She sat hard on the bed as light crackled under her eyelids. Her face stung as she lay on the too-soft goose down mattress. Her ears rang like a bell and echoed in the bones of her skull. The building around her creaked as it shifted, giving up some of the cold of night to the warming sun. Soon the sun would be far too weak to make the hotel shrug, even under its noon gaze.

She reached out to the hot sparks of lives in cabins climbing the hill behind Dawson, in the diggings along the creeks, and on the gravel island of Klondike City. Moaning from the whore cribs of the Segregated District flitted through her ears before she was distracted by two souls rising toward violence over a disputed claim in a saloon in Grand Forks, ten miles away up Bonanza Creek.

Against her will she returned to Alice Mary. Perhaps Lorelei should meet Fred Dodge wherever he chose to drink this night when she awoke from her dreams, perhaps not. It depended how she was feeling. She had plans. Still, she could do a service for the girl by taking Fred on a little trip into the hills, and she should consider it. After a necessary but boring night with Jack Finley, she was feeling rather mean. Fred's very existence was so irritating.

She yawned and rubbed her eyes. There was much to do before winter. She had to find a man worthy of her company amongst the hordes who had come north seeking their fortune. Perhaps a poet, or at least someone with a tendency to honor the finer manifestations of love as well as having the proper physical endowments. Perhaps even a virgin. That would be a relief, not to mention convenient.

Of course there were the Indians, but this winter she didn't feel like Indians. She was tired of playing the Sacred Being, the Secret One whose name was always unspoken. It would be fun to be the Whore again. After all, it was a gold rush.

II.

"OUCH!" THE BRASS BED CREAKED AS ARIZONA CHARLIE STRETCHED his six-foot-six frame across it and threatened to break as he pushed the heel of a foot against a post. He swore as he sat up and massaged his left calf.

A soft hand danced across his neck, and fingers walked down the hollow of his back. "Got a Charlie horse, Charlie?"

"Damn straight!" He grimaced, "Shit, what time is it?"

"I dunno... day."

"Lily, you got a way with words."

His comment was answered with a giggle and a dimpled grin on Lily's fair features. She sprang off the goose down mattress and snatched up a puffy pink robe, held it coquettishly before her as she slipped into it, and prepared to open the hall door to the water closet.

Charlie smiled. "Ain't nothin' to hide from me. You sure look fetchin' though."

She answered with another giggle and disappeared down the hall.

Charlie massaged his calf, tossed back shoulder length brown hair, and fumbled in the humidor beside the bed. He took out a cigar, lay back with the unlit maduro between his teeth as he stared at the brass lamp hanging from the ceiling, and stroked his neatly trimmed beard as he gave a long sigh. Lily didn't know she'd be sharing bosses tomorrow. Charlie had sold half-interest in the Grand Opera House, and now his proud showplace was to become the Palace Grand Theater. Even though he'd still be running the saloon and gaming tables, it kind of hurt to be giving up most of the shows to Sid Grauman and his troupe from the Standard Theater. It had been less than a year since Charlie had dug down to permafrost to lay the foundations and less than half that time since April's fire had burned his first fine showplace to ashes with the ground still frozen.

The shows popular in Dawson City weren't his cup of tea though. Arizona Charlie Meadows had cut his teeth on real Indian fighting and had the scars to prove it. He'd been in Wild West shows all over the damn world including Buffalo Bill's and had done fine with his own circuit. He was a crack shot and the champion lassoist of the whole god-damn world. Up here though, where it was *still* the frontier, the people with money wanted just the opposite. The proper damn Canadians were clambering for Operas and fancy plays, or at least those chatty vaudeville acts that Sid put on. They turned their noses up at Charlie's bawdy jokes and only seemed to laugh at fellows in derby hats and spats spouting stuffy dandy-ass lingo. The Yellowlegs had even charged him for a goddamn permit just to use a pistol.

Last night had clinched it. He'd been shooting cigarettes from his wife Mae's mouth with wax loads from his favorite Peacemaker just like a thousand times before. He'd shot six in a row, reloaded, and switched to shooting glass balls from between her fingers.

Damn. He must have been awful hung-over. After working his way up her hand, the fourth shot went and took Mae's thumb clean off at the knuckle. You wouldn't think a wax bullet could even do that. Mae was sleeping like the dead above the theater right now from a tincture of laudanum and a half-dozen belts of good Tennessee whiskey.

Charlie had been too keyed up to sleep, what with the deal to take in partners and shooting poor Mae like that, and right out of the blue sweet little Lily had been more than willing to help him lose some of his tensions in those long hours of the night which was when such things just seemed to happen to a fella.

Damn, she's tight. So tight that Charlie, being both a big man and a considerate sort, had been afraid of hurting her. Lily seemed just fine this morning though.

Charlie frowned at the ceiling. He had to make sure Lily didn't start acting all lovey-dovey at work. He should get her a job at the Monte Carlo. Swiftwater Bill Gates owed him plenty of favors and Lily wasn't a shabby prospect by any means. She was just Bill's type anyway: seventeen and blond. Christ, he'd be doing Bill a big one and it oughta come back around with interest. Lily made plenty for the house and did just fine for herself while she was at it, but the spiffy new Palace Grand Theater was going to use the boxes exclusively for watching plays, not assignations. Charlie was going to see a high-tone place that the newly rich could bring their wives to now that women besides goodtime gals and dancers were showing up in Dawson, and he'd given over management to folks who wanted the same. He'd performed at Buckingham Palace, and would tell anyone who wanted to listen that the Canadians were even more British than the Brits. Mountie bigwigs could sit with their snooty wives, or whatever they preferred to call their consorts, and peer through their mother of pearl opera glasses at plays. Maybe they'd even loosen those goddamn stiff collars when no one was watching, and he wouldn't have to worry about some tart shrieking in the next box while a miner went after her like a wolf on a fat calf in January. He'd made a good profit, he was still front man for the place, and some of those stuffed shirts would drop a good deal of that gold they'd skimmed off American miners in his saloon and gambling operation without a doubt.

He rolled the cigar in front of his face. Lily would like the Monte Carlo, although she and the Lamore sisters might not click right off. *Christ,* he *had* to get rid of her before she became a habit. Lily was too young, too much fun, and Charlie Meadows dearly loved his wife. Come spring Lily could be married, got somebody killed, got such herself, or just be one of the town pumps over in the Segregated District. She was too young to tell and way too pretty. That long blond hair made her look like a damn angel, all naked in the lamplight.

He had to check on Mae. She could be waking up right now and hurting like the devil. Mae had stood by him come hell or high water and had toughed it out coming over the trail from Dyea like a trooper. A twinge of guilt rippled through him as he lit the cigar. He groaned and stretched again. You couldn't find a decent bed in a place like the Empire Hotel for a man his size, or anywhere unless you made a goddamn project of it.

Charlie blew a smoke ring and watched it ripple and disintegrate against the red velvet-covered walls. That wallpaper had cost a pretty penny. He'd lost most of his first outfit with doodads for a showplace when a glacier had calved a thousand tons of ice on his burro train out of Sheep Camp. Some folks died, others lost their outfits, and some had turned back right there, but it hadn't slowed him down but a few days. Nothing like that could keep Arizona Charlie down. He'd weathered the previous winter and the near-famine in the overcrowded town by making hunting trips himself to return with caribou and moose, and doling out the meat to the right people. Hunger had made meat better than gold and put a good stake together of the latter, and he was looking at this winter from a far better perspective. Charlie was one of the top dogs in Dawson now with claims on Bonanza, Bear, and Little Skookum creeks, and he had the grandest showplace in the north to boot.

The scent of Lily tickled his nose from the bedclothes, and he was aroused before he knew it. She ought to be back any moment; Mae must be sleeping, and Joe would have the sense to give her more laudanum should she awake. He grinned at the sound of Lily's footsteps in the hall.

———

A cold front spread darkness across an ancient sky. Lorelei tossed in her sleep, listening to the bellow of beasts long gone from the land, creatures whose bones were even now being tossed aside from hills and creeks as hordes of miners moiled for gold. Her nostrils flared as she inhaled the living scent of mammoths, simultaneously seeing their time-stained ivory glistening in shining arabesques as it was pried from permafrost to greet the sun for the first time in eons. She stood on cliffs of grey ash watching an anvil cloud rise from the distant Wrangell Mountains as a great volcano turned the earth inside out and the sky grew dark as the belly of a burnt-out log. Ash fell for days until no living thing could breathe. A child choked in darkness, crying out to his mother as creeks filled with the bones of wood bison, moose, and brown bear. Eagles fell from the sky, with their wings cloaked in ash.

Lorelei's attention was taken by a sound like the very sky falling as it awoke a girl child centuries later. The earth trembled as a great slide broke loose from the ridge above where Lorelei now lay, spreading out on a cushion of air across a village of a people who called themselves Han, and into the river beyond. The girl's bones cried out to her from the shattered serpentine stone and mud beneath Dawson. Her restless voice echoed in Lorelei's skull.

What was her name?

The present broke into her dream with a living girl's laugh. Three doors down a young woman was taking on a big man, gritting her teeth as she accepted his lust and swallowed it in the maelstrom of her own while tearing trails across his back with purple nails.

With familiar ease Lorelei slipped into their moment, and with the lightest touch brought their union to a place neither had ever known. It might well create problems in their lives later as they sought to find that moment one more time, but for the *now,* they were utterly happy. Selfless lust was rare amongst the couplings of short-lived beings, and was something to be cherished.

Glorious laughter erupted in Charlie and Lily's souls. They trembled like a chime struck with a sun's ray of gold as their strangled gasps echoed throughout the Empire Hotel. A miner swore and pounded on the wall, and Lily let loose a loud giggle to be joined by Charlie. The thin walls shook as they rolled off the bed onto the floor.

Charlie lay beneath her with the breath rattling in his chest. Lily's mouth was against his right cheek as he stroked the damp skin of her face. The sweetest breath caressed his other cheek, followed by the touch of soft lips, and a blowing in his ear. Charlie jerked up with Lily on top of him.

"Whatsamatter?" she mumbled, still locked on him with a grip he admired.

He yanked up the tousled sheets and peered under the bed. "Damn weird!"

"What, hon?"

"I swear! I felt somebody on the other side of me, like I was layin' 'tween two women."

She exploded in laughter. "Charlie!"

He gazed at her mouth and sighed. "I know it sounds crazy... but I swear. Somebody was right here, right *next* to me, Lily."

"Well, I *guess,*" she gave his manhood an appreciative squeeze and peeled waist-length hair from a face pink from exertion. "You just never got so far with a woman I'd wager. Your mind is awash with passions and humors, and is presently prone to visions, sir."

Charlie put hands behind his head and examined her nipples. He let out his breath and nodded. "You might have a point there, ma'am."

"And that was absolutely wonderful, Mister." She pressed a damp cheek against his shoulder.

He ran a hand through the tangle of her tresses and traced the doe-soft skin of her throat with a fingertip. "Damn." He shot a glance to his left, but there was only the underside of the bed, scattered piles of lint, and a fat cigar butt.

"You have gotta be gettin' home soon." Her breath bounced in the hollow of his throat as the room spun, and they lay locked together like dogs after the rut.

Be wonderful to stay like this, Charlie said silently to the unseen sky above. He could feel its vastness as if he were rising up through the roof of the Empire Hotel to gaze down at himself and Lily like some immortal being, and the walls around him seemed to fall away. He felt as if he were stretching across the universe.

Reach for what is offered. Nothing lasts forever.

He sprang up with a start. "Who the hell was *that?*"

Lily's body gave up his penis with a soft sucking sound, and her face fell. "Huh?"

"Damn, Lily, somebody just spoke to me!"

"Honey, you think maybe you're a tad light-headed?"

"Damn!" He stood up and yanked hair from his damp shoulders.

"What?"

"Gotta get back, Mae's gonna wake up sure as hell. Christ, I shot her fuckin' thumb off."

"I like Mae."

He gave her a bemused expression.

"Better take a bath first. Let me wash your hair too."

Charlie deferred to the wisdom of his teenage companion with a nod. He ran hands through damp locks and glanced about the room. "Gotta hurry though."

She massaged his shoulders. "Its all part of fate, I guess. Kismet."

"Huh?"

"That's like fate, Charlie, I heard it in a play once."

"I seen that one too." He yawned, "Where are you from anyway?"

"I thought you'd never ask."

.

III.

A⎯T DUSK THE *JOHN G. BARR-* PACKED TO THE GUNWALES WITH ANOTHER load of gold seekers, nosed up to the docks. Beside it the *Victorian* was leaving its spot at the quay under a cloud of smoke for the fifteen-hundred-mile journey to St. Michael, carrying others to the beach strikes of Nome, or a ship Outside. Some were rich beyond their dreams. Most were fleeing before winter locked them into cold and darkness in the prison of the North.

Loud pounding rang from the foundations of a metal cable tower for spanning the river under construction as workmen drove a last few bolts. The sharp clang of steel on iron echoed through the dirt streets and off the bluffs across the river. Shouts of men and neighing of horses mingled with voices from the decks of riverboats, saloons along Front, and the barking of dogs. The town was built on a swamp, and the smells of horse manure, dog shit, and mud filled the chill air.

Lorelei rubbed her temples and groaned at the pain behind her eyes. The frenzy of day in Dawson had rippled through her time-spanning dreams, and the babble of voices and the minds making them made her toss and mumble against her pillow. Tonight she'd be ensconced in rooms above Jack Finley's saloon, where thick log walls would dampen the physical noise, and once she'd found a proper lover, she could dampen the cacophony of passionate souls swarming like bright flocks of birds through the blazing sky of her dreams. After finding a companion, things should settle back into proper perspective. She could focus on a single special soul and devote two centuries of practice and talent to cultivating him. She parted the curtains on a deep pink evening in the southwest. The disappearing orb of the sun burned her face through the crystal air of the subarctic as it set beyond the broad brown river.

Jack was a most unsatisfactory meal. Try as she might, she could find nothing interesting in his nature beyond his desire for wealth. Lorelei had run the gamut of his entire life and memories, and had come up bored. His blood had supplied her most basic needs, but her spirit was hungrier now than if she'd never eaten.

Damn.

That man Charlie down the hall—now there was a union worthy of its name. Not only was he a magnificent specimen of physical endowment, but his spirit was afire with a million dreams worthy of her indulgence. Even his youthful killing of Apaches was understandable, as they'd slaughtered most of his family, and he'd partnered with Lakota and Pawnee since in Wild West shows and discovered a brotherhood near lacking in the rest of the world. Charlie Meadows had more than enough character not to carry his early feelings from the Apache of Arizona to the Athabascan of the Klondike. She chuckled. Little did he know the volcano of her churning dreams had driven the Apache and Navaho south from this, their homeland, long centuries before.

There was a knock on the door.

"*Dzaa,*" Lorelei said to the Athabaskan maid Esther in her own tongue. She had Esther draw a bath, then slipped down the hall unseen and lowered herself into the not-too-clean cast iron tub.

After her bath she dressed for the night in a ruffled silk dress with a corset and a big hat with three plumes of ostrich feathers. She didn't need the corset, and a bustle she couldn't tolerate at all. Fortunately they were out of style, and she could live another century without wearing one. Lorelei stood before the mirror running a belt of heavy gold chain with an array of nuggets through her fingers. Three spots were empty, as it was the custom of women entertainers to leave them for enamored prospectors to fill. Goodtime girls stashed some of their prize nuggets and left conspicuous holes on their belts for men to fill again and again. With any luck a girl would know first when a particular rich fellow was back in town, and return his gift to its place of honor while in his company as if she'd kept it close all the time since.

She'd bought the belt off a dancer in Circle City who was heading Outside, exchanging it for more paper money than it was worth. That, along with the diamond and nugget necklace around her white throat would mark her as a denizen of the palaces of pleasure and carousal. Someone whose flashing eyes, smile, and company could be purchased with gold, with the implication a lucky miner might purchase more.

Jack's eyes widened as a young blonde entered the Golden North and hesitated in the nimbus of attention she engendered. He loudly cleared his throat, and her eyes met his. Jack stood, bowed, and motioned her to his table. "A fine day indeed Miss, if I'm makin' your lovely acquaintance. Just arrived in our Eldorado of the untamed north, I take it?"

"Yes, sir." She extended a gloved hand, which he immediately took in his own and brushed with tobacco-stained lips. "Mary Johansson, sir, of San Francisco."

"And I am John James Finley, most commonly known to one and all as Jack: entrepreneur, raconteur, purveyor of fine entertainments at the estimable establishment which bears my name, and woefully dining alone at the moment. Would you care to partake of breakfast at my expense?"

Mary's fair face lit up. "Thank you sir, I should be delighted." She removed her heavy brown overcoat; Jack hung it, and she sat across from him.

His eyes skipped off the cleavage in her lavender dress and returned to her wide blue eyes. "You haven't come this far alone, I expect."

"Oh no sir, my mother is with me. We have plans to open a laundry here, or perhaps in Grand Forks."

"Indeed? When someone such as you could find wealth far faster and with much less unpleasant work I'd wager. Those lovely hands would be debased by the rough trousers of miners and scalding water I fear, not to mention their unmentionables."

Her cheeks bulged as she toyed with a cigarette in her lead-beaded purse. "Well, I have also done some vaudeville."

"Indeed?"

Mary had been off the Victorian but an hour, but knew a highroller when she saw one. "I worked at the Thalia on Pacific Street in San Francisco. We did shows, but it was rather loud there. You always had to yell to talk to the joh... uh, the customers."

Jack tugged at his moustache as his face split in a grin. "The Barbary Coast, lass, been there."

———

Lorelei frowned at the heavy sensation of Otto approaching from Jack's place. He felt like a bull in his size and dullness. She sighed, resisted the impulse to turn him elsewhere and made ready, pulling her trunks out of the closet and placing them where he'd have access.

She really ought to kill Fred Dodge. She couldn't get that smirking face out of her mind. She should give that Han Hwetch'in girl Esther some gold before she left too. Esther was the only pleasant thing about the Empire Hotel. Amongst the noise and cigar smoke, she was always sweet and steady, had lovely dreams of the wilderness, sang songs in the privacy of her thoughts, and should bear fine children. Lorelei ignored a tiny flash of jealousy at the thought of children as Otto's knock came at the door.

"Come in."

The big Austrian entered, pulled at his beard, and froze when his eyes fell upon Lorelei. She caught a sharp flash of his wishing he'd taken a bath, and her cheeks dimpled. Otto swallowed and shuffled in place, struck dumb in her presence.

"Here are the trunks, dear."

As he bent to lift one, a twinge of pain shot up his back, and Lorelei fought the urge to save him the trouble. She could carry Otto and her baggage at the same time, something that would send ripples of astonishment across Dawson City as fast as news of another strike. Instead she led the straining behemoth out the door, who stumbled while maneuvering her steamer trunk into the hall. Otto was far happier tossing loud men of small stature into the muddy street outside Jack's saloon, which was why he'd been hired in the first place. Once in the hall, he hoisted the trunk on his shoulder.

Her hand shot out to steady it as it nearly slid off. "Careful, dear."

"Gott verdamnt!"

She let loose a laugh that tickled his spine and guided him as he staggered toward the stairwell groaning with each footfall. When he made the porch, Otto stood adjusting the load as Lorelei examined the crowd of tired-looking men with eyes riveted upon her, men who had left homes months or years before with dreams of gold. Their faces showed the strains of their journeys and the labors of the Bush. Lorelei tasted the chaotic mix of desperation and elation surrounding her, inhaling it with the cool air. With such different feelings occupying the same space, and amongst such passions, she could always find the right lover. She'd turned back to Otto when a white burst of awe from someone froze her on the porch, and her gaze jerked back to the street.

The flair of emotion came from a sandy-haired boy of seventeen shod in worn rubber gum boots who was standing in the churned earth of Queen Street. Lorelei graced him with her smile and turned away, but the depth of the young man's wonder continued to tickle her spine as she guided Otto to the wagon. When Otto had put the trunk in the wagon, she sent him for the other and examined the boy, who stood rooted where her first glance had planted him. A dog team pulling a sled on wheels skirted him, and the driver cursed.

"Hello, love."

Joseph swallowed, and shifted from one foot to the other as mud sucked at his boots. He shivered as sweat dried under his clothes. He'd spent the day in the hills cutting wood for the stoves at Charlie Meadows' theater, desperate to raise money to get out past the crowded diggings of Bonanza and Eldorado on his own. Visions of spending the winter working a claim drove his every waking moment. His dreams wouldn't founder in the muddy streets of false front saloons, stores, and whore cribs where stinking water pooled between the buildings and men died without purpose. Joseph had no intention of becoming just another laborer trying to get hired on—except as a step toward his own inevitable Eldorado.

Joseph had arrived three days ago, having bluffed his way past the Mounties checking outfits heading over the Chilkoot Pass to make sure people had enough gear and food for the winter. He'd persuaded two men to pretend their large outfit was partly his own by packing twenty-four loads for them up the brutal White Stairs, and had nearly drowned in Miles Canyon on the journey north, yet the world was a wondrous frontier with near-death but another name for adventure. He had nothing of his own save the twenty dollars the men had given him, his hope, and his youth.

A familiar feeling percolated through Lorelei's nerves. She let out her breath. "Hello, Joseph." The first thing she'd do was give him a bath. "I could use someone to do things. Would you like to make some money?"

He stood hat in hand. "I, er, I'm making ten dollars a day now ma'am... and how do you know my name? Do we know each other? I owe Charlie Meadows the work I'm afraid. I gave him my word."

"Don't worry, I'll tell him. Charlie is a friend of mine. How about twenty dollars a day, with food and lodging to boot? You'll need it, if you're to hook-up with a claim before winter."

"How do you know my name?"

Her cheeks dimpled. "I've heard what a hard worker you are from Mister Meadows and those fellows you came over the pass with. Word travels fast in the Klondike."

"Um, what do you need me to do?"

Her smile nearly blinded him. "You can start by helping Otto with that trunk he's trying to get down the stairs."

"Yes, ma'am!" He sprang up the porch and onto the stairs, to be greeted by Otto's curses.

Lorelei laughed. "Otto, he's with me, let him help."

"Dunt need no damn little boy helping me!"

"You shall."

Otto let Joseph take an end of the trunk, they moved it to the wagon, and Otto got in the seat behind a skinny horse that had some-how survived starvation coming over the Chilkat Mountains. Joseph held out a hand to help Lorelei up, and something coursed through him in a hot tide at her touch. Before he knew it she'd lifted him onto the trunk behind the seat. Sparks filled the backs of his eyes, and Joseph rubbed them and fought light-headedness. He shook himself, adjusted the thin volume of Tennyson he'd carried all the way from Oregon in his back pocket, and shivered with the cold.

Otto flipped the reins, and they traveled the muddy street toward the saloon of Jack Finley. Joseph gazed at the woman in front of him, shook his head, rubbed his eyes again, and tried to clear his vision.

Her silhouette seemed to shift and ripple in the yellow lights of Queen Street, as if she were changing shape. Joseph inhaled the marvelous scent that seemed to surround her, ran a hand across his face, and shivered again.

IV.

H ONEY BEE GAZED IN THE MIRROR AND TOUCHED THE CORNER OF HER
mouth with a fingertip. "Ow." The sore was larger and made her
full lips lopsided with its presence. "Oh, damn." She pouted to examine
her favorite expression and sighed. There was no way to hide it, not
that some customers would give a damn... just the better ones. She
swiped at her long auburn hair with a boar bristle brush and groaned.

Three spots of dried blood formed a triangle on the spruce plank
floor. Honey Bee grabbed the rag she'd staunched Alice Mary's nose
with, wrung it out in the basin, and scrubbed it clean while thinking
about her favorite customer, a handsome young Mountie who was
polite as all get-out and made her feel like a lady. She'd have him give
that Dodge fellow some real hell after their next *assignation*, which
was what her Mountie called it, and maybe even chase the lug out of
the Territory completely, but her Yellowleg savior was in Fortymile
at the moment, chasing a load of whiskey and somebody named Big
Dan McCain.

Swiftwater Bill Gates had given her some vague reassurances when
she'd taken the problem of Fred to him, but had shushed her and cut

her off when his lover Gussie Lamore had appeared coming down the wooden sidewalk before Honey could explain. Bill had scooted Honey Bee into the alley behind the Monte Carlo in company of one of his men, who'd escorted her back to the Segregated District where girls plied their trade with one hand exploring her backside and that was that.

Alice Mary was her dearest friend and they both despised working for others, be they madams or pimps. Honey was a Pederson from Minnesota. Her family must never know what she did here just as some future husband wouldn't. She sighed. They probably thought she was dead anyway. Did they even care?

Alice Mary was just Alice Mary: a hot-blooded product of old Virginia who didn't brook a sideways glance from anyone. They'd both been abused by relatives, and had struck out young and alone to end up in the Klondike which was about the farthest place on earth—birds of a tattered feather, but together at least. They were sisters now, and lovers, who braved the roll of the dice each time they gave their bodies to strangers.

Mornings were for long talks after servicing the newly rich miners who shopped the Line. They talked about customers, other girls, and their frequent close calls. Honey shared a dented once-burgled, hand-me-down safe under her bed with Alice Mary that had been given to her by its previous owner for a night's pleasure. They counted their nightly take together as they fantasized about what they'd do with their riches and fell asleep in each other's arms.

Someone stopped at the window of the crib to peer through a gap in the curtains. It was a bear of a man who had a thick black beard that reached to his waist. Honey drew knees under her chin and backed into the shadows against the wall on her bed behind the half-wall that gave her a modicum of privacy. He was too big, and no matter what he had between his legs she wasn't going to have that one atop her. She didn't feel like working anyway. Better to treat Alice Mary to a nice dinner to salve her friend's sorrow, maybe even get Swiftwater Bill to let them hide out upstairs at his place with some decent champagne and perhaps a little opium. Bill had a soft spot for both of them, they'd made use of it before, and she still had to get him alone to explain their situation. Getting out of the District was what they needed, and when Bill heard Alice Mary's tale of Fred Dodge's cruelty added to her own, he might even loan them a couple of his fellows to set things right. If they could get him away from the Lamore sisters for a while, it should be easy. Bill loved the young ones, he was protective of his women, and they both were sixteen.

"Fresh as a flower in the Lord's fields, my precious Norski angel."

Her mother said the same thing every Easter as she tied the ribbon of a hand-sewn bonnet under Sonya's chin. She'd stood listening to it again at twelve, freshly ravaged by a cousin, yet mute like all her kin when confronted with things beyond speaking. Her mother's wan complexion was the face of her future: a gray road of misery worn to leather in western Minnesota with the cold prairie winds for company and eventual marriage to some silent farmer whose idea of joy was a full silo and Sunday dinner.

Her first cousin Johan, who went by John, was an up-and-comer at the bank, the pride of the family, and the first to go to college. He sat in his shiny suit in the family pew smiling broadly when she came to church that Easter morning: the same man who'd taken her to the barn the night before and held a calloused hand over her mouth while the Holsteins mooed at their troughs. He found pleasure in her vulnerability, her fear and her pain, laughing and grunting as he finished. She'd rolled away from him when he finally got off, and he'd slapped her bottom with a laugh and left. She'd heard that laugh from other men since and she despised them all.

Three years later she'd jumped at an offer from a traveling lawyer heading for Saint Paul and gave him what he desired gladly to escape. He was invariably polite and seemed rather shocked when she actually provided it. Sonya exulted in her new power and relished her head-long plunge into the unknown. He commented over and over on how young she was as he flipped the reins over her head in his lap on the seat of his wagon.

Saint Paul was so big and Minneapolis even bigger. The lawyer gave her ten dollars along with a droning speech about being a better woman when they'd arrived. She'd managed to acquire enough for a train to Seattle from the next fellow. Once there it was easy to fall in with the stampede north, and she'd joined a troupe of 'actresses' she met at a combination bordello and melodeon a block from Skid Row being rounded up by Mattie Silks for her new bordello in Dawson City. The other girls called her Baby and watched out for her in their way, and she'd found favor from the richest man on the ship to Skagway to the envy of the other girls. She'd worked for Mattie just long enough to have something of her own, and had taken over a crib on the Line this past summer. *To hell with bosses.* To hell with *anybody* who thinks they're better. She and Alice Mary would show the world when they left the Klondike in style. Alice had a book of colored pictures of Nob Hill in San Francisco, and they dreamed aloud of buying a house there and making it a refuge for girls like themselves. They spent mornings fantasizing about it, laughing with a laugh no one else shared but them as they decorated their dream castle on a hill where they would reign supreme.

Honey Bee laid out her best crinoline dress, anxious to get to Alice Mary's crib before a customer. She could see her sitting with the door barred, playing with her Bowie knife, and imagined her friend letting someone in who turned out to be awful, somebody who pushed her beyond her limit. Honey hoped Alice would never let that thing coiled inside her loose that was the source of her pain, though she knew somehow it was the very same thing that made her a wonderful lover. She imagined Alice's black-painted nails around the ivory handle of her knife and what would follow, and Honey Bee began to hurry.

They were going to have a time together and forget the goddamn Line tonight. She—

Honey jumped as the door creaked open. She was sure she'd locked it after Alice Mary left, but the silhouette of a man was there, backlit by the glow of kerosene lamps from the un-electrified shacks of the Line.

"Where's the little scamp?" The gravelly voice of Fred Dodge boomed off a Currier and Ives print of a New England Christmas above the tiny table and rattled the glass in its frame.

"She's not here!" Honey's voice was shrill at the return of the man who'd used both her and her lover so cruelly, and she swallowed as if trying to pull it back out of the air.

"Whatsamatter, Honey-Beeee, don'tcha like your job, little chicken? Looks like you can use a pluckin' too I'd say." He stabbed a tobacco-stained finger in her face, and she flinched. "You're her girl, eh? Betcha want her for yourself, Don'tcha?"

"I'm her friend! Go away! I know Mounties, and Charlie Meadows... and Swiftwater Bill! My man is a Constable and he's coming back right now, and he'll—"

Fred slammed the front door and Honey Bee sprang over the bed for the back one onto the alley. Her hand seized the handle just as he caught her long hair and he yanked her backwards with a shriek. She bounced on the thin feather mattress with a yelp and her hands ready to claw his eyes out, but he grabbed her wrists so hard she thought they'd break. "Whores ain't got no friends!" He ripped off her dress in one motion with that same laugh, "We'll see what friends you got!"

Lorelei set Joseph to work making the room above Jack's saloon into her abode. He helped her broom cobwebs off the ceiling and began to hang her collection of clothes in a dark closet built against the outer wall from which the smell of damp wood and mildew issued.

"Whoa," she held up a hand, "let it air out. Leave them in the trunk for the time being."

She laid a heavy nugget belt with a diamond and nugget necklace across a wolverine pelt spread on the oaken dresser and ran a bath, having had Otto stoke the boiler downstairs. Joseph marveled at the apartments, which were the crowning glory of Jack Finley's establishment, existing solely for Jack and whoever had the privilege of this room. Through a window of expensive double-pane glass, Joseph could see the mouth of the Klondike River and snow-dusted mountains with the aurora rippling under a fat fall moon.

Lorelei pulled a curtain of gold silk across the brass rail separating the bath from the bedroom. "Undress Joseph, I shant peek." She pointed to a steaming clawfoot bathtub, "Get in, and I'll scrub your back when I return."

Joseph hung his clothes on the door and peered into the room where she'd disappeared. He stood for a moment, tested the water, hissed, and poured some in from the pitcher beside the tub. The water in the pitcher was as cold as the tub was hot, and upon emptying it he found the bath just right. He put a foot in the water, sighed, and slid into the welcoming water to stretch muscles tight from the labors of the day. He rubbed his eyes and yawned.

Lorelei appeared in a robe of blue silk with her hip-length hair rippling in the buttery lamplight like a raven's wings in summer sun as she placed a stool beside the tub. "Now let's get you presentable," she said as she put a bar of soap, a green bottle, and a wash cloth beside the tub.

"For what?"

"For me, Joseph."

The robe slid off like water over ivory shoulders, exposing breasts surmounted by stiff nipples over a stomach as flat as his own. He'd never seen a woman like that, but he hadn't seen any naked either except his little sisters and the occasional glance at his mother through a door. He tried to look away, but his eyes were drawn to the dusting of hair leading to a pink mouth offering the mysteries of the universe. A shiver ran up his spine as goose bumps rose on his skin.

She poured shampoo on his sweat-matted hair, and Joseph closed his eyes as her fingers ran across his scalp and the hot water ran down his neck. Her fingertips made trails of sparks in the hollow of his back. She began to wash his thigh. The blood rushed to his groin with a shout, and he made a motion to cover his stiffening cock.

Her laugh was like warm honey. "It's all right, he knows what's about." Her fingers closed around it, and a rush shot through him. "And he'll behave just fine, I promise. Now stand up." She poured more water across his head and shoulders and dried him with the towel. Joseph swallowed and gazed into sea-green eyes sparkling with flecks of red. Long dark lashes blinked back as light purled in her pupils, and lips parted on a shell-pink tongue. He smelled her breath and wondered if she'd been dining on flowers.

"Oh, damn!" His hands slid across the silken skin of her throat, up her smooth cheeks and into her hair. For a moment he was conscious of their roughness, before an answering giggle ripped that white throat saying she knew his thoughts and all was fine. His mouth found hers and that impossibly sweet breath flowed into him, setting off explosions in every cell and lighting his nerves like a thunderstorm on a hot summer day. He swept her up in his arms. She was as light as a feather as he carried her to the bed.

———

Lorelei ran a finger down his nose as he dreamt and muttered in his sleep. Joseph had been more than satisfactory, giving her both sexual sustenance and the balance of spirit she so craved, but day was coming. She laid her head on his chest and watched the tiny hairs dance on his arm with each breath. She should set him free before things got complicated, give him some gold, and cloud his memory of this one night beyond pleasure until he was an old man far from this place, and she could return with absolution for all the wild things he would do in his life from seeking that which she had shown him and then hidden.

No. She'd keep him for a while *and* let him remember. Joseph was her consort for the winter. *Who shall know?* All her kind on earth were gone besides she and she alone, and it wasn't anything she hadn't done before anyway. Jack was cold putty she could mold with bored familiarity, but Joseph was a joy. The only thing that had made their loving less than perfect was some girl crying somewhere in the chaotic nest of souls that was Dawson City.

She yawned, letting her attention drift from her lover for the briefest of moments, and the hollow whistle of bloody breath rattling out of Honey Bee's slashed throat erupted into her consciousness.

"No!"

Lorelei was gone even as her shout rippled through the logs of the building, and Mary jerked awake beside Jack in the next room.

———

Mary rubbed her eyes, shook her head, glanced about, and groaned. Jack lay next to her with his mouth open and one foot sticking out from under the quilt. He snorted and pulled the covers over his face. She stared at the mound beside her and sat up with another groan holding her head. Jack couldn't help using liquor, drugs, or something on a woman even if she were wholly willing. Mary understood that, or at least expected it. She'd been hoping against hope that Jack would be different, but she'd been with such men before.

She wrapped herself in a red Hudson's Bay blanket, walked to one of the double-pane windows, and gazed over frosty rooftops at the Klondike River where it met the broad Yukon. Cold mist rose in the gray light before dawn. Mary scowled as she ran fingers over bruised flesh, staring at the twin stacks of a riverboat with two columns of smoke rising straight into the frigid air. Jack might now consider her his property and she really should have encouraged him to court her for a few days at least. That had been her intent, up until the ride back from Grand Forks in that fancy wagon when he had plied her with that French brandy that made her head spin.

She was horribly thirsty, arose, and glanced about for water. She pulled back the curtain in the middle of the papered wall separating the room from the bath and examined the door on the other side. The place was silent but for the ticking of the stovepipes running up through the middle of each room.

The bathroom held a green enameled tub on cast iron lion's feet with a faucet over it, a sink with two faucets, and one of the only flush toilets in Dawson with an expensive oaken water box above it. A green pitcher stood beside the tub. She went to the sink, turned the handle on the right, and was relieved to feel cold water. Mary dropped the blanket, cupped her hands, and drank, splashing water on her face.

A pale wraith stared back from the mirror. She eyed her freshly cut hair coming midway to her neck and sighed. Her breasts looked mottled and uneven in the shadows, and her nipples were sore from Jack's ministrations. She vaguely remembered her protests and his rough laughter, until she had yielded to his mouth and the thrusting of his body. A growl rose from her chest. He *definitely* had slipped her something. She felt like a brick. Mary had been planning to give herself to him in time of course, but now she felt quite used and unhappy.

Her lip curled at spying the bite on her neck. *That* should make her look like some little Jezebel while walking the streets of Dawson. "Goddamn it!" To make things worse, the pearl-handled five-dollar derringer she'd carried from San Francisco had been taken by the Mounties upon disembarking from the riverboat. She *slept* with that gun, and now she was amongst a horde of randy miners and grifters without it! Mary sighed and scratched her head. At least Jack was a rich man and he could make things happen if he wanted to. Perhaps—

A sound made her catch her breath and turn around.

Joseph wobbled as he stared at the girl's breasts, and his eyes wandered down between her legs before he stepped back, blinked, stumbled on the rug, and swallowed. The girl snatched up a red Hudson's Bay blanket on the stool and threw it around herself, and his face burned as he pulled an identical blanket draped around his shoulders tighter. "Oh, I... excuse me!"

Mary cleared her throat. "Do you live here?"

"No, ma'am, I just... woke up over there," he pointed behind him, "and was, I... don't know." He shook his head and began again, "A lady brought me here last night, and it's really not proper to say what's happened since."

"Jack Finley brought me here. What lady?"

"Miss Lorelei, she was in the other room, and I thought she might—"

"As is Jack in that one." She tossed back her hair and looked him up and down. "Did you pleasure her?"

Joseph's mouth opened, but the words were slow in coming. "I suppose you could say that, I really—"

"Well, you did or you didn't. Did she slip you something in your drink?"

"Didn't drink a thing save water."

"Then she's a damn sight better than Jack." She chuckled, "The man should have been an apothecary." Obviously he was but a youthful diversion for the woman in the other room who must be one of Jack's investments in the demimonde whoever she was, perhaps an actress, or another mistress with a claim to his time which could complicate things. "What's her name again?"

"Lorelei, Miss Lorelei. She had me cleaning up her new digs here and..." Joseph's knees buckled and the blanket slipped to the floor.

Mary reached out to stop him, and her blanket joined his. "Damn you're heavy!" She put a shoulder under his arm and sat him on the stool as Joseph moaned, and his head fell between his knees. "Are you all right, fellow?"

"Awfully sorry, just a bit dizzy."

She ran water in the pitcher and held it to his lips. "Are you sure?" Mary put down the pitcher and stood with a hand in his hair, rubbing his neck with the other.

He took a breath. "I apologize. I'm feeling rather weak for some reason... and powerfully hungry."

"Well, I should love to have coffee and breakfast myself after a bath." She examined him one more time and let out her breath. "Would you care to join me?"

"For breakfast?"

"For both if it doesn't offend you. We'll be lucky to have enough hot water for one I'd suspect. We're both here for the same reason I suppose. Oh, I'm Mary." She twisted the faucet on the left above the tub, felt the flow of water, and nodded. "Not too hot, but a damn sight better than cold. We're definitely sharing."

"I'm Joseph."

When the tub was full, she helped him in and slid in with her legs around his back and her feet against his thighs. She massaged his neck and shoulders and he sighed, leaned into her hands, and stared at the ceiling as he snuggled against her breasts. Mary flinched as he put his weight against sore nipples. No matter what, it seemed that being around a man always brought these little moments of discomfort. It was a woman's lot. She hummed a rhyme and ran fingers through his hair. They took turns rinsing each other off, climbed out giggling, and toweled one another dry as a rooster crowed above Dawson.

V.

HONEY BEE BLINKED INTO FOCUS THE PALE COUNTENANCE ABOVE HER. Her chest heaved as blood gurgled down her windpipe and sparks danced in her vision. She summoned the last of her strength and raised a trembling hand toward the face of an angel.

Lorelei clasped it to her breast. "Oh! I was lost in my own pleasure and didn't *listen!*" A sob wracked her as she touched the ragged hole in Sonya's throat. She could heal it if given time, but there wasn't any.

Honey Bee stared through that beautiful face at the shining void beyond. There was so much pain in this angel. Honey tried to smile for her sake.

Lorelei's wail shook the shacks of the Line, and men and the girls who serviced them jerked upright to peer out curtained windows. Honey Bee could feel them as Lorelei did and let her know it with her smile. There was no anger left, only acceptance. She was little Sonya on a prairie meadow, watching cloud dragons in an endless sky as the words from Sunday school echoed in her mind: *Suffer the little children unto me.* Why *suffer?* The pastor said it meant to *allow,* but she'd never believed it. She'd suffered so much before at the hands of her own kin and since, yet there was no angry father awaiting her now. Only the light of love... and an angel.

Don't cry angel!

Lorelei lifted her up like a fragile leaf and carried her to where Lorelei could not follow, where she was but a mote of dust as the roar of that river grew louder and the light blinded her. When she regained herself, she kissed the empty husk born Sonya and returned to the saloon of Jack Finley like the breeze. Fred Dodge was gone from Dawson City to his claim on Hunker Creek and day was nigh, but his time would come. Tears froze on the wooden sidewalk as she rushed to shelter from the coming day, holding close the reflection of the soul she'd been privileged to aid in passing.

VI.

MARY SLIPPED INTO JACK'S ROOM AND RETURNED IN A BEIGE DRESS AND heavy cotton petticoat over high leather boots. She had a red woolen shirt and fresh socks for Joseph, and he put them on over clean flannel underwear Lorelei had left on a chair. Mary took one look at his stained canvas pants and fetched fine corduroy ones from Jack's closet, then stood staring at Lorelei, who lay unmoving under the flannel sheets as Joseph donned the clothes. A dark stain of blood was barely visible at the edge of the woolen blankets.

Joseph tapped her on the shoulder, and Mary rubbed her eyes and followed him out of the room.

In order to avoid Jack's minions, they decided to take the outer stairs and stepped into crisp morning air. Ice-coated heaps of barrel staves and rough-cut lumber sparkled in a thick coat of frost. They shivered and laughed in a cloud of breath as they skirted the doors of the saloon and headed through scarlet leaves of blueberries across the hillside beneath the tent camps of Klondike stampeders until they were out of sight of Jack's place. They glanced back at the saloon when they reached the corner, where people were already drinking at the polished mahogany and oak bar that glowed through cigar smoke in the early morning sun streaming across rooftops to the south.

They walked into the cold shadows hand in hand, headed downtown, reached King Street, and stepped up on the wooden sidewalk. Saloons, cigar stores, outfitters, markets and hotels lined both sides of the street to the Yukon River, and a hundred telephone lines buzzed from leaning poles. A dog team hitched to a sled on wheels sat loaded with furs at the edge of the plank sidewalk.

Joseph gulped the fall air. "I am fairly starving."

Mary nodded. "Me too, I've got some money here." She reached into her lead-beaded purse and pulled out a handful of silver dollars, two twenty-dollar gold pieces, a small poke of dust, and a roll of bills. "Enough to buy one hundred breakfasts, Joe."

Joseph eyed the money in amazement.

"Jack won't miss it. He's got a safe-full, and this was just lying around. Besides, I'm still paying for it. Notice how those fellows looked at me with this big 'ol hickey on my neck?"

"Your neck is lovely none the less."

"Why, thank you sir."

A plank palisade of whipsawed boards began at Fourth Avenue that had been erected by decree of the North-West Mounted Police around the whores of the Segregated District. Posters and handbills covered the fence advertising showhouses, saloons, various outfitters, breweries, and the coming and goings of steamboats. Beyond the fence the gaily painted cribs of the Line filled both sides of the street, each a little log or clapboard house with a front window and curtains. Most had girls' names hanging over the narrow doors embellished with yellow, blue, purple and red flowers. A few girls stood yawning before their respective portals even at this hour.

There was a shriek, and two girls bolted toward a crib a block away. More cries and wailing followed. A half-dressed young woman came running in their direction, screaming, "It's Honey Bee! Call the Mounties!"

Joseph took Mary's arm. He put himself between her and the chaos of the District, and she snuggled up to him as they passed the windows of a dry goods store. Behind the glass were dresses of crinoline, silk and taffeta, as well as huge hats topped with ostrich feathers along with iridescent green and red quetzal plumes. Several well-dressed women were going in and out of the place, both respectable wives and members of the demimonde. The women of proper social status stared straight ahead as they passed their more numerous opposites, most of which were better adorned as well as more attractive.

Mary gasped. "What lovely things. I saw that dress at the City of Paris, but how strange to see it so far away in this northern wilderness." People shouted behind them, and she quickened her pace toward the river, "Let's not ruin our morning with whatever brouhaha is going on back there."

"Where are you from, Mary?"

"San Francisco, Joe, born and raised there."

"I should like to see it after I have made my fortune in the gold fields."

Mary's laugh was as high-pitched as a child's. "You're doing all right already I'd wager. That lady who took you in is something to see."

Joseph rubbed his eyes as they continued down King, and two Mounties galloped from the direction of Fort Herchmer down Third Avenue to wheel their mounts toward the Line with a savage yank of the reins. "Yes, I still feel rather odd about it though."

"What do you mean?'

"I don't know. It's as if things have been knocked ajar, and I was floating almost. It's... rather hard to explain, Mary."

"Well, she's certainly one of the most expensive of the demimonde, and is presently lavishing herself upon you it appears. She must be quite an experience, that's for sure."

"Do you think?"

"Fella, I haven't seen a classier looking lady in this town, even sleeping, and without her fancy clothes. And that's coming from another woman you know."

"Pshaw, you're but a girl yourself."

"A girl who grew up around the Barbary Coast and the Tenderloin, and who went to a decent Presbyterian school when my mom had the money too. I've seen the lives of the nabobs on Nob Hill as well as the hoi polloi. I've been in some of those mansions even, and I've seen the parlor houses—at least from the outside of course. San Francisco is where the great demimonde become wealthy and respected, and lead lives of their own choosing. I'm telling you that she *has* to be one. I mean... she's in Jack's place, isn't she?"

"I suppose. Where are we going to eat?"

"There's a good place on Front."

"Joe! What's cookin' son? You up for some work today?" Charlie Meadows stood thumbs in his belt with a long black cheroot dangling from his lips just inside the door of the Grand Opera House as men erected a scaffold beside buckets of paint and piles of boards on the sidewalk, and he directed the work with a fat glass of whiskey in one hand.

Mary caught her breath as she took in the countenance of Arizona Charlie with his flowing brown locks draped across the shoulders of a beaded and fringed buckskin coat that would do Buffalo Bill proud.

Charlie removed his broad-brimmed hat. "Your pardon, young lady, didn't mean to speak like that before makin' your acquaintance. Sometimes a man forgets himself."

Mary let go of Joseph's hand and put hers to her breast. "You're... Arizona Charlie Meadows!"

"I am indeed."

"Oh my gosh, I saw you in Oakland when you shot the cigar from the mouth of that fellow from that beautiful white horse. That was the most amazing thing I have ever seen, Mr. Meadows!"

"Thank you kindly, ma'am. His name was Lightnin', a damn good horse, got him from a 'Rapahoe. And what, pray tell, might your name be?"

"It's Mary Johanson, sir."

"A pleasure to make your acquaintance. Would you and your young friend, whose reliable assistance I could certainly use this morning, care for a cup of fine Italian coffee?"

"Actually we were heading to the Golden North. We both have had a hard night and are in need of breakfast," she flashed a coquettish smile, "in the company of one another actually."

Charlie winked at Joseph as the workmen exchanged envious glances. "In that case I'll let you take my best worker, but bring him back if he wants to make a few dollars."

"Mr. Meadows," Joseph spoke up, "Miss Lorelei said you knew that she had retained me."

"Miss Lorelei?"

"Yes, sir, she said you were well acquainted."

"Well, I'd certainly like to be. How did you meet that tall drink a' good whiskey?"

"Pure happenstance, but I am helping her prepare her—I have been retained by her, to work under her, um . . ."

"Say what?"

"I—"

Mary tugged on Joseph's hand. "Joe's sorely in the need of a meal at the moment. It's a pleasure to have met you, Mr. Meadows."

"And you, young Mary. Are you employed?"

"I'm not sure."

"Well, if you want to work at the new Palace Grand Theater let me know. You're one who obviously isn't shy or afraid to speak her mind, or make a man dance to her tune I'd wager," Charlie's voice rose as they began to leave, "we can always use a girl like that!"

"Thank you Mr. Meadows," Mary laughed, "I surely shall keep that in mind!" As they walked down the block, she continued to chuckle. "The Klondike's full of offers."

The wharves were crowded with riverboats and barges emptying cargos or loading before the journey downriver to St. Michael. Several were docked in a slough across the river, soon to freeze fast for winter. Men tramped off a sternwheeler bent low under kits and duffels, and Joseph wondered where they'd put themselves at freeze-up. Another crowd was jostling to board a boat with **BEACH STRIKE IN NOME!** painted on a banner draped from the wheelhouse. The Klondike rush had peaked, and a new rush was spilling toward the shores of the Bering Sea.

Most of the newcomers stopped to stare at Mary, amazed such a fresh-faced girl could have beaten them here, and some boarding the boat shot her sullen looks as if she were the embodiment of all they would never attain.

"Where are you from, Joe?" she asked as they walked into the tented side of the restaurant and sat at a table.

Joseph studied her bright features and scratched his downy inkling of a beard. "From Oregon. My father raises wheat, potatoes, apples and cattle. He's got a feed store that pays the bills too. I wanted to go to the University in Eugene to study literature, but my older brother got the money to study engineering." He shrugged, "Three brothers and six sisters. Ma and Pa have done the best they can, and she makes the best apple pie in the world. Ever hear of Cottage Grove?"

"No."

"It's a few hours' ride south of Eugene where the University is, if you've heard of that. Up in the mountains to the east there's the Bohemia Mining District. I used to go up there on camping trips and grew up dreaming of gold. My uncle's got a claim in the Siskiyou Mountains in Josephine County where the big placer strikes were in the Fifties, and I used to help in the summer so I know what to do here. They paved the streets in Cottage Grove with tailings from the Bohemia Mines, so they say the streets were paved with gold. It's in my blood, I guess. I headed here the moment I had the chance and spent every dime on my passage to Skagway."

"How old are you?"

"Seventeen."

"Same for me."

Tzu Bai was at the table. "You lookee hungry."

Joseph nodded vigorously.

"Get anything you desire," Mary laughed. "Better give us whatever's good and fast, Suzy. He's wilting away as we speak."

"You eva have caribou sausage?"

They shook their heads.

"Very good, German man make it right here. How 'bout caribou sausage with eggs, and fry potato, and fresh bread... lots of blueberry—"

"Yes, fine," Mary nodded, "and coffee with cream and sugar please."

Tzu Bai hurried back to the kitchen.

The smell of food was making Joseph's stomach growl and twist. He had a dull ache in his groin and couldn't remember being so hungry in his entire life. He closed his eyes. Lorelei was staring back as if she were standing before him, with tiny slices of vermillion glittering between the blue-green stroma of her irises like flecks of red gold. Her eyes grew larger and became pools he began to sink in as lovely laughter rippled through him.

"Joe?"

He jerked upright. "What?"

"Has anyone ever told you that you're quite handsome?"

"Um, thank you. You're a fine looking person yourself."

"Isn't it strange how we met like this? I mean in such a place as a bath above Jack Finley's saloon?"

"I guess. It's all rather quick, that's for certain. I've never bathed with a lady before."

Tzu Bai put down a chipped earthenware platter full of sausage, eggs, and potatoes in front of him, and he picked up a piece with his fingers.

"Too late to be shy now. Besides, you were engaged with Miss Lorelei before that. She left a nice scent upon you."

"Um... how did you end up at Jack's?"

Mary made a face. "I went with him to see Grand Forks in the diggings, and he poured his funny brandy down me on the way back." She waited for Joseph's reaction, but he was engaged with the sausage and she sighed, "My Ma wants to open a laundry there, but I can do a lot better."

"You mean . . ."

"Yes and no. I don't intend to be one of those girls who sees countless fellows if that's what you're thinking. Neither do I intend to work in one of the showhouses for the time being, although it's tempting and I've done it before. Rather I should consider a relationship with a prosperous businessman or entrepreneur, someone like Jack if not Jack himself. He's rather a cad, actually."

"If he's using funny brandy, he's worse than that."

She shrugged. "Still, I intend to find a fellow who can support me in a proper manner."

"I suppose that would be one way to do it..." Joseph's voice trailed off as he grabbed another chunk of sausage and stuffed it in his mouth.

"She must have starved you."

"I'm juth 'ungry," he put a hand to his mouth, swallowed, and grinned, "pardon my manners."

"Seen worse." Mary accepted a mug of coffee from Tzu Bai, who put down the silverware, a can of evaporated milk, and a small cone of hard brown sugar in a bowl. Mary sawed off four pieces with an ivory-handled knife she produced from her bag, dropped them into her cup, shook the thick yellow milk into the mug, stirred vigorously as it overflowed on the table, and lifted it to her lips. "Oh that's good!" She wiped pale goo off her lip. "So here we are in the Klondike."

"Yes, here we are."

"What are you going to do today?"

"Me?"

"Yes, I mean what are your plans? How can you get grubstaked before winter? It's almost freeze-up, you know. Shouldn't you consider the opportunity right before you?"

"Huh?"

"The *opportunity*, Joe. Did Miss Lorelei like you?"

He took a gulp of coffee, stirred in more cream, and looked up. "What?"

"You can be her fancy man if you put yourself to it. I saw what you've got there between your legs you know. We were both naked if you'll remember, and I've been around a couple of fellows myself as I'm sure you've gathered by now. Dare say I've known a few too, and I must say that you are exceptionally well-endowed sir."

Joseph choked on his coffee and put a hand to his mouth.

Her smile broadened. "I grew up where such things are the way of the world. Of course she must really *like* you. She did scratch your back. Did she cry out your name when you pleasured her?"

Joseph's face reddened and he glanced around. He stared into the wide blue eyes of the girl across the table and inhaled. "I can't really say. I know we were somewhere I've never been before, that's for sure. There was all this brightness... and," he shook his head, "for a very long time it seemed. Almost as if it were forever."

"Sounds like you can hold your fire anyway." She winked, "Keep giving that woman what God gave you and she could probably set you up. What do you want to bet some miner will drop the deed to a claim for her favors, and you can have it for your own?"

He picked at a splinter on the table and sipped his coffee. "Think so?"

Mary cut herself a bite of sausage and grimaced. "Want mine?"

"Yes, thank you." He speared the sausage and began to demolish it.

"That'd be fun. I shall have Jack or someone like him, and you shall have Lorelei, and we could be friends on the side seeing as we're the same age and I find you quite attractive."

Joseph stopped eating and studied her face. Her throat rippled as she drank her coffee, making the bruise quiver. His gaze fell to her freckled breasts. Mary was inviting him to take her as a lover, and he felt an answering thump between his legs.

The blast of a steam whistle made them jump. His coffee splashed, and he grabbed the mug before it went over. A dog team exploded in howls on the other side of the canvas wall, and they burst into laughter. "Oh, what the hell."

"Yes Joe, what the hell. We're both in demand it seems. I'm used to it, but you're in an odd way." Mary fingered the bruise on her throat. "We had a fellow in San Francisco called the Barbary Chicken who entertained the demimonde. He was legendary. They actually *bid* against each other for his favors." Mary winked, "If you don't mind me saying so, I could give you some lessons in using that thing." She cracked her back and yawned, "I wonder where my mom's got to?"

VII.

ALICE MARY ADJUSTED THE GOLD CHOKER ONE LAST TIME AND PUT A palm to the glass side of the hearse. Two black horses pawed at the muddy street as curious onlookers watched from the sidewalk. She studied her palm print floating before the polished coffin on the other side, whispered, "Love you," and stepped up onto the wooden sidewalk through the doors of the Monte Carlo. Girls from the cribs weren't allowed in the showhouses, but Swiftwater Bill Gates had jumped all over the Yellowlegs when they'd tried to enforce it today, and with a little gold in the right hands someone had made an exception.

Other girls from the District were there. Three-Way Annie gave her a little wave, and Molly Fewclothes hugged Alice Mary when she saw her. Laura and Hermine, the Belgian sisters, were standing with Gussie Lamore and her little sister Nell, two of the blond belles of the Monte Carlo, speaking in hushed tones. Emile the Belgian girls' pimp wasn't anywhere to be seen. Honey Bee hated him, so it was all the better.

The working girls all had their hair in proper buns and smelled of lavender and perfume. Swiftwater Bill saw Alice Mary and nodded. Arizona Charlie Meadows tipped his hat. She was the closest thing Honey Bee had here to family, and people who knew their relationship gave her the deference accorded to a grieving spouse.

The girls of the District had all thrown in for the funeral. Mattie Silks, who'd brought Honey Bee to Dawson, had paid for the mahogany casket, and they'd bought up all the roses the German man in West Dawson grew in his greenhouse across the river. An auburn-haired Klondike Kate wiped violet eyes as she handed a bouquet to Alice Mary and kissed her cheek. Red roses covered the coffin, and Honey Bee would have squealed with delight to see them. Alice Mary held some flowers up to hide her face, closed her eyes, and inhaled.

"Folks," Swiftwater Bill stroked his beard and held up his hands, "It's time."

With a murmur, the crowd piled onto Front Street and began to fill carriages, wagons and mounts. The man from the funeral parlor motioned to Alice Mary and patted the seat beside him on the hearse. Charley Meadows held out a hand for her and nearly tossed her over the seat when she took it. "Whoops, sorry ma'am. You don't weigh more'n a sack a' feathers." She settled next to the driver, who gave her his best sad undertaker's smile from between gray muttonchop sideburns as he flipped the reins.

They headed down the curve of Front to the disturbed waters of the Klondike River and followed it along the base of the ridge behind Dawson past stumps and tents until they reached the road up Midnight Dome. Alice Mary examined the crowd behind her. A lone representative of the North-West Mounted Police accompanied the procession and the young Corporal looked uncomfortable in his dress uniform amongst the nocturnal residents of town and kept pulling at his blond mustache. Swiftwater Bill Gates rode in his own black carriage with Gussie, Grace, and Nell Lamore. Arizona Charley rode a beautiful white horse that Alice Mary had never seen before, with Mattie Silks and her Mexican lover Cortez following in a black buggy. Diamond Tooth Gertie rode beside Edith Neal, the tallest woman in town, known as the Oregon Mare, and Cad Wilson the actress, with Cad's 'servant,' a shaven-headed Negro known as the Black Prince, driving the wagon. Three wagons full of goodtime girls followed behind, several of whom looked drunk. Jack Finley was recumbent in a rented carriage driven by his doorman Otto with a pretty young redhead beside him. He tipped a bottle of champagne to his lips as the girl's head disappeared in his lap and waved at Alice Mary, who fought the urge to curse him. She ground her teeth and gazed up at the hill where Honey Bee would be laid to rest. *Well... we're whores, ain't we?*

They made the half-hour ride to the new graveyards on the ridge and stopped at a freshly dug hole between two impressive monuments bought by wealth the owners hadn't had the chance to squander in the saloons and cribs before fate found them. Dawson City was a jumble of log and lumber buildings below with its false-front showhouses, warehouses, and stores clustered along the Yukon River. She could see the buildings and parade ground of Fort Herchmer and the brightly painted shacks of the Line on Fourth Avenue with the fence encircling them. The valley of the Yukon stretched in both directions between mountains capped with fall's first snows, and V's of geese called as they headed south against a clear blue sky between pillars of smoke from steamboats at the wharves. One looked just like the one she'd ridden on as a little girl on the Ohio River at the western edge of her childhood world. Her father was back from leading a company of infantry in Cuba and spent the trip smoking big cigars he'd brought home. Of course he went away again, and was never there to protect her from his nephew. The boat had a blue wheelhouse with its name in gold letters and red spokes on the stern wheel with the name again: *VOYAGER*. Alice Mary wanted to be on it.

Golden birch leaves coated the fresh hole in the earth and glowed against the damp gravel within. They swirled in the breeze as Alice Mary swatted at a tiny red fly buzzing around her face. The Episcopal preacher from St. Andrews stood in his black cassock before the grave, waving at gnats and little red flies as the procession disembarked. People crowded around as Alice Mary stepped off the hearse. Once again Charlie Meadows was there, lifting her gently to the ground this time. She hugged the roses as he brushed her cheek with his lips. "We won't forget her, young lady," he whispered in her ear. Alice Mary blinked away tears. It was the first time someone had called her *lady* in Dawson City, and most likely the last.

Molly Fewclothes tossed a mass of black curls out of her face, adjusted her silk dress with embroidered flowers over large breasts, and seized Alice Mary's hand. "Come on hon, you're sposed to be in front."

Alice Mary stumbled on the soft ground in her black patent leather boots, stopped at the edge of the grave, and kicked a clod in. Soon all would be frozen solid and Honey Bee would be one with the cold ground. Alice felt the leaden dark of winter on her shoulders and swiped at her eyes.

The preacher looked bored and shifted from one foot to the other as the procession arrived. Alice Mary tried to make eye contact, but he wasn't having any of it. He'd been paid after protest to be here by Swiftwater Bill, and maybe even strong-armed a mite by Charley. She smirked. He caught her expression and gave her his best *To Hell* look in return, before he cleared his throat. "Ladies and gentlemen," he began, "we are gathered here today to give back to the Lord she who was taken by most foul deed from our midst and commend her to his bosom. Alas, but a child of sixteen who fell from grace and dwelt amongst the wretched of the earth, yet a child of God nonetheless."

"Amen!" came from the Oregon Mare as she towered over a cluster of goodtime girls on the edge of the crowd.

67

Three-Way Annie sobbed. Klondike Kate turned violet eyes to the sky and bowed her head. Charlie Meadows stood beside Alice Mary with his big white Stetson hat to his chest. He reached down for her hand and she took it.

"Are there those present who would care to say a few words over our departed sister?"

"Damn straight!" The Oregon Mare's voice echoed off birch stumps and the monuments of dead miners. "This weren't no lost soul; she had a whole life ahead of her, and family. May the dastard done this be hunted down like the mad dog he is... and every girl in the District oughta get herself a pistol for that matter!"

A roar of approbation came from the assembled goodtime girls.

The Mountie at the back of the crowd raised his voice. "Ahem! In the name of the Crown, there shall be no talk of pistols within the confines of Dawson City!"

An uncomfortable silence fell as saloon keepers and sex workers comported themselves before the authority of the Crown. Alice Mary finally spoke. "'Spose Ah'm a lost child myself, and Ah'm her closest kin hereabouts 'cause of it. Her name was Sonya Ann Pederson, and that's the name should be on her marker. Ah thank y'all for showin' the respect she didn't find here in life and Ah want y'all to know she was dead set to make good after this. She come from a farm in Minnesota and she didn't have no chance to be who she was if'n she stayed. Her own family done her in, just like my family done me. Preachers and teachers didn't do her no good, nor give her no help when her own cousin was havin' his way with her, and nobody ever—"

"That shall be quite enough!" the Parson commanded, "we are here to ask for forgiveness for her soul, not to roll in the reek of sin and debauchery!"

"Fuck you."

The Mountie gasped and pushed through the crowd, but Arizona Charlie put his six-foot six frame in front of him and held up a hand. "Now calm down, Corporal Pippin, the girl's a mite upset."

"That base woman must cease her—"

"Have it your way, Mr. Yellalegs." Alice Mary's angry stare was reflected by the preacher's in spades as the saloon keepers and show-house owners shifted uncomfortably and checked their watches. The goodtime girls closed ranks around Alice Mary beside the grave. Arizona Charley held her hand as the coffin was lowered and the Oregon Mare took her other hand. Alice Mary tossed in the roses.

VIII.

THE OREGON MARE BLINKED AWAKE IN A SHAFT OF SUNLIGHT. SHE reached for the man she'd retired with and swore as her hand stretched across the flannel sheets. She sat up and yawned. The sound that had awoken her came from somewhere between the bed and the wall. She peered over the side with her long legs dangling over the other.

A prostrate form lay between the bed and the window, naked but for woolen socks. His hands were wrapped around a bearhide poke clutched to his hairy chest as if he were laid in his grave with something precious, and his waxed mustache quivered beneath a pronounced nose. A gold tooth flashed as his upper lip trembled before a drawn-out snarling shook the walls.

"Damn." She yawned again and scratched under an arm. It was a shame George didn't trust her any more than that. His gold was safer with her than any bank in town. Miners left their pokes with the best goodtime girls all the time for safekeeping. She would simply take what was agreed upon and guard the remainder with her life, and anybody who wanted to take on all six feet of the Oregon Mare was in for a very hard time indeed. "Oh, well."

George was a North-West Mounted Police Inspector who hadn't yet learned the finer points of etiquette in regard to her profession. He'd only been in Dawson City a month, and it was her good luck he'd succumbed to her charms rather than arresting her for working outside the District. She glanced at the pile of dust and flakes on the nightstand crowned with a nugget the size of a pigeon egg. How did a Mountie come by that? Of course, that wasn't any of her business.

Diamond Tooth Gertie kept a fine house and Edith would tidy up before she left. The place had gold brocade curtains between the parlor and bedroom with pictures on the walls of lush southern plantations complete with ladies and gentlemen dressed in antebellum finery on the balconies. Gertie was from South Carolina and used her accent to good stead. She called every fellow she met 'Sir' with a lovely tilt of her head and a curtsy that would do Queen Victoria proud.

"It's all in the packaging." Edith said to the recumbent George as she poked the embers in the stove with an iron. After stirring and blowing on it, she added a scoop of coal. Once she'd heated water and bathed, she would send him on his way, leave Gertie a nice note and a pinch of dust for the use of her house, and drop the sheets at the laundry.

Edith Neal didn't have a crib and wasn't going to get one. She danced, took gold from men, and stayed wherever and with whomever she damn well pleased. She'd gotten through the last winter in style, and there were a lot more rich fellows in town in this one with more saloons, hotels, and naive Cheechakos to boot. Besides, to be called a whore and live in the Segregated District wasn't her cup of tea. At the cribs they just lined up at your door, and she'd rather pick and choose in the resorts and showhouses. Of course if the Yellowlegs caught her plying her trade out of the District, she'd be forced to do laundry at Fort Herchmer just fifty yards south of Gertie's for the hypocritical sonsabitches while enduring some prune-faced Chaplain's noise. She put a hand to her mouth. *Inspector of the North-West Mounted Police.* It offered an opportunity for payback on some of his peers, should she play it right.

Gertie's house stood on Church Street in the shadow of St. Paul's Anglican Church that was being rebuilt after the last fire, and the house had a back door that George or any other 'respectable' fellow could slip out of into an alley just yards from the Commissioner of the Territory's palatial residence. His bright red coat and tan hat hung on a chair, but he'd hung his creased blue pants with yellow stripes in the closet. *Mr. Yellowlegs.*

Edith sat up, took a deep breath, and let out a piercing whinny.

George sat bolt upright on the floor with his hands fluttering on his chest as his eyes shot around the room.

"Good mornin'!"

George rubbed his eyes and set to looking for his clothes.

"Your proper 'ol clothes are properly hung, Guv'ner."

George coughed and shook his head. "Zounds, Edie, no wonder they call you the mare!"

She cocked a purple-painted toe at his face. "And proud of it, Mister Queen's Law."

He cleared his throat. "I must admit the way you kicked that Dodge fellow halfway across York Street would do a stallion proud, Madame." As he stood, the poke landed on the floor with a thud. George scooped it up and held it in front of his privates.

"That sonofabitch got a mean streak towards women that could use some permanent fixin', if you ask me."

"Lucky I stopped you then before someone got hurt."

"Too bad, actually, although it was an interesting way to meet. You know, George, you don't have to worry 'bout your gold around here. Clarence Berry gave me a sack that would break a man's back to sit on last spring and he ain't even a customer. He was goin' to Fortymile, the banks were closed, and he knew I was trustworthy. Didn't even look at it. I just put it under the sink at a trusted friend's place. Got all wet and the burlap rotted by the time he came back. Clarence laughed like hell and said he was glad I didn't store it in the crapper. Said I could take my pick o' nuggets he did."

George stepped into his pants. "Well, I'm not one of the Eldorado Kings like Clarence."

"Oh, I know, you got to keep your red coat clean and all. Must be hell watchin' all these folks havin' such a grand ol' time and having to make them stop at twelve a.m. Sunday mornin'. That's lunchtime in my book. Anyway I hope I helped you make up for it just a bit."

"That you did, ma'am," George tipped the hat he'd returned to his head, "I am fairly wrung out. I didn't know a woman could be so rough-and-tumble to be honest."

"Well, now you do."

"Indeed. Um... if you'll excuse me I must be returning to the Post as I am to take a detachment to Fort Constantine this very afternoon. Some half-breed blackguard has shot a man on the American side and is under guard there. Sergeant Fitzgerald was tasked to do it, but he has been assigned to patrol the Segregated District, as some miscreant murdered a poor girl on the Line and the rest are nearly hysterical."

"I know all about it."

George's mustache quivered again, and he exhaled. "I must accompany the criminal from Fort Constantine all the way to Skagway for a boat to Juneau."

Edith snorted. "Damn sight easier to hang him here. Hell, George, we both know there's hangin' goin' on that nobody gives a hoot about. There's a couple lugs in this town I'd pay to watch swing. Some of us even know where you bury 'em, sweetcakes."

George gave her a bemused glance and nodded. "I wholeheartedly agree, but unfortunately the minutiae of international diplomacy does not allow for it in this situation."

"A Mountie's work is never done," Edith's eyes lost focus for a moment. "Hope your boys find the fuckin' bastard who killed Honey Bee. That little girl never shoulda come to an end like that."

George cleared his throat and reached into his poke. "We shall, I assure you. Perhaps you will accept this as a further token of my esteem." He produced a piece about the size of a nickel and offered it to her with a flourish.

"Seen bigger nuggets stuck in the cracks of Frank Dinsmore's outhouse, sweetcakes."

George's face puckered as if he had bitten into something sour.

"The way we do it around here is like *this,*" The Oregon Mare took the poke, lifted the tasseled coverlet of the nightstand, and spread the contents across the little table, "Hum," she poked a finger amongst the glittering prizes and selected the second largest of the bunch, one just slightly smaller than the pigeon egg already crowning the pile from the night before. "This should do, dearest."

George swallowed, "Yes, of course."

"Thank you my sweet." She kissed him on the forehead. "Now, you should be gettin' along to the Post. Watch out for Commissioner Steele's cleaning lady; she's usually beatin' the rugs this time a' mornin' and can see a good piece down this way. You're lucky he's in White Horse. I shall dream of you in the long nights 'til we meet again." Edith opened the poke and pushed the remaining dust, flakes, and nuggets into it from the edge of the table, making sure to spill some on the opposite side as she did. She handed it to him, and with her other hand on his shoulder escorted him to the back door, opened it, and shoved him into the alley with a peck on the cheek. "Ta-ta, love."

George froze on the steps, and his head swung from side to side in terror he'd been spotted leaving the abode of Diamond Tooth Gertie before he stalked off down the alley tugging at the sleeves of his red coat.

Edith slammed the door. "Cheap sonofabitch." She slapped her hands as if cleaning his spoor from them and began to pick gold out of the carpet behind the nightstand.

———

Afterward she filled a thin brass pipe with opium and took a bath in lavender salts, stretching her long legs in the tub under a mantle of white smoke. George had been rather intimidated by her, and she'd had no luck in satisfying herself whatsoever. Now she felt like taking on the biggest strongest sonofabitch in Dawson City... as long as he had the money. She slapped the water and it splashed on the floor. She shouldn't give it away to some good looking fellow with a hard luck story. She was primed for it after her night with George, who after all was here to regulate and harass all the hardworking pilgrims like herself. Edith sighed. She was too damn soft-hearted for this job... or her own good for that matter.

She dressed for the sleepless streets of Dawson in a pink silk dress with her trophy belt of nuggets and examined herself in the mirror, running long-fingered hands through short brown hair as she adjusted a golden choker around her neck. Some diamonds or sapphires would stand out so much more than gold in a town like Dawson. The next time she hooked up with one of the Bonanza or Eldorado fellows, she should get him to buy her some stones from that Jewish jeweler on York Street *before* a bed. She felt rather mean, and quite unfulfilled, and admonished herself not to get out of hand this evening.

The Monte Carlo had a party Swiftwater Bill was throwing for Gussie Lamore, and Gussie owed Edith fifty bucks from bailing her out of a fix at the docks with two teamsters. The Grand Opera House on King was changing names, and although the official party and renaming weren't scheduled until October, plenty of highrollers would be there drinking to Charlie Meadows' health and the success of the Palace. Miners would be gambling over at the Standard Theater while some vaudeville act of Sid Grauman's was on stage. He owed her a favor too. Nigger Jim Daughtery at the Pavilion was throwing a birthday party for one of his favorite girls, her friend Belinda had let her know there was a fellow from Eldorado Creek staying at the Fairmount who always dropped a bundle, and Eddie Doland had told her that the Savoy had a new show from Seattle that ought to snare some of the big fish from Bonanza looking for girls with a little breeding.

She'd start at the Monte Carlo and get Gussie to have Bill cough up a couple bottles of good champagne for her and whoever she chose to get into one of the balcony boxes. Bill was crazy about Gussie and would do almost anything that woman asked. Last winter he'd found her having breakfast with another man, and in a fit of jealousy had bought up every egg in town because she claimed she couldn't start the day without them. He'd had them fried up and thrown to the sled dogs on Front. People had been calling him King of the Golden Omelet ever since. After the Monte Carlo she'd go to the Grand... the *Palace,* to see what was up. Too bad Arizona Charlie was married to Mae.

She blinked at the wicked grin in the mirror. Mae was full of laudanum and whiskey recovering from a gunshot. There was an opportunity to hook up with him if she took it, although she wasn't the only one with that idea. If some little tart got in her face when she had him primed and ready, she'd rip the hussy's hair out. Charlie was a big man and he deserved a big woman like the Oregon Mare. The two of them would do a hell of a job to a bed, and it would more than make up for a grueling night with George. A night with Charlie would be something to remember: the King of the Cowboys and the Oregon Mare for one helluva hard ride. She could even have their picture taken over at Hegg's studio for a keepsake.

"Oh, *stop* it!" she shouted at the mirror. Here she was going off to dreamland about somebody who hadn't even given her more than a wink and tip of his big Stetson hat. Charlie had twenty beautiful girls working for him and a hundred more who would jump at getting him in a bed behind Mae's back. The boys were standing in line for any old girl, but Charlie Meadows was someone any goodtime girl in Dawson would pay for.

"Good men are hard to find," Edith admonished her reflection before she left for her night on the town.

The songs of wolves roiled the marrow of her bones as Lorelei kept her vision far away from the town her body was in, relishing the joy of a young wolf bursting from the company of her elders to chase a snowshoe hare between birch trunks. The scent of the rabbit and tang of crushed leaves as she sped through the brush was a tonic in her wolf's nose, as for a short and precious time Lorelei had the light of the sun all around her and its balm filled her being.

The Sun.

Lorelei exulted in its heat on a thick fall coat and crisp air rolling over a lolling tongue. The hare ducked under a cottonwood's roots. The young bitch wolf let out a yip of frustration and sat down to chew at a dry spot at the base of her tail.

With a flick of her will, Lorelei made the wolf turn her face toward the light in the sky. The animal flinched as if from a blow, closing her eyes as it beat upon their lids as Lorelei luxuriated in that last warmth before she let the young hunter trot back to her family.

Day was shrinking by a half-dozen minutes with each rising and falling of the sun. If she took the day now, she might yet have twelve hours to know the light. Yet whatever the time she chose, if she would have a day the price would be the same.

Day was easy. All she had to do was find one good man, a man who was worthy and loving, whose life and substance were at the cusp of his existence and all she could expect of his kind: a young man like Joseph. She would use the allure of perfect flesh and flashing eyes to take him where he wouldn't rise again, use his mortal life and immortal soul as the tender she must give back to the Light, just as all her kind had done for millennia.

Lorelei moaned. What once was the holy *right* of her kind was now her curse. That perfect *Taking* was the greatest pleasure she'd ever had or ever would know, yet she detested killing good men. In her youth she'd awoken from the afterglow next to the empty flesh that had been her lover to find herself drifting alone in the deepest, darkest place in all creation... her own *Hell*. "Shit."

Sun shone through cracks in the curtains and her eyes squeezed shut against her will. Lorelei forced them open, staring at the golden traces of day tantalizing her from between the thick drapes while painful flashes of lightening bounced in her retinas. Her eyes closed of their own accord.

It had been a year since a young seer had given her a day, someone who had done all things right in regard to her, and she was helpless before the power of it. He was the youngest son of Chief Charley on the Kandik River, and with the ancient knowledge of blood had commanded her to do her most holy duty in the name of love and submit to his bidding. With an irresistible will he had woven his power upon her, for he would become as Raven, and for one day restore the sun to the sky with his own blood. His love was beyond denial, her surrender ordained.

She shuddered as his reflection flowered to life from where she kept it. *The taking of a soul,* a beautiful soul dwelling in her forever, but only in part. She drew her knees under her chin and examined her toes. Joseph could give her that day. It was easy with a virgin.

I will not do it!

She would not... she could *not* steal the promise of the life he carried within him like some selfish bitch mindful only of her own satisfaction. Only a few nights ago she'd let Sonya die at the hands of a fiend while she was engrossed with Joseph and loathed herself for the loss.

There are too many.

Lorelei was born to take them, born to survive on the spirit and blood of men, yet only when a powerful and good man discovered her on his own in what was meant to be by his own nature, and with his full knowledge commanded it, could she accomplish her ancient purpose anymore.

The golden promise of that young seer's life on the Kandik was gone from the world, and his people, faced with the tide of newcomers from Outside, needed him more than they would ever know. Because of this, far more than the hatred and burnings of her kind for centuries, she must remain hidden. It was why she had abandoned the Han/Gwich'in clan on the Kandik, even though the long nights were coming when she could move without impediment.

She groaned. Why hadn't she been born a thousand years earlier? Her mother never had these attacks of conscience in Ireland or in the Massachusetts Colony where Lorelei had been raised two hundred years ago in the forests of the old frontier.

Night was swelling like a wave swallowing the world, and now she had this awful hunger to take another good life for the selfish love of a single day and of the taking itself. It was a thing she had no regret in the doing, but only in the endless years of reflection afterward and the awful loneliness of living on.

She seized the brass lamp on the nightstand and crushed it in a seemingly soft hand. She growled, unwound her fingers from the twisted metal, and put the thing back on the table but it fell off. She would find Fred Dodge when he returned and rip his black heart from his chest! She should have paid *attention!* She should have *known!* She would ignore the need for a *Taking* and hope it would abate. Lorelei groaned. The Klondike needed all the good men it could get.

IX.

EVENING FOUND JOSEPH AND MARY ON THE SECOND FLOOR OF THE EMPIRE Hotel. Mary's mother Jane sat on a maroon couch. She wore her strawberry blond hair in a proper bun that she kept touching as she greeted him with exaggerated courtesy tinged with disbelief. She'd talked Jack Finley into renting the apartment for the winter on the promise of returning Mary to his company, and upon Jane's none-so-subtle reminder of the arrangement, Mary gave a drawn-out sigh and took her mother into the adjoining room.

Joseph waited on the sofa in the tiny parlor sipping on a glass of sugary lemonade. He'd been eating all day and could still smell the waffles and coffee at a little stand on Front Street they'd passed earlier. He'd done nothing in regard to Lorelei, yet he felt sure they'd meet this evening and all would be right with the world. He closed his eyes and imagined her bathed in a nimbus of golden light like some kind of angel.

Who are you?

Anticipation of his first experience with a woman had been part of the thrill of his adventure. He'd listened in silence at the bawdy tales men told on the journey north and had considered the whores in Skagway, but had stubbornly held onto his virginity with the notion he'd encounter someone better. He certainly had... but why was it so hard to remember what had happened with her? He sighed and drained the lemonade with a sip that left the paper straw flat.

It sounded as if Mary's mother was arranging another tryst with Jack. That didn't seem strange at all. He hadn't seen a better-looking girl than Mary in Dawson City except for Lorelei, who would surely appear at the perfect time and snatch him back to her bed, which was the only place he wanted to be.

He'd learned in White Horse that all the rich claims had been staked in '97. Two years on, latecomers were working for wages along Eldorado, Bonanza, Hunker and Sulfur Creeks with ten men for every job. He'd have to wait until next season if he were to make his own strike on some distant creek. Fifteen dollars a day was the going rate for hacking holes in the permafrost, some ten times the wages Outside. Men worked by the light of storm lanterns in the winter, sat in dark smoky cabins when they weren't in the ground, and shoveled gravel all summer into sluices and rocker boxes while living on beans and pilot bread as mosquitoes and flies hung in biting clouds. Most spent every dime in town when freed from their labors, only to return to the creeks to make the claim owners rich. Now, Lorelei was paying him twenty dollars a day and all he had to do was be her lover, which was priceless. There wasn't any sense in heading to the diggings when he had that kind of arrangement.

What if she grows tired of me?

He wadded up the straw and shrugged. The thought didn't have any weight against a sense of contentment that was unshakable. In the whole world, the only things plaguing him were a gnawing hunger he couldn't sate and the fact that he couldn't remember anything at all after he'd entered her. Women spoke of swooning at such times, but the idea he might be prone to the same thoroughly irritated him.

As the sun set in the south, nightfall brought a sense of her growing closer, as if she were a beautiful flower blooming in the shadows. He closed his eyes and felt her breath and the softness of her kiss.

Lovely laughter tickled his spine.

Joseph sat up, rubbed his eyes, and gazed across Queen Street. The lights were coming on in Dawson, and a Mountie stood with a well-dressed young woman in front of the Pioneer Drug Store who was arguing heatedly with the Constable. The red-coated man shook his head and pointed toward the Segregated District. Voices grew louder in the other room and a door closed. Mary returned, sighed, and plopped down beside him on the couch. "Joe, I must return to Jack."

"I surmised as much."

"We shall have our time together."

"That's all right," he smiled, "she calls to me."

"What?"

"Oh nothing... I mean I don't know. I just feel all things shall work out between us. Joseph kissed her cheek, and Mary responded instantly on his lips.

She pulled away with a loud sigh. "As do I." She went to the door, but instead of stepping into the hall, she pulled the chain across it. "Would you consider me forward if I should care to use the short time we have remaining as your paramour?"

As she began to remove her clothes, he again heard a peal of laughter, and his eyes jerked to the window. Joseph ran hands through his hair and peered into the street for the source of the sound.

"We should close these." Mary stood in a white lace bustier and petticoat as she drew the drapes across the glass, and Joseph caught the slack-jawed stare of a bearded miner on the wooden sidewalk. "Well, Joe," she smiled, "we don't have all evening. After we have pleasured each other, I must bathe and hurry to meet Jack."

"I—"

Take her, love. Lorelei's voice caressed his left ear and her breath was against his cheek. Joseph's nostrils flared. He could smell her. *You're not imagining things. Only you can hear me.*

"How?"

Mary stepped back and eyed him.

You'll grow to accept this. I thought you could appreciate Mary when we aren't together. She's never had a companion of your caliber, and it will make you feel useful also. Just don't... oh never mind, I'll keep an eye on things. I think I should make you a rich man before winter is over, Her laugh rippled through him, *Look down.* He did and saw the bulge in his pants. *Things could be much worse as you've already concluded. Now, might I suggest you devote yourself to the task at hand?*

Mary unbuttoned his pants and he let out his breath.

Alice Mary stared at the aurora dancing over Moosehide Slide and brought the bottle to her lips. The whiskey burned on the way down, but that was what she wanted. Honey Bee's killer hadn't been able to open the safe in his haste to leave their crib, and Alice had hauled all the keepsakes from the family who knew her as Sonya to the big new post office on King Street and mailed them to Minnesota by the Royal Mail. *The Royal Mail.* She liked that. She'd exchanged Honey Bee's gold for paper money and sent that too. She kept a few things they'd shared and a sepia picture of the two girls together draped in gauzy silk slips and ropes of nuggets that Swiftwater Bill had talked them into taking at Hegg's Studio and paid for. She'd had it framed and mounted on the wall.

She'd sought out the oldest scotch in Dawson City to toast her soul mate. It took the aid of a man of course, since the Yellowlegs wouldn't allow a girl of her years to purchase it, although servicing the men who drank it was another matter entirely. She could have had a Mountie buy it if she'd been willing to spend the few minutes it took to please him. "Yellaleg shits."

Two men looked up from their negotiation with the Belgian sisters Laura and Hermine across the street. "Sorry! Ah'm not workin' fellas!" The men continued to examine her, before returning to the older and plumper inventory, who promptly dragged them inside their crib and shut the door.

Alice Mary rocked on the wooden sidewalk and kicked a half-frozen chunk of horse droppings with her patent leather boots. She held up the bottle and examined it. Swiftwater Bill said it was sixteen years old and had gone on about some place in Scotland and peat moss or something. She could read the numbers herself. "Same age as me," she took a long pull and gasped, "same as Honey Bee!" She wobbled into the shack, slammed the thick birch rod she used to bar the door, and fell on the bed. The bottle began to roll out of her hand, but she caught it and pressed the cork down tight. She rolled it back and forth across her lover's Norwegian quilt and curled around it like a cat. She really wanted a cat.

Alice Mary jerked erect at a keening noise like a dog in pain and grabbed her Bowie knife. She scanned the windows and checked the door before she realized it had been herself. "Fuck it!" She threw her knife into the log wall and it sunk with a sound like something breaking.

Green light pulsed against the stars as day faded, arching over Polaris as it rose above the moonlit jumble of the Ogilvie Mountains. The arc grew as it began to drip toward the earth, and red appeared in its folds as the night came alive.

Lorelei stroked her hair with a boar bristle brush. Its mother of pearl handle glowed in near-darkness. She closed her eyes to feel the churning above. Dawson City seethed around her, filled with the souls of outnumbered young women planning how they might offer themselves to the newly rich, while planning their escapes should the meetings prove unsatisfactory.

The Oregon Mare sought her prey on Front Street as she approached the Monte Carlo, where Gussie Lamore sniffed cocaine from a green vial in a box above the dance floor beside Swiftwater Bill Gates and her sister Grace. Lorelei felt excitement and ambition boiling in a violet-eyed Klondike Kate Rockwell as a Greek bartender named Alexander Pantages told her she was the most beautiful woman in the world, and meant it. A hung-over Lily awoke in a room behind the Tivoli next to a man three times her age and cursed, casting about for her clothes. In a room above the Palace, Mae Meadows flinched and swore at the sting of iodine on the end of a mangled thumb. Mary was climbing the narrow stairs at the back of Jack's place, approaching Lorelei's room.

———

Mary stopped with her hand on the door of the arctic entry, opened it, and stood for a moment in darkness amongst dusty mackinaws and dirt-caked gum boots.

"Come in."

Mary opened the inner door onto the dim room. Lorelei was dressed in a blue crinoline dress and ostrich-plumed hat. Her hair was in a ladylike bun, and she wore the gold nugget belt of a goodtime girl with two diamond and nugget dog collar necklaces around her slim throat that glittered in the low light. Pendant earrings hung from her white lobes, each a large nugget set with a diamond. Her eyes glowed as Mary shut the door.

"Is Jack here?"

"He's downstairs. Are you in a great hurry to see him?"

"I am young, but I can feel the bite in your words."

"You're a smart girl. Did you enjoy Joseph?"

Mary swallowed as she tried to adjust to the dimness. Lorelei's eyes were the brightest thing in the room. Mary felt no threat from her, but neither could she puzzle out how she could possibly know, at least not yet. The curious comments Joseph had made in regard to Lorelei came back. "Pardon me, but you strike me quite oddly, ma'am." She glanced toward Jack's room. With any luck he'd be late and drunk. Perhaps he'd even fall asleep before he touched her.

"I thought you and Joseph would make useful friends."

"Well, we have."

Lorelei laughed. "Indeed. You might live long if you continue to listen to that part of yourself that knows what men cannot say, or most women for that matter."

"You surely do speak in riddles."

"Quite literally, love. Would you prefer to spend the night in my company?"

"I should—"

"You needn't linger here like Jack's chambermaid. I'll make sure that whatever you choose to do, he accepts it. He's easy. Besides, you're dying to get back down into the thick of it and see what Joseph's about, and you would dearly love to flirt with that fine specimen of a man Charlie Meadows." Lorelei's cheeks dimpled, "Then again, perhaps you'd rather stay for the goings-on at this establishment."

"How can you make Jack behave?"

"An inherited trait."

"I get a very odd feeling about you, Lorelei, if you don't mind my saying so."

"I appreciate it. I am consumed with an endless need for the company of youth, for as you discover the depths of passions you have never known, I myself am justified. Well, I suppose I should dress you properly if we are to see the town together. You would be stunning in either green or violet with your fair complexion."

"Do you have something that would fit me?"

"I just happen to have come across two outfits in exactly your size, green and violet perchance, and of course, jewelry." With the flash of a wooden match, Lorelei lit two kerosene lamps upon the dresser.

Mary gasped as her eyes lit upon a braided golden belt across a cloth of royal blue velvet, with its nuggets throbbing in the flickering lamplight. A necklace of seed pearls interspersed with nuggets lay beside it in the glow of the flames, and two matching nugget earrings sat in the middle.

Lorelei draped the necklace around Mary's throat, then stood back and whistled. "I must say you're stunning with this."

Mary stared at herself in the mirror as her fingers caressed the gold and pearls. "Oh, my God . . ."

Lorelei lay soft palms on Mary's shoulders. "I could let you keep these little trinkets if things work out. I shant even demand your favors... at least not at the moment." A trill of laughter rippled her throat.

Mary stared in the mirror. "But, why?"

"Why question? If I were a rich man, you would simply consider yourself fortunate as well as deserving. As I said, I find pleasure in your experience and could use a companion this evening, one who can cloud men's minds with her charms of course."

Mary giggled. "I suppose I could consider myself your protégé then."

"In a way."

"Well then, what's not to like in that?"

"Very little love."

X.

EDITH SPIED A HIGHROLLER STEPPING OUT OF A BARBER SHOP AT THE corner of Front and Princess. He wasn't a bad-looking sort, being tall with a newly trimmed reddish beard. He kept putting a finger in the tight starched collar of the boiled linen shirt he'd purchased that afternoon, and had the smell of one of the newly rich whose fortune was burning a hole in his poke.

Edith seized him by the hand, and he meekly followed her into the Monte Carlo. She steered him to one of the upper booths and handed a nugget to the waiter, who winked and went for a bottle of champagne. She asked him his name, which was Jim, sat him down above the still sparse crowd out of sight of the bar, and planted a kiss upon his lips. By the time the second bottle had arrived, he was telling her the story of his life and proposing marriage. They hit the Palace an hour later with the Mare attached to Jim's arm and his poke in her possession for safekeeping. Edith planned to fill a couple gaps in her nugget belt with two of his finest trophies, perhaps three.

She handed the poke to the waiter, a sturdily built olive-skinned fellow named Alexander who'd come over from the Monte Carlo for the evening as his violet-eyed girlfriend Kate was onstage. Alex had a trick worked out with Edith: she would pour her champagne into a clean spittoon placed under her seat for that purpose, and when Jim went down to the water closet, Alex refilled an empty bottle from it through a funnel he kept stashed to sell it again. At the same time he made sure to weigh the gold in plain sight at the bar so as Jim could see from the balcony and return the poke each time to its upright keeper, the Mare.

When Jim stumbled back from the WC, he nearly ran into Diamond Tooth Gertie, who was of a stature nearly as imposing as the Mare, forty pounds lighter and considerably more attractive. Gertie was preparing for her turn on the stage, but wasn't too busy to put her arms around Jim's neck and give him a taste of her perfume. The diamond wedged in the gap in her upper teeth sparkled, and her long blond hair hung to a remarkably slim waist girdled with a nugget belt that was the envy of Dawson. Three places on it were conspicuously empty, no doubt to be filled by helpful miners come morning.

Gertie was pressing her breasts against Jim when Edith appeared and seized Jim's hand in her own. "Come on, sugar, we got another bottle of the real French stuff upstairs." Edith's voice was cloyingly sweet as she threw Gertie a mild flash of annoyance over his shoulder.

"Sorry Edie, didn't know he was taken."

As soon as Edith had Jim in the booth, she put hands around his waist and her lips to his. "Stand still, honey." She removed his coat, released the pressure of the tight collar, and loosened his suspenders. With a deftness born of experience, she undid Jim's belt and yanked his new herringbone pants down around his ankles. He stood speechless, staring at the top of her head. "Now sit down." The Mare wasn't going to lose her mark for the evening.

Joseph rode his Appaloosa through emerald grass as strange birds wheeled and cried in the hot summer air. Grasshoppers exploded from the grass and crackled like popcorn in the heat. He reached the pond where he did his best thinking, slid off his mount, and reached for his notebook. It was important he write something down before he forgot.

A musical laugh made him glance up. Lorelei stood naked in the pond. Joseph blinked, and her reflection in the green water danced like a white flame in the backs of his eyes. He put a hand up to shade them, and she laughed again.

He awoke from the dream with a headache. He moaned to the empty room, staggered to his feet, and hurried to the water closet down the hall to empty his bladder with a groan. Joseph saw a brief flicker of red in the dim light, but when he rubbed his eyes, it was gone. He returned to the room and searched for something for what felt like a crack in his skull that had appeared upon waking and was threatening to become a yawning canyon. A brown bottle of Bayer's Aspirin sat on the bedside table. Joseph examined the German words, sighed, tore off the paper cover, and pulled the cork. He shook five of the pills into his hand and washed them down with water from the pitcher on the nightstand.

Be sure and eat before you join us. Your blood is too thin.

He glanced about, though he knew he'd find no one. "What manner of woman are you?"

My, I'm tempted to call you bitchy.

"Christ, I'm hearing voices, and my head hurts!"

They say aspirin does wonders, but I shall send Esther the maid up with a tincture of opium just in case. She's a dear, so be nice and do not curse. I'm going to have her give you a bath.

A chuckle rippled his lips. "That shall be the third bath in a row I'm taking with a different woman." He fell on the bed and rubbed his temples. "I'm going crazy."

You'll get used to it. After you have bathed meet me and Mary at the haberdashery across the street. I've got to dress you properly.

"Why?"

We're spending the evening at the Palace Grand Theater. Mary looks simply stunning by the way.

"You put us together—as lovers."

Yes, her laughter rippled through his nerves like fingers on the strings of a harp.

"To what do we owe this honor? I mean... why?"

Due to your own nature which I did not create, and despite your present whining you're quite comfortable with it.

"I'm not in the least sure what you even mean, Lorelei." Joseph sat up at a knock on the door. The pain between his ears twisted into a knot and he gasped.

"Excuse me sir, I'm here for your bath."

Do let her in.

"All right." He went to the door.

A pretty Indian girl wearing a maid's brown dress and white apron stood holding a green bottle, with a rough-looking fellow in the hall behind her holding a pile of clean towels. Ester directed him to place them on a chair, and the man left, giving Joseph an envious glance as he shut the door behind him.

"That's—" He eyed the bottle.

I told you. Take only a spoonful with some water.

"All right."

"Your pardon?"

"That's opium tincture, Ester."

"Yes, Miss Lorelei says to—"

"Take only a spoonful."

"Yes," Ester put a hand to her mouth, "she says I am to wash you."

"Well, all right. I shant bite."

———

He was fed, dressed, and at the Palace in the company of Lorelei and Mary by eight. The place was crowded to the walls around the faro tables and the long teak bar. Cigar smoke drifted in a layer head-high to be parted by two beautiful young women who entered with a young man on their arms looking uncomfortable in a wing-collared shirt, silk tie, and double-breasted herringbone suit.

Don't be nervous, love. They envy you.

His back twitched. Lorelei was right there beside him, but it was the same voice she'd used when she wasn't. He couldn't for the life of him guess how she did it. Her lips parted with a flash of white teeth, and he forgot to breathe as he stared at the pale curve of her cheek and the glow of her eyes. Something bright flashed behind his own eyes—a memory, a place... he couldn't tell. With a yank Mary pulled him through the crowd, and they made their way toward the stairs.

They were placed in a four-seater behind a red damask curtain by a waiter with slicked-back dark hair. The box had upholstered gilt chairs with red velvet cushions. The waiter left, reappeared with a bottle of Mumms Extra Dry champagne and an ice bucket, and stared at Joseph.

"This is on me," Lorelei said, eliciting a bemused expression from the man. "You'll get a good tip, Alexander. Just make sure each bottle is sealed when it gets here." She said something to the waiter in a language neither of the youths could make out and handed him a nugget.

Alex weighed it in his palm, put it in his vest, and nodded. "Certainly, Madame." He left the booth.

"What were you talking?"

"Greek, love."

"Sure was to me!" Mary said, eliciting a laugh from Joseph. She squeezed his hand.

On the stage below Diamond Tooth Gertie was finishing a risqué song to the howling and clapping of men on the floor and the boxes above. She scooped up two dozen nuggets tossed at her feet along with an entire poke and disappeared in a swirl of golden fabric.

There were several girls with men in the other booths. As Joseph glanced at the one across from them, the head of the Oregon Mare arose. She gave him a wink and disappeared. He laughed.

A pretty red-haired girl appeared in a flowing pink dress and feather boa, and a hush fell over the crowd as she glided across the polished boards of the stage. An electric spotlight came on with a kaleidoscopic lens, throwing colored patterns on a sheet draped across the back of the stage as it illuminated her bright complexion with its shifting colors. Her fair cheeks glowed, but what caught Joseph's attention was the remarkable color of her eyes. They were the most amazing violet he'd ever seen. She seemed to look directly back at him as a fellow with a handlebar mustache and arm garters in the piano pit began to play.

The girl smiled around the theater, put her hands to her breast, and began to sing in a sweet trilling voice *She's Only a Bird in a Gilded Cage.* She wrung delicate hands before the deep cleavage of her dress as she stared into the balcony boxes, then directly into the light shining from the rear of the theater as it shifted to blue. Joseph craned his neck to examine the fellow standing high at the back of the room as the man slipped another colored filter over the light, and the girl was bathed in an amber glow. Her voice rose in pitch.

A gray-bearded man seated on the floor below let out a howl of anguish and tossed a nugget as big as one of his bulging eyeballs upon the stage. It bounced once and rattled at the girl's feet, to be joined by dozens more from about the room. Whole pokes joined them. A large one landed with a thud, resounding to the rafters over the music of the piano. The woman in the opposite booth had arisen beside the miner she'd been servicing, and was staring in amazement over the balustrade.

Joseph's gaze returned to the redhead on the stage. "Who is she?"

"Kitty Rockwell, Joseph, she's quite a little dish."

Mary gasped. "I should like to have it come so easily!"

"Kate, Queen of the Klondike!" A miner shouted as he stood up in a box between two girls and almost toppled into the crowd below. They seized his arms and sat him down between them, but he let out a howl, leapt back up, and tossed a huge nugget at the stage.

The nugget landed amongst the auburn tresses of Klondike Kate and bounced off her scalp onto the boards with a clatter. She staggered and put a hand to her head. "Ow, damn it!"

A roar of voices and laughter came from the audience, accompanied by shouts for silence as Alexander shoved his way toward the stage. Kate felt the top of her head, checked her fingers for blood, and waved off her man as she motioned for the piano player to resume where he had left off.

"Sorry, lovely!" The miner who had thrown the nugget called and tossed a whole poke in a gentle arc to land at her feet with a loud report.

Kate broke a smile, blew him a kiss, and the room erupted in cheers and applause as she began to sing again.

When the song ended, Charlie Meadows appeared on the stage in his best buckskin coat and white Stetson hat to present Kate with a bouquet of red roses wrapped in gauzy pink tulle. Kate smiled at the crowd and blew kisses as more gold landed upon the stage.

"Where in God's name would somebody get fresh *roses* around here?" Mary blurted.

"She's beautiful," Joseph mumbled.

Lorelei chuckled, "Yet a slave for that little Greek. He plays her like that man in the pit plays his piano, just as she plays these men. Desire is an endless dance that knows no permanent master, only the players seduced by their own youth into believing theirs is somehow an eternal thing preserving them from the same fate." She sighed, "Only the dance lives on."

Charlie Meadows left the stage, the lights dimmed, and Alex appeared to scoop up the gold and place it in a black satchel. Kate brushed his cheek with a kiss and whispered in his ear before she walked back into the single spotlight and curtsied to the crowd, eliciting another roar. More gold landed at her feet as the little Greek waiter darted about, careful to keep out of the glare. By the time she left the stage, it was clear of gold also.

XI.

LORELEI TOLD THE WAITER ALEXANDER IN HIS NATIVE GREEK TO PROVIDE whatever her young friends wished, and slipped away during the next performance. "Don't re-pour the champagne or ask them for any gold. You'll be rewarded by me." She fixed him in her gaze, and for emphasis, put a hand on his. Her eyes flashed a glimpse of red. Alexander stiffened when something ran through him like a wave, and she released his hand. "You have your own gifts. Perhaps I should put them to closer inspection, or at least let you remember some things we have already shared." She brushed lips across his and departed the balcony as he tottered, drinking her scent.

Lorelei passed amongst the men downstairs like a breeze, clouding the moment. She was in no mood to flirt or to attract attention. When she reached the sidewalk, she headed up King past the gate of the Segregated District and turned right into an alley that paralleled the back entrances of the cribs. The alley was used to enter and leave the rear doors of the little houses and, unlike the colorful entrance on King Street, was the most discrete method for customers with some social standing to depart after visiting the girls who worked there.

The alley was unlit and she made the half-block in one bound, sensing the impending damage to a terrified girl like a blister swelling in her flesh. She was but a blur and a breath of night air on the faces of drunks as they staggered from cribs. Lorelei slipped inside the little shack and stared at the tangled brown hair on the back of Fred Dodge's head. She felt his rage and sadistic pleasure as he raised a hand over the cringing girl pressed against a red papered wall who was holding a hand to her swollen lips.

A white rage surged up her spine, sending Alice Mary naked from the bed as she sprang to swing a tiny fist at her tormentor. A scream erupted from her chest as she stared into Fred's blue eyes and drove her hand with all her might into his smirking face. Then he was gone.

Alice Mary landed on the floor, yelped, and twisted to ward off the blows she felt coming. Her hand darted under the goose feather mattress and her fingers closed around the ivory handle of her Bowie knife. Honey Bee's face flashed before her as Alice Mary yanked the knife out and turned about the room with her breath rasping loud in her ears. The polished tip trembled in yellow lamplight. She swallowed, peering into the tiny parlor where she'd greeted drunken men many times her age. The house was empty. The door was shut.

Alice Mary sprang to the door and slammed the bolt. She moaned, sat on the bed, let out a sob, and the big knife slipped from her hands to sink point-first in the floorboards between her toes.

Cold air caressed her. Her fine dress was forgotten somewhere in the night, yet her belt of nuggets, earrings, and golden necklaces adorned her. The man she carried was the least of her burdens. His terror was a tonic, and the scent of his fear fed a fire in her that flared high in her heart. Lorelei shivered, not with the cold, but with knowl-edge of herself.

The aurora rippled over moonlit mountains like a bonfire of the gods as her beloved brethren sang from their crests. Each of their braided voices was a golden thread holding the heart of a wolf. Lorelei's own heart unraveled the fabric of their song as she bounded to the top of King Solomon's Dome carrying her unwilling sacrifice in one hand like a child's doll of straw to drop him amongst the frosty leaves of blueberries. Air exploded from his lungs as he hit the ground, followed by a tearing sound as if a thick cloth were being ripped: the sound of mindless terror flavored with the gibbering of madness.

"You have truly earned my attention Fred!"

Fred Dodge lay under bright stars staring into eyes luminous as the moon above and the color of blood. Foam bubbled from his mouth. His eyes were wild, what mortal men would call those of an animal. Lorelei knew full well they were those of the least of men as he stared at the aurora without comprehension.

"You damnable little worm! Don't tell me you're not even going to pay attention to your own *killing!*"

She ran white hands through waist-length hair and sat down hard on the ground. Fred wasn't even responding to the sight of a preter-naturally beautiful woman against the glowing auroral sky. His years of drink, drugs and cruelty were shattered. He saw nothing. Lorelei's breath made a cloud on the breeze as her lips curled in disgust.

She grabbed his hair and jerked him upright. "Honey Bee! Do you remember her? Do you remember her terror, her pleading for mercy? How it aroused you, you goddamn worm? You fucking killed her and you were going to do the same to Alice Mary! Damn you," her chest rumbled, "do you *hear* me?"

Fred made croaking sounds as a rope of snot twisted toward the ground from his nose.

"Her name was Sonya... and she's *watching!*" Lorelei drove her left hand up under his ribcage, and Fred shuddered as long white fingers tore through the slippery membrane surrounding it and closed upon his beating heart. She tore it from his chest in a black arc of blood that sparkled in the moonlight and steamed as it painted the frosty ground before his dying gaze. With a grunt of effort, she hurled it down the valley of Gold Bottom Creek out over Bonanza, across the log buildings and lights of Grand Forks, and over the ridge beyond to the unseen surface of the Yukon River as his body slid from her grasp.

There was a distant splash, and Lorelei threw back her head and howled to the wolves. On a nearby ridge a pack pricked their ears and held noses to the air at the message of a feast atop King Solomon's Dome.

———

She returned to the Palace in an outfit of green silk and a silk hat topped with iridescent quetzal feathers. Her hair was in a proper bun and her pale skin flushed, imparting a pleasant color to her cheeks. She graced Charlie Meadows with a smile, and he grinned back from where he towered over the crowd at the bar. Men parted and bobbed in her wake as she floated to the balcony with all eyes upon her.

"Damn cold, to be out without a wrap," Charlie muttered as he poured another drink from a bottle of scotch.

Joseph and Mary didn't hear her. She stopped at the portal of the booth to watch them, inhaled their scent, ran a hand across her lips, and chewed a knuckle. She'd expended a great deal of energy and was in need of Joseph's contribution immediately. She was painfully hungry, but it would be a shame to break up these two just now. She could have killed Fred by consuming him, but shivered at the thought. The mere idea of taking on his wretched soul for whatever time it took to pass it on to a well-deserved oblivion was beyond repugnant.

Lorelei had begun to back out of the box when Mary glanced up with a dazed look. "Hi!"

Joseph blinked. "You changed your clothes."

"I thought I'd freshen up."

"How did you change so fast?" Mary marveled, "I mean, with a corset and all?"

———

Lorelei left them with a kiss and headed to Fourth Avenue. She spied a nervous half-breed dressed like a white man as he lingered beside the colorful plank fence of the Segregated District who was steeling himself to approach one of the girls before a Mountie caught him where he wasn't allowed. Lorelei dragged him into an empty crib whose owner was gone for the evening and greeted him in his Cree tongue, and before a surprised Five Pelts could respond, shut the door behind him. "I hope you're ready." She shed her clothes like a dry skin as they fell to the floor, and she spread her arms.

He ran a hand across his face and whistled. "Goddamn... how much?"

"Nothing, and all you've got." She pulled combs and barrettes out of her hair. A very white woman stood before the young Indian like an apparition in the night, blessing him with her smile and eyes like the morning star. "I wouldn't have to put my hair up at all if I'd stayed with your people."

He fished in his poke. "Hell, no!"

She held up a hand. "This is on me."

Five Pelts nodded. He knew a gift of God when he saw one.

XII.

PINK DAWN GLOWED THROUGH THE FROSTED GLASS. "I'M GOING TO THE diggings."

Mary yawned. "Can I come with you?"

Joseph rubbed the spot his breath had made on the glass and peered outside. "Do you have proper clothing?"

"Yes, Joe, I came prepared you know. I have riding pants even. Besides," she bounced off the bed, "I could buy them. Starving again?"

"Yes." That was true, but not with the all-consuming hunger of yesterday. This morning he had a healthy appetite, but no more.

"Wondering where your patroness has gotten off to?" Mary stepped into the bath without waiting for an answer.

He put hands behind his neck and stretched. *Where might she be?* A jagged pang of jealousy caught him unawares, as if a blow had come to the gut of someone going about his own doings and he was unprepared for the violence of it.

"What's the matter?" Mary appeared behind him and slid her arms around his middle. "You're feeling abandoned by her, aren't you?"

"I—"

"She has her own business to which we're not privy, Joe. Besides, we just spent a lovely night in her bed together. I should be grateful. I mean; here I am at Jack's, and just as she said I haven't spent a moment with him since yesterday morning. I don't give a damn for the fellow and she seems to have him well in hand for our benefit, and my mom hasn't a clue, and is enjoying her rooms at the Empire Hotel." She kissed his cheek, "We should be grateful."

"I suppose you're right."

"Of course I am." She laughed. "And now we're going on a tour of Grand Forks and golden Eldorado like two rich tourists rather than working." She kissed his neck. "Should I rent horses?"

Joseph scratched the hint of a beard and shrugged. "Here I am in the far Klondike, yet I feel somewhat like a gigolo in a pampered parlor."

"Don't complain, fellow."

"Oh," he grinned, "I suppose not."

"We take for granted what we are given, especially at our age."

"You sound like Lorelei."

"She's impressed me. It's strange that I feel no jealousy over your obvious longing for her at all, as if she were outside of all normal measurement of such things. She hands us gold as if it were dross... and I feel so safe around her. You know, Joe, she's not like us."

He turned to the window as sunlight touched the hills above Moosehide Village downriver. "She often speaks to me in my head when we're not together, with a voice like music, and so very clear." He spun to stare into her eyes, "Doesn't that sound like I'm subject to madness?"

"And I get this strange sense of peace around her that makes me accept such things. Doesn't that sound queer also?"

Faint shouts came up through the floor. It was Otto, roaring at someone. There was a crash.

Mary's fingers entwined in his. "I believe she is a creature of another realm to be honest."

"I know that you're right."

"So what does that mean for us?"

Joseph rubbed his chin. "That we shall visit Eldorado in leisure instead of working for a living, I suppose."

'Like finding gold at the end of the rainbow." She grinned. "I'm glad my mom's taken up with one of the Eldorado fellows at the hotel. She's talking marriage and he wants to build her a house on his claim. That should keep her out of our hair."

A blazing sky filled with birds flashed for a moment across his vision and Joseph blinked it away, regained the real sky, and exhaled. "We should enjoy it while it lasts, at least."

"That is the most mature thing I've heard from your lips."

"I suppose."

———

Footsteps pounded up the stairs as they finished dressing, and Jack shoved open the door stinking of whiskey. He stumbled and stood blinking with the cold air wafting in around him. Jack stepped sideways, caught his balance, and scowled at Joseph. "What the 'ell 'er you doin' in me digs, ya fuckin' scamp?"

Mary slid behind Joseph and grabbed his belt.

'I'm... fixing the boiler, sir. I came up to test the hot water. Otto has it stoked, if you'd care for a bath."

"Ah-ha!" Jack growled and shoved the door shut. As his back was turned, Mary slipped into Jack's room and down the inner stairwell. He wiped his reddened nose and snorted. "Where'd that little tart get to?"

"She's gone to the W-C, sir."

"Christ, me 'ead is splittin' like a goddamn melon!" Jack waved a tobacco-stained hand in Joseph's face. "Get outta 'ere, boy!"

"Yes sir." Joseph went down the stairs as Jack staggered into his room to flop on the bed with a groan.

———

They rented two well-mannered mules from a stable on Craig Street and had waffles and coffee at the little stand on Front. It was a tent on a spruce plank platform with a knee wall that a woman and her adolescent daughter ran. The girl handed Joseph a steaming mug with a hand burned from cooking as his feet crunched ice. What would they do when winter came? He gave her a five-dollar gold piece of Lorelei's money and waved off the change.

They took the narrow bridge across the Klondike over ice-silvered mudflats and rode past a sawmill churning out lumber beside shanties crowding the island called Lousetown between Dawson and Klondike City. The line of telephone poles running across the bridge buzzed like excited bees.

Mary buttoned her coat to her neck, blew on her hands, and put on gloves. The river valley was stripped of trees but for a few tiny willows and birch. Hoof prints and wagon ruts were everywhere, and narrow gauge train tracks ran up both sides of the river. South-heading water-fowl circled, crying in dismay over the condition of their traditional abodes as wagons laden with lumber headed for the diggings where miners hurried to finish whatever must be completed before winter.

They followed the Klondike Road for a couple of miles and turned up Bonanza Creek with telephone wires crackling overhead. A Mountie astride a fine black horse appeared with a rifle in a scabbard and a big Webley revolver sticking out under the leather flap of its holster. He halted, eyed Mary's riding pants critically, and pulled at his thin nose. "Ah-hem!"

They let a wagon loaded with burlap sacks guarded by four Mounties carrying shiny Lee Enfield rifles pass. "This is quite acceptable garb for a lady riding, sir," Mary spoke up, "and there are no sidesaddles to be had this day anywhere in Dawson City."

"I see." The Mountie glanced at the wagon, which was disappearing around the next bend.

Joseph saluted. "That's a fine Winchester, sir."

The Mountie nodded. "A Model eighty-six, big enough for man or beast." He glanced at the receding wagon. "Carry on!" He saluted with a glove to the brim of his squarely worn hat and kneed his well-fed horse, "But don't let me see you behaving in such a way in the better parts of town. And no bloomers!" he intoned over his shoulder.

Mary let out a laugh when he was out of earshot. "Stuffy fellow."

"Sure are a lot of 'em."

"They tax the poor miners like the dickens they say."

"They want to make sure everyone pays their ten percent when they weigh their gold in town. This territory keeps the whole British Empire afloat I bet."

The hills ahead were criss-crossed with roads, trails, and fans of dirt in hues of grey, pink, and white like faded mounds of Neopolitan ice cream. Mary shaded her eyes from the sun to stare at a flume running down the side of the valley.

Joseph pointed to their left. "That's the white gravel lode. It's from a riverbed left high and dry ages ago. Some Swede started digging there after all the good claims were staked down on the creeks and people thought he was crazy. I hear he's washed out a million dollars in the last year. Now that whole band of gravel is being mined on both sides of the valley."

"A million dollars!"

The smoke of Grand Forks hung where Bonanza and Eldorado Creeks met under a snow-dusted dome. Two streets on the left of the creek were packed with log buildings and a few frame ones where canvas-sided tents were giving way to more permanent structures. The sounds of hammers and saws, the braying of mules, shouts of men, and rattling of cables echoed in the cradle of the hills. Joseph's head turned from one slope to the next as he tried to imagine where the golden lodes lay around him.

Mary stretched in her saddle. "Jack took me to the Grand Forks Hotel. Belinda Mullroney owns it. It's the best place if we get hungry.

She owns the company that put up those telephone lines and has the Fairview Hotel in town. She owns the Dawson Telephone Company, the water company, and several claims too. I would guess ten score men work for her at the least."

"What does her husband do? Is he a miner?"

"She has none. No man is her master, although many would like to be."

"Then how did she get the claims?"

"Through hard work, Joe. It must be wonderful to be a woman here and accomplish so much."

"I guess so."

"I would break my back to have what she does, and with nary a moment on it with anyone I didn't care for." Mary caught his expression and grinned, "Not you Joe. What can you give me besides your company? I'm simply speaking as to a close friend. I have no girlfriends here, and my mother has her mind made up as to what I should and shouldn't do, so I am speaking to the only one I possibly can do so with. Do I offend you?"

"No, I have simply never heard a woman speaking so frankly. It's refreshing, to tell the truth."

"Good. Here a woman can show her mettle and be as tough as a man. Not that we aren't anyway." Her cheeks dimpled, "The prospect thrills me."

"Well... it seems reasonable."

Mary pulled off her riding bonnet and ran hands through her hair. "Let's be partners."

"In what?"

"Something that's fun, and full of adventure, and makes us very rich of course," She glanced around. "I wonder who amongst these noble miners would like to show a pretty girl his prize nuggets?"

"Most of these fellows are hired labor. You've got to get out past Bonanza to find someone who's working their own claim, maybe over on Hunker Creek."

They spent the morning riding from claim to claim watching men stoking boilers and driving steam points to thaw frozen ground beneath the thin soil. Holes were everywhere seeking the bedrock where gold had collected over millions of years as rocker boxes and flumes worked the black gravel brought up from beneath the creeks.

On Eldorado Creek they spied a neat two-story cabin with painted window frames and lace curtains. As they skirted a flume, the sounds of a fiddle and guitar rose above the pounding and rattling of the mines. A woman sat in an oaken chair on the solid porch playing a guitar, and a balding man with an unlined face sat across from her on a stool wearing a bow tie and holding a fiddle. At the sight of Mary the woman stood, and the man laid the fiddle on a barrel head. "Good day, ma'am!" He reached for a nonexistent hat as if to doff it.

"Hello, is this the famous claim of Mr. Berry?"

"It is, and I am that fortunate fellow, and this is my wife Ethel."

The Berrys were most likely the two richest people in the Territory, but seemed no different than the simplest homesteaders or prospectors aside from their clean clothes. They obviously no longer had to climb into holes to hack at the permafrost, chop wood, or slave over boilers thawing the ground. Clarence pointed out where he thought the big and as yet un-tapped lodes might be, and Ethel made a pot of English black tea and served it with little bowls of cream, sugar, and lemon. They drank it on the porch and ate warm scones with real butter and wild blueberry jam.

When they finished, Mary dabbed her mouth with a napkin. "Mr. Berry, is it true that you found nuggets the size of your fist when you arrived in ninety-seven?"

"It's a fact." Clarence glanced around his property hesitantly, looked at his wife, and Ethel nodded. "Would you like to see some?"

"Oh yes, please!"

He disappeared beneath the floor of the cabin into a hole that had been one of his diggings and returned with an iron-studded oaken box. Ethel leaned her guitar against the wall and placed a double-barreled shotgun across the table beside the fiddle. Clarence grunted as he hefted the box onto the floor and shoved it across the planks with some effort before shutting the trap and throwing a rug over it. He stood up, wiped his pants, lugged it into the sun, and glanced around again before opening it with a flourish. "My babies."

A collection of huge nuggets washed and cleaned of all impurities nestled in a lining of red velvet. The one in the middle was shaped like a potato and indeed was the size of a respectable russet.

Joseph whistled.

Mary gasped, "There must be a king's ransom here!"

"Jus' 'bout. 'Course, the real money's from all the little stuff 'cause there's more of it, but these just tend to set a body's heart to thumpin' don't they?"

"I should say!"

———

They climbed King Solomon's Dome with the mules' hooves crunching fresh snow. Ten thousand geese flew across the ridge tops like phalanxes of an aerial army with their shadows making dark splotches on patches of dirt from the diggings. Mary's mount let out a snort and pranced sideways at the sight of three ravens that cawed from the summit.

Joseph's mule shivered under him, took a step backward, and he drew up the reins as Mary did the same. White-mantled mountains surrounded them. No mining had gone on this high, and all was as it had been before men had found gold except for a single spruce pole with a tattered Union Jack at the summit. One of the big black birds landed on the broken top of the pole, as another picked at red-stained bits of cloth in the snow.

Mary's mule was rolling his eyes and backing up. "What's got into you? It's only ravens."

Joseph dismounted, handed Mary his reins, and walked to the level summit. The big black bird held its ground to the last moment and flew off with a bit of bloody cloth in its beak. At the spot the raven had vacated, a hank of brown hair lay in the remnants of a bloody shirt with a swarm of the red, white-footed flies called whitesocks circling it. Joseph slapped at one biting him on the back of the neck as he stooped to inspect the hair. A sparkle caught his eye, and he pulled a gold chain from the thin mantle of snow. He held up a pocket watch dangling from its golden fob and snapped it open. "Fred Dodge."

"What, Joe?"

"This belongs to Fred Dodge. His name's on it."

Mary sat astride her mule, blinking. "How could he get up here? I saw him at the Palace bar at eight or so last night, drunk as a skunk and mean as hell. Charlie Meadows threw him out, and he headed for the cribs, probably to take it out on some poor working girl."

"I know." He let out his breath, "Bet you anything it was him killed that girl in the cribs."

"Honey Bee?"

"Yes, maybe this was somebody else he killed, and he dropped his watch."

"Why in the world would he haul them all the way up here? I should—" Mary shrieked, "Look!" She pointed to something glistening like a mushroom that protruded from the fresh snow.

Joseph approached it and rolled it over with the toe of his boot. It was a skull, with bits of pink tissue in the nasal passages and damp scraps of scalp clinging to it. A gold incisor flashed in the sun. "Shit." He gingerly picked it up and examined the marks made by wolves that had gnawed away the flesh.

"Yuk!" Mary made a face, "Those are Fred's corduroy pants... at least part of them. I saw him wearing them last night! And that gold tooth is just like his!" She slid off her horse, knelt, and pulled a glittering object from the crust of snow that sparkled as she ran it between her fingers. It was a gold nugget earring, set with a diamond that hung from a fine gold chain at the end of a hook. Mary fingered the nugget. "Lorelei wore this at the Palace! She showed it to me before the show. This isn't somebody Fred killed... it's *him*, Joseph!"

Joseph put the skull down, wiped his hands in the snow, and snapped the watch shut. "She knew he killed Honey Bee. I bet you anything he was about to do the same to some other girl and she stopped him." He gazed down the trough of Gold Bottom Creek. "We're most likely the last ones up here before winter." He turned around with his teeth in his lip as he took in the panorama of their surroundings. "The wolves have scattered things thoroughly. This is probably all that remains with Mr. Dodge's name on it." He slipped the watch into the pocket of his canvas pants, striving again to part the curtain that kept him from remembering where Lorelei had taken him during their lovemaking.

Who are you? He said to the endless vista of mountains. Why wasn't he afraid? Well, Fred Dodge most certainly deserved it.

Mary gazed down Gold Bottom Creek to Bonanza Creek and the distant Klondike River. The cries of geese echoed in the dry air as she waved at the buzzing whitesocks and shook her head. "That's an *awfully* fast ten miles."

Joseph sat in the snow and ran hands through his hair as the honking of geese echoed over the hills. *Who are you?* He tried to still the pounding of his heart. "Only eight or so, if she went straight up the ridge." He felt a senseless grin on his face and swallowed. "I should like to see it when she moves like that."

"How marvelous. She even had time to bathe and to change her clothes." Mary stared into space and turned at his approach with a start.

Joseph put hands on her shoulders. Mary's eyes showed no fear at their discovery and he wanted to kiss her for it. "Let this be our secret."

"Of course Joe, she trusts us," Mary gazed at the skull, "Although I shouldn't care to anger her."

XIII.

THEY DISMOUNTED AND HITCHED THE MULES TO A RAIL AT THE GRAND Forks Hotel. Mary cracked her back and scratched a gangly young Saint Bernard sprawled on the porch. The dog leaned into her and almost knocked her down as his wagging tail lifted dust from the boards.

Inside was a dining room with a bar at the back that doubled as an office where room keys hung beside liquor bottles. The logs of the building were hidden by wallpapered boards above a wainscoting of shellacked birch and hung with pictures of castles and verdant landscapes. The tables had white tablecloths.

Joseph hesitated. "This place looks expensive."

"In a way, the food is half the price of Dawson but the liquor's double. Miss Mullroney believes in being fair with the essentials I'm told, and uses the liquor profits to give folks a good deal on the grub."

"That's decent."

A florid-faced blond woman appeared from the kitchen and smiled. "Drinks?"

Mary nodded, "I should like a beer, please."

"Um, make it two."

The woman went behind the bar and returned with two bottles of Rainer's beer and two mugs. They sat sipping beer, staring at each other. The big clock on the wall ticked as its bronze pendulum swung in a glass case. Mary reached into the pocket of her riding pants and pulled out the earring. She dangled it in the afternoon light coming through a window and the diamond sparkled in its house of gold amongst dust motes. It glowed before the round rise of her breasts as her lips pursed in thought. "How strange. . ."

Joseph took Fred Dodge's watch out of his pocket and rocked it on its fob. He glanced at the nugget earring and imagined it hanging from the white lobe of Lorelei's ear. He'd kissed that ear. He could smell her skin this very moment, even as his own rose in goose bumps.

Where are you taking me?

A dark-haired woman in her early thirties entered the room, wiped her hands on a towel, tossed it on the bar, and tacked toward them as if a wind blowing her on some errand had shifted. "Hello, kids."

Joseph slid the watch into his pocket and the earring disappeared in Mary's fist as he rose. "Hello ma'am."

"Sit down, you're the guests. Nice to see two young people out together for a change instead of the girl being all gussied up like a china doll on the arm of some fellow who could be her grandfather just because he's got a fat poke. I'm Belinda Mullroney." She held out a hand rough from work and shook Joseph's with a grip as firm as any man's, then Mary's.

"Miss Mullroney, I was mentioning to Joe here how I should love to do one tenth of what you have this very morning, while I was telling him about your enterprises."

"There's more to do than any one of us can grab hold of, and that goes for a woman if she's got the moxie. You kids have full names?"

"Oh, excuse me. I'm Mary Johansen, of San Francisco."

"And I'm Joseph Walton, of Cottage Grove, in Oregon."

"Come to seek your fortunes no doubt."

"That seems to be the reason everyone's here. It's hardly the climate."

Belinda chuckled, "Where are you staying?"

"Um," Joseph began, "at the Empire Hotel and in apartments above the establishment of Jack Finley at the top of Harper Street."

Belinda scowled, *"That* man. Not a very secure place for the winter I've got to say." She turned to Mary, "Are you the one he brought here the other day?"

Mary blinked. "Um, yes, Miss Mullroney."

Belinda stared out one of the two windows and shook her head. "A girl like you above the saloon of Jack Finley. Watch out that he doesn't slip you one of his damnable Mickey Finns."

"Actually we are guests of Miss Lorelei, who is renting the room at—"

"The tall woman with black hair and very fair skin, who has those remarkable eyes."

They nodded.

"A stunning lady to say the least. She came by the Fairview the other night, and my guests spent the rest of it speculating as to her origins. Is she Irish?"

"I believe so, by way of the East Coast I believe."

"Perhaps she's one of the landless gentry whose parents were driven to America by way of the Hunger." Belinda shook her head, "Jack Finley is a dozen notches too low for someone of her caliber, or at least what she appears to be. Whatever does she see in him?"

"She's only renting the apartment. There are few accommodations that would do her justice in Dawson City this winter."

Belinda took a beer from a dripping ice box behind the bar, pulled a chair up, and put her arms across the back of it. "And you Mary, it may seem inappropriate for my asking, but you're not the plaything of that uncouth lynch from the hedgerows of County Cork I hope."

"What's a... lynch?"

"Er, no, Miss Mullroney. My mother is staying at the Empire Hotel and we intend to open a laundry, although I must admit I am quite taken with the success of some of the performers hereabouts. Klondike Kate is amazing. I saw men throwing a fortune at her feet just last night."

"Oh, the stage. Do you have any training?"

"I... yes. I sang as a youngster in a couple of melodeons in San Francisco and worked a bit in a vaudeville troupe to help earn our way here, at the Midway Plaisance on Market Street. It's run by the same fellow who ran the Midway at the Chicago World's Fair and is quite reputable. Have you heard of it?" Mary grinned, "It's all rather fun, actually."

Belinda ran a hand through her hair. "Jim Daughtery is looking for players at the Pavilion. You might check with him. Tell him I sent you if you'd like."

"Is that the one they call Nigger Jim?"

"Yes, from the blackface skits. He's a friend and I could put in a word, although when he takes one look at you he'll hire you." Belinda sighed, "You're a very pretty girl, and it isn't hard to surmise you've been around a bit too. The temptations of wealth here are great, but sweet Jesus, you're still as shiny as a new penny. Please, do be careful."

"Oh I shall, Miss Mullroney, thank you for your concern." Mary smiled, and her thumb caressed the nugget in her palm.

"And what of you, young man? Are you presently employed beyond accompanying this young lady to the goldfields?"

"I, um—"

"Miss Lorelei is retaining him as a Jack of All Trades and a Go-For, Miss Mulroney."

"What?" Belinda put a hand to crooked teeth, "That's a quick retort. So, the mysterious Miss Lorelei, the most beautiful woman in Dawson, has picked this strapping youth here as her... *Go-For.*"

"I—" Joseph's tongue seemed stuck against the roof of his mouth.

"You're cut of the same cloth it appears. Have the Mounties given you much trouble? They are damn proper you know, and I doubt you can explain what you're about to them any better than to me."

"Well, actually, Miss Lorelei will take care of that."

Belinda blinked, and after a long pause she shook her head and took a sip of beer. "You certainly have faith in a rather strange and wealthy woman who obviously doesn't need any help from someone your age. Have you some special relationship with her?"

"Um... in a way, ma'am."

XIV.

*T*HE YOUNG MAN STOOD KNEE-DEEP IN GREEN WATER AS A DRAGONFLY THE *size of a hummingbird droned overhead. He lay down his precious bow and quiver, and watched them bob in the gentle current before they drifted away in the reeds. He took a breath and straightened for inspection of the Goddess's rainbow eyes. They became the color of blood. He shuddered, but kept his gaze upon them and prayed aloud to his ancestors.*

A smile blossomed on her face. Something erupted within him, and a swelling arose in his breast as her voice rose in song. Birds rose from the reeds in a roar of wings as Inanna, great mother of Lilith, held his soul cupped within the chalice of her own: a shimmering draught of light amongst the endless red halls of her heart. With the song of the Sun she held out her hand, and he stepped to an altar above the river Euphrates where he would joyously give his blood as a million feathered souls circled and sang in the high blue vault of day.

The rattle of Jack's cough broke into her dream. Lorelei frowned, clinging doggedly for a moment to the memory of her ancestor and the glorious warmth of a sun on skin long gone. She ground her teeth and willed his mouth shut. Jack sneezed through his nose, mumbled drunkenly, and belched.

"Damn." She arose and went to the window. Snow was falling from a sky that held only the last vestige of light. A pain welled in her breast, a pain more real than the song of her ancient ancestors in dreams. She so longed to feel the burn of day on her skin, to feel the sting of healing beyond pain as she was anointed by daylight. At such moments, she would do anything to salve her longing. Lorelei drew the curtains.

You know the price.

She imagined traveling to some island to live like her forebears as a hungry Goddess taking a good man's life each night and dancing in the sun each dawn as bright birds sang in the trade winds. How long would that last before people burned her as a witch or whatever the custom of their particular culture was for an imagined being of Hell? Even staid Protestant missionaries might be prodded into Puritan fury by the existence of Lorelei, daughter of Lilith, a living *Liliot* at large in their world. She'd watched at fourteen from the forest as they'd hung her mother, raging in silence against her mother's last command that she remain hidden as they burned her body that she might not arise in the night.

She bit her lip and tasted blood. She might yet take the chance if she weren't the last, if she could just get past the feeling that taking those glorious lives was no longer her *right,* for unlike her fortunate ancestors Lorelei lived with great and awful doubts, ones that grew stronger as the years passed.

She ran fingers down her stomach and closed her eyes as she imagined life swelling within. She thrust out her hips and rubbed her navel as if she could call it forth. Her breath grew loud in her ears as she tried to feel what every mother before her had known. It was an inherited memory that she couldn't even touch at the moment, perhaps from Jack's irritating presence or the shear stress of trying.

Bearing her child would take the life of a good man, as no other would do. When that time came, she would cast doubt aside and exult in the taking. He who came to her on that unknown day would be the chosen of her line, blessed to live on in her beloved daughter and her daughter's daughters. His sacrifice was *ordained:* a holy thing. The renewing of a world rode on that soul and it was beyond question. Lorelei was the future when it came to her kind, and she must bear a daughter. She was the last. She flopped on the bed with a sigh and turned her attention to Joseph.

⸺⁓⸺

The young man she touched straightened in his saddle.

"Whatever is it Joe?" Mary's breath was a sparkling cloud as their mounts' hoofs echoed on the planks of the Klondike bridge. "It's Lorelei, isn't it?"

"Yes."

You're consumed with knowing the truth. I hope it won't make you afraid of sharing my company.

"You should know what we've decided in regard to that, Lorelei." A musical chuckle tickled Joseph's nerves as Mary jerked upright on her mule in the dusk, eyes wide.

I'm speaking to both of you now so listen; I am at times vengeful as that too is my nature, but please don't think it the sum of me.

"Oh... how marvelous!" Mary clapped her hands, "This is better than I could have imagined! Lorelei, tell me; are you some kind of witch... a spirit... a *Goddess?* I mean—"

Your mind is filled with the stiff and musty images of classical tomes. I see the pages of books you devoured while schoolmarms watched over your shoulder and smell the yellowed paper, but I live. The blood in my veins is hot and red, and my loves and lusts are of this world to a degree

119

I often loathe. I haven't come into your lives from some other realm, but live in yours, even if my heart carries the burden of another, her sigh bounced on the chill river air, *I suppose I must educate the both of you now, if we are to remain acquainted.*

Mary made a nervous laugh as they turned on Craig Street toward the stables. "That would be wonderful, and I am so glad you killed that vile cur Fred Dodge by the way. I mean... *really.*"

There was a warp in the air: a huge and wordless void of sorrow filling them with a deep melancholy.

Even such as he was once a babe at his mother's breast and cradled in her arms. I was acting on impulse as my thoughts were for a girl whose life is of particular concern to me, and in righteous revenge for another. I shall probably regret ridding the world of even that man soon as all things have consequences. I'm weary of killing. Please don't let it tempt you in your youth, in spite of my poor example. It might make your hearts beat louder for a while and can deafen the soul with its noise, but leave such things to someone like me who can avoid the consequences that follow... at least for now.

Mary glanced around. "Well, I shouldn't suppose I'm cut out for such as *that,*" she said quickly and turned to Joseph in the thickening snow, "whatever is the matter, Joe?"

He's a bit jealous that you hear me. He considered me his special secret: his gift. Joseph, you're my lover, but I can never belong to you in any way. Such is the nature of my kind and the sorrow of all whom we have touched until they accept the transience of all things. Loss is the other side of joy in mortality's shadow.

"I... I just—"

However tonight you again shall share my bed, which is what you wish to hear.

Joseph slid from his saddle with a burning face.

Mary laughed.

Lorelei made Jack go away. She had them bathe together and sent Mary to her mother with a lingering kiss, then turned eyes glimmering with red upon Joseph as she took his hand and drew him to the bed. A sliver of fear within him that could become a chasm in his soul yawned before her, and she fought an instant of self-loathing that had become all too familiar after a killing. She centered herself, closed her eyes, put a hand to his cheek, and let her breath pass into him.

He trembled, as a young man had on an altar ten thousand years before with the knowledge that the woman he held was more than all others. Life and death met here with her kiss as the vision of a skull atop King Solomon's Dome arose in him. He inhaled her breath and cast off fear, yielding gratefully to the demands of his heart and body. He heard the roar of a river that was the unbroken line of her kind: that ancient song, whose present voice was Lorelei's in all her beauty. The faces of terrifyingly beautiful women appeared in his mind, but he could not focus upon them.

A ripple of envy caught him by surprise. *Look,* her voice ran through his bones, *here's what you see and I cannot. You see lives that might issue from me, those yet unborn.*

He tried to speak but was lost in the roar of their blood as a white flare of love burst within him, feeding her hungry soul to be answered in kind. Lorelei gazed into the eyes of that one who'd died selflessly before the first city was piled up from the mud of Eden and felt tears, not knowing if they were remembered ones or running down her cheeks this moment. All the lovers in eons since who had been her ancestors' and her own, who had become one with her kind in death, merged as she fed on the one within her. It took all her will not to take him totally, not to consume him in a shout of pleasure and passion and grace that would leave him an empty husk on the creaking bed and leave her adrift again in a hellish loneliness.

Lorelei sundered her heart in parting. She lay gasping, staring at the ceiling. Joseph would awaken weak and aching and possessed of a mortal hunger after the dawn, but he would awake. She drew the coverlet over him as a rivulet of blood trickled down one white thigh and stained the carpet. She went to the window and opened it wide upon the night, letting the chill turn their mingled sweat to crystals on her pale skin.

XV.

"MISTER GATES, PLU... EESE!" ALEX STUTTERED AS HE HELD UP HIS hands to ward off a blow.

"Out, you sonofabitch! I knew you were skimming since you and Gertie fleeced that Swede from Sulfur Creek in July, but this is the damn *end* of it!"

"Not on my life, Mr. Gates, I—"

Swiftwater Bill slammed his palms on the teak bar, and Alex stepped back. Bill's sandy mustache wobbled over prominent upper teeth glistening with saliva, and a drop hung from his neatly trimmed beard. "Then how in *hell* did the gink drop six thousand dollars in one evening without me seeing any more than twelve goddamn bottles of champagne? *Five hundred a bottle!* You chiselin' sonofabitch! Where the hell's the *money?*" Bill straightened and stared at his reflection in the mirror behind the bar. He took off his derby hat, ran a hand through his hair, and swiped at his mustache with the back of a hand. "I'm gonna let Charlie Meadows know you chiseled him while you were working the Palace. How much did you take, Pantages?"

"I swear to you, we didn't—"

"Then how in hell did he spend six thousand dollars?"

"I... ask Gertie, she's—"

"If Gussie hadn't taken a liking to you, I woulda tossed you out on your goddamn Greek arse a long time ago. I know you've been tryin' to get your filthy hands on Nell. She's but fifteen! If I can help it, you won't be runnin' your game anywhere in this town!"

Alexander fought the urge to strike out and forced his voice into a semblance of calm. "Mister Gates, I have never had intentions toward Nell Lamore. I've been as loyal an employee as anyone you've ever had, and I do not appreciate—"

"You've got three hours to clear out! Now get your kit and git!" Bill pointed a shaking hand toward the stairs, pulled his sleeves down over the white cuffs of his boiled linen shirt, and straightened his coat. "If any of my boys see you in here one minute after five, I'm givin' them orders to toss your arse in the street and rearrange your face doin' it!" He turned away as if Alex no longer existed.

"What... what about Kitty?"

Bill spun on his heels, "What the hell *about* her? Miss Klondike Kate Rockwell is the prime attraction here! You think she'll follow an unemployed waiter into the gutter and leave the finest rooms in Dawson? I'll raise her stake to make sure she don't, you sonofabitch! Winter's comin' you fool! Now git!"

Alex shook off his paralysis and bounded up the stairs. When he reached his room, he took the key from his pocket with a shaking hand, and it bounced on the floor with a rattle. "Gamo'to!"

He let himself in, went to the closet, and began tossing clothes on the bed. With a grunt of effort Alex seized the corners of a black iron safe and pulled it away from the wall. He spun the dial, but had to start over three times. *That arrogant sonofabitch!* Bill Gates had a lot of nerve accusing *him* of having his sights on Nell Lamore when everyone knew Bill used every chance he had to be in the girl's company when her sisters Gussie and Grace weren't around. "Bastard!"

The door opened exposing bags of gold dust and flakes, nuggets, gold watches, nugget-studded money clips, gold doodads, piles of American, Canadian and British bills, a jewel-studded dirk with Cyrillic writing on it, and a stack of gold coins. Out of habit he began to count, stopped, swore, and began to stack the hoard in a black leather suitcase with heavy brass hinges and leather straps that he'd gotten from a gambler who'd lost one too many hands at the Monte Carlo. He put some clothes on top of the loot, shut the case, locked the locks, and cinched the straps. Alex stuffed the bills in his silk vest next to his derringer and began packing his other belongings in a trunk. He'd have to get someone to help him move the safe, maybe Otto from Jack's place.

When he was done he sat on the bed, ran hands through his oiled hair, and took a breath. *What am I afraid of?* This was nothing for one who had been born Peracles Pantages on the Isle of Andros, where once gods and heroes walked. Getting thrown off a tramp freighter in Panama at seventeen delirious with malarial fever... now that had been a crisis.

He closed his eyes, and was again that youth staggering across hot sand to collapse at a stream flowing from the jungle to drink, feeling the scales of a huge green snake sliding across his cheek as he lay weak and trembling. He'd sprung back with a shout of terror to sprawl on the beach crying out to God, then all the Gods of his ancient ancestors, to save him from this nameless place where he was cast away to die. Alexander had lain for who knew how long in the glare of the equatorial sun, staring into the vault of heaven as he sunk into a delirium whose other side was death.

That was where the Goddess had found him, for of all he'd called on in the pantheon of immortal beings she alone had heard his plea. The voice that had awakened him from his slide into death was more beautiful than music, like a cool stream washing over him. Her laughter filled the sky and rose from the sea to dance amongst the tangled trunks and vines of the jungle. Birds cried out and took wing at her voice. The earth quaked as he stared into eyes that sparkled in all colors in a face that thrilled him to the bone: a face beyond mortal beauty. He felt her lips on his as her sweet breath flowed into him. Alex had put hands to his chest to hold his heart within its house of flesh and bone, lest it rise from him in joyous offering to disappear in the fires of the sun itself.

That was where Esmeralda found him, and men had taken the delirious young man to the village of Sangre del Mar. He was Odysseus upon an enchanted isle, and Esmeralda was the mortal vessel of the Goddess who had shown mercy at the sound of his prayers.

Sweet Esmeralda was two years younger than him, and her mother Maria was a saint. Alex spent a healing season on the edge of the jungles of Panama beside the sea, and with the blessing... indeed the *will* of the Goddess, the virgin Esmeralda had become his lover: the gift of one whose name he did not know. He crossed the Isthmus to the west coast in the spring leaving in the night a girl big with child. Esmeralda awoke in the hot dawn weeping, but Alexander Pantages had worlds to conquer and fortunes to be made.

Alex wondered what child bore his blood in the tropics. He must be a young man now. Alex didn't even consider it could be a young woman. He blinked, shook off his reverie, and stood. He had to find Kitty. Alex lugged the suitcase down the hall to the suite of rooms Kate occupied overlooking Front.

He stopped at her door. *What if she spurns me?* He wasn't a handsome seventeen-year-old anymore. Alex imagined the blue sea of Panama frozen solid and covered in ice. He shook off the vision, muttered a wordless prayer to the nameless Goddess who had saved him, rubbed his nose, and squeezed his eyes shut. He let out his breath and knocked.

"Who is it?" The girlish voice sounded much too young for Kate's twenty-five years.

"Me, Alex!"

"Oh," a bolt slid back. Kate stood in a quilted blue satin robe with her auburn hair down to her waist. She saw the expression on his face and put a hand to her mouth. "Whatever is the matter, dearest?"

He hurried in, shut the door, and propped the heavy suitcase against her dressing table. "I am cast out, Kitty!" He sat on the bed and buried his face in his hands. "Swiftwater Bill has heard from someone how me and Gertie put that fellow from Sulfur Creek to the routine without giving him his share, and says he shall ruin me in Dawson!"

"He what?"

"Of course he wishes to keep you and shall offer you more money to stay, but he has fired me and given me three hours to leave the Monte Carlo!"

Kate let out a gasp. Alex held hands to his face, glanced at her leg through his fingers, and inhaled her scent.

Kate sighed, sat down beside him, and her arm went around his shoulders. "I *shant* let you be cast adrift! We shall find another venue, Alex, *together!*" She pulled his hands away from his face and pressed a damp cheek to his own with tears at the corners of her lovely violet eyes.

"Bill says he shall tell the other resort owners not to hire me, Kate."

"Then... whatever shall we do?"

"You know how I have dreamt that one day we would open our own showplace?"

"Yes, but—"

"The fellow building the place two doors away is strapped for cash and near bankrupt. He'll bolt south if given half the chance. We can get friends like Frank Dinsmore and Diamond Tooth Gertie to throw in and start our own resort. It already has the beginning of a stage and a fine teak bar. You know how I've always talked of opening a theater. You shall be the headliner, and we shall have a full repertoire of acts, good rooms upstairs, gambling, and a fine saloon."

"Our own... theater?"

"I should like to name it the Orpheum after he who brought music from Apollo to mankind, even if he was hounded and torn to shreds by the seductions of the Manaids who were sent by Dionysus out of jealousy for his craft."

"Who were they?"

"Young women of supernatural beauty and appetites Kitty, though I'd wager not as lovely as you."

Kate sighed. "I so love it when you speak of such things." She put a hand to her breast and stared out the window, "I have quite a bit saved, but I am not experienced in the management of an entire theater and saloon, and it is already snowing."

"I've been planning this for a long time, Kitty. This is but a turn of fate sent by God to spur us onward my love. I beg of you, trust me."

Kate ran a finger across his cheek. Her upper lip trembled. Her delicate nose flared, and Alex kissed her. Kate kissed him back with abandon.

Unlike most performers in Dawson City, Kate had never been known as a goodtime girl who would shed her clothes for a man, and Alex had been forced to act satisfied to have her as his erstwhile girlfriend and partner in working the miners in a relationship that had remained unconsummated. The mere sight of them together had opened doors all over town, but just the same he would become terribly aroused, and often had left for a visit to the whores of the Segregated District. His hand began to explore her thigh, and he readied himself for her to push it away.

Kitty shrugged fair shoulders, her robe fell across the bed, and she sat naked beside him. "I shall go with you, Alex! You have my word, just as you shall have me."

"I... now?"

"I have never used these fine rooms for their best purpose, and I feel it entirely appropriate to do so with you before I abandon them entirely for what fortune may bring in your company... if that be your wish."

A trilling laugh ran through Alexander like a flash of lighting sent by his ancient Gods, like a sparkling brook pouring from some hidden place. A wall seemed to fall away, revealing a vast space on the other side from which that laughter came, the same laughter he'd heard in Panama while teetering on the brink of death.

"Dearest, what is it?" Kate gazed at him with concern, at a loss to his hesitation.

"I... *Gods!*" He kissed her and again heard that laugh, this time from above him as if in the very room. Alex glanced up toward the tongue-and-groove boards of the ceiling.

"What in the world's the matter, Alex?"

"I heard the most lovely laughter, Kitty."

Kate's laugh mingled with the one from beyond his world as she seized his head in her hands and brought his lips to her own.

XVI.

"JOE! WE'RE GOING TO WORK WITH KLONDIKE KATE ROCKWELL IN A brand new theater!" Mary tore open curtains upon the day. She was clad in a black skirt over high black boots, a tailored blue blouse, and a too-small straw hat held upon her hair by pins. Another young woman identically attired accompanied her with her blond tresses pinned up under a matching hat. They stood over the bed and giggled.

Joseph groaned and rolled away from the buffeting of cold air that came with them, followed by a blade of daylight cutting his dreams to the bone. His head hurt mightily, yet he reached out for the vision that had been snatched away and the lovely voice that had faded with the entry of two flesh-and-blood girls.

"Oh, this is Lily, we met at the Monte Carlo. She's working there but is coming to the Orpheum as soon as it opens. Klondike Kate and her boyfriend Alex have lined up Diamond Tooth Gertie and a whole bunch of girls to work with them, and *we're* going to be there too! Isn't it exciting? Joe?"

'Ah...' Joseph pulled the covers over his head.

Lily exploded in giggling, and the sound drew Joseph's head from under the covers to peer at the girl who stood beside Mary with hands on her hips. "Hello, Joe," she plopped down on the bed beside him and Mary did on the other. Their weight pulled the comforter tight, and he groaned again even as he felt a steady response in his loins.

"Is he really as good as you say? Looks plumb wrung-out to me, girl."

"He's been with Lorelei. She leaves him rather disoriented and wracked with humors."

Lily giggled again, "Sounds like me and Charlie Meadows. That is some *hunk* of a man! Bet he'll try and get me back over to the Palace somethin' pronto."

"What did he say when you told him?"

"He was pretty straight-faced. He has to be with all those people around... and Mae and all, but I could tell what he was thinkin'. I just hope he don't come and pester me all the time at the new place."

"What new place?"

"The Orpheum!" The girls shouted.

"Where's that?"

"It's on Front, just two doors down from the Monte Carlo, but it's not finished yet Joe."

"Then how can you work there?"

"We're part of the new company. We didn't have any money to put in, but we signed six-month contracts with Kate and Alex, and will be at the grand opening. They—"

"When is it going to open?"

"Sometime this fall, before Thanksgiving for sure. In the meantime we got jobs for a couple of weeks with Sid Grauman's show at Nigger Jim's Pavilion. It's not all blackface and pratfalls you know. He wanted to dress us up like Chinese girls, but we're going to do the two sisters act that Ned Foster's run for years at the Bella Union in San Francisco. I did it at the Midway Plaisance on Market with a friend, and the sailor boys loved it! Showed it to Sid and he busted a gut. We're going to be Itzy and Bitzy, the, oh," Mary turned to Lily, "I can show you how the hoochy-kootchy dancers at the big melodeons do this thing with their hips, Lily. It makes the fellows crazy I'll tell you right now."

Mary stood up, put her hands behind her head, and began to grind her hips to the laughter of Lily, who clapped her hands in time. "Look: they wear these little shiny skirts that show their tummy like this," Mary lifted her blouse to expose her navel, "and rotate it just so." Her stomach rippled with the effort and Lily gave an appreciative shriek. "Have you seen Little Egypt? She came to San Francisco from the Chicago Worlds' Fair. I was only twelve, but I snuck into the balcony of the Thalia on Pacific and watched from a booth while she did the Belly Dance and the Dance of the Seven Veils. I'll tell you right now that girl could *shimmy!* That's when I decided to learn to do the same. You should see the boys' faces!"

"Very impressive."

"Thank you sir, then do you think we're qualified to work at the Orpheum alongside the great Klondike Kate and Diamond Tooth Gertie?"

"Perhaps they'll run out of gold if you're upon the stage first."

"You do so know how to speak to a girl," Mary put a finger to her lips, "Oh, and I shall need a stage name, a *handle,* as they put it. What shall I call myself?"

"Barbary Mary?"

"*Lily!* That sounds like a wrinkled old whore in the cribs! *Really!*" Mary huffed and turned to Joseph. "Any suggestions?"

"Klondike Mary?" Joseph scratched under the covers, and his fingers found a spot of dried blood on his stomach.

"That's been done. I want something unique, something that both rolls off the tongue and is memorable."

"Gold Bottom Mary?"

They burst into laughter. "Lily! Maybe if I had a bottom like Diamond Tooth Lil, or Babe Wallace!"

Joseph chuckled. "It really isn't my preference."

"What else?"

Lily shrugged, "I like your bottom."

Mary winked. "Well, I suppose I can think on it while we're eating. You hungry, Joe?"

"Need you ask? I am fairly starving."

"Lorelei sure takes it out of you. Care for a bath first, Mister?"

"Yes, that would be perfect."

"Then we'll run you one." Mary jumped up and motioned for Lily to follow. They went into the bath, from which the sound of water came to him mixed with giggling.

Joseph stared at the ceiling and stretched until he was spread-eagle on the bed. He seemed to float on the goose feather mattress, and the sound of his heart was a hollow drum as if it were in a deep canyon below. Was it the sound of his heart... or Lorelei's? Where did such a question even come from? He listened until his head again began to ache.

When the girls emerged from the bathroom, Mary had a scrub brush and bar of soap, and Lily had a towel draped over her arm.

Lily's cheeks bulged, "Ready for yer baa-th, sir?"

"Am I to be bathed by the both of you?"

"Yes, do you mind?"

"No, ah, this is so strange though. Everyone told me how women were in such short supply in the Klondike, yet I have never been around so many in my entire life."

Lily grinned. "Suppose it depends on your luck, Joe,"

Mary shrugged. "Fate is a cruel mistress at times. At others she is lavish with her gifts. Don't question her plans, good sir."

"I should thank Lorelei."

Mary nodded. "She knows what we're up to anyway."

"Why in heaven's name are you two talking about some older woman as if she were God or something? *We* are the most desirable women in Dawson, Mary. We're not uneducated whores, and we're quite good-looking," she tossed her head, "and we're young."

With the pulling of two pins, Mary removed the straw hat from her curls. "We do seem to be having the most fun I've got to admit."

"You are golden beings upon the passing stage of life, Goddesses who dance amongst mere mortals suffering travails and darkness as they moil for gold."

Lily raised an eyebrow. "You sound like a man of letters, Joe, or a playwright. Do you wish to write plays for us?"

"Me?"

"Well? You sound far more learned than the average rude miner who 'moils for gold' or whatever. Your compliment sounded quite well-spoken to me."

"Do you think?"

"Yes, and by the way, did Lorelei take it all out of you, or do you have enough left for us poor 'mortals' in need of a proper stallion?"

"Lily!" Mary fluttered fingers on her breast, "You are so *forward!"*

"Mary, hon, if half the things you have told me are true, I see no reason why we should pretend otherwise, or waste time for that matter," Lily put a hand to her own breast, "I am fairly dizzy with curiosity."

"What have you been telling her?"

"Only the truth, Joe."

"Can we ever know that?"

"I'm not talking philosophy. I just know things are going our way at the moment. Life is quite a bowl of cherries, so to speak."

Joseph rubbed his neck. "Well, if you speak of what I think, I suppose I shall be ready for it. This is all so strange and sudden, but actually I'm quite excited by the prospect of both of you. Um... that *is* of what you speak, isn't it?"

Lily pursed her lips and curtsied. "You're getting smarter all the time, fella."

"First a bath then, and I must brush my teeth." Joseph hesitated before rising from the covers.

Lily grabbed the comforter and snatched it away. Joseph made to cover his crotch as he lay on the sheets, but not before she caught an eyeful of that with which he was endowed. "Sheesh!" She fluttered ring-covered hands and whistled. "You weren't pullin' my leg, girl!"

"That weren't what I was pullin', sister. Well, come on Joe." Mary motioned toward the bathroom.

Joseph stood up with his hands before him. "Am I to be the only one without clothes then?"

Lily put a foot on a chair to unlace a tall boot, Mary did the same, and the girls took turns unlacing each others' bustiers and slipping out of their clothes. Lily stood naked trying to mimic modesty with her hand in Mary's, and grinned. "Well, fella, do I gotta yank on that thing to lead you to water?"

<hr>

Joseph's stomach was rumbling like a freight train by the time they entered a restaurant on Princess Street. The eyes of two miners who were wolfing down caribou steaks widened as he passed with a girl on each arm. The scowl of contempt from the one about his age caught him like a blow, and Joseph froze for a moment.

Lily huffed and tightened her grip. "Don't pay a bit of attention, hon." She tossed back a lock of hair that had come unpinned, "They'd give their whole stakes and right arms too, to be where you are right now."

"Damn gigolo," the young man muttered.

Lily smirked as she and Mary guided Joseph to a table. The scent of the girls' sex came back to him from beneath the smells of food and cigars, and his blood began to pound as he pulled out their chairs. He found himself grinning back at the young miner. The man glared like he wanted to kill Joseph before his stare fell on Lily, and he ran a hand through a thin beard as his attention wobbled to Mary's breasts.

Mary squeezed Joseph's leg and yawned. "I wonder what winter holds for us besides the fact it's going to be awfully cold."

"Whatever we wish!" Lily said brightly.

"She has blessed me," Joseph whispered as his hands squeezed their soft thighs under the table. It was to the entire crazy young town around them, to the fabulous and fearful hills of gold, to the cold shades of winter growing within vales and crags, to the shafts of sun coming through the dark bellies of clouds like the gaze of beings beyond imagining. It was to half-lit memories of his time with Lorelei that he fought mightily to recall. He felt the shaggy shoulders of beasts for which he had no name heaving beneath his feet as if awakening from a sleep of eons. Joseph felt a thousand things of which he could not speak, of which he might never be able to, as if he'd come unstuck in time and was in a place where all things existed at once, but only came into sight when he chose to focus on them. He sighed.

"What are you thinkin' Joe?"

"That I am quite hungry I suppose."

XVII.

KATHLEEN ELOISA ROCKWELL STARED AT THE TRACKS OF WORKMEN IN yellow sawdust and listened to the echoes of activity presaging a future she both dreaded and wished had already happened. A draft tickled her legs under the flannel petticoat and she crossed them, tucking the folds of her pink dress between her thighs as she adjusted her position upon the wicker-bottomed chair in the unfinished balcony box. Kate leaned on the unvarnished balustrade and put hands together as if in prayer. She clasped a delicate nose between fingers graced with long purple nails, stared at her newborn stage of birch planks, and imagined bright lights burning as she stared into the wide eyes of starving men.

Starving men?

She chuckled. Yes, they truly were starving... for what Alex had been starving for when she'd tested him, even though she knew he had snuck off countless times to the whores when she'd refused him. She chuckled. It wasn't the act itself they so wanted but the woman, and she was more than all the girls in the cribs put together to those men. Above all entertainers in the Klondike, Kate had assumed the mantle of an angel: someone whose mere presence reminded them of all things womankind could be even in this harsh clime so far from wherever they'd come. Only a select few she'd bestowed that gift upon since joining the troupe in Seattle two years ago, though only after some serious grooming of her suitors and at a very high price, and an oath of silence none had broken. *They didn't dare.*

Alexander was sanguine he was the first to have her, and in character she had acted innocent and fearful past the point that said she was in unfamiliar territory, only becoming passionate in lovemaking after he'd cajoled her repeatedly. She even had a well-honed story of an incident on a horse he seemed to believe, or at least wanted to. She felt a smile on her lips and shifted on the chair.

It had made his time with her all the more valuable. That was for certain. She only hoped he hadn't gotten some disease from the working girls, and of course that she wouldn't become pregnant. She hadn't used any of the lozenges she'd purchased from Mattie Silks, but it wasn't her time of month anyway.

A door banged downstairs, and she jerked on her seat as the sound echoed through the building. Kate ran a finger in the film of sawdust on the railing and frowned at the space the gaming tables were taking. That would certainly limit seating for her shows, but then again she'd be making money off those fellows even when she was elsewhere just like every other resort owner. Alex was going to charge $12.50 or an ounce of gold for an orchestra seat on opening night, and it was already booked. All their money was going to be sunk into this building, and if another fire like last April's came, they might be left destitute when the nights were endless and the river locked in six feet of ice.

Perish the thought!

"No, we shall be wealthy beyond imagining, damn it!"

"Your pardon, ma'am?"

Kate turned with a start. A handsome sandy-haired young man stood at the top of the stairs with his thumbs rubbing the insides of his fingers as if his hands were looking for something to do. He blinked in her violet-eyed stare and rocked on his feet. "I was told to come here to help out, but I'm not sure what for."

"Oh? And who told you that?"

"Miss Lorelei. She told me I'd find you in the balcony."

"That gorgeous woman who resides above Jack Finley's saloon . . ."

"Yes ma'am. Oh, my name's Joseph Walton."

"And mine is Kathleen, although Kitty and Kate have been my handles for some time now. You're quite a good-looking pup, Joe. Seventeen, are you not? I can see why she keeps you."

"Pardon?"

"Everybody knows you're her fancy man. There's no need to be shy about that." She chuckled, "I don't feel like playing the Belle of Dawson or the Queen of the Klondike or all that fluff at the moment. Sometimes I envy Edie. She doesn't give the lie just to be accepted by high-tone hypocrites who sneak off to her and her compatriots when they think nobody's looking. She doesn't even mind being called the Mare." Kate shuddered, "I would detest that." She batted long lashes as her rose-hued orbs appraised him, "Joseph Walton, it's obvious to those of us who make the night their day that this Miss Lorelei keeps you for your prowess in a bed. She's the only woman in this entire town of such exceptional looks who isn't working the miners and she certainly must have financial holdings elsewhere. I saw her dressed like a goodtime girl the other night, but she wasn't working a soul. In fact she was spending money on you like you were a goodtime girl and she was one of the Bonanza Kings, and on that little dish Mary besides. What is she really, some European gentry, or perhaps an heiress slumming as a lark in our Eldorado of the North?"

"You're quite perceptive Miss Rockwell. Was it so apparent?"

She nodded, "To all the hard-working girls who watch other women even closer than they watch men, it was. The Mare told me about your doings in the balcony. Of course none of the men would notice a thing beyond her looks. She is extraordinarily beautiful and I'm rather relieved she *isn't* working. There'd be a lot less to go around for the rest of us anywhere she chose to plant herself. That's a certainty."

"Both of you have the most remarkable eyes."

"She does also, doesn't she? Mine are renowned for their violet hue and I quite enjoy seeing them in the mirror myself if I don't sound too vain. One discovers quite young what they do to others you know, but I have never seen or heard of eyes like that woman's. They seem to change like slivers of glass in a kaleidoscope: shifting colors as when one twists the tube." She shook her head, "Quite remarkable."

"That's a wonderful description."

"A metaphor, Joe. Do you know what that is?"

"Sounds like a simile to me."

Kate put a hand to her mouth. "Then you're somewhat educated I suppose. Well, I shouldn't think she'd pick anything else when she has her choice of men. So what are we to do with you, and what is your price as a laborer?"

"She pays the price, and my services are yours."

"How could one refuse that?" She stroked her chin and looked him up and down, "Hum, of what use could you be?"

"I'm a hard worker. I can do carpentry and the like."

Kate stood up and slid hands down her dress to get the wrinkles out. She slapped it, and a cloud of dust arose. "I must point out that you haven't denied your relationship with this Miss Lorelei, but if Cad Wilson can get away with that Negro boxer they call the Prince for a 'servant' I suppose your situation is relatively mundane." She pursed her lips. "The man has the body of a Greek god and he lives right in her apartments." She slid the dress and petticoat up her thigh, kicked off a moose hide moccasin as she extended one foot toward him, flexed her leg, and pointed purple-painted toes at his face. Since long before she'd arrived here, Kate had trained in gymnasiums. It was mandated by any good theater company for all the girls, and a gym had been established in a warehouse on Duke Street for the performing troupes to use. She continued to do so although it was horribly drafty and very cold in the winter, but the effects of such discipline were well worth it on men, as well as keeping her from damage while doing some of her more strenuous acts.

Joseph's eyes traveled up her leg to her face, and he grinned.

She chuckled in return. "You know this will be the grandest place in Dawson City, although not the largest as the Palace has that honor, but it shall be the *best*. Do you know how much money I take in on a good night?"

"Quite a bit I suppose."

"I made seven-hundred and fifty-six dollars on Friday."

Joseph whistled, "That is... in one *night?*"

"No mucking about the diggings or squatting over a frozen hole to relieve oneself for this girl," her upper lip rippled in a raspberry curl, "and all because men want a piece of tail that they shall never have."

Joseph's face began to color.

She laughed. "Now don't tell me you didn't jump, Joe, when that woman offered you her favors."

"No, I... yes, but I have never heard women speaking in such a way until the last few weeks in Dawson City, and not just the base tarts of the cribs, either, but women like Lorelei, and Mary, and Lily, and you, Kate."

"I am being more than forward. I don't even know why I trust you so to speak in such a way. There is something about you which causes me to cast aside all deception with abandon and to confide in you as if you were my paramour." She shook her head, "It's quite strange, and rather disquieting."

"I bet you say that to all the fellows."

They broke into raucous laughter, and the hammering downstairs stopped as workmen turned their heads to the balcony. Kate leaned over the balustrade and fixed the foreman in her gaze. "Well... what are *you* looking at?" The men made haste to return to their labors, and she turned her back on the doings below. "You would be wasted working with these lugs. Let's go to the Palace for some champagne."

"Well all right. She did tell me to come see you and to let you decide what we should do."

"What for?"

"She doesn't say in so many words; she just suggests things. I was dining with Mary and Lily when she, oh never mind."

"Well, she must be something if she sends her fancy man to see other women. She's not plotting anything, is she?"

"Oh no, she's quite secure in her person and knows that I shall return at the proper time. She looks upon us as children I think."

"Perhaps you. I may look nineteen, but I'm actually twenty-five." Kate put fingers to her lips, "Why am I telling you these things!"

"Um . . ."

"How old is she?"

"She's, um... thirty or so I believe."

"My *word!*" A hand fell to her breast. "I should like to find out what she does for her skin. Nary a blemish, or a line on the girl's neck or around her eyes. It must take some doing to find the cosmetics and the like, especially here. What a fortune she must spend. You're one lucky boy to be snatched up by the likes of her. It's marvelous. It's as if you were one of the new girls who had the great fortune to have found the richest and most handsome of the Klondike Kings the very moment you arrived." She winked, "Actually Joe, you're quite the gigolo."

Joseph's gut clenched. "I beg your pardon!"

His flash of anger rippled through Kate's features as he saw her stiffen from a momentary thrill of fear. "Miss Rockwell I apologize, I didn't mean to scare you. I just... that's so odd. I intend to prospect in the hills come spring and make my fortune through honest endeavor. Miss Lorelei is someone who has taken me into her confidence and her bed it's true, but I'm not some parasite from the haunts of depravity I assure you. To be honest, your friend Alex looks far more like—"

She let out a shriek that again stopped the workmen in their tracks. "Oh, that's good... it's *true!* Alex appears a swarthy scoundrel with a closet full of secrets, doesn't he?"

"Um, well—"

"And I am the Queen of the Klondike drenched in innocence and purity, whose golden love he has stolen from all these *far* more worthy men," she laughed. "What a turn of fate!" Kate did a pirouette, her cheeks took color, and her violet eyes glowed. "Isn't fate grand?"

"I suppose."

"Come, let me show you my new apartments." She seized his hand, dragged him to the stairwell, and led him down and up another set of stairs to three unfinished large rooms at a corner overlooking Front. They stood at windows newly set in their casements, gazing out over the riverfront commerce of Dawson. "There will be a stout door both at the bottom and the top of those stairs, and far richer men will but dream of entering here where you stand. Oh look, there's Johnny Matson, gazing up here like a hungry hound." She pointed to a short-bearded miner standing on the sidewalk below who was staring at Kate. "He follows me from one venue to the next, never raising his voice like the others, but always leaving gold. He's a shy one that Swede," Kate sighed, "and I'm his angel of salvation I suppose, his dream of hearth and home when he's back in his dark cabin, and the wind howls outside filled with only the cries of wolves and the driven snow." She waved at the little Swede, whose face was upturned as if in prayer or supplication as he stared at Kate through the falling flakes.

Joseph took a breath. He was so far from the dream that had brought him here, adrift on a strange sea scented with the perfume of Lorelei's skin, inhabited by lovely voices that kept him company in dreams when she wasn't there, and surrounded by young women when he awoke. He squeezed his eyes shut and shook his head.

There: her laugh again.

"Whatever is it, Joseph?"

"Um, excuse me. I was just trying to imagine exactly what the future holds."

"Money, Joe."

"Is that the whole of it?"

"No, silly, it's only a means to an end."

"What end, Kate? Isn't the life you live, the excitement, the blind adoration of men, and the envy of women what you truly crave? I've seen you upon the stage and walking amongst the crowds. Your heart beats harder and your eyes sparkle. They bare your very soul at such times. When that ends will money alone buy happiness? And isn't the passion of a lover your secret and greatest joy as the nights grow longer outside these walls? Youth is your sustenance just as is the living of it. I may be quite young myself, but Lorelei has revealed that to me. Honestly... where will you ever be happier or more fulfilled than now, Kate?"

Kate turned having forgotten the man in the street. She put a hand to her breast and sat on the windowsill against the glass. Her bare shoulders jerked away from the cold, and she turned violet eyes rimmed with dark lashes upon him sparkling in the fine pale skin of a girl's face framed with chestnut hair. Her tongue touched her lips. Her upper teeth bit her lower one as her feet scuffed the unfinished floor in beaded moosehide moccasins. "How can you know these things? You speak as someone far older and wiser, as if it isn't even the voice of a young man that touches me so but something else entirely. Quite honestly, it frightens me."

"Really?"

"Yes, it's as if you were some daemon or incubus sent to sway me from the path I've chosen and the whole future of this endeavor, yet you make me feel a great excitement also."

"I assure you I'm no demon, and I can't recall what that other thing is at all at the moment, Miss Rockwell."

"And what do you mean when you speak of your lover Lorelei?" Kate's eyes narrowed, "You said she's shown you such things. What things?"

Joseph found himself reaching out to Lorelei and the comfort of her voice for an answer, but there was only the pounding of hammers below. He gazed out on Front, searching for the face of the lone miner whose unrequited love of Klondike Kate made him appear like a pale wraith warning of winter's arrival. There was only the passing crowd, oblivious to the two of them above. "She is no demon either, although she is far more than one could imagine."

"Well, at least at your age," she rose from her perch on the sill, "one might suspect her of being a succubus anyway if you know what that means. You're quite a perceptive young man that's a certainty, although you still make me feel rather un-at-ease."

"My apologies, Miss Rockwell."

"No bother," Kate snatched up a pink pastel parasol that matched her dress, pointed its brass tip at him, and smiled. "Well, let's be off to the Palace for a sip of champagne."

Joseph followed Kate as she took dainty steps down the stairs and out of the theater.

———

If he'd thought the company of Mary and Lily gave him no privacy, Joseph found that walking down the street with Klondike Kate was like strolling into church naked. Every eye was upon them and remained so. The same two miners who had glowered at him in the restaurant but an hour ago were staring from where they sat in front of the Canadian Bank of Commerce on the riverfront, smoking cigars while the NWMP was overlooking the weighing of their gold and taking the

Crown's ten percent tax. Their faces were blank as Joseph and Kate approached, but he could feel their bone-deep envy.

Arizona Charlie Meadows was coming down the sidewalk in the company of his wife Mae, who had her right hand held up before her wrapped in gauze. Charlie had a wry expression on his face as he tipped his big Stetson hat to Kate and winked at Joseph, "Howdy, Kate."

"Mister Meadows," Kate twirled the parasol and smiled delightfully, "and dear Mae! How is your poor thumb?"

The pretty brown-haired woman gave her a wan expression. "What's left of it hurts like the fucking devil, Kate."

Charlie examined the sidewalk. "I'm givin' up the trick shootin'. Reflexes aren't what they used to be, I guess."

"I am so sorry!" Kate said in the most appropriate tones as she pressed a cheek to Mae's. "If there is anything I can possibly do—"

"If you see any good thumbs tossed on the stage, let me know—female ones preferably." Mae grinned weakly. Her face was ashen, she swayed on her feet, and Charlie put an arm around her shoulders to steady her. "I need more of that laudanum, Charlie, and a little shot of whiskey perhaps."

"After you get some air and have something to eat, my love."

Mae sighed loudly, Charlie excused the two of them, and Joseph and Kate continued down Front.

"Poor Mae," Kate said. "Living with such a man as that must be something though."

"He's quite a fellow."

"Like a damn stallion with the torch of Apollo in his eyes. Did you see that look he gave me?"

"Um... no."

"You're young and someday you shall notice such things. You know, he's seeing Diamond Tooth Gertie and that little blonde filly Lily as well."

"I didn't know that."

"Yes, rumor has it Lily is with his child."

As they turned into the Palace, a vision of Lily's flushed face as she sat astride him with her lovely breasts swinging to the thrusts of his body replaced Joseph's view of the room. *Good God... might she be pregnant with mine?* He stumbled and caught himself against the bar.

"Whoa!" Kate took his arm and led him to a table near the gaming tables being cleaned by a fellow in red arm garters who had rushed to it from behind the bar. "No standing at the rail for this girl."

The man pulled out her chair, and she sat in a flourish of pink. "Miss Rockwell, how are you?" the bartender asked as he swiped the table with his rag.

"Fine, Danny, bring us a bottle of Mumms, the dry kind."

"Certainly, Miss Rockwell."

"Kate, damn it."

"Sure Kate."

Joseph examined the afternoon crowd as the rattle of a roulette wheel's ball came from behind him, with the shouts of men calling out as if commanding the thing to yield to their will. As it stopped there was a chorus of muttering and cursing followed by a single cry of triumph.

A pretty, rather plump young woman appeared in the doorway with her breasts half-tucked into a purple outfit a size too big that seemed to have something underneath. She moved somewhat stiffly as she glanced about the room. "Where's Mel?"

One of the men at the bar spoke, "He's wrestlin' with that gold, Lulu. He's got two fellas to help him and one to tote a shotgun. They oughta be here real soon."

"Good," Lulu hopped on the bar. A crowd was beginning to form obstructing Joseph's view of the goings-on, but he caught a glimpse of Lulu putting a hand behind her neck and posing as if someone were taking her picture. "What of the scales?"

"Couple fellas from the Alaska Commercial Company are bringin' one right this minute," another said, "Mel promised he'd have it back by closing. Ain't many big enough to fit a woman on that can be moved easy."

"More's the shame doll. After all the times a girl's got her weight in gold, you'd think one of these so-smart resort owners would have one permanent-like for such occasions. It would do great business for the lug."

"That's a good idea," Kate whispered, "I'll have Alex find one and have the Kinsey brothers take pictures when we do it, and have Stroller White write us up in the Klondike Sun... and we'll print posters. We'll get all these weighings at our digs."

"What's going on?"

"Lulu's auctioned herself off to Mel MacDonald from Gold Bottom Creek. He's paying her weight in gold for her hand in marriage."

"Really?"

"Sure, it happens quite a bit. She'll give him a year and either leave the country or just pop up in the saloons again. But a man gets a good time complete with cooking for the interim. See her clothes? I bet you anything she's wearing something underneath to make herself heavier. There's an old vest of Chinese chainmail from the tongs in Frisco that goes around amongst the girls for just such an occasion. It's worth its weight in gold as they say. I'd wager my stake in the Orpheum that she's got it on right now."

"What do the tongs use them for?"

"To stop bullets."

Two men in suit coats wheeled in a big scale with two brass pans swinging from its arms. They were followed by a crowd of more men, dance hall girls, shopkeepers, and excited boys. The men steadied it, braced the wheels, and one of them placed identical weights in each pan, then adjusted the dial in the middle of the contraption until the two pans were of equal height.

"Wahoo, here comes the gold!" shouted a short, furry man who'd been finishing a drink left on the bar by a patron whose attention was riveted to the goings-on.

Four men pulled up in a wagon, and a stocky fellow with freshly barbered red muttonchop sideburns dressed in a new three-piece pinstriped suit jumped onto the boardwalk and brushed snow off his shoulders. Another dropped the gate and began lugging heavy sacks off. They carried the sacks into the Palace as the driver got down with a short double-barreled shotgun and tied up the team with his free hand.

The crowd had thickened around the selling of Lulu to Mel Mac-Donald, including a few whores who had drifted over from the District. Klondike Kate was forgotten, for here was great entertainment combining the lusts for gold and women into one spectacle that men would speak of for years to come, and women would dream of.

When the gold was stacked next to the opposite pan, Lulu slid her round bottom upon the brass dish nearest the bar and let out a yip of excitement, "Pile away, honey!" Mel hefted a sack, dropped it on the empty pan, and it landed with a thud to be followed by another. "Stack away!" she yelled, "we ain't near there yet!" She leaned back with a hand on the center post and waved to the bartender, "Gimme a glass o' bubbly, will ya sweetheart?"

The bartender poured Lulu a glass of champagne. She downed it in an instant and threw the glass upon the floor to smash into glittering pieces. "No bother Danny, I'll pay for it and tip you like there's no tomorrow!"

"Wa-hoo!" shouted the furry little man who was finishing others' drinks. He held out an empty glass for champagne, and Danny poured him some. Danny poured Lulu another as a sack dropped upon the pile made her sink down and bounce a bit, spilling her drink. She giggled.

Danny swept up the glass as Mel looked at his diminishing pile of gold and shook his head. He looked at Lulu, opened his mouth, and clamped it shut. Two sacks were left. With deliberate slowness he hefted one and let it down gently.

Lulu sank down and rose again with her feet swinging. She crossed her arms and wiggled her toes, "Hope ya brought enough, Mel! Sure am lookin' forward to tonight!"

"To hell with it!" Mel seized the last sack, dropped it on the pile, and Lulu rose in the air to balance on the opposite side of the gold with her red high-heeled shoes kicking. The crowd erupted in a chorus of shouts and laughter. A look of relief crossed Mel's face, "Drinks for the house!" he shouted over the din, and everyone converged on the bar.

Kate and Joseph remained at the table. She put a hand on his arm. "I hope it works out."

"What?"

"Wouldn't it be nice if they actually stayed together?"

"Certainly, do they ever?"

She sighed, "Occasionally I hear."

"That would be a happy ending, wouldn't it?"

"Women are supposed to crave such an ending aren't we?"

"That's what I've always heard. Presently I can't say, Kate."

"You know how you spoke in the balcony about this being *it?* I mean, how the very living of this life is what I truly love the most?"

"I was just rambling."

"Maybe for you, but it sticks in my mind." She stared at the ceiling, "I want to marry Alex and live a respectable life with children and a home. Truly I do."

"Then—"

"Do you know what déjà vu is?"

"I sure do. I've known more of that feeling in the past few days than in my entire life up to now."

"That's what I felt as you spoke to me, as if I were a very old lady remembering that moment and agreeing that this *was* the epiphany of my life... right *here*... right *now.* That's what scared me, because then

what do I have to look forward to? It was as if you were some supernatural messenger sent from the future to tell me it's all downhill from
here."

"I hope not."

She ran a hand across her face, "It makes me want to say to hell with
it all and take you into my bed right this minute."

"Oh."

XVIII.

JOSEPH LEFT KLONDIKE KATE IN THE COMPANY OF DIAMOND TOOTH Gertie and stepped into the October afternoon. He shoved hands into the pockets of the red plaid mackinaw and walked Front toward the mouth of the Klondike River through the frenzy of people racing a fast-coming winter. He had no rush, no wood to cut or logs to chink against the bitter cold. He had Lorelei... or did she have him? The street was churned to frosty mud under horses' hooves and the wheels of wagons, and he stopped to clean his boots more than once.

He bought a waffle and coffee from the stand on the riverbank. The adolescent girl serving him clutched her shawl in a gloved hand and shivered as she poured him a cup. Her mother had a hacking cough. What would they do come winter? Joseph dug in his pocket and his hand emerged with a five-dollar gold piece he didn't know he had. He dropped it on the plank counter and left as she searched for change.

The bridge across the Klondike loomed out of the river's cold mist. Joseph stepped up on it, kicked mud off his gum boots, and hugged the rail as two wagons passed. When he reached the middle, he leaned on the railing and watched a cloud hugging the top of Midnight Dome against the clearing sky. A shiver ran through him as if for a moment he felt straining backs of miners probing the dark hearts of the hills, and something deeper and far older that seemed to be awakening as they did. "I felt that, Lorelei. I know it was you."

Those hills held the mortal remains of Fred Dodge and a host of far better souls who had come here seeking a future of wealth and happiness only to go in the cold ground. He closed his eyes and heard the low rumble of beasts long gone from the land whose bones were being brought up from the frozen gravel this moment. "Damn... how do you make me feel such things?"

They run through me like the blood in your veins, and as you come to know me it's natural that you begin to know them as I do.

"I knew you were watching. I can feel it when you gaze on me now."

Yes, you're much more sensitive than many a man. Why do you think I picked you?

"This isn't easy. I feel all adrift and without mooring. I dreamed of death, and I felt as if I were in some far away place long ago and I knew it must be from you. I quite often wonder if I am going mad."

I know love, believe me I do, but trust me, you are becoming sane.

"Klondike Kate thought me frightening though I was only speaking of what came to me."

Yes, but look how she is enthralled with you... and see how she makes herself available to you without question.

"That seems to go with being your lover."

It does, her chuckle tickled his spine, *I've taken you far from your intended path and for that I apologize. It could be called selfishness, but I honestly relish your company.*

"My body anyway."

An exasperated gasp buffeted his face with the scent of flowers, *Oh please, your soul! The company of your soul is what keeps me alive my love. Otherwise, I could have a different lover every night for a thousand years.*

"I apologize. That was childish of me." He rubbed his cheek, "One could call me possessed I suppose, yet why am I not afraid? This is all so unbelievable anyway."

Perhaps because you crave the pleasure of me, perhaps because you are young and your innocence when we began was a clean palette for my brush. Perhaps because in your heart you have always known this was meant to be.

"You offer me these possibilities like multiple choices on a test. Sometimes you sound like a schoolmarm, Lorelei."

Her laughter danced in the voice of the river, *Your youth is my greatest pleasure as well as my sustenance. The answer then: choose all of the above.*

"Why do you speak of your sustenance so? And for that matter... why have I never seen you eating?"

There was a long silence while Joseph watched his breath drift on the breeze. He gazed at a twisting pan of ice with a single golden leaf upon it sparkling in the last rays of the sun as it bobbed against the bank. The air seemed to warm until he could feel her breath again and catch a scent of her. Soft lips brushed his cheek. He blinked and turned to look. There was only an overloaded wagon making its way from town.

You know in your soul what the physical bond between us is. You have from the start, but your mind has hidden from the brightness when we are not together.

Vertigo seized him, and he gripped the rail as something rose in his gorge. Joseph stepped away from the river lest he fall in.

"Watch yerself!"

He stepped out of the way of a wagon's wheels and stared into the eyes of a teamster whose grey beard waggled on a head wreathed in cigar smoke. The man grunted, glanced at the opposite bank, and shook the horses' reins as the planks groaned under the wagon's weight.

The bridge swayed. Suddenly the boards heaved like a blister about to burst, and a terror of falling seized him. Joseph grabbed the railing and fell to his knees. He was going to be sick. His whole self, his whole being was washing away in a river roaring from within and without—dissolving his very bones in a headlong rush as if he were lost in a maelstrom welling beneath the surface of what he *thought* had been the world. He was going to be sick and put hands to his mouth with a moan.

A soft hand lifted him up, and he was that golden leaf on its crystalline raft, breaking the light into rainbows as he bobbed on a familiar river of souls.

Say it, love.

"You're feeding on my life's blood."

Yes, for you are my chosen, yet the love you feel is no trick or illusion. In return for your companionship, I will give you knowledge and long life and the love of strong and vital women until your dying day. You shall never be content with less, but you must do this willingly now and come to me with knowing to grow into this as have those who came before you that I and my kind have chosen. It can be no other way. Otherwise, I must go.

"You would leave?" His voice sounded like the croaking of a toad, and Joseph slapped himself. He wiped tears from his face. "Don't!"

Not until you're prepared anyway. Eventually of course, but we're quite unfinished and I'm responsible for your present state of affairs. Your blood is my own, my precious love, but you've known this in your heart since the beginning.

"Yes... I did."

You are that golden being, who has always given himself to the coming night that the day might be born anew through his love.

"Yes, Lorelei."

You're safe in my keeping and blessed by a power beyond my own. I mean you no harm whatsoever, and neither will I let it come to you if it is in my power. Such is my vow, my love.

"Yes... thank you."

But don't act all giddy or half-mad in the presence of others, I beg you. This is our secret as lovers chosen by fate. You're partaking of the mysteries of a love older than the hills around you, and no other shall understand, not even Mary.

"Of course."

Good, now please get off your knees. There's a Mountie at the end of the bridge and he thinks that you are drunk or ill.

Joseph wiped his cheeks and glanced toward town. "Where are you?"

If someone entered my room above Jack's saloon, they would see me sleeping, yet I watch over you constantly.

"That sounds too much like my mother."

An exasperated sigh echoed in the æther, *Whatever... anyway you're my special project, remember?*

"I suppose I'll get used to it."

You already have. I'm going to let you deal with this on your own now. I don't want you talking to the air when that man approaches.

"I—"

"Ho! Are you all right fellow?"

Joseph turned to the Mountie, who had reined up his horse but a few feet away. "Yes sir. I dropped my watch on the bridge, and it nearly fell through the cracks."

"What watch?"

Joseph fished in his pocket and produced the golden watch of Fred Dodge.

The Mountie crossed his hands over the pommel of his saddle and glanced at the sky. "It is clearing. The lights should put on a glorious show tonight."

"Yes sir. I was just thinking how all this gold hereabouts has lain hidden for a million years."

The Mountie nodded. "And the savages have run around on top of it for who knows how long without digging a penny's worth."

"Um, yes."

"Are you employed? The winter is upon us and transport Outside is nearly over."

"Oh, yes sir."

"Where, with a mine?"

"No, although that's why I came. Presently I am employed in the opening of the Orpheum Theater on Front Street."

"Indeed? I hear Klondike Kate is moving there."

"Yes she is."

"A fine specimen of a woman I must say. Not like the base strumpets crowding the saloons or mopping the floors at Fort Herchmer when we catch them pestering good citizens with their solicitations outside the Segregated District. She's from a fine family in Spokane I hear. Her father is a doctor and it's said she went to a good Catholic school. You can tell she has breeding. I've served in Australia, India, and all across the north, and I must say that woman has the most beautiful eyes that I've ever gazed upon... and when she sings . . ."

"She's well educated. I was speaking with her today and she used a couple of words of which I wasn't sure of."

"Indeed? Where did you speak to her?"

"In her new apartments above the Orpheum."

The man's eyebrows rose, "And what were you doing there fellow?"

"They are under construction and I'm doing carpentry. Miss Rockwell was showing me what she wished done. She is very particular about what shall be done and where."

"Oh, indeed. Tell me, is she... oh, never mind. Carry on!" The Mountie saluted and kneed his horse toward town.

Joseph turned back to the lapis-blue sky. Polaris burned brightly above the pale scar of Moosehide Slide. He shivered and rubbed his arms. "My life's blood feeds you and I relish it. I can't help but wonder what God must think of this whole situation."

There was only the sound of the river and the bite of the cold, and he headed back toward town. Electric lights were coming on in the Eldorado of the North as green phosphorescence arced over the mountains, and a curtain of cold fire spread across the sky as if a great dark place that was always there but hidden had been torn open to spill its treasures across the vault of night.

When he reached the end of the bridge, he nearly ran into two men as his attention was riveted on the aurora. They parted and stopped on either side of him. "Hey, it's fancy man!" the one on his right said. It was the miners he'd seen in the restaurant and later on the street with Kate. The one about his age was on his right, and the older on his left. "Hey... you a pimp, Mister?"

"No call for that, Daniel."

"Why not? Maybe he's one of them girly men the whores and show gals keep around for sport 'cause they never want a piece a'tail. Don't ya think?"

"I am none of those things, sir. Now, I'd appreciate it if you would remove your person from my direction of travel."

He saw the fist at the last instant before it crashed into his right eye, and there was a flash of sparks as he went down on the steps at the foot of the bridge. Joseph's head hit the boards and a loud *crack* echoed in his ears.

"Danny! Damn it!"

"To hell with the fancy-arse sonofabitch!" Danny spat as he stepped up on the bridge and slapped his palms together.

Joseph grabbed Danny's ankle as he did and sprang erect as Danny went sprawling. He swung as Danny rose and felt his fist connect with satisfying solidity against Danny's nose in a meaty *whack* that stung his knuckles as blood sprayed in a glistening fan across the planks.

"Enough!" Big arms wrapped around his chest, and Joseph was lifted off the ground by the man behind him flailing and kicking. "Don't, goddamn it!"

Danny was getting ready to charge while the other man pinned him. "You hit him while I got him and I'll kick your arse all the way back to Twenty-One Above! I swear it Danny!" The man's beard rubbed against Joseph's cheek, smelling of smoke and liquor. "Hey, you got him," He muttered in Joseph's ear, "now both you young scrappers stop your fussin' and let's end it."

Without waiting for an answer the man let go and Joseph landed on his feet. Danny tottered six feet away, alternately wiping his nose and balling his fists.

The big man laughed, "You come back good, kid. Danny here's just all wound up 'cause you were with all them fine lookin' dames. It was kinda getting' to me for that matter. Guess Dan and me need to dip our wicks real soon." The man pulled out a handkerchief from his pocket, handed it to Danny, and put a hand on his shoulder, "How 'bout I buy us both a woman 'fore we go back to the claim?"

"Gee, really, Pete?"

"Hell yes. Let's go to the District and get us a couple a' young ones. That oughta settle you down some."

"Damn... thanks!"

Pete turned to Joseph. "Wanta come with us? It's on me, pilgrim."

"Um, no, thank you. I've got one... or some."

The man's teeth flashed, reflecting the lights along Craig Street. "Yup, I guess you do. Sorry 'bout the ruckus. You're pretty Skookum in a fix anyway. Have a good night kid. Come on, Dan."

"Hey, I'm sorry Mister." Danny shook Joseph's hand.

"That's all right. Have fun."

Joseph waved as the two headed back into town and were lost to view on Fifth Street. He felt the side of his face, then put a hand to the back of his head. He winced as he touched a bump there. He rotated his head, and his neck cracked. "Why weren't you watching out for me?"

I'm not your mother, remember?

A hand touched his arm and turned him into the rainbow gaze of his lover. Her lips touched the side of his face, and the stinging abated. Joseph stood holding her in the night, not cold, not hurting, and not asking the universe *why* any longer. The rest of the world had disappeared and it didn't matter.

XIX.

GEORGE BRUSHED SNOW OFF THE WOLVERINE FUR RUFF AND HANDED THE pretty coat check girl his caribou parka trimmed in Gwich'in beadwork. He slipped a weather-burnt finger under the tight boiled collar of his red dress tunic. It was oppressively warm inside after the bitter winds without. The girl smiled and handed him a yellow tag with a hand burnt from making coffee and waffles, then hung the parka with exaggerated care below a plethora of headgear from bowler hats to wolf fur caps with the ears peaked and stiffened by bone stays, and adorned with gold nuggets where the eyes had been.

George had arrived early, both to watch who came in and to avoid embarrassment that he was unaccompanied. All the girls he'd planned to ask, respectable or for pay, were taken. He'd only returned from Skagway yesterday, and everyone from the resorts and theaters seemed to be here to see how Pantages and Klondike Kate had turned the place into the newest mecca of pleasure and carousal just two doors down from Swiftwater Bill's Monte Carlo. Now that the weather had locked up the river in ice and shut the passes in snow, the selection of female company was growing both limited and expensive. The brand-new

White Horse and Yukon train was stalled at Lake Bennett from avalanches, and the interior had returned to the isolation of previous winters but for dog sleds. Fortunately, George had made White Horse on the last train over the mountains.

He was limited by economics to the open seating in the balcony and had been lucky to get a ticket at all. It had come with a small poke of gold in return for looking the other way after a fellow had made a scene at Mattie Silk's place and her lover Cortez had tossed the man out a second-story window. Of course George wouldn't have taken the money and given the erstwhile favor if the fellow thrown out the window had been in the *right*. He'd been a real troublemaker, one that George felt no compunction about throwing into the lockup at Fort Herchmer after a trip to the hospital. George's standards were sorely challenged by the peoples and distances of the Yukon, but he was learning the ways of the Klondike and needed to acquire a bit of cash. The Mare had taken his last big stake while his mind was softened by her wiles and he'd been pinching pennies since.

He ascended the carpeted stairs amongst the murmur and buzz of voices, checked his seat number, and sat on a chair sheathed in purple wool. He examined the seat next to him and ran a hand across the dark carved back that swept down to lion's claws on the armrests. *Scotland.* George grunted his approval just as a familiar voice rose from the floor below.

Edith Neal was guiding a sturdy if presently meek miner to one of the tables. She sat him down and flicked a hand at one of the waiters, who brought a pewter ice bucket and tripod stand with a bottle of champagne. Edie seized the bottle from the waiter and laughed. "You'll get a good tip, Johnny," her voice boomed, "just let me open the damn thing!"

George winced, remembering her laughter as she had shared his bed, how it had excited him even as he worried someone might overhear their conversation. He fought a momentary surge of envy as

Edie fiddled with the wire stopper. It appeared to be good French stuff although George couldn't read the label. She popped it, shrieking as it foamed up from the shaking she'd subjected it to in jerking it out of the waiter's hands. Edie grabbed a gold linen napkin, wrapped it around the neck of the bottle, and poured it into two fluted glasses, spilling a good deal in the process as her companion responded with a baritone laugh.

"This champagne's just rarin' to go, sweetie. Kinda like a fella I know, eh?"

The miner's high forehead reddened as he glanced about the room and muttered something to the Mare.

"Oh, pshaw!" She whispered in his ear, and he laughed.

The crowd thickened until every table was full. To be seated down there, that Greek fellow Pantages was charging twelve-and-a-half dollars a pop or an ounce of gold. It was extortion pure and simple, just like every other fandango and exhibition this winter, but it was the way of highrollers to show off their money by spending it. What good was a pile of gold up some creek when the ground was frozen ten feet deep, the sun hardly peeked over the mountains in the south for a couple of hours, and you were in a dark cabin smelling dirty clothes while listening to your partners belch and fart... without even a good window?

Four teenage girls appeared on the floor dressed in golden gowns with low-cut necklines. They carried bouquets of paper flowers that they placed on tables in crystal vases, leaning provocatively across the male customers as they did so. Some men acted unaware if accompanied by certain females. The rest howled. At each table the girls smiled and curtsied as pinches of gold dust and small nuggets were lavished upon them for their mere presence.

The girls appeared on the balcony to hang gilded paper wreathes before each box and across the balustrade. One with a complexion as white as a ceramic doll smiled at George. He cleared his throat and sighed. She looked like an angel. It would be something to have young things like that working for you, and he imagined them coming to him with their big doe eyes and perfect complexions at every turn of events. The tall fair-skinned one with long black hair and blue eyes looked quite Celtic and had high cheekbones fragile as carved glass. He—

"Inspector MacAtee! What in hell are you doin' over there all by your lonesome?"

George turned toward the resonant voice of Charlie Meadows, then stood at the sight of Mae and bowed. "Mister and Mrs. Meadows, how nice to see you."

"Get yourself on over to our box, pardner. We've got six seats and only four filled. You can be five." Charlie glanced around and winked. "Maybe one of these girls Pantages stole from me could make it an even half-dozen."

"Charlie, we're doin' fine without them."

"Sure, Mae, but that little Greek is a hell of a hustler. Just you watch. He's gonna try and make another raid on our inventory if this goes over."

"You'd do the same, you big sonofabitch."

Charlie laughed and kissed Mae as she held her right hand out of the way with the remains of her thumb sheathed in a golden jacket that had a nail and knuckle sculpted into it held on by golden chains around her wrist.

George watched the two Americans, rather put off by their language. The coarseness of their conversation was just part of their nature he supposed, but it never failed to amaze him: the result of having left the civilizing influence of English society and the Monarchy. Still, a fine little woman like Mae should attempt to change it, rather than joining in a continuing repartee of vulgarities once married to the man. George sighed. *The cockneys of the frontier.*

"You comin', Inspector?"

"Certainly, I should be honored."

"Good, come on."

He followed the Meadows to their box on the right of the stage that had red, white, and blue bunting interspersed with British and American flags draped from the brass railing. George sat to the left of the Meadows, eyeing the empty seats.

"You won't believe this lady that oughta be along in a hot minute—" Charlie began. He stood at a rustle of the curtains, at long last doffing his white Stetson hat to hold it before his chest as he bowed to someone coming through the purple damask drapes.

An image of beauty appeared like the sun parting clouds on the darkest day, and George sprang to attention. His chair bounced off the back of the box, and he reached to steady it as two eyes like he'd never seen in his life examined him from a flawless pale diamond of a face. Her porcelain nose flared over full lips spreading in the loveliest smile he'd ever seen or imagined as she extended a white-gloved hand and a wrist sparkling with diamonds. Without hesitation George bent one knee to the floor, raised the hand in his own, and kissed the back of it.

As he inhaled her scent, a roaring erupted between his ears. His head spun. George held that glorious hand for a moment longer, utterly without will or ability to let go. He finally did and rose.

Her eyes blazed like gems, seeming to grow larger as he stared. "Hello, George, I am Lorelei."

Her voice was as he'd expected, as he'd *known* it would be, like celestial harps from some symphony in a realm beyond the mortal coil. Mozart's life work was no more than the buzzing of ants in comparison. It was manifestly the voice of an angel.

"My, you are quite the poet and embellisher with your thoughts. You really should turn your talents to music yourself, or perhaps to writing." Her cheeks dimpled, "We might have another Lord Byron in our midst."

"Did... did I speak?"

"No you did not. Sit down, George. Your head is light enough." She flicked a graceful hand, and he felt a soft pressure upon his shoulders as he folded into his seat.

A sandy-haired youth appeared in a starched white shirt and gray bow tie, gray silk suspenders, and brown herringbone pants. He clutched a matching coat and had a faint sheen of perspiration on his forehead. When he saw George, he extended a hand. "Hello, sir, Joseph Walton."

George stood again, "Inspector George MacAtee, North-West Mounted Police."

"Pleasure to meet you," Joseph said as he sat beside Lorelei.

George watched the young man's right hand entwine in the left of Lorelei's and inhaled, trying to regain his bearings. He glanced at the side of her face with the gold curtain of the stage beyond her: a perfect profile of a perfect woman. He rubbed his eyes. One such as she in a place like this was astounding. He was dying to ask her if she were descended from one of the crowned heads of Europe. Such beauty simply *reeked* of the regal.

"Pardon me, Mademoiselle Lorelei, but you most certainly remind me of someone from the peerages of Europe by both your demeanor and obvious breeding. Are you, perchance, of noble blood?"

A trilling laugh rippled her white throat, and George sat transfixed as those eyes turned to him. *What color were they?* Her lips parted to speak, "I actually *am* descended from a noble line, one whose roots are as deep as the veins of gold torn from the flesh of our mother the earth. We've had many a title applied, but none are accurate, not to mention worthy. However, know that I have the blood of an Irish Lord and his secret mistress if it shall assuage your curiosity, as well as a host of others whom speaking of would only confuse and disturb you."

George sat puzzling her words. Here he was in this edifice of sybaritic diversions at the edge of the civilized world, being teased for his good manners by a woman whose beauty was beyond question, but whose allusions were doubtless to kept women and illegitimate consummations. He blinked and pulled at his mustache.

Oh... and what of the Mare?

George jerked erect and glanced over his shoulder.

Joseph let loose a laugh.

"Well," Charlie said as he poured a glass of champagne, "how about some of this Frenchie bubbly 'fore it goes flat? Damn stuff cost as much as a good horse in Tucson." He offered a glass to Lorelei, then to Mae, and poured one for George and Joseph. Charlie poured himself the last and held it up, "To the success of goddamn everybody, and for the gold to hold out, hope to God."

Lorelei took a sip. "For a while anyway."

George put his glass down. The champagne was excellent: crisp and dry, with a subtle bouquet that blended with the exquisite scent of her. He put his hand to his mouth to try and hide a belch just as Charlie let out one that drowned it anyway, and turned to Lorelei. "What do you mean? Do you think the gold is to run out soon?"

Her smile spoke of mysteries he longed to probe as her white shoulders rippled like a cat under a stroking hand. "Nothing lasts forever. Much of the hottest blood has left for the beach strikes of Nome already." She put a hand to the bun of her raven locks, "It's all so fleeting. Only one thing remains the same."

"And what, perchance, might that be?"

"Love, George. Only love is forever."

He was about to ask her what she meant when the lights dimmed and a riff of notes pounded out on the piano below the stage. The cacophony of voices fell to a murmur as a spotlight fell on a lone figure, illuminating the glistening black hair of Alexander Pantages as he gazed over the crowd and took in the cream of Dawson. His eyes met those of Swiftwater Bill Gates, who was ensconced with Gussie, Grace, and Nell Lamore in a box to the left of the stage. Bill played with the end of his mustache and winked.

"Ladies and gentlemen of the Klondike, the mighty Yukon Territory, and the great Territory of Alaska," Alex shouted in English only slightly accented with his native Greek, as he had practiced this speech from this stage since the first planks had been laid, "I bid you welcome to the Orpheum Theater!" A chorus of shouts and whistles erupted. Pantages raised his hands waiting for the noise to die down as staid Brits, Canadians, and a few Americans hushed the rest, "And to the esteemed proprietors of other palaces of entertainment and diversion who are our honored guests here tonight, I bid you welcome!

"Tonight's entertainment will include the terpsichorean talents of a host of the best performers to ever enliven the hearts of those who labor under the aurora for gold, toiling in—" he was interrupted by a roar of approbation from a miner, "anonymous sacrifice, that they might return to civilization with the golden—"

"Get the hell on with the *girls,* fella!"

". . . fruits of their labors, and—"

"Shut up, Davy!"

"You shut up, ya goddamn cheat! You got seven feet of my claim when you filed and ya know it! How so? You slip some greasy Yellaleg a fat poke at Fort Herchmer, Mr. fuckin' swindler Nelson?"

"What? You sonofabitch! I'll—"

The man's retort was interrupted by the landing of a fist on his nose, and he went sprawling between the tables flailing at the other miner who was upon him. Shouts went up from the crowd as men sprang at both of the combatants. Another fist was swung, and a chair was brought down on a man's back with a crash. A woman screamed.

"Bloody hell!" George sprang up, "I must put an end to this!"

Lorelei raised a white hand.

The silence below was deafening as people righted their chairs and sat down with military precision. They all were exactly as they'd been moments before waiting for Pantages to finish his speech, who went on exactly where he'd been interrupted.

"... that he might find that which is earnestly sought: the honest rewards of hearth and home, protected by the wealth of our great land with the blessings of almighty God that he might live the rest of his days in comfort and be blessed with the laughter of his grandchildren. Ladies and gentlemen, I give you the Orpheum, which like its namesake, who was blessed with the gift of music by Apollo, and entered even unto the depths of Hades to retrieve his mortal love from the darkness of death, shall be alight with the fires of laughter and wholesome recreation during the darkest days of winter. It is my fervent wish that you too shall find joy within these walls, and I bid you welcome!"

Thunderous applause erupted from the crowd.

George MacAtee stared at Lorelei. Her eyes flashed blood-red for an instant and ice surged through his veins. He glanced about for anyone who took notice of what he'd witnessed with his own eyes: a fight that had ended suddenly and without comment. George searched for the slightest ripple of awareness amongst the participants, but no one seemed to pay it the least heed... or even *remember.*

Charlie and Mae were watching the stage and sipping champagne, but Joseph was smiling, watching George. Surely he remembered.

Lorelei blew George a kiss, "He does."

He inhaled her breath, almost as if her insides were lined with flowers, fighting the urge to be mesmerized by her preternatural grace even as he felt that chill.

"But neither shall you George, neither shall you."

On the stage Mary and Lily appeared scantily dressed for their routine as Itzy and Bitzy, and there was another roar from the crowd. George stood, blinked, and tried to remember why he had risen from his seat before he excused himself and sat down to watch the performance.

XX.

THE MOON'S IVORY DISK ROSE OVER BLUE-WHITE MOUNTAINS TO SPREAD its light across the ice of the Yukon, pushing shadows across the pale swath of river as a chorus of song erupted from twelve wolves. A dog team winding its way along the ice near shore answered in a cloud of breath, with their voices cut short by exertion. The wolves yipped, laughing at the dogs' attempts to sing as their wild kin, and the huskies broke into loud barking as the aurora blazed green and vermillion across a million stars in the blackness above.

Jack McCreedy didn't notice the sky and heard only noise from his team. He was lost in contemplation of the gold he'd acquire from the grateful denizens of Eagle City. He'd heard from Wada, the Japanese prospector who'd been everywhere, that the last riverboat coming upriver had been laid up in ice at Holy Cross. Her provisions had been diverted to Nome, where thousands of stampeders coming for the beach strikes were draining goods of any kind, and anything that came over the Chilkoot and White Passes went straight to White Horse and Dawson.

Older gold towns like Fortymile in the Yukon, Eagle, Rampart, Chicken, and Circle City in Alaska were getting only the tail end of things this fall, and their residents were hungry for a drink and anything else good times entailed. Jack was going to provide it, at least the liquor. He'd tried mightily to talk Alice Mary and Three-Way Annie from their warm cribs on Fourth Avenue with the prospect of making a winter's worth of loot for a week's work, but the two working girls greeted his proposition with thin smiles, only expressing a mild interest in his report upon returning. Skinny little Alice might suffer a bit on the journey, but Annie had enough meat on her bones to show up ready for work he was sure. It was too bad. Those girls were just too comfortable where they'd landed and didn't have the proper spirit of adventure as far as he was concerned. He'd been hoping for a bit of sport with them too.

Jack grinned. Alice sure could take a rough ride for such a little thing. She'd been extra cautious for a while after some blackguard had murdered Honey Bee, but had been downright perky lately. He fished in his parka for the cigar he'd light upon reaching Eagle. Appearances mattered after all. Jack balanced on the runners as the sled hissed along, luxuriating in the ride after running alongside in the snow while circumventing the army post at Boundary. He took the flask from his parka and shook it to hear the slosh of good Canadian whiskey. It was music on a night like this. He took a long pull and let out a satisfied "Ah!"

Jack was singing *She's only a Bird in a Gilded Cage* when he came around a shoulder of rock the Han Indians called Old Woman where a ridge marched into the river next to a frozen creek. "Gee!" he bellowed, and the sled moved away from the place where water had made passage that was roofed with only a thin layer of October's ice around a still open lead as his team expertly sought the firmer surface away from the danger made by the creek's flow.

Jack lifted the flask and sucked air. "Damn." As he tried to slide it back into his parka, it slipped from his gloved hand and clattered on the river ice behind him like a schoolhouse bell. He shouted, "Whoa!" and stood on the snow brake.

The sled lurched as the wooden brake gouged ice for which it hadn't been designed, and the dogs slowed as the sled began to tip on its side. Jack went sprawling, spewing a storm of monosyllables as the load rattled and shifted, followed by the sounds of breaking glass. The left wheel dog yipped in pain as the sled slid into her hamstring and jerked in her lines, and the others set off a howl, bolting across the ice with the disintegrating load bouncing behind them. Whiskey bottles went skittering every which way in the moonlight accompanied by the bellowing of Jack as he attempted to get to his feet. He fell down again as he made a lunge for the handles of his sled that was weaving behind the panicked team like a scared cat and dumping his precious whiskey all over the mother river of the north. The dogs were heading for the open lead where water steamed in the frigid air.

"Stop!" Jack bellowed, "Dammit, *stop,* ya stupid fuckin' dogs!" He slipped again, went down on his back, and air rushed out of his lungs as he hit the surface. Sparks flashed under his eyelids and there was a loud crack.

—⁓—

Someone rudely shook him from blackness, and Jack opened his eyes. He blinked and tried to get his bearings. The sound of his team had ceased, meaning they either were around a bend in the river, they'd calmed down all at once, or something was wrong with his ears. His fingers explored the knot on the back of his head, and he winced.

"Get up," a lovely voice said as the sweetest breath rolled across his cheek like a warm breeze.

Jack rose on one elbow to stare at two beaded mukluks beneath a robe of caribou hide. It was an Indian squaw. "Thank God, my Athabascan friend! You've just earned yourself some good whiskey and my eternal gratitude if you'd like to help me with my team. I—"

A bare white hand seized him by the shoulder, and Jack was lifted to his feet to stare into eyes like pools of fire in a face white as the moon framed by a curtain of raven hair. He caught a scent that put his head to reeling and his heart to racing, and his mouth fell open. He closed it before he frosted his lungs and wiped frozen breath from his beard. "What the hell?"

"I'll help you, as you might well die if I didn't. You would have stayed unconscious until you froze, Jack." She gestured downriver, "We're going in the same direction, and your load can be of some use when we get to Eagle."

"What the bloody hell is a white woman doin' out here at the end of October?" He glanced past her at his sled, which was a few feet away and upright with his team watching him in the untangled lines, ready for travel. His lead dog Skookum yawned, and his tail began to beat a rhythm on the ice.

There was a musical chuckle, "Saving your bacon, so to speak."

"Who the hell are you?"

"Does that matter? You'd be laying there knocked out without my intercession, and your team would be downriver delivering what's left of your whiskey on its own. Besides, I'm keeping you alive, Jack," her eyes were huge, "and you won't remember this anyway."

She wore no head covering nor gloves. Jack stared at her bare hands in the moonlight and the ivory glow of her skin. "You ain't for real!" He snorted, "You're some kinda spook conjured up by the whiskey. I'm asleep or somethin'. Damn, gotta wake up 'afore I freeze to death!"

"You're awake, but you do have to get to Eagle. I've returned the unbroken bottles to your sled and secured the load. Between the two of us we have everything Eagle City dreams of, Jack."

"What the hell?" Jack stepped back as strange visions erupted in his skull like a string of firecrackers. He sensed things, strange things that he didn't want to touch on. "You're too perfect. You look like some kinda—" He glanced at the full moon and stepped back, "Sweet Jesus... it's Halloween, ain't it?"

"Halloween, Samhain, La Samhna, All Hallow's Eve, yes, Jack, it's the night before the dawn of a new year for my kind as the nights wax longer. My grandmother was so angry when your Church stole tomorrow and named it All Saints' Day, one thousand years ago tonight, that she killed thirteen men out of principle and sunk them in a peat bog."

"I *knew* it... I *know!* You're some spawn of the Devil sent to lure me to the pit! To hell with you, ya goddamn witch!" Jack seized the index finger of his right glove in his teeth, yanked it off his hand, and tore open his parka as he fumbled with the butt of his .45 Peacemaker.

The gun flew from its holster in a flash before his fingers closed around it to spin into the night and land in the snow beneath bluffs a quarter-mile away. Jack stood speechless with the fingers of his right hand aching with the cold.

"Put your glove on and get on the sled."

As if in a dream he obeyed. The woman stood on the runners behind him, and without calling 'mush' or any other command, the dogs resumed their journey. Jack leaned against the groaning pile of bottles, staring over his shoulder at the apparition in command of his team who was carrying him like so much baggage to Eagle. He rubbed his eyes as the cold wind beat his face.

He reached under the tarp and levered a bottle free, twisted the cork out with yellow teeth, took a long swallow, and sighed. At least the whiskey tasted the same. *Whiskey burnin' down my throat in a dream?* He put the cork back and shook his head. "To hell with this." Several dogs glanced over their shoulders at the sound of his voice, and the she-creature behind him let out a musical laugh.

Jack closed his eyes. *All right,* he was being escorted by a demon down the Yukon River on a night as bright as day. *Are we even headed for Eagle?* A chill colder than the air around him crawled up his spine, and he sat up. *Jesus, Mary, and all the Saints... what if she's takin' me to HELL?* He glanced at those glittering eyes and felt a knot in his middle.

———

Lorelei drifted as the team guided itself. The songs of wolves were a symphony on the night air, and the moonlight was a balm. It was sad she couldn't share such things with the terrified man on the sled. There were ancestors in his Irish bloodline that would have gratefully given their lives and souls for such a chance and responded with song and poetry, but not Jack. The moon danced in her pores as she breathed in the night. It was Samhain and there was a *Taking* coming, but she must be careful not to finish off any of those whom she chose. She must leave them all alive if rather weak come dawn, for this was a night when killing would come far too easily. She must pace herself and be prepared in case selfless sacrifice arose in some soul and beckoned to her fiercely. If he did, it was her duty to refuse him. She'd *promised* herself. The moon burned in her eyes like a flare. Lorelei yawned and closed them.

———

Jack's right hand fiddled with the pack lashed to the sled as he fished for the butt of a small pearl-handled Smith and Wesson that he'd bought from a bartender in White Horse and kept for a pinch. He slipped off the thick glove, got his fingers around the gun, and froze. If that spooky bitch could move as fast as she had when he'd reached for his Peacemaker, she'd most likely stop him. Demons were said to be good at protecting themselves, but she wasn't going to take Jack McCreedy to Hell if he had any say in the matter. It wasn't going to happen. Instead of pointing at her, he raised the gun in the direction of travel and winced as he squeezed the trigger to shoot his good ol' lead dog Skookum in mid-stride.

The dog let out a strangled howl and went down on his chin with a trail of blood that steamed in the moonlight. Jack moaned as he emptied the gun into the other dogs, and the sled ran up on them, throwing him into a screaming, yipping tangle of wounded, dying, and terrified animals. Teeth seized his left hand and bit through the caribou glove, and Jack let out a roar of pain as the sled ran up on the pile of writhing bodies and tipped.

"Gods!" Lorelei sprang over the chaos, landed on her feet, and turned toward the melee as she slid to a halt, "You fucking fool! Those dogs didn't have to die!" Jack was too involved in avoiding slashing teeth to hear her. Lorelei ran hands through her hair as she watched the lives of dogs flicker and bleed away like her breath in the night. "Goddamn it!" She nearly seized Jack by the throat to snap his neck, but shook her head, took a breath, let it out, and set to work cleaning up the mess.

———

No one heard the sled approaching Eagle but the ever-present dogs of the north. Strangely they all were silent, though their ears were pricked at sharp angles and the thunder of their breath was loud in their own ears. The scent of blood made the hair rise along their spines yet another scent hovered over it, commanding them to silence.

Lorelei pulled the sled next to a skiff locked in ice, dropped the lines, and sat down hard in the snow. Jack and the living dogs were on the sled, tangled under the blankets in their mortal frailty. "Shit," she gazed at the lights of a roadhouse where a Halloween party was underway. The scent of her drying sweat wafting on the breeze was like strewing candy for mortal men, it was Samhain, and she was horribly hungry. She hadn't planned on playing the part of a sled dog at all.

She slipped into the Eagle Hotel and clouded the mind of the man nodding at the desk. She put Jack in a room upstairs with a thick balm of sleep upon him that he might not awake, and with some irritation cleaned his wounds. She preferred to let him heal on his own, but his hand kept bleeding, so she shut her eyes, put her hand on his, and closed up the holes, giving him a good week's start on the slow rate of healing mortals were prone to and making herself even hungrier with the effort. "You're a sonofabitch Jack, but you're not bad, just superstitious. You've never hurt a woman anyway," Lorelei ground her teeth, "if I killed every fool who hurt a dog in this territory, none of you would be left. You're going to regret it for the rest of your days anyway. You were afraid, and Skookum was your best friend."

She came to him in a dream as little Alice Mary, Jack smiled, and she left.

Three uninjured and two wounded dogs waited on the sled. Four were dead, and she'd left them on the ice, as the wolves could use them. She sat amongst the furry heads and stroked them. One turned his face to the stars and closed his eyes in bliss as she scratched him under the chin. Lorelei yawned. "Well kids, I'm going to a party."

XXI.

H ALLOWEEN WAS AN EXCUSE FOR A PARTY, AND THE HEAVY LEAVENING of residents in Eagle of Celtic extraction assured that such an occasion would be used to its full extent. Old Pat — who had been in the bush fourteen years trapping, prospecting, bartending, running mail and whatever else it took — was telling a ghost story. It was a version of one from his native Ireland combined with Han lore about a woman who'd died awaiting her man's return on that last October night. The man had fallen down a well in the Irish version, but Pat made it the ice of the Yukon and told how he was saved by a rope braided with auburn hair like his wife's, thrown to him as he was being swept away in the current to certain death. When he arrived wet and freezing at his cabin, the man had found a skeleton picked clean by mice beside a long-cold stove. A braided rope of auburn hair was in the skeleton's hands, and a pair of shears upon the table.

There was silence as those around the stove took in the story. It was broken by a heavy sigh from Sadie Pingo, the Gwich'in Athabascan girl who was married to John Robedoux the trader. She crossed herself like a good Catholic, then put a hand under her caribou hide blouse to clutch the talisman hanging between her breasts with a bit of her umbilical cord made by her grandmother after her birth seventeen years before. Sadie had two children by John, both of whom had similar bundles made by Sadie's mother. She shook her head. "That's scary!"

The men broke into laughter at her comment, with their manly courage fired by a magnum of Chilean Pisco brandy John had provided. Unfortunately it was running out.

"Such things happen on All Hallows' Eve." Pat had a look of satisfaction on his weather-burned face as he took another sip of brandy and held his near-empty glass in libation to Robedoux. "The dead awake for things unfinished and often make great mischief... but sometimes return to save us from our own peril."

"For love."

"Yes, Sadie, for love."

"I'd hate to meet the shade of that man they hung on American Creek who murdered that goodtime girl Annabel from Seattle who was so nice."

The men in the room exchanged glances and shifted in their seats. "Better not to mention such things. What's done is done, lass. He was an evil man who did unspeakable things to that poor girl, a' for the wrath of Providence caught up with him in the form of our good neighbors."

"He must be burning in Hell, anyway."

"If there's justice."

"Let us hope."

They ceased speaking as the outer door creaked open, carrying a frigid wind through the half-shut inner door of the arctic entry. In came Bruce MacGregor with his arms full of bottles and a grin as wide as the Yukon River. "Whiskey, I found *whiskey* piled in the snow!"

Those in the room rose as one.

"Whose is it, Bruce?"

"Don't know, Pat. It was stacked neat as you please right in front of the damn door, and it's not even froze yet. Lucky Judge Wickersham's in Circle City." Bruce paused upon spying the two women in the room. "Your pardon ladies for my language, I—"

"Open a damn bottle!" shouted Portland Lucy, being half the whores left in Eagle this fall. Having her choice of customers, she'd become rather picky as of late to the consternation of some. She'd attached herself to the proprietor of another roadhouse and was getting ways about her some would say. Many wondered if she'd abandoned her trade entirely. The only other whore was Babe, a fat bottomed thing who could be showing up any time, as she had a nose for liquor.

Bruce unloaded his burden onto the table, set the nine bottles in a line, and whistled, "MacNaughton, all the way from Edmonton. I wonder who the hell put it there?"

"Some angel, obviously," Pat scooped up a bottle, "or perhaps a daemon who wants us to enjoy his holiday afore he makes his appointed mischief." He popped the cork and took a long swallow, "Ahhhhh!" Pat passed judgment and handed the bottle to Lucy.

"Whoever left it," Robedoux said, "I hope they're not planning on coming back for it."

"For the glass anyway," Pete French wrapped a big hand around a bottle and raised it over his head. "To our mysterious benefactor and their obvious good taste."

"Ya!" Lucy chimed in as she slid on Pete's lap when he sat down, "You boys all look a mite lonesome tonight."

"You been too took-up with Ched Dunham to give a damn lately," Pete retorted as he slid an exploratory hand to her crotch.

Lucy giggled and scrunched down on it, "It's a damn pity Ched's layin' his head at the Westminster in Dawson City tonight, now ain't it?"

"That's what I want to hear!" Pete stood up with Lucy in his arms and made for the stairs. Lucy kicked her legs, laughed, and the two disappeared with her swinging the bottle.

"I guess Pete's gettin' a night of it."

"Not a night, John. She'll be back down in an hour you can bet. Looks like she's back in business anyway."

"Think I'll take some of that," Bruce said.

"Don't know, hear tell she's got the clap."

"Naw, she was at the doctor's in Fortymile before freeze-up, cured her with mercury."

"She's half of all there is to choose from anyway."

Sadie Pingo got up and made for the door.

"Hey Sadie, our pardon, we didn't mean to chase you off."

"Goin' to the outhouse."

"Oh," the door closed with a blast of cold.

"We need some music. Hey Robedoux, how 'bout playin' that piano?"

"I should like some accompaniment. Pat, do you have your fiddle?"

"Of course John, with me gear. Suppose I could fetch it if you don't mind me takin' this bottle with me. Helps me night vision." Pat took his heavy black bear coat off a peg and placed his wolf fur cap upon his head with the ears stiffened and standing up. With his beard he was a study in fur. A cold gust from the door made him turn.

Radiant eyes stared back at him from a white face like a statue of pale marble as a woman of incomparable beauty stood naked before him. The nipples of her breasts were lavender as if the cold of the night had colored them, yet had failed to raise a goose bump on her perfect flesh. Pat's eyes fell to the dusting of hair beneath her belly, his eyes rose back to hers as his nostrils flared, and he took in the most marvelous scent he'd ever imagined that seemed to come from every pore of her skin.

A voice like warm honey in summer sun filled the roadhouse, firing the glow of the kerosene lamps until it was as bright as noon in July. "Each of you will remember this night, but only on your dying day when your secret is safe from the world. This night is between us, so live it now with all your hearts. All life is a fleeting moment, so drink of me as I shall drink of you."

"Jesus, Mary, and Joseph!" Pat tried to cross himself, but his hands hung at his sides as the eyes before him seemed to grow larger. He heard a great roaring as if a river were rising up under the floorboards, as if the frozen ground below were melting away in one great warm rush as her laughter filled the room.

"Damn, fella!" Lucy's voice echoed from upstairs.

———

She went back to the night as a plume of incandescence rose from her that awoke ravens in the dark spruce. Her bare feet melted the ice of the Yukon, leaving footprints in its wind-polished surface. Lorelei danced under the moon as wolves broke into a chorus that was answered by the dogs of Eagle, and she howled back.

The aurora danced on green snow and rippled across the stars. "Twelve men, Mothers, twelve men give their blood to your daughter, the bearer of your flesh and memory... yet I've left them *living!*" The thunder of her voice sent cascades of snow down the steep slopes of Eagle Bluff to the river but it didn't matter. All in town were sleeping like the dead but for Lorelei, the ravens, the dogs and the wolves.

She felt a stirring from when great Nations sent their finest to her embrace, when hearts bled red in the altars of her many temples. Lorelei gazed through the eyes of a girl who had stood upon the rise of Eagle Bluff ten thousand years ago filled with that power. Tonight all was as it should be. It was good New Year, and she'd fed as those before her but without killing a soul. She sure could use a drink though.

XXII.

JOSEPH STARED OVER MARY'S HEAD THROUGH FROSTED GLASS AT THE RIVER beyond. It was a glowing plane of ice under the moon, a luminous road where Lorelei had journeyed beyond his senses.

"Thinking of Lorelei again?" Mary's breath bounced in the hollow of his throat.

"You know I am."

"She's got her own business, Joe," Mary sighed. "I do so wish they wouldn't make us close up at midnight on Saturday, and on Halloween to boot. That fellow from Bonanza was a hell of a spender, but I didn't want to go to the Fairmount with him. Now I'm bored."

Joseph ran a finger around her ear and rocked the nugget earring from King Solomon's Dome on the lobe. He lifted it on the tip of his index finger and watched the light break into a million colors in the depths of the diamond. She'd had a mate made for it by the Jewish jeweler on York Street with a nugget and another diamond she'd gotten from an infatuated miner that now hung from the other ear. "Why didn't you go with him?"

"Call it intuition. I didn't trust him. A girl's got to watch herself you know."

"Oh," his gaze returned to the window.

"You can't see a thing out there."

"I know."

"I thought you might be glad I didn't.... Joseph?"

"Um?"

"Don't you ever get jealous?"

"No, at least not of you. I'm sorry, but the only one I can feel such things for is utterly beyond my ability to do anything about, or even find a way to *think* on. I'm in a state of disbelief I suppose. Nothing surprises me anymore, but I feel as if it's always been this way, as if I just didn't know it, as if I were a vessel for something or someone far older than myself. I feel that I've always loved her, Mary, through lives uncounted." He stretched on the couch, "I suppose that really is the word for it... *eternal.*"

The footfalls and chatter of the Orpheum's employees echoed in the hall. There was the laughter of Diamond Tooth Gertie, followed by a low comment from Klondike Kate, before loud laughter erupted in the adjoining room.

Mary sighed theatrically, "She has you entirely."

"How else could things be? All we are, all we have or may be, is but a passing play to her. There is no one like her, truly. Men have said such things about women since the dawn of time, but in this case it's beyond doubt."

"She must be something in a bed."

"Beyond telling."

"That makes me feel awfully small, Joe."

"I'm sorry. It's just that she really is beyond all others. I mean she's immortal... or at least blessed with a span beyond any but the biblical patriarchs whom I am not at all certain endured as the Bible says anyway. And she's so much wiser than we, Mary. How else could I feel about such things?"

There was a knock on the door, and before they could say "Come in," Kate Rockwell leaned in with her shiny auburn hair loose and violet eyes aglow. "Do you two want to go to a Halloween party?"

"Yes!" Mary jumped up, "I am going crazy with boredom!"

"Good," Kate swept into the room followed by Gertie with the diamond between her teeth flashing. "Cad Wilson is having a little get-together at her place above the Monte Carlo for us nocturnal types who need recreation when the Yellowlegs won't let us play in our abodes of wholesome and uplifting entertainment on such a fine Saturday night, and it's Halloween to boot."

"It's Sunday morning," Gertie interjected, "you depraved and wanton woman."

Mary clapped her hands, "I've got to find Lily. She says Cad is the best actress in Dawson."

Kate nodded, "Cad's a thespian in the legitimate regard, but I think Lily's already there."

Joseph noticed Gertie eyeing him and grinned at the implication of a diversion. He couldn't imagine being out in the diggings anymore. If only Lorelei were around. She hadn't even spoken to him with her special voice.

"Come on Joe," Mary pulled him toward the door, "and I don't want to hear about Lorelei for the rest of the night!"

They were let into the party by a tall and smiling Black Prince, an imposing Negro with a shaved head wearing a white tuxedo and a build that bespoke his career as a boxer. All the denizens of the saloons and theaters knew him to be Cad's lover. In her apartment above the Monte Carlo, they could relax, and when Joseph shook his hand, the man's grip was like iron and his teeth flashed a brilliant white. The place was festooned with orange and black streamers, paper cutouts of witches, and skulls. There was a crystal punchbowl on the table surrounded by cakes and ladyfinger sandwiches and champagne cooled in tin washtubs filled with snow.

The Mare towered over Jack Finley with a glass of champagne in her hand. She slapped his hand off her behind, hugged Kate, and spilled champagne on the rug. Swiftwater Bill Gates was sprawled on a couch, wedged between Gussie Lamore and her little sister Nell. Eddie Doland, the manager of the Tivoli, was deep in conversation with Cad, who ran hands through her short red hair and nodded. Charlie Meadows was there sans Mae, smoking a dark maduro cigar and cradling Lily in one big arm on another couch while talking to her in a hushed voice.

Babe Wallace, who ran a string of girls, was bent over a little lacquered table by the window with a tiny blonde who looked nearly a child and had come with her from the District. The girl's green eyes skipped about the room as she stood in the corner looking small. As they fell on Joseph's he felt an inexplicable thrill, and she quickly glanced away. He turned to watch Babe's huge breasts swing over a thin brass Chinese pipe that hissed like a snake as a small black object was pressed into its bowl.

Joseph and Mary found room on an overstuffed couch and scrunched in together. The pipe was lit and passed to Bill. He took a long drag and produced a thick cloud of white smoke that wreathed his head as he sat between the Lamore sisters trying not to cough.

"I think I shall try some opium Joe, how 'bout you?"

"I don't know."

Mary reached for the pipe, but it was snatched out of Bill's hand by Lily with a flash of her blue eyes. She took a long drag and passed the pipe to Mary as she rocked on her feet. "S'good!" She got out with a grunt, accompanied by a gush of smoke.

Mary put the mouthpiece to her lips. Smoke rattled in the thin stem, and her cheeks bulged before she handed it to Joseph with her face swollen like a chipmunk. He accepted the sizzling bowl gingerly.

Charlie struck a match on his blue denim pants and cupped it over the bowl as Joseph put it to his lips. "There's a good piece left. See it bubblin'? It's like a little piece a' tar that takes a while to smoke up. Take a long one, and hol' it in. I promise you won't turn into some sleepy slant-eyed Chinee fella in a puff 'a smoke, pilgrim."

Joseph took a drag and the pipe rattled as his lungs filled. He wanted to cough, but tightened the muscles of his chest and held the smoke as he sank on the couch. Mary's arm was around his shoulders, and his limbs felt like rubber.

Having fun?

"Lorelei!" Smoke exploded from his mouth and he coughed, "Where the hell are you?"

People in the room stared at him and a girl's laughter echoed in his head like a brass bell. Joseph glanced around, but couldn't focus on who had made it.

You're providing entertainment for your compatriots anyway. I'm quite distant at the moment, taking care of some things.

"Where?"

Where men yield to my needs and history won't record my deeds. It's a rather special night for me.

"Halloween."

Yes. You know that I'm the last of an elder time although younger myself. Yet I have a burden, a yoke that must be loosened on nights such as this. Otherwise life would become unbearable.

"Where are you?" He noticed Lily's amused face, who along with everyone else in the room was staring at him. Mary winked, and Lily burst into giggling.

"You're talking to the air, fellow," Eddie Doland said. "That stuff knocked you for a loop!"

Jack's laugh was the loudest in the room. "Best in the territory, Eddie," he hooked a hand in his belt and reached for the ample bottom of Babe with the other, "costs a pretty penny too."

"You're lucky the Yellalegs didn't catch you with it. They're snooty about smokin'. They say it's Chinese devil stuff and would take it away just to watch you holler 'bout it."

"That's quite unnecessary, Edith."

"Edie, please," Kate said. "Anyway best to smoke it up so no bloody Redcoat sonofabitch hauls you off to Fort Herchmer for a fine and a lecture 'cause you didn't pay some damn tax or the like. They can't figure a way to tax it proper since it's too easy to sneak in, and are beside themselves thinking something is being used without proper damn tithing to the Queen."

"Saw you with that Inspector MacAtee last Wednesday, Edie, givin' him the full Mare I'd wager."

"So what, Babe? His gold's good as anybody's. You'd hump a bear if the critter would pay enough."

The room erupted in laughter.

Edie rose to her full six feet and grinned, "Besides, he's privy to what's about from Skagway to Fort Constantine, and Circle City and Eagle too. He told me a fella found a twenty-pound nugget on the Fortymile before freeze-up and give me the lug's name."

Babe was eying the Mare and trying to find a comeback for the bear comment. She turned away, scowled, and tottered toward the ball of opium sitting on the table amongst a litter of cigar butts and glasses.

Charlie stroked Lily's neck and raised a lock of her hair to his nose. "You gals oughta treat each other with respect. We need you all. Without you there'd be no Palace, no Tivoli, no Monte Carlo... no—"

"No Dawson!" Gertie shouted. "The ginks would go Outside if it killed 'em! What we got right here," she patted her behind, "is what men truly labor for, though they claim it's wealth and prestige and all that foofaraw. Without this a man ain't a man."

"Thank God," Edie muttered.

"Damn straight," Babe chimed in.

Lily had molded herself into Charlie's side and was fooling with his belt. He stroked her cheek and looked around the room. "Anybody got a ghost story?"

People shifted in their seats as the sound of the pipe rattling and hiss of the stove filled the room, then the coughing of the Black Prince who'd been smoking the pipe next to Cad as he stroked her leg. Klondike Kate chewed a knuckle and stared at the muscular Negro. He grinned back.

"Kate, where's Alex anyway?"

"He doesn't come to many get-togethers, Cad."

"I should say. What does he do, just sit in your rooms counting his money?"

"He has grand plans to build a theater in Seattle after we're finished here, and another after that. Alex looks at everything in the long term. It's a part of his heritage, being from an ancient civilization and the like."

"Little greaser oughta loosen up!" Bill Gates glanced around for approval, stroked his mustache, and grinned as he returned Kate's stare, "Well? He's gettin' your pretty tail and a good share of the gold hereabouts, isn't he? Fella oughta pay some back like the rest of us. Throw a party or something."

Babe nodded, "That's true, Kate. What goes around comes around they say."

"Especially when we're sittin' on a fella's lap and holdin' his poke, eh Babe?" The Mare added.

The two goodtime girls locked eyes for a moment and laughed.

Kate stared at Bill with her teeth in her lower lip. Her violet eyes looked daggers.

"Here," Joseph refilled the pipe and handed it to Kate, and she ran her free hand through his palm as she took it.

"Ah got a ghost story." Alice Mary, the young whore who'd accompanied Babe, spoke up from where she sat in a corner.

Charlie nodded, "Good, where's it from?"

"Right here."

"Is it 'bout Injuns... or miners?"

Kate put a hand to her breast and her voice dropped, "Is it about Honey Bee?"

"Isn't... but *is*. It's somethin' happened to me."

Charlie let out a whoop, "Good, tell it, little Alice!"

Alice Mary glanced around, took a breath, and moved to the arm of the couch beside Joseph. A bruise purpled her thin neck. He reached out to run his finger down her throat, and she didn't seem to mind. "Well, you all remember that sonofabitch Fred Dodge."

"Sure," Charlie nodded, "bet you girls are glad that weasel's gone."

"I'd like to kick his arse one more time, personally," the Mare growled. "Fuckin' pieceashit."

"And you could, Edie!"

"He came to my place," Alice Mary went on, "you know, my crib, in September, mean drunk and lookin' to hurt me. Anybody with a thimble a' sense knows it was him kilt Honey Bee," her lower lip quivered, and she ran a hand across her face. When she took it away, her mouth was set like stone. "Yellalegs woulda said the same had they the time to figure it out."

"You're right!" The Mare barked, "They—"

"Ah wouldn't a'let him in, but he waited 'til this fella left and grabbed the door 'fore he closed it. The other fella walked off just like it weren't nothin' to see that big ol' bastard pushin' his way into my crib for the next crack at me. Once a man got what he wants it's like a girl ain't there no more Ah guess." She scowled, "Wish Ah'd had a damn pistol. He wanted to hurt me and Ah stood up to him, and he was gonna really lay into me, maybe kill me. He laughed 'bout Honey Bee... he *laughed*, and Ah was lookin' into the eyes of a killer with me up against the wall

all by my lonesome." Alice's green eyes brimmed as she stared at the ceiling, "God, Ah *hate* that man! You know he raped me 'afore but that's another story. He just laughed, said you can't rape a whore, and slapped my mouth. Honey Bee stood up to him and she died for it. There was just him and me, and Ah was backed up on the bed against the wall . . ."

She glanced at the women in the room. Such violence was an experience they seldom spoke of in public, meaning in front of men. Gertie had a hand to her mouth as if trying to hide the gap in her teeth. Kate tapped her foot on the carpet, bit her lip, and stared out the window. The Mare stared in fascination with her chin on her palm.

"Ah was prayin' to get my Bowie knife, jus' staring in the eyes of that god-awful dog of a man. There weren't no soul there behind them eyes Ah swear. He raised a hand to hit me, and—" Alice Mary blinked, and her eyes darted about the room.

"And?" Babe blurted.

Alice Mary let out her breath, "And then he just... *disappeared.*"

"What do you mean, disappeared?"

"There was this gust a' wind, but all the doors and windows were shut tight. Ah thought Ah saw a flash of somethin' white. Coulda been my mind playin' tricks on me, but he sure was gone jus' like that, and not a single soul has seen him since that very night."

The Mare nodded, "Nobody."

"And no word of him at his claim, toward White Horse, or downriver either. The Mounties have been checking every cabin and bunkhouse," Cad added.

Jack snorted, "So what happened? That's no ghost story. Bet you were bloody whacked on opium or blind drunk or something. Maybe he had his way with ya and you just forgot it. Hell, I—"

The Mare stiffened. "Shut up, Jack!"

Kate lifted her skirts, dropped to one knee, and put a hand on Alice Mary's. "What do you think happened, dear?"

"Ah don't know, but I felt somethin'... or someone. Ah know full well Ah'm just a little whore to most of you even though we sit as friends here. When some of you leave this place and Ah return to the District, you will only speak of me in whispers in public places. Ah've known some of you men right in this room and will probably see you again." Her child's face hardened, "Couple'a you lugs look like you can't keep it in your pants right this minute. Ah know personal things 'bout you that you wouldn't want spoke to your friends or your women and Ah don't care who they be, which jus' makes me worse for you to know Ah guess. But Ah don't think there is nowhere else Ah can tell this story and even come close to somebody belivin' me. Ah swear to you, Ah *felt* someone. Ah almost *saw* her... Ah *swear!*"

"Her?"

"Yep, it was a she, that's damn certain."

"Why?"

"Ah could smell her perfume, or somethin' real nice anyway, and Ah could feel her, and hear her laughter clear and sweet as spring in the Virginia woods when Ah was a little girl who thought the whole wide world was good once upon a time. Ah know damn well it was a woman's voice. Who else would come to the aid of a whore and ask nothin' in return? Even in the nether world Ah bet a male ghost would want my favors. Ah'm only sixteen, but Ah know men too damn well."

"Sounds to me like you had truck with the Devil, lass."

"Shut up Jack." The Mare blew smoke in his face.

XXIII.

L ORELEI HELD A BRASS PIPE IN HER HAND AS SHE GAZED OVER THE wind-polished ice with Pat's bearhide coat draped over her shoulders. Jack had cached some opium in a moosehide pouch and she was going to smoke it. She lifted a bottle of whiskey to her lips, drained half in one gulp, and wiped her mouth. She ought to let her young lover along with those goodtime girls, gamblers, rodeo stars, fancy men and rough-tough sourdoughs at the party see *that,* but to sit amongst them, to be one of them, was something that could never happen.

She took off the caribou skin gloves, struck a match with her thumbnail, and a tiny piece of phosphorous caught under it. She flinched, and in the brief moments it took her flesh to heal, she thought of the burnings, and each and every one of those souls who'd suffered that fate. She closed her eyes and was a girl proclaimed a witch, laughing at the faces ugly with hate as flames blistered her flesh. Searing heat invaded the girl's lungs and Lorelei felt them collapse.

She'd hidden two hundred and six years earlier at the age of four-teen in the forest west of the Massachusetts Colony and watched her mother burn at the stake. Until then she'd never known such death but for the memories her mother had passed on to her. That death was within her too until the end of her own span, whatever that might be.

Lorelei touched the flame to the bowl and puffed, watching the shadows of smoke on the moonlit ice as they made dark bubbles on its surface. She sucked it to ash in one inhalation. She ought to show those gathered in Cad's room above the Monte Carlo that. She held the smoke in and let it pass into her blood. Normally she'd prevent it, not allowing herself to become so inebriated for fear of exposure, but tonight she let control slip away as she stared at the aurora in a glorious sky.

What the hell, it's Halloween.

She could feel Alice Mary closing like a hound on her scent but couldn't blame her. Lorelei was just taken aback at the *depth* of the girl. Alice was one of those who once touched could not turn away, and would seek her out no matter what the cost to herself.

Lorelei rose unsteadily to her feet and slid on the ice until her legs spread wide. She giggled. The rush of blood from so many men was heating her like a torch. She slipped out of the coat, dropped the woolen shirt and caribou hide pants, and stood naked beneath the stars. She finished the whiskey in one pull, slung the bottle like a bullet across the river, and a cloud erupted a half-mile away in the moonlight before an avalanche of snow spread onto the ice.

She could hear a sled coming downriver from Fortymile, and Lorelei saw the thinning ice before it and felt the swallowing rush of freezing water in the man's future as his head drooped in exhaustion. In an unfettered instant, a filament of her soul leapt out and struck the driver like a slap across the face.

The man's head rocked back as he gasped, spied the open lead before him and shouted, "Gee!" to his team. They wheeled left but moments before breaking through.

She exploded in laughter, "Close call!" Her bare feet slid out from under her, and she sat down hard. "Whoops!"

There was a sharp crack, and Lorelei plunged into the dark waters of the Yukon.

PART TWO
The Golden Gift

XXIV.

IT WAS A LONG JOURNEY FROM THE KANDIK COUNTRY AND PETE WAS tired. The smooth surface of the river was a pleasure after the unsettled hills to the north, and he had to remind himself to watch for weak spots in the ice. The dogs had settled into an easy lope on the last few miles to Eagle, sensing the end of a long day's travel. He gazed at the lights in the sky that had shone over his people forever and savored the chill air. Pete wiped mooschide mittens across his face, rubbed his eyes, and laughed. White men wore wool masks on fine nights like this and looked like wooden statues awaiting someone to breathe life back into them.

The face of a girl who lived in Ketchumstuk Village arose in his mind, and his pulse quickened. At sixteen Pete was not too young for a wife and he was a good provider... although he'd very much like to have the experience of *having* a woman first. Thoughts of the white girls in Eagle and Circle City who would play as a wife in return for gold tickled his imagination for the hundredth time, and he sighed. The gold hidden under the load of furs would buy him every girl in Circle many times over.

He'd set out from Charley Village in a hurry, entrusted to take his uncle's gold to the trader Robedoux, who would give him just what had been agreed upon earlier in the season. Pete had a list the half-breed Skookum Sam had written out for his uncle in French, just in case.

There was no protection for those of the First Nations who found gold and sought to sell it. The country from which it came would be invaded by Whites with their brutal and confusing laws at the first hint of a strike, which was why *Vitii,* Uncle, had sent Pete. Pete was quick and strong, and could beat any man out of Eagle who tried to follow him. He knew in his bones that his people had been here since the world began and was at home in the winter night. Even a blizzard that drove white men into a frightened frenzy and sent them circling like blind dogs chasing their tails would come as his friend. He could weather one wherever it caught him and find his way on a starless night back to his village over what the Whites would call trackless snows.

"Ay yai yai!" he shouted at the shining peaks, *to hell with those arrogant people! But, some of their women . . .*

The luminous rise of *Tthee Tawdlenn,* which white men called Eagle Bluff, loomed ahead. Pete wiped ice from his lip and cracked the rest off with a grin. Robedoux would have a warm bed for him upstairs, and his cousin Sadie Pingo would leap from her own bed to fix him a hot meal as soon as she greeted him with hugs and kisses. Pete could smell moose meat browning in a skillet already. He'd mush to Ketchumstuk tomorrow to settle his uncle's debt with cousins, then down the Fortymile River and on to Dawson City, but tonight's journey was nearly done.

Wolves broke into song from the phosphorescent crest of Tthee Tawdlenn, and his dogs gave voice in return. Suddenly his lead dog let out a yip, threw his feet out, and slid on the ice. Dogs piled into one another, tangling their lines and barking as they slid to a halt. Pete stepped gently on the snow brake as not to tip the sled and spoke sternly to the dogs. The team had halted at a thin patch of ice where his lead dog Arrow circled, sniffed, and began to bark. Pete inched forward, laying hands on the dogs and speaking in a calming voice. Arrow was a good one. Vitii had picked the pup and told him he'd be such an animal, but why was he still barking?

There was a scraping from beneath the ice, and Pete caught his breath as the stories of beings with their siren songs that dragged children under dark waters during *Divii Zhrii*, the Moon of Rivers Freezing, awoke. He felt a thrill of fear that no wild animal had ever given him and no drunken hateful *vaanoodlit,*white man, could hope to make him feel. He inched forward and spied a loose piece of drift ice that nudged the bottom of winter's roof. Pete let out his breath and chuckled: only ice, jostling in the current beneath winter's roof.

A vibration erupted beneath his feet before his mukluks slid from under him, and there was a loud crack as he landed. Pete caught his breath and spread his weight out, staring at his own reflection in dark water beneath the treacherously thin ice.

Two red eyes stared back at him from a face white as the moon as bubbles of breath streamed from a pink mouth to weave amongst black hair dancing in the current. The hair on the back of Pete's own neck danced, and he rose to his knees with his breath again catching in his throat. He put mittened hands on the ice of the Yukon as he gazed at the face of a woman more beautiful than life itself.

Help me!

The voice echoed in his bones and the roots of his heart. Shock percolated through him, and Pete wondered if he were going to swoon like a frightened child, but it was the river spirit's eyes that grew green with fear. Pete slapped his face and forced himself to look. He pulled a mitten off with his teeth and spread fingers on the ice. A white palm rose to press the bottom of the ice, almost touching him as her mouth cried *"Please!"* in his own Gwich'in tongue.

"Aiiiieeee!"

Pete slid backward, stood, and tore the covering off his sled. He grabbed an axe and, not six feet from the luminous face, brought it down upon the ice. With a report like a gun, a fissure appeared. He glanced up at the subarctic moon, "Keep me safe from evil," he cried, "guide my hands in this! Whatever being she may be, I *cannot* let her die! My heart will not *allow* it!" He swung again, and a piece the size of a beaver turned in its hole. Water lapped out, and Pete slipped on the wet surface and fell to his knees.

A white hand rose from the water, and he grabbed at it, but it slipped from his mittens. Pete tore them off, lay on his stomach, and reached again. There was only cold dark water lapping in the hole. "Do not die!"

A hand rose from the river and white fingers found his bare ones. They were not cold. In that first morning of November from the frigid waters of the Yukon, Pete felt a warmth that he had never known, one that leapt through him in a flash of light. With a great heave he pulled a naked woman from the river and edged backward, clutching her limp body as ice trembled and cracked around him.

She was a thing of ivory under the moon with her black hair trailing as crystals formed in it. He could not see her chest move nor any breath coming from her delicate nose and mouth. Pete dragged her away from the hole, shaking with a cold that crawled toward his core and sought to wrap hands around his heart. He laid her upon his sled and bundled her in a blanket and, with hands like two blocks of wood, wheeled his tangled team toward shore where smoke rose from a lone cabin's chimney. The dogs moved slowly, confused by the state of their harnesses, but his hands were too numb to free them.

Pete staggered to the door and banged frantically. He fumbled with the latch and almost fell on the floor when it opened. The cabin was empty, and the red glow from cracks in a cast iron stove was the only light as he hurried inside and laid her on a bunk at the back of the place.

He opened the stove with the toe of a mukluk and thrust his hands in. He could do no more until he regained feeling. Pete shook, bouncing on the balls of his feet as ice crunched in his mukluks and layers of hide pants. When he could move his fingers, he stripped off the wet clothes and shoved more wood in the stove. He found two lanterns, lit them with a sliver of wood from the coals, and turned to the woman.

She was as he'd left her: white as the snows and very still with her beautiful face staring at the ceiling. Her eyes were blue as a summer sky and without the fog of death. Her round breasts were tipped with nipples that were lavender and sparkled with cold. Her raven hair was a curtain that fell to the floor and glittered with ice. With rattling teeth he lay his face against hers to feel for any breath upon his cheek. He put an ear between perfect breasts to listen for her heart. There was no sound.

Pete let out a quaking moan and shook. He put his lips upon hers and tried to breathe life into her. He lay down beside her and put an arm and leg around her, trying to use his own meager heat to warm her. He pulled a black bear hide and a tattered quilt over them, shivered, took a quaking breath, and closed his eyes.

There was a great roar as if a river was rising beneath him. Perhaps death had come for both of them, but he had done what his heart commanded. It was a good way to die for he had been true to himself. Pete let go and drifted, letting that mighty river take him.

He heard singing as he floated in a great warm sea. He'd never seen the sea, but welcomed it. Laughter and crying were all around him like the billow of heat from flesh when it is opened to a winter sky in the hunt, like countless souls rising to the stars across the vault of night. The voices grew louder until they bent the very light around him, filling him with their songs and the drums of his Nation. He heard his ancestors, who were singing, who were pleased.

The heat of their hearts was a coal that he blew upon and it became a flame. The voices rose to a great shout like a hot river bursting through cold stone, followed by the sounds of exultation. Something burst in Pete's chest as a torrent of souls met those of his ancestors to merge forever within him.

He felt tears upon his cheeks. He inhaled the kerosene smell of the lamps and smelt the sweetest breath caressing his face. He heard laughter like tiny bells on a spring breeze and gazed upon an endless field of flowers under a huge red sun.

Pete gasped, "Am I dying?"

"No my beloved, no... we live!"

XXV.

B EFORE THE DAWN OF ALL SAINT'S DAY, SHE TOOK HER LOVER'S LIFE AND gave it back. Again and again she took and gave of herself in total-ity, exulting in the embrace of this innocent whose love had resurrect-ed her, of this boy whose soul was as clean as the snows. To him she would bestow a gift he would carry for a century to come. The ancient Sabbath of her kind had sought her out as always though she'd hidden in a fog of opium and whiskey, yet her birthright had found her. All things were of less substance; all other things held no meaning against this shining sacrifice that she'd been gifted.

Lorelei was born back to the world.

She walked on the river ice in the light of the sun, and the sky was a coral vault over pink mountains. She threw back the hood of her parka to let it fall upon ivory skin. It was not a burning she felt this day, but a balm. She had found a day in the sun yet had left her lover living. Lorelei shook with the wonder of it and let out a trilling laugh. "Amen!"

A flock of finches burst into song in the bare branches of willows along the shore. She turned rainbow eyes upon them and wiped a tear from her cheek. "Sing to me of morning. Sing for one who has not the sun tomorrow and praises this gift of this day with all her heart!"

The birds' song rose in volume.

She sat on a log, threw back her hair in the breeze, and listened to dry grass rattling a mile away. She closed her eyes and felt the sun as a shining lover, penetrating to the white-hot core of her soul. Lorelei sat for a glorious hour as it rose in the south and finches danced amongst bare branches to wander downriver singing. The sound of someone chopping wood echoed off the bluffs as she listened to the barking of dogs and smiled at their conversations.

A hissing arose from upriver. Lorelei shaded her eyes and squinted across ice brilliant with the light of day. Minutes later a lone figure came around the bluff: a man with a red scarf around his face riding down the middle of the Yukon on a bicycle. He wore a brown derby hat and a taupe herringbone suit coat. He'd taken off his parka and fur hat, and had lashed them to a pack over the rear wheel beside two spare tires. The hard rubber wheels were making the hissing sound she'd heard.

She laughed.

The man jerked upright, scanning his surroundings for the source of that utterly feminine voice. He saw her, began pedaling in her direction, and ten feet away stopped and stepped off the bike. A grin spread his young face covered with four days' stubble as he laid his bicycle against a log and tipped his hat, "Hello!" bubbled from wind-burned cheeks as he unwound the scarf, slapped his hands together, and stomped his feet. "What in the world is a lovely lady such as yourself doing here... on such a winter's day?"

"And what is a fellow such as you doing riding down the frozen Yukon on a bicycle?"

"Going to Nome!" he fairly shouted, and rummaged in his pack, "care for a mint?"

"No, thank you. You're riding all the way to Nome, on a bicycle?"

"Yes. The river froze before I could book passage, and to be honest I didn't have the financial wherewithal anyway, but I want to be there on the beaches to be set up by spring. Did you know the very sands are full of gold?"

"So they say," Lorelei blinked, and her eyes became emerald green, "I might drop in on someone there myself. Josephine is her name, though she's known as Sadie. She and Wyatt her husband are opening a saloon. She's a remarkable beauty whose soul is worth knowing, is cunning to a fault, and her dreams have touched my own," she grinned, "and her husband is rather renowned of his own accord."

"Wyatt Earp, the Marshall and pistolero from Arizona?"

"The same. They have named their establishment the Dexter Saloon I believe."

"Ah, a saloon." The young man gazed at her with hesitation, "To be honest, you don't look like one who is used to such nocturnal carousals. I mean, with a flawless complexion such as your own."

Lorelei let out a laugh that became a shriek and put fingers to her lips.

He gave her a bemused stare, "I—"

"Excuse me. I'm just a bit giddy with the day. I do so wish I could let you know how much this all means to me."

"It is lovely, isn't it? By the way, I stopped in Eagle City just upriver and found the chaps all asleep, even the dogs. They must have tied on a mighty one last night."

Lorelei blinked at the realization she hadn't known the man's thoughts whatsoever and bit her lip. "What's your name?"

"John, John Johnston. Not very original, but one doesn't have a choice either of names or mothers when one is brought into the world, does one?"

She nodded, "Not at all. How far are you going today?"

"I was hoping to make Miller's Camp by nightfall but I don't know if I shall or not. It's all an adventure you know. The soldiers at Fort

Egbert gave me a hearty breakfast after laughing their heads off. They're mortally bored in those cold tents, and I suppose I provided them something to talk about." He smiled, "They took bets on whether I shall perish before reaching my goal. I stayed last night in a cabin at the mouth of Boundary Creek and left the owner a thank-you and a small remuneration. I hope to reach Saint Michael within four weeks. I hear the crossing overland from the delta is a tad rough, but I believe the sea ice shall be sufficient to cross over Norton Sound by then."

"Wonderful... you're really going all the way."

"Yes, of course. I have two spare tires and sufficient provisions, and find it quite stimulating. A pack of wolves ran alongside me for a goodly ways yesterday as if I was one of their own and I felt no fear whatsoever. In fact I felt closer to a far older sense of divinity than in quite some time. Ever, actually."

"John, you're a charming and sensible man," her cheeks dimpled, "and I think I'll assist you to Nome." Lorelei stood, stretched, and grinned at his expression. "Don't worry, we'll both fit on your bicycle. In fact you needn't pedal at all as you could use a rest. I have so few days like this to enjoy and I should like to spend some of this time with you."

As if in a trance he mounted the bicycle. Lorelei sat on the pack behind him with her hands around his waist, put her chin on his shoulder, and the bike began moving of its own accord.

"Wha... ?"

"Rest your feet on the handlebars. You don't even have to hang on. I'll take care of the steering, and I'm very alert to thin spots in the ice today I assure you."

"This is... quite remarkable!"

"It is," she nuzzled his ear, "just as fate has made you my companion on this wondrous day."

"I feel absolutely at ease, as if I were floating on air almost. Tell me, how do you do it?"

She chuckled. "All right. I'm the last in a long line from a time when tribes roamed across their mother the earth and gave their finest young men for our survival. For thirty thousand years all honored us. Good men like you were our sustenance then... and still are, although things have been getting rather rough for the last five millennia. It was my ancestors who brought art and music to those roaming the ancient forests hunting creatures whose names you haven't words for now. Europe was our refuge until the Romans came, and when the Christians won they turned on our ancient groves with a fury... and the Jews have a grudge against our Mother as well that the Christians kept in spades. My own mother was hung in the Massachusetts Colony and her body burned in sixteen ninety-three when I was but a girl of fourteen."

"Sixteen ninety-three... you're holding up rather well I must say."

She laughed, "I headed west and hid amongst the Indians for decades but there's nowhere left to go. I live at night in order to maintain a life for myself without stirring things up." She sighed, "In fact, I must normally take the life of a good man as my lover in order to have but a single solitary day in the sun."

Lorelei felt a tremor of fear in the man she held and enfolded him in a nimbus of softness to calm him. "It's quite all right. Although it's a great renewal, I can hardly bear the loss of a promising soul, even though I keep part of him within me. That particular facet of my existence has come to wear on me terribly: taking a good man's life just to get a little sun."

"Oh, then... did you take a good man's life last night?"

She enfolded him in her warmth again and felt him relax. "No I didn't. He saved mine and returned it to me in far better shape than I'd left it actually."

"Well, it's a damnable modern world we live in, eh?"

"Yes it is, love."

He sat up, "Ah-ha, Halloween!"

"Yes, John. I appreciate your mind by the way. You're assuming all the right things about me without giving yourself over to fear, and it's lovely. I see you're from a learned family. A proper education can do that." She inhaled his sun-warmed scent, let out a trill of laughter, and turned her eyes to the sky, "This is such an amazing day!"

"If you have killed fellows as you say, why am I so at ease in your company?"

"Because all men are when they're at their best, and my heart is washed clean by the sun besides. Because I'm here to speed you on your journey and not to end it."

"Quite remarkable."

"It is, and tonight I have a gift."

As the sun rose over mountains in the south, John donned a pair of smoked glass spectacles he'd bought in Dawson. After a moment, he took them off and offered them to Lorelei.

"No, thank you. I want as much sun as my time allows."

He shrugged, yawned, put them back on, and snuggled against her as if in an easy chair. Lorelei kissed his cheek as they floated along, skirting open leads and passing the occasional cabin. They passed a dog sled, and the driver stared open-mouthed as they disappeared around a bend in the river. They passed the settlement of Nation in an hour and headed toward Circle City. Lorelei could make the bicycle go much faster, but the chill of the wind would cause him harm, so she kept to a pace where she could warm him with her breath. She might as well get him a goodly ways on his journey. She stroked his hair and laughed. Tonight was going to be something for the both of them, and she luxuriated in the backwash of his joy shining from the near future. It was such a beautiful day.

XXVI.

THE MERCURY FELL LIKE A STONE IN THE FIRST WEEK OF NOVEMBER AS THE residents of Dawson burrowed deeper into whatever shelter they had found. The whiskey poured in saloons increased, fueling the desperate passions of men come in from lonely diggings for want of a woman's company.

Alice Mary had been busy. She was one of the youngest goodtime girls in Dawson and better looking besides. Her biggest problem was what to do with the pile of gold dust, flakes, nuggets, silver and gold coins, and bills of two nations she was accumulating for an uncertain future Outside.

The Mare loaned Alice the use of her safe in the back of Gertie's place, although she wouldn't give her the combination. Alice couldn't blame her though. They didn't know each other that well. In truth she was quite good for her word and determined to prove it by her actions. Alice Mary was honest as the night is long in November and a trooper besides. She would take a turn with two men, a man and a woman, or a woman alone, which she'd done several times in strict confidence that she'd never violated. It didn't matter. Everyone seemed to enjoy her and she seldom had to coax some fellow's little soldier to stand up and do his duty. Much to the contrary they were all ready it seemed, and she hadn't even caught anything bad yet. *Knock on wood.*

She rapped on the polished teak bar of the Orpheum.

Alex looked up from September's *Seattle Post-Intelligencer* that he was reading for the ninth time. He'd been working at reading English during the last year while bartending, sitting in the barber's chair, or within the fast-enlarging rooms in which he'd been staying after counting his money. That newspaper had saved him in Skagway when he'd arrived destitute after losing all in a card game on the steamer north. He'd hired someone to read it and charged a dollar a head for men to hear the copy he'd brought off the boat read aloud to them. An old newspaper had paved his way to Dawson, and he'd nurtured an affection for them ever since, scrounging every copy he could as well as paying Stroller White to write a few friendly takes on Kate and the Orpheum in the *Klondike Nugget.* "Care for more coffee?"

"Yes, thank you, Alex."

He poured a steaming stream in the chipped brown mug and slid a can of condensed milk and a little wedge of dark brown sugar in a porcelain bowl in front of Alice Mary.

"Thanks."

"It's nothing." He put a palm on the bar and rubbed his eyes with the other hand, "How was your night?"

Alice blinked eyes the color of spring leaves and shrugged. "Guess you're askin' to be nice since you pretty much know," she yawned. "Had a go-round with two fellas at once who were thinkin' they were gonna save money."

Alex whistled, picked up a rag, and began to polish a whiskey glass.

"Ended up givin' me all they had anyway. One of 'em was a bear to finish off though. Too much whiskey does that to some. Said Ah was his angel when we were through," she ran a finger through the ring left on the bar by her mug and shifted on the stool. "Big 'ol sonofabitch left me sore."

"That's a bit hard to hear, Alice, from such a pretty young thing as you."

"For now, anyway." She put the mug to her lips and winced as the heat contacted a sore at the corner of her mouth.

Alex was watching her in that way, before he came back down the bar and leaned across it. "You know, you could work at the Orpheum if you quit the life. I'd vouch for you to the Mounties. Such a frail thing as—"

"Ain't a dancer, and too many men know me to see me all dressed up with a drink in my hand," she smirked. "Besides, Ah ain't old enough for drinkin's what the Mounties say."

Alex sighed and returned to wiping the bar. "Well, you certainly can take a sturdy fellow for your size."

"That's in regard to yourself, Ah presume?"

He grinned, "Well . . ."

"You did get rather excited as Ah recall, and you know for yourself that in spite of my size Ah can take a very large fella. Some lug thought he was gonna kill me last weekend with that thing he had and Ah just laughed. Afterward, he tol' me he loved me. Men say they love you sometimes, jus' 'cause you can handle 'em. Sometimes the sound of your voice is enough to get them to do just about anything afterward... for a while." She yawned, "That's a sweet spot a girl's gotta learn to use, but most treat you as less than dirt soon as they done their business." She examined him in the mirror behind the bar, "You know, Alex, you better not let Kate know 'bout friends like me, no matter what she says when we're all together. She's quite a find for a fella like you."

"Do you think?"

Alice Mary's mouth twisted into a smirk and she dabbed at the sore on her lip. "You visited me and how many other workin' girls 'fore you two threw in so thick, but now you're a kept man."

"Why do you say that?"

"She's your ticket and you know it. Don't play me no games just 'cause Ah'm young. Kate is the angel of a thousand men's hearts and she don't have to smell their sweat to do it. If you were to cross her, the whole shebang you got built around here could drop on your head like a ton a' bricks. Lotsa fellas envy you, and that makes for some dirty dealin' too, if given half the chance." She grinned, "Neither one of us trusts people just 'cause they say one thing when they're around. That's why we're alive: me a little girl from Virginia, and you some Greek lug they jus' don't understand. Other fellas mutter 'bout you in a bed, you know."

"Who? Bill Gates? What do they say?"

She gave him a mildly surprised look and shook her head, "Not Swiftwater Bill. He's kinda inclined to admire you now, although he still calls you the Little Greaser."

"He is?"

"Yep, don't say nothin' to the Lamore sisters though; they'd throw a red fit if they knew he was lettin' off some steam in my direction. All three of 'em," she chuckled, "although that's what the lug deserves, tryin' to have three wives 'round here," a full laugh rippled her throat. "Gotta hand it to him though."

Alex ran a hand across his face. When it returned to the bar, he wore a broad grin.

Alice Mary leaned toward him, "Where was Lorelei the other night?"

"That Irish girl comes and goes like I've never seen anybody do in this weather, not even the mail sleds. Haven't seen her leave or enter town once, but often she's simply nowhere to be found."

"Funny that nobody mentions her when she ain't around."

"Why?"

"She's the biggest looker in the Territory for one, and for two everybody's the subject a' gossip. Fellas should be talkin' her up in the bars all night long, and workin' girls talk 'bout everybody when they're not workin'. It's borin' just sittin' around waitin' for some fella to show up, but nobody ever seems to talk about *her.*"

"Well, you're talking about her now."

"Ah know," she sipped her coffee, "but it takes a real effort, like she was standin' behind a curtain or somethin' in my mind. Ain't you felt that?" Alice Mary shook her head, "Ah gotta fight for it jus' to keep her in focus." She ran a black nail around the top of her mug and licked off a bit of sugar, "Had a dream this mornin'."

"I dream every night, Alice."

"No, this was different. Saw her in the crib Ah used to use with Honey Bee on Fourth 'afore Ah moved-in with the Mare at Gertie's. She was standin' there all naked, lookin' at me with them wonderful eyes—"

"Dressed for work, eh?"

Alice's green eyes paled, "Ah'll drop it."

"No," he held up his hands, "I'm sorry, go on."

"She had blood on her hands, Alex, and... and anyway she smiled at me... and then she held up Fred Dodge's heart."

"His *heart?*"

"Yep," she nodded, "torn from his body and still beatin' like a damn bloody drum."

"How did you know it was Fred Dodge's heart? I mean, if there was only a bloody heart and all?"

"Ah jus' *knew* it," she glanced at the ceiling, "Ah don't know, maybe she tol' me. It was all real strange. Don't even know why Ah'm tellin' you this. You must think me daft, but it's part of somethin' that's goin' on all around us, at least for me."

"It's a strange dream. I can certainly see a man having dreams about her. I have myself, but—"

"Ah know," she glanced at her cup, and he poured more coffee. "Thank you."

"You're welcome."

"Ah think she's a witch... or a spirit."

"Say what?"

"Ah been watchin' her. She does things other women can't and then makes people forget what she's done, or where she's been and what she's about, like people is jus' like stuffed dolls that she's playin' with."

"What do you mean?"

"You ain't noticed she only comes out at night?"

"So do we!" Alex roared with laughter and slapped the bar, "What about you? Never seen you during banker's hours either."

"Ah mean when it's *dark.*"

"She sure likes that young buck Joseph for a spirit, I'll tell you that."

"Ah think that's how she feeds."

"What?" Alex stared at Alice Mary. She stared back. After a painful pause, he broke into strained laughter.

"Laugh, if you like," she slipped off the stool, and her heels thumped on the plank floor as a nugget rattled on the bar.

"Coffee's on the house Alice, I don't have change—"

"Keep it. You dropped a way bigger one outta your boot when you were kickin' 'em off in my crib last July. You musta been kinda loopy for a fella like you not to notice somethin' like that."

"Oh," Alex scooped up the nugget.

Alice Mary's elfin face broke a thin smile, "Where's Joe?"

Alex glanced at the bronze clock on the wall. "Probably above Jack's place with Mary, or perhaps with Lily upstairs, he's rather in demand with those two."

"Could be with both. Ah'll try here first if you don't mind."

He waved at the stairs, "Go ahead, last door on the left."

"Thanks." She lifted her skirts to her ankles as she climbed the stairs. When she glanced back Alex's eyes were smoldering and Alice attempted to give him another smile, but her face froze in a half-grimace. She waved stiffly, walked down the hall to the last door, and knocked. There was no sound, and she knocked again.

Joseph's groan came from the other side, accompanied by Lily's sleepy mumble.

"'Cuse me, it's Alice."

"Who?"

"Alice Mary! I must talk to you."

"Um... just a moment."

After several minutes a tousle-haired Joseph in a quilted bathrobe opened the door. Over the smell of cigars rising from the saloon below, the smell of sex rose from his damp skin. Alice Mary slid around him into the room and nodded at Lily, who was in bed with the covers to her chin and her golden hair splayed across the pillow. "Hello."

Joseph yawned, "Hello."

Lily sat up, letting the covers drop to reveal the rosy marks of Joseph's mouth on her throat. She took a pearl-handled brush off the nightstand and began untangling her hair. "Hi, Alice."

"Hi, Lily, where's Mary?"

"Doin' her duty with Jack I guess."

Joseph scratched a hairless chest. "What brings you here so early?"

"Ah got to ask you 'bout Lorelei."

Joseph's face went blank. He studied Alice for a moment and shrugged, "About what?"

"You know her better than anybody else here, Ah'd guess."

"I have the privilege."

"What a gentleman you are," Lily grinned at Alice Mary. "Don't you hope he would speak of us in such a way when out of our company?"

"Nobody speaks a' me in such a way, Lily."

"Oh, sorry."

"Joseph, you know why Ah'm here."

"What do you mean?"

"Ah saw you and Mary when Ah 'tol that story at Cad's party. You knew exactly a' what Ah spoke, didn't you?"

"I—"

217

"Has she took you into her confidence?"

"About what?"

"'Bout the killin'."

"I don't know what you're talking about."

"Then why are you so nervous? Ah've had men lie to me all my life beginnin' with my stepfather who used and nearly kilt me, and Ah damn well know when someone's lyin' so don't do it. Lily called you a gentleman a minute ago and Ah should dearly love it if you would tell me what you know like one."

"About . . .?"

"'Bout Fred Dodge. She kilt him, didn't she?"

"How would I know that? Besides, Lorelei was at the Palace with me and Mary that night, and she—"

Alice Mary folded her arms, "Then how come you know the night Ah'm talkin' 'bout, jus' like that?"

"I don't... I mean no."

Alice sat in the maroon overstuffed chair by the window, and Joseph returned to the bed. Lily put arms around his neck and kissed his shoulder as he scowled at the wall.

"What is she, Joe?"

"She's a woman of great wisdom and beauty, Alice."

She nodded, "She's that and far more, and you sure do wanta tell me. Ah can see it so why don't you? Look: Ah owe her my life. Ah *know* it was Lorelei. Ah've sought her in my dreams and she's teased me an' tried to hide from me, but Ah *see* her. It's in my blood. It's in my heart! Ah'm like her more than anyone else in the whole world, and Ah *know* it! Besides, this is drivin' me crazy!" Alice Mary glanced around, as if Lorelei would suddenly appear from the closet, "Where is she right now?"

"I don't know."

"How did she leave Dawson, by sled? For where? Where would she go in November? Tell me, Joe. Ah know that you know, so why are you hidin' her?"

"Whoa," Joseph strode to the water closet, shut the door, and the sound of him urinating into a pewter basin on the other side was loud.

"Ah ain't leavin' 'til you tell me!"

"Why do you so much want to know?"

"Ah 'tol you!"

"What the fuck are you two talking about?"

Alice gave Lily a green-eyed glare, "Can't you feel the power in her?"

"She's got a lot of money, honey."

"Money ain't nothin' to her, can't you *see*? Ah see her in a forest in my dreams runnin' with wolves. Her eyes are red as blood and she laughs with the most beautiful laugh Ah've ever known. She's—"

The door to the WC flew open with a bang, and Joseph stood staring at her.

Alice Mary stared back, "Well? You know Ah ain't crazy."

"I wouldn't bet on—" Lily began.

Joseph let his breath out with a groan, "You're not crazy Alice, not at all." He sat on the bed, held out a hand to her, and drew her next to him. Alice Mary was as light as a leaf. Lily ran a foot along Joseph's leg and kneaded his thigh with her toes as Joseph stared at the ceiling, opened his mouth, shut it, and groaned. "I wish she would tell me what to do!"

"Does she speak to you when you're apart?"

"Yes, Alice, she speaks in my mind when we're apart."

"She's the one what kilt Fred Dodge, weren't she?"

"Yes... *yes,* Alice, and returned to the theater in a brief few minutes though she ran with him to the top of King Solomon's Dome and tore his heart from his chest. She threw it across the valley of Bonanza, all the way to the Yukon River."

Alice Mary jumped up off the bed, and Joseph and Lily bounced when she landed. "*Ah saw it beatin' in her hands!* Can you speak to her now and tell her that Ah *must* meet her?"

Lily drew her knees up under her chin. "What the hell are you two talkin' about?"

"She's not a witch and she's much more than a spirit. She is flesh and blood like we, but far older and wiser. Her youth is in a way our own, and, and she is the very last of her kind upon this earth, Alice. I—"

She grabbed his hand and held it to a trembling breast. "What is she?"

"God forgive me, but I can only call her a Goddess."

Lily snorted. "You sure you ain't just plumb-all crazy about some tail, Joe?"

Alice Mary blinked. "Shut up, Lily."

XXVII.

A PUNGENT STENCH AND GUST OF FREEZING AIR ASSAULTED JOHN IN HIS bed of stiff robes. Ice crackled on the bear hide thrown over wool blankets as he let out a groan, rolled over, and peered at his surroundings.

A tin can hanging from a pole bobbed overhead, protruding through a hole in the tent through which icy air was blowing. A rag was stuffed in the can, from which the acrid odor wafted.

"Dammit!" John leapt up in his woolen longjohns, seized his Green River knife from under the coat that served as his pillow, and the tin can dropped on his cot with a rattle.

His tent mate shouted, "Chloroform! It's chloroform!"

John swore again, stumbled over his bicycle propped against the tent pole, and sprang through the hole, ripping it wide to spy two forms running down the dark alley toward River Street. One let out a barking laugh and waved a middle finger in defiance as John slid on the ice and grabbed for the leaning tent pole. "Damn you, you blackguards!"

"Fuck you!"

John tottered in the frigid wind listening to the breakers crashing amongst ice blocks beyond the saloons of Nome's Front Street. He shivered, hugged himself, and almost lost his balance on another glacier of frozen urine that was encroaching on the spot where he and Ted had erected their tent. "This is *wonderful!*"

"We cannot stay here!"

"I've never been anywhere in my life where so many thugs and cutthroats abound with such utter impunity!"

"It's the ships. They can step off of a lighter on the roadstead but a pistol shot away. Some of these lugs haven't walked a mile since the Barbary Coast I'd wager. Wait until June. There must be fifty thousand coming."

"By then we should be rich, Ted."

Ted answered with an exhausted grin and rattle of teeth, "I should hope."

John examined the wreckage of their tent. "Good God in heaven, what shall we do for the rest of the night?"

"Perhaps we can find lodging nearby."

"I shant leave a thing here, not even a tent pole!" John stamped his feet and pulled on the rest of his clothes, "I wish I had a pistol! We'll get a room at one of these places for the night before we freeze to death."

"Good idea. I'll repay the favor at the soonest opportunity, you have my word."

They gathered up their belongings and left the tent in favor of not freezing to death. The saloons and hotels of Front Street were bustling as they made their way toward the board sidewalk, careful not to slip on the glaciers of yellow ice covering the ground around newly built log and frame buildings.

As John walked his precious bicycle, a vision of sunshine and warmth erupted. He stared into rainbow eyes and blinked. In an instant they were gone, but not before a familiar laugh tickled his spine accompanied by a fleeting sense of contentment. The stench of piss wafted into his nose and banished the vision. "This place is hell!"

"I concur, Mister Johnston."

They broke into tired laughter and skirted a cabin from which the panting of a man and moaning of a woman issued.

"I still can't believe you rode that thing all the way from Dawson City."

"It was easier than you think. I still don't know how I made it in seven days."

Ted chuckled, "That's quite impossible, but perhaps your memory was influenced by events. Didn't you say you tied one on in St. Michael?"

John's shrug became a shiver, "Where shall we stay?"

Ahead, a two-story structure rose above the log cabins and wall tents, alight and beckoning with a sign proclaiming *DEXTER SALOON*.

"There," John pointed, "they have rooms upstairs I'd wager."

"That's Wyatt Earp's place."

"Wyatt Earp, how strange."

"What?"

"Something about Wyatt Earp just rang a bell. I don't know, I feel as if I were meant to come here. He has a wife, doesn't he?"

"Dunno, never heard of one."

"I'm sure of it Ted."

"What does that have to do with anything?"

"I don't know, but let's make haste. I'm freezing!"

———

Sadie tossed a gold double eagle on the green baize tabletop, "Thirteen, black, on thirteen!"

"Sadie, you sure?"

"Shut up, Hoxsie," Sadie laughed as she tossed her dark hair over a bare shoulder and low-cut red velvet dress, "I'll bet *where* I want, *how* I want, and *when* I want to."

"Just like you'll do what you damn please any other time, Josephine," Hoxie pulled at his mustache and grimaced at the spinning wheel. "Don't know how Wyatt..." his voice trailed off as he pushed her chips on the marker for thirteen black.

"What did you say?"

"I said: I don't know how Wyatt puts up with you sometimes, Sadie!"

"He has no choice, sugar."

Hoxsie grunted as he scooped up the roulette ball with his croupier's stick and readied it for the next turn of the wheel.

"Hurry up Hoxsie."

Hoxsie turned toward two young men who had approached asking about rooms and waved them toward the bartender. "You're lucky fellas. We have one left for ten bucks."

"Ten dollars!" The taller of the two stepped back, wrenched his gaze from Sadie to contemplate the sum, and put a hand to his chin, "Our tent was ransacked by vandals but minutes ago and we have nowhere to stay, but... ten dollars!"

"I got a game to run, gents. You can sleep in one of the missionary tents if they've got the space. These are the finest rooms between here and Dawson City, or anywhere in Alaska 'cept maybe Juneau, and that's sixteen hundred miles by ship after breakup if you've got a mind to try." Hoxsie turned back to the roulette wheel and the crowd waiting for him to set it spinning, "It's your play. Go talk to the bartender and see what's up."

"I don't—"

"Here, fellow," Sadie sashayed around the table and dropped a twenty-dollar gold piece in the tall man's hand, "Go warm up and get some sleep. You look like you need it."

John's mouth fell open, "I—"

Hoxsie groaned, "Sadie, you let Wyatt see you throwin' it away like that and he'll cut you off. For Christsake, that's the price 'a *two* rooms!"

"It's my damn money. I make it too, you know. And Wyatt isn't kicking his lady love out in the street like you'd do these poor pilgrims. Now spin that thing!"

"Sadie—"

"*Spin it!*"

Hoxsie set the wheel to spinning and released the ball in a silver blur under a layer of cigar smoke. Voices shouted numbers and colors at the polished implement as it mesmerized the men around the wheel like mice before the gaze of a serpent.

Sadie stared, willing the ball to the color black and the number thirteen with her teeth white against red lipstick as she bit her lower lip. She was deep in the hole, and Wyatt would be roaring and stomping about their rooms when he found out. He might even punch the wall, but she had no fear he'd hit her. Wyatt wasn't that kind of man. When things were tough in Arizona, San Francisco, or on the long journey here, one or the other of them would always manage to pull money out of the hat. Wyatt had his reputation, and Sadie had her looks. A million dime novels Outside praised his courage and made a grudge fight in Tombstone years ago into some kind of myth, but they'd been stretched awfully thin when they'd arrived on this stark and bitter coast of the Bering Sea after a miserable winter stuck on the frozen Yukon River in Rampart. Now they were going to get out rich, and then back to San Francisco or a ranch somewhere and respectable lives. Here in Nome, Josephine Sarah Marcus Earp was worth more than gold. Sadie was a truly beautiful woman at thirty-seven, to the point some muttered she had truck with the Devil. Wyatt had won her from the Birdcage Theater in Tombstone where she'd performed as both a dancer and more by killing her previous man, and he still came close to doing the same with any prospective suitors, but this was their last chance. It was the Big One, and it would only work if they pulled together. Time had become their enemy now, but they were born lucky.

"Black, on thirteen!"

"Whoop!" Sadie sprang in the air, clapped her hands, and bent over with a howl to scoop up her winnings while giving the boys a peek at her cleavage in the tight red dress, "See, Hoxsie, *see?* When one gives to the right soul in need, the Muse of Luck is sittin' on your damn shoulder!" she giggled, "or perhaps some other part of my anatomy."

Sadie turned toward John and Ted, who were at the bar having watched the proceedings, "Got it back fifteen-fold fellas! You two better clean up and get back down here for a drink before I spend all this pretty gold."

The taller of the two tipped his derby hat, "Thank you again, Miss—"

"Mrs. Josephine Sarah Marcus *Earp!"* Hoxsie barked.

Sadie winked at John and shot Hoxsie an awful glare.

The room was huge, being some fifteen feet on a side and lit by five kerosene lamps. It had Turkish carpets, two beds, a night stand, a closet, and two chamber pots. An earthenware crock of fresh water was on the dresser with a large mirror above it, and the closet had five polished hangers from England.

Ted bounced on a bed, pulled off his boots, and stretched on the quilt, "This is great, the best room in Nome for free, and ten dollars besides!" He put his hands behind his head and stared at the ceiling, "Can you believe it?"

"That's Wyatt Earp's wife."

"Looks like it, didn't even know he was married," Ted grinned from ear to ear, "she's a dish, that's a certainty. Didn't you say something about him having a wife? Wonder where the man himself is? I'd like to meet the fellow in the flesh. He's killed twenty men I hear."

"That's dime novel stuff. He's killed four, maybe five."

"Five more than me."

"That's some filly he's got."

Ted laughed. "And she wants to buy us a drink!"

"Wonder where the bath is? I'd like to clean up."

"It would be lost on most of these lugs."

"I wasn't thinking about them."

"You're not planning on getting friendly with Mrs. Earp, are you?"

"Well . . ."

"John... "

"Just presentable, that's all. She does seem so... familiar, almost as if I'd known her previously."

Ted chuckled, "I should like to tell myself the same, but it might take a few drinks first."

"Well, we're to be her guests in the bar anyway."

"With the way that fellow Hoxsie talks, I don't think we should dawdle. She could be broke again by the time we get downstairs."

"That would be something."

"How old do you think she is?"

"Can't tell. Older than we I suppose."

"Must be something, having a woman like that in a place like this."

"It's Wyatt Earp Ted, no one would cross him."

"Good to hear you say that John."

———

Sadie was sitting at the bar when they returned. She brushed off the men on either side of her like bothersome insects and patted the suddenly vacant stools. Sadie had insisted that Wyatt have stools installed since she refused to any longer stand at a bar, and the red leather seats were her private domain when she was present. Her hazel eyes were alight with the bath of men's attention as well as the effects of whatever she'd been drinking. "Hey, boys," she said as they sat down, "gonna be the next millionaires?"

"At least we're here earlier than the Klondike," John offered, "and the beach is open to anyone and can't be claimed. We're going to build a rocker box as soon as we find permanent shelter and begin working the sand at low tide with a tent pitched and a stove so the sand doesn't freeze in the riffles. I saw it done today. By the way, I certainly shall reimburse you for the money and I shant forget it. You have my word."

"Takes a lot of fuel to run a stove and finding it is a chore in itself. Maybe you'll have a coal barge run aground with a couple cases of whiskey to boot," Sadie grinned, ignoring the comment about paying back the money, "Dawson... we were going there when the river froze. Spent a winter in goddamn Rampart, then we turned around when the river thawed and headed for Nome. Glad we did."

John nodded, "You've done well."

"Indeed," Ted added, trying to keep his eyes off Sadie's low-cut dress and failing, "more than well. How long have you been here?"

"Six months," she shrugged, "and this could be the very last gold rush boys." Sadie motioned to the bartender, who put down a bottle of whiskey and three glasses, "And by those standards I shouldn't even be wasting time with two Cheechakos who don't have a pot to piss in, but I never was too smart about such things."

"You were smart enough to throw in with Wyatt Earp."

"You mean he was lucky enough to throw in with *me,*" Sadie put her hands behind her neck and thrust her breasts out, enjoying the effect it had on men at the bar just has she had for two decades across the West. "When a man has killed other men and folks he's never even met make up tales about him, it changes him. Wherever he goes, whatever he does, people have their minds made as to who and what he is. It's always out there waiting for him, and some crazy sonofabitch might come out of nowhere and try something. You have to always be watching over your shoulder, and I'm his eyes and ears as much as he is. Maybe more," she sighed, "it's something to love such a man, but then I do love men."

There was a murmur in the crowd as a tall fellow hung a bearskin coat on a peg that had suddenly become vacant. He wore a bowler hat, and a heavy brown mustache salted with grey covered his upper lip. His eyebrows rose as he looked at Sadie, then at John and Ted. He squinted as if he were looking down the barrel of a gun as he lit a half-smoked cigar with a flash of a match off his pants leg.

Sadie slipped off her stool and sashayed over to meet him with an embrace. John watched his big hands wrap around her tight little bottom and couldn't help but stare as those cheeks were squeezed. The thick gold wedding band on the man's left hand flashed against her red dress and lovely derriere.

"Got to be the man," Ted whispered.

John nodded.

"Don't ask for anything to cover a bet!" Wyatt growled in an ear from which a gold nugget earring protruded from the curtain of her hair.

"I'm way ahead, sugar."

"Then quit."

"Pshaw, that ain't any fun."

"Dammit," Wyatt nuzzled her neck before the appreciative crowd, "What am I gonna do with you, Josephine?"

"Well, sugar, we *do* have the biggest bed in Alaska."

Several men in the crowd chuckled, but were silenced by a glance in their direction. Wyatt took Sadie's hand and led her across the room to a back table that had been hastily cleaned as she gave John a last glance over her shoulder and winked.

"Might as well finish this," the bartender slid the bottle between John and Ted where she'd been sitting. "She'll not be back if he's here, but she'll cover your drinks."

"Thank you."

"Hell, thank her. It's a wonder there's any profit left in this place when she gets a hair. That room you've got sells a lot of champagne when a fella orders up a girl, and the girl always tips the staff if she works a fella too. You two don't look fixed for that kind of sport right now."

"Not tonight, although I see a great event in the making over there."

"Watch it, pilgrim."

"Sorry," John shrugged, "the world is built on dreams you know. Anyway, I shall be back here after I make my first ten thousand dollars to tip you all."

The bartender laughed and refilled John's glass. "You and everybody else, but you never know. After Anvil Creek was all claimed up, that beach is a godsend. Seen bums make enough to buy a house on Nob Hill. Speakin' of Frisco, I hear Lucky Baldwin is opening a place here."

"Who's that?"

The bartender gave John a look as if his appraisal of him had dropped a few notches. "He's the great entrepreneur from San Francisco. Lost his first theater and hotel on Market Street in a fire, and every wife he's had has tried to kill him, but he still finds a fortune everywhere he goes. He and Mr. Earp promoted horse races and prize fights in Oakland, and at the Mechanic's Pavilion in Frisco. Wyatt's refereed John L. Sullivan, Gentleman Jim Corbet, you name it. It's a good omen that Lucky's here."

John laughed, "He doesn't sound that lucky to me."

Ted leaned over his drink, "I bet he's had more women like that one in his bed in a week than we have together in a lifetime, John."

"Perhaps you're right, Ted, although one would do." A ripple of musical laughter tickled John's spine, and he straightened.

"Hey, you're spilling the whiskey. What's up?"

"I just had a... I felt as if I *had* had a woman like Sadie, only better."

"Dream on, partner."

John grinned at the bartender, "You're right about building on dreams. How poor we'd be if we could not." There was a crash across the room and he spun on the stool.

Wyatt Earp stood with his right hand extended and his knuckles speckled with blood, and a man sprawled with one foot on an over-turned table before him as a bottle of amber liquor slowly burped its contents onto the floor. Someone snatched it up as Sadie leaned back in her chair with a glass in her hand. She caught John's eye, winked, and proceeded to smooth her blood-red dress across her legs.

"That woman's poison," the bartender muttered, "you fellas want a beer to chase that down?"

XXVIII.

"I'LL FIND THAT LITTLE WHORE AND RIP HER GUTS OUT!" A HOARSE VOICE echoed through the hallway above the Orpheum like the blast of a trumpet, rousing bartenders, waiters, actors, and actresses with the threat of impending violence. Someone swore. A door slammed.

"Shut up!" It was Diamond Tooth Gertie.

"Who the hell is yellin'?"

"Alex! Some gink wants ta do a lady in!"

The shouting rose again as the sound of someone kicking a door and a woman's scream roused the last denizens of the Orpheum from their beds. Eddie Doland, the manager of the Tivoli, leaned out of a room with a Colt Peacemaker in his hand and glanced up and down the hall. Another door opened a crack, and Alexander Pantages peeked out with a scowl.

"Whatever is it, dear?" Kate asked from behind him.

"Some girl got the best of a fellow, I suppose."

"Here," she put a pistol in his hand, and his fingers closed around the butt.

"Where is she!"

"I don't *know,* now get the fuck *out,* goddamn it!"

"That's Mary!" Kate hissed. She snatched the pistol out of Alex's hand and stepped into the hall with her pink chiffon robe clutched around her and her auburn tresses hanging to her waist.

A big, bearded man was backing out of a room two doors down with his face alternating between fear and rage as he held hands up in front of him, "Hey, sorry! I just want to find that little whore who robbed me, and—"

"Get the fuck out!"

Mary appeared flush-faced in a black bustier, lace panties, and one black silk stocking. She had a short-barreled shotgun pointing at the man's groin and her blond hair was mussed from sleep, "You *ever* bust in here again, your goddamn guts will be all over the wall! Ya fuckin' sonofabitch!"

Klondike Kate laughed.

The man turned, saw the gun in Kate's hand, Eddie with another, and glanced at the stairs. He took a step backward, stumbled, and grabbed the banister, "All right! I'm sorry! I'm leavin'!" The Adam's apple bounced in his thick throat as he bounded down the stairs.

Kate waved the heavy pistol at the empty hall and handed it back to Alex. "What the hell was that about?"

Gertie stepped out from behind Mary with a diamond-studded sneer, "Gink was lookin' for Alice Mary, said she robbed him or somethin'."

"Alice Mary may be a whore, but she does not rob people." Kate scowled, "Somebody should warn her."

Gertie nodded, "She's at my place. I'll send somebody with a note. That sonofabitch is dangerous."

Kate glanced at Mary, "Where's Joseph? He's the quickest."

"Out."

"I'll go myself then."

Alex took her arm, "That fellow is big and mean, Kate. You can't go out there if he's lurking around just waiting for one of you to go looking for Alice Mary."

"Then I should appreciate it if you would go yourself Alex, here," she pushed the big Smith and Wesson into his hand, "put this in your belt under your coat and don't let the Yellowlegs see it when you cross the street."

Alex sighed, glanced at the other faces in the hall, and nodded, "I shall get dressed."

"Thank you dearest."

Ten minutes later Alex was on the street. He pulled his wolverine fur hat down over his ears and buried gloved hands in the pockets of his heavy black bear coat as a cloud of his breath shrouded him. He avoided a big dog by stepping off the wooden sidewalk, slipped on a chunk of ice peeled off the underside of a wagon, and cursed loudly as he went down in the snow to the laughter of two adolescent boys. "A *real* city would have some taxicabs!" he shouted at the facade of the Monte Carlo as he stood up and slapped at his pants. That was an idea actually. Perhaps they should invest in some.

An upstairs window rattled open on the side of the Monte Carlo. "What's the matter Alex, Kate throw you out?" Lace curtains billowed around Gussie Lamore as she clutched a quilt around bare shoulders with her long blond hair floating in the frigid breeze like a pale Nordic goddess.

He took off his hat, "No such luck, Madame Lamore."

Gussie blew him a kiss, shivered, and slammed the window.

He was nearly frozen by the time he reached Gertie's. The chimney had a column of smoke rising straight in the icy air, and it looked like the stove had just been stoked. Alex knocked on the door, bounced in his mukluks, and shivered. His blood was too damn thin for this climate, even with a diet of meat and whiskey. There was no answer from within, and he groaned. He wanted to warm up for the walk back whether or not he could deliver his message.

The red silk behind the tiny window in the door parted momentarily before the sound of a chain rattling brought his head up. The pulling of a deadbolt was accompanied by the door shifting in its frame as he stomped his feet. "Hurry up!"

It opened on Alice Mary with a small chrome revolver in her hand. Alex eyed the gun as he stepped in, and Alice Mary shut the door and slammed in the bolt. "Hello, Alex."

"Hello, Alice." He hung his coat, took off his gloves, and hurried to the stove rubbing his hands.

"Take off your mukluks, please."

"Oh, sorry," he returned to the entry, sat on the bench beside the door, and pulled off his footwear.

"He's been to the Orpheum."

He glanced up, "Yes."

"Ah knew he would, knew you were comin' too."

"Oh?"

She put a finger to her lips. "Edie's sleepin'. Yep, knew you were comin'. Ah dreamed it."

"That's handy," Alex squeezed around the back of the stove and rubbed his hands.

"Ever since Ah realized she saved me from that damned Fred Dodge, I been havin' these wondrous dreams."

"Who did?"

"You really don't know?"

"No, Alice."

"Lorelei, Alex, Lorelei did."

"What makes you think that? Kate said you told those at Cad's party it was a ghost rescued you."

She folded up on the couch and stroked her hair with a boar bristle brush. Her wrists seemed so thin that Alex wondered if they might break with the effort. "She came to you once."

"Who? What do you mean?"

"You were alone under a burnin' sun at the edge of a green jungle. Never seen a jungle, but that's where you were in my dream. You were pretty much 'bout my age, and cast off a boat, Ah believe."

Alex turned from the stove with a face noticeably paler. He sat across from her on a footstool and leaned toward her with the whites of his eyes wide around dark irises. "How did you know that?"

"Tol' you, Ah dreamed it."

"No one here knows of that time."

"You had a young lover. She gave birth to a daughter after you left her cryin' on a awful hot and humid night. The girl's name is Alexis Maria. She's a whore for the French, who are tryin' to build a canal. She dreams of you often Alex, but she can't never see your face. It makes her cry."

He sprang up and knocked over the stool, *"Stop!"* The big Smith and Wesson revolver fell out of his belt and landed on the floor with a loud thunk.

"Careful that thing don't go off."

Alex scooped up the gun and stuffed it back in his belt, "What tales has Kate told you?"

"Kate? She don't know 'bout that time, and your lover under that burnin' sun. She don't know 'bout the laughter you heard that day or the day you first had her above the Monte Carlo either. Ah do," the look on Alice Mary's porcelain features bordered on sympathy, "Ah see her more clearly each night now whether she wishes me to or not and Ah see those she's touched too."

"Who?"

"Ah tol' you Alex."

"Lorelei? Lorelei is simply a beautiful and rich woman who keeps to herself and dabbles in younger men."

"Where is she at this moment?"

"I have no idea."

"She's in Nome, simply to know another woman."

"*What?*"

"She is."

"You are daft, Alice, and who told you about Panama?"

"Panama, is that where it was? Boy, that was a big 'ol green snake. Scared the bejesus outta ya, looks like."

"*Stop it!*"

Footsteps echoed from the back of the house, and the Oregon Mare peered from the door of the bedroom. She spied Alex, put down her revolver, and muttered, "Damn."

Alex turned, "Excuse me, Edie."

"What the hell's goin' on?"

"Esmeralda. That was your lover's name."

"Stop it!" Alex put hands to his ears, "You cannot know her *name!*"

"Lorelei can't hide her tracks from me, for Ah too am a hunter in dreams: a hungry wolf in the night that's starvin' for to know what Ah really am. Ah'm trailin' her scent, Alex. You're a man, and don't tell me you ain't never noticed her scent."

Edie glanced from Alex's stunned face and back to Alice Mary, "Honey, what in the hell are you two talkin' about?"

"You are mad!" Alex ran to the entry, yanked on his mukluks, and grabbed his coat, "Stay away from the Orpheum! Keep all your filthy doings out of my establishment and your filthy, dangerous customers away from my help! Do not even talk to me, ever *again!*" He dashed into the alley without putting on his gloves or buttoning his coat. Alex's wolverine hat was still on the bench by the door.

Alice Mary went to the door, shut it, and shrugged, "Men."

———

Night fell at three in the afternoon. Alice Mary was in the bathtub smoking opium and watching the last pink colors on the hills through the fogged glass of a tiny window. Someone banged on the door and it rattled in its frame. She rose from the bath, wrapped a purple towel around herself, and seized the little chrome pistol and her Bowie knife from the dresser.

She knew who was there as surely as if she could see his face. The fool was Donald, who was convinced she'd robbed him of an extra poke he'd never had upon her entering his room at the Empire Hotel. She'd risked arrest just going there. If the Mounties had seen her delivering herself to him at the hotel, she'd be at Fort Herchmer right now doing laundry while listening to some Anglican priest spout about Jezebel and Satan and the like, maybe even being deported to Skagway because of her age.

It didn't matter. Donald had spouted off to enough people in saloons that he couldn't turn away from his tale now and keep face. He must find her now for his simple man's pride and was committed to exacting some kind of revenge upon a girl he outweighed nearly threefold. He probably believed it himself by now, the fool. She gazed at the ceiling and sighed. Edie was gone and Gertie hadn't returned. Alice Mary slipped into longjohns and a blue flannel dress. It would be nice to put some pants on, but the Yellowlegs wouldn't have it and would stop her on the street.

She heard Donald walking around the house trying to peer into windows as she stood in the parlor holding her knife. Finally he grew cold, or bored, or perhaps had decided to have a drink or lay in wait for her somewhere else, and he headed down Church Street toward the river.

She pulled on high boots and yanked a wool stocking cap over damp hair before climbing the ladder to the attic. Alice lifted the cover of the tiny vent and peered out. Donald had turned up Second. She sprang down the ladder and pulled on gloves. She slid the knife in its sheath and hung it on a thong tied to the back of a tight nugget dog collar necklace so it rested in the small of her back. She yanked it out quickly a few times, like she'd done a thousand times before. It felt like a part of her. She hesitated with the pistol in her hand before she put it back in the drawer of the nightstand. Alice Mary donned a red woolen Hudson's Bay coat, stepped out of the house, and locked the door with the big brass key Diamond Tooth Gertie had entrusted to her.

She ran to the corner, but stopped before she turned on Second at the sudden vision of a look of glee on Donald's face as she came around the building, followed by rage as he seized her in his big hands. His face became Fred Dodge's and she saw the flash of a gold tooth. Alice Mary felt a cold surge of hatred crawl up her spine and began to tremble. She took a breath, closed her eyes, stilled herself, and leaned out to peer down the street.

Donald's bare head was visible over a sea of beaver and fur hats as he headed toward Queen Street. She pulled her coat around herself, pulled the hood over her face, stepped out, and followed. He turned right on Queen. He was going to his hotel.

She stopped at the corner where there was a Mountie standing on the steps of the British Bank of North America and turned so he couldn't see her face under the hood. There was quite a crowd in the darkening afternoon, and she hoped no one would recognize her or call out her name. Alice made a right on Queen just as Donald entered the Empire Hotel. She crossed the street, walked north, and cut between buildings into the alley behind the hotel. Bertrand the Belgian baker was emptying grease into a can, but went back in his bakery without a glance. A yellow mongrel gave her a wary look before he nosed off the lid and shoved his head into the container.

Alice Mary made the stairs at the rear of the hotel and climbed to the second floor. The rickety porch creaked loudly. She shivered and grasped the railing. She took a breath and tried the door. It was locked. Alice swore softly, pulled her knife, and inserted its tip into the crack of the door. The bolt popped in an instant, allowing her a brief smile of triumph before she hung the knife behind her back and stepped in.

The hall was empty. She made her way to the room where yesterday she had given Donald her body for a twelve-dollar ounce of gold. Hopefully he hadn't lingered downstairs. There wasn't a bar, but he could have paused to scan a paper in the lobby if there were pictures in it. There was movement inside. Alice Mary closed her eyes, swallowed, and knocked.

"Who is it?" came the deep voice of Donald.

"Me."

Heavy footsteps preceded the door being flung wide, and the towering form of Donald Johnston stood before her in a stained undershirt with his mouth open in surprise.

She stared fixedly into his face and shut the door, willing all his attention to her eyes, willing his soul. *Yes...* that was what she was doing, she was capturing his *soul*. She'd done it a million times before, for ten thousand years, and she knew it.

"What in hell?"

"Ah've come to put all things right between us."

"Damn."

"Ah will give you far more than what you have lost and you shall have me besides. Ah'll love you with all that Ah am, Donald, and all Ah shall be."

Donald broke a yellow-toothed grin as she dropped her coat. Alice Mary inhaled the rank breath she'd barely tolerated when he'd gasped and lost his seed in her but a dozen hours ago. She tightened the muscles of her stomach and stitched a smile across her lips.

"You're a gutsy little chicken I've got to say. We'll see how you pay... but where's my gold?"

She slid up to his chest, opened his dirty undershirt, and put her face against damp flesh. She barely came to his hairy nipples. Alice

Mary kissed one and felt a tremor run through his body, "Where it has always been, my love."

"Hot damn," his right hand closed around her tiny bottom, almost touching the tip of the knife. His left cupped her right breast and pinched the nipple hard. His right fumbled under her dress and pulled at the longjohns before blunt, dirty fingers began to probe her.

Alice Mary rose on her toes, and her left hand wrapped around the hilt of the knife. The blade made a soft hiss as it left the sheath. She pulled away from his grasp and grunted as she drove it with all her strength into his stomach, jerking it up toward his heart.

Donald let out a gasp that was cut off by a rush of air as his esophagus was severed by the blade. He dropped to his knees, twisting the knife from her hands. Bright arterial blood spewed from under his ribcage, and she sprang away to avoid being drenched by it. "You can go to hell! You shit!" She put her foot on his heaving stomach and pulled on the knife. It was stuck, and she tugged and twisted, cursing. A big hand grasped at her and she ducked her head. A woof of air from his chest blew droplets of blood in a cloud around her, and he toppled like a tree. She stepped away as he fell on the hilt of the knife. The blade appeared out of his back as he landed on the floor, driven through by his weight with a glistening crescent of vertebrae impaled upon its tip.

Something shot up Alice Mary's spine, and the top of her skull tingled. She vibrated like a bell. White sparks flashed in her eyes, and there was a roaring in her ears. She fought her way through the fear, through the trembling, and blinked the world into focus. With a grunt of effort, she tried to turn the heavy body over. After several attempts she pulled the knife from under his ribcage with a heavy sucking sound, followed by a last bright arc of blood.

She gulped air and held the knife over her head, "Ah got the *right,* Lorelei!" she shouted at the ceiling as blood ran down her arm and made purple spots on her blue flannel dress.

Quiet! You must flee, and lose your bloody clothes!

"Yes, you *know,* you *see!"*

Watch your voice! Be that as it may I would prefer that you escape. Do as I say, and I shall hide you.

"Thank you!"

Shhhh! And please... you must promise me here and now that you won't make this a habit!

"Ah suppose."

Beautiful laughter erupted from a distance to flit about the room and fade quickly, but not before Alice Mary heard it and laughed back. "Ah am a witch also, Lorelei!"

Perhaps so, but there have been foolish witches my friend, and seldom have they lived long or prospered. This was a terribly rash act.

She shrugged, "You did the same for me and for Honey Bee... and Ah know it."

I doubt you can carry him faster than men can see to the top of a distant dome and be done with him. You can hardly turn him over, let alone clean up this mess. You must leave now if we are to keep you from being discovered.

"Ah can learn."

A sigh shook the air, *You're an ambitious girl but please do as I say. This is such a mess! I'm going to have to get you out of here somehow.*

A radiant smile spread Alice Mary's face. She wiped blood from it, pulled the red woolen coat over her blood-stained dress, slid the knife back in its sheath, and stepped into the hall.

XXIX.

S ADIE JERKED UPRIGHT IN THE DARK, SHIVERED, AND PUT A HAND OUT TO Wyatt. He groaned, let out a gust of whiskey breath, and rolled away, pulling the covers off her as he did and pinning them with his weight.

"Shit."

She squirmed out of her bondage and found the chamber pot, squatting to pee while holding her long hair away from the splash. Sadie stared at the frosted-over windows and yawned. *What a strange dream.* She'd been running with a woman through a landscape that shifted from the Bird Cage Saloon in Tombstone, to the Palace Hotel in San Francisco, to the Dexter Saloon in Nome. She couldn't see her face no matter how hard she tried, just her white hands and hair, and the echo of bright eyes that seemed to linger in the back of her own. That made her mad, yet she sensed it was someone who knew the loneliness of a life spent at night with too many men, and the joys of unfettered lust too.

And there was that laughter. Sadie vaguely remembered a blond girl with an angel's face killing a giant, yet the fleeting feeling of a better place went on and on and remained, as if time could be stopped in those selfless moments in a bed. It was all there at once in her mind. She tried to seize a piece and force it into focus.

She'd danced in and out of her vision, but Sadie could almost see her... someone who never had to leave that perfect place but who could stay there forever... and those *eyes.*

A ripple of laughter made her jump and she almost knocked over the chamber pot. Sadie stood up, wiped herself with a rag, and glanced about the room. That was strange. Was it her imagination? She could still feel the dream, almost smell it over the sharp odor of her own piss. Sadie threw on a heavy quilted robe, stepped into thick wool slippers, and tied the sash around her waist. This cabin behind the saloon was their private abode, kept blissfully secure by Wyatt's reputation. All was silent in the wee hours of the morning but for the hiss and tick of the stovepipe and the snoring of her husband.

What was that laugh?

It must be the tail end of her dream teasing her. Sadie wandered to the stove, opened the door, and slid in two scoops of precious coal that had come on the last steamer from Katchemak Bay before freeze-up. She sat in the diamond willow rocking chair in the small parlor and scratched an armpit. Wyatt had been too drunk for sex, and since it was so damn hard to heat enough water to stay clean in this fucking cold, she'd let it pass. Of course they'd been together for over a decade now, and that just seemed to happen sooner or later. They were getting older after all.

"To hell with that."

She spat at the flickering light coming through cracks in the stove and watched it hiss on the hot iron. Nobody ever thought she was thirty-seven, but she could feel it. There was a level of tiredness growing larger, born of too many fast times and too many lovers. That was why goodtime girls got married, after all: for the security of a man and his money after her youth was spent and all she had was a million secrets, even if a girl really didn't trust him.

She still wanted a baby, but by now the prospect scared her. She'd had two stillborn already, but just as soon as they returned south, she wanted a child. If she gave up on the cocaine and laudanum and quit drinking like the doctor had told her, things might be different this time. She should cut the gambling too. It never paid in the end. Sure was fun though. Sadie loved the rush of fear when she was afraid of losing everything and the lift she got when she didn't. It was like going to bed with a strange, handsome man who could be the best lover in the world or a killer. It was all a roll of the dice, but Sadie knew she was born a winner.

That fellow John came into her mind. There was a man she would have grabbed and rode like a bronc without question a few years back, just like she'd done upon meeting Wyatt. Of course that particular assignation had gotten her previous lover killed at Wyatt's hand, which did tend to make one a bit more conservative as time went by. But just the same, something about John was so stimulating.

The red light of the stove pooled in the ring on her finger. That diamond was worth enough by itself to buy her a start somewhere if she ever needed it. You never know. She rubbed her hands together, put them on each side of her nose, and exhaled. She ought to get back to bed.

Sudden warmth radiated down on her shoulders as Sadie felt a pleasant pressure, stretched, began to rub her neck, and touched smooth fingers upon it. She gazed down at white hands that slid toward her throat softly as feathers, sending warmth throughout her body.

"You have known life growing in your womb, Sadie. In that how much richer you are than I. Even your loss, I envy." The fingers stroked her cheek and the hands withdrew.

The owner of that voice came before her. Sadie gazed into eyes that were blue and green and sparkling with tiny facets of the deepest burning red like embers or the light in a kaleidoscope dancing off the crystals within. The woman was nude. Her flesh was white as ivory, but the light of the stove rippled across her body and long raven hair like the red stripes of a tiger in a jungle of dreams.

Sadie stared for an endless moment, then blinked. The vision held. "Why am I not afraid? Why do I feel I know you? Is this a dream?"

"You are far too strong to pretend it's a dream," the woman broke a smile, "do you ask for your own amusement? You already know. Yes and no then. I walk in your dreams and I walk in your room." Her smile was glorious, yet tinged with a sadness made all the more obvious by her beauty, "This coming night you will conceive for the last time and I am here to share it even though you will not bear a living child," A flash of melancholy deeper than the ice-choked sea beyond Front Street rippled across her face, and she gazed at the sleeping form of Wyatt, "I know such emptiness a thousand-fold."

Sadie gripped the arms of the chair and shook hair from her face, *"Why?* What in hell *are* you? *Who?* You seem as who I would be if I were given the gift of making thought flesh. An Indian gave me some bitter black tea in Arizona once, and I saw things like you. You're too damn perfect, as if created by the mind of God himself... or the Devil."

"Through beauty I survive beyond your years though I too shall die. I suspect through violence, as it has found all my kind. I accept that, as I ask you to accept your own fate in regard to motherhood. I am but a wretched child who cannot yet conceive herself. You have, but have never brought at child to birth. In that you are as I."

"But... what *are* you?" Sadie pressed against the hard chair and heard her teeth grind in her mouth, "No tricks, bitch!"

That was met with a gale of laughter. Sadie stared for a moment, put hands to her mouth to vainly stifle her own, and felt sudden tears. "I so long for motherhood, and yet you tell me it shall again come to nothing but a child still and dead," a sob wracked her chest. "Are you the Devil then come to torture me? Why in hell are you doing this?"

The woman shook her head and pursed lips that Sadie wanted to kiss, "I mean you no suffering. I have simply longed to know that moment for generations of your kind. We are of the same heart and flesh, and for that I stand before you cursed with a loneliness you have never known if only for its duration."

"But, why . .?"

Lorelei knelt and put fingers to Sadie's cheeks, "I too am tired, tired of countless lovers who have only known as much of me as their hearts allowed, tired of those who knew my foremothers before I was born, yet whose memories remain with me and are a burden. You are as I in passing through life and I am drawn to you by nature. I long to share with you the memories hiding in your bones and for you to know them in your waking days, so listen: once more you shall conceive a child who will never come to term, but you will give me the experience of that conception as you lay with your man in a union like you have never known. We shall exult in it as I will be there with you as spirit and return to comfort you in your loss in the future. That I promise."

"Jesus Christ, *why?*"

Lorelei chuckled, "You're as stubborn as I. A man would have folded like a cheap napkin by now." That brought a snicker from Sadie. Lorelei brushed a curtain of hair away from her face and smiled, "We share the loneliness of those whose hearts and bodies have held far too many lovers, yet we would die without their touch. Such a sweet pain we must bear yet it cuts us to the quick. Know that life shall begin in your womb but hours hence, and only for a short time you shall know her within you, so seek her in the silence of your soul and cleave to her in your heart. Yet how I envy you!"

Sadie raised trembling hands to Lorelei's throat, felt the living pulse of blood there, closed her eyes, and felt tears roll down her cheeks. She kissed Lorelei, inhaling the breath of she who was real beyond dreaming, and a river of voices blazed up like a coal blown upon bursting into flame. Sadie shook like a leaf as Lorelei lay her on the bear rug and their hair made a curtain around them, a shining raiment of which Sadie was a perfect thread. She pulled away from Lorelei's mouth with a gasp, "Damn, this is different!"

"Thought you'd had it all, didn't you?"

"Well, I guess."

XXX.

JOSEPH SHIFTED IN A CLOUD OF BREATH AS HE LIFTED A PEWTER FLASK OF whiskey to his lips from under the bearhide coat. He gazed across the river's ice as the wan white sun of noon beat it into silver with just a hint of gold as the barking of dogs echoed off the Yukon's bluffs.

He'd fled to the woods to think too many times to count, having grown up in Oregon, but the mossy rocks and towering trees of his home were far from this. The welcoming roots of an ancient maple weren't like this cold stone in the middle of Moosehide Slide. Lorelei had told him that beneath it, the bones of children lay.

Town lay below with its myriad smokes rising straight into the air before arching over the crowded slope behind Dawson as a breeze off the river bent them. Joseph stared downriver, wishing her to appear. He imagined her driving a team of wolves with her hair flying in a black pennant behind her in the light of day, laughing.

How I miss that laughter!

She hadn't spoken to him since Halloween.

He felt a void, an emptiness growing with each day that yawned wider until each waking moment left him teetering over an abyss. Sleep was worse. He could hardly sleep anyway, and he used Mary and Lily until they begged him to stop. Joseph had begun going down to the saloons to sample the showgirls. Something Lorelei had done to him made it almost too easy, and he'd become a satyr, mounting nymphs whose faces blurred together until they were like one. It was never enough, though. It wasn't Lorelei.

He stood and wobbled unsteadily in the snow atop a green serpentine boulder. "Speak to me!"

All right.

"Lorelei!" Joseph stumbled, slipped, and grabbed at the lip of the bolder as he almost fell into the jagged rocks below.

Watch yourself!

"It's you!"

Who else?

"Where in the hell are you?"

The familiar music of her laughter filled him. *Not in Hell, I'm in Nome.*

"Alice Mary said that, how in hell did she know?"

She's been stalking me and it's rather irritating. And for that matter, you could speak with me more often if you would quit feeling sorry for yourself and whining all the time. It hurts our connection and I'm disappointed. Here I've brought you these two beautiful girls and many more to make love to according to your inclination, and you haven't even taken the opportunity to enter their souls, there was an exasperated sigh, *they're there for the knowing.*

"Well excuse me. We're not all spirits you know, or goddesses, or whatever. You could have told me."

I just did, which is giving in to your desire for being pampered far too much. You're a young man and I suppose I can't expect miracles, but they happen occasionally.

Joseph felt blood warming his face.

There was her laughter, *Good, you're embarrassed! You're in such a unique and fortunate situation my young love. I got sidetracked after Halloween and ended up here, which is how things happen sometimes. It was quite unexpected as I'm really not all-knowing or any of those things. I'll be back, but my own impulses in regard to one worthless person have stirred things up more than I expected, and I would appreciate it if you would make use of the gifts I've given you in the meantime. You're going to put them to use quite soon.*

"I appreciate the girls, Lorelei, I love them until they—-"

Another exasperated sigh roiled the frigid air around him, nearly knocking Joseph off his perch again. *Not that. You could have known their souls and you've only known their bodies. Anyone can do that. I expect more of you.*

He brushed hair out of his eyes and shrugged, "I guess it takes practice. I certainly satisfy them. They—"

When their hearts are open, don't dwell on me; pass into them. They hold the secrets of creation and our most ancient memories also. They just don't know it. Help them remember and fulfill both our purposes. I have seen it done since before my own birth, and in doing so you shall find your own redemption.

"Redemption? Are you starting a church now? They still couldn't make the top of King Solomon's Dome in five minutes like you."

It's not a race. This is like training a puppy sometimes. Perhaps I should make you sit up and roll over, but I'm afraid you'd fall off that rock, another sigh made the air tremble, and a sense of melancholy hovered around Joseph's shoulders threatening to join the black funk he'd just stepped out of upon hearing her voice. *So you think that you're sad. You don't even know what pain is yet. I wish you didn't have to learn. Oh... not really, it builds character.*

"When will I see you?"

Start by treating those around you better. You will have the opportunity to prove yourself this very night as you're needed by a young lady in distress.

"What? Who?"

Alice Mary. You're going to spirit her out of Dawson.

"What? That little whore? You said *lady!* He grimaced, "What has she got into now?" Only the cold breeze answered, buffeting him on the boulder. Joseph sighed. "I'm sorry for saying that."

Not yet you're not but you may be soon. You must help her flee Dawson, and I'm trusting you'll acquit yourself well. She's a remarkable young woman who's found me of her own initiative, so don't bind her with your judgment. Believe me, you don't know enough to try. Besides, you two are going to be in very close company soon so keep an open mind.

"I suppose you would know."

That's right.

There was a soft popping on the breeze and he knew she was gone.

"And where the hell am I to take her at this time of year?"

———

By the time he scrambled down the chaos of Moosehide Slide and reached the mission at its feet, night was falling, and the sun was a pink glimmer in the south coloring the mountains with its last rays. The lights came on in Dawson, setting it aglow in the dark of the Yukon's night like an island of dreams.

Why must I leave this?

There was no answer, only shouts and laughter from the saloons along Front Street. Joseph shoved his hands further into the pockets of his coat and trudged between the frozen droppings of horses and dogs. The barking of a team tied to pilings echoed off the empty wharfs. Small shacks and tents stood on the ice of the river over holes where men had been fishing. One had smoke rising from it. It was Saturday night, and the bars were full of men hurrying to drink themselves into a stupor before they were closed by edict of the Crown at midnight on the first minute of the Sabbath.

He nodded at the Oregon Mare as she escorted a miner from the Floradora Dance Hall toward Gertie's house and Edie winked back. Joseph grinned. This was his town. He no longer felt anything but at home in the saloons and in the company of such women.

At the corner of Second and Queen, a crowd had gathered where a dozen sets of blue legs with yellow stripes were visible under heavy brown overcoats. It appeared the Mounties had the entire area around the Empire Hotel blocked off, and a goodly portion of Dawson's population was at the barriers.

"What's happening?" Joseph asked a passerby.

"Murder... murder most foul, hear tell!"

"Who?"

"Fella from Hunker Creek that was on a tear last night, who got chased out of the Orpheum just this mornin' they say."

"The Orpheum?"

"Yep," the man glanced at the Mounties and put a hand over his mouth, "they say Klondike Kate drew a revolver and chased him out herself."

"Did he hurt anybody?"

"Nope, but he was lookin' for little Alice Mary I'm told. Said he was gonna wring her pretty little neck like a chicken's."

"Do tell."

"Yep, somebody musta took offence and squared up with the lug. Hear tell he's been gutted like a fish."

"That's something." Joseph turned around and headed for the Orpheum.

———

There was the usual crowd around the bar and gambling tables. Gertie was onstage. Kate laughed with a glass of champagne in her hand between two infatuated miners. Lily danced with a fellow in a three-piece suit and bowler hat to a ragtime tune being played up-tempo by a new piano player, a skinny black man with a goatee who was smoking one of those tiny cigarettes that were becoming popular Outside in places like New York, but still considered rather effeminate in the north. He wore a pin-striped shirt with sleeves held up by arm garters, a battered derby hat with an ace of spades in the band, and had a sheen of sweat on his forehead. Joseph paused for a moment to listen and watch the man's fingers fly across the keys.

"Hi, Joe!" Lily's hand was on his arm.

He kissed her cheek, "What happened here? Who got chased out?"

"This morning? Oh, some sonofabitch thought Alice Mary robbed him and came in early wakin' us all up, shoutin' and threatenin' like the devil. Said he was gonna kill her. Mary had a shotgun, and Kate and Eddie had pistols, and they chased his mangy arse outta here somethin' pronto. It was a hoot! Wish you'd been around," her voice dropped, "think the Mounties will search the place for handguns?" She leaned closer and whispered in his ear, "there's a good bit of hard stuff Alex ain't paid duty on, and the Yellalegs don't take to opium or coke much either when it's not in a medical way. Buncha pansies," Lily eyed two strangers who had entered behind Joseph, "maybe I oughta take my stuff to Gertie's for safekeeping."

"I don't know. Did you know he's dead?"

"What?"

"The fellow who was looking for Alice, somebody gutted him with a knife in the Empire Hotel."

"Oh," Lily put a hand to her mouth. "Gosh. Well, I'm not surprised. He was a mean sonofabitch, that's for sure. They know who did it?"

"Not yet."

"Oh well."

"Where's Mary?"

"Upstairs."

Joseph headed to the rooms and found Mary on the bed reading a dime novel about Wyatt Earp in the one they shared next to Alex and Kate's. She put the book down and smiled. "Hi, Joe."

"Hello Mary."

"Where have you been?"

"I took a walk in the hills."

"Brrrrr, that sounds cold."

"It was, but I had to think."

"Hear from Lorelei?"

He bounced on the bed beside her, put his hands behind his head, and grinned at the ceiling, "Yes."

"I wish she'd speak to me again. Sometimes it seems but a dream."

"It's no dream. I should be grateful she didn't just use me for one night and cloud my mind afterwards. That's her way when she doesn't want to bother with things. I've been quite a child about all this she says."

Mary giggled, "I love her opinions."

"I suppose."

"So what does she say?"

"That I must escort Alice Mary out of Dawson."

Mary rose up on her elbows, crossed her legs, and put a hand under her chin, "Why?"

"I don't know, but from the crowd at the Empire Hotel I'd say she gutted that fellow who was looking for her."

"*What?*"

"He's dead, stabbed this afternoon."

"Oh my God."

"Lorelei says Alice Mary has pursued her in dreams and is far more than what she seems," Joseph ran a hand across Mary's bottom and cupped a cheek in his fingers, "I'm sure it's her that killed him."

She giggled. "Well, she's more than a whore for shore."

"That's lovely," he ran hands through his hair and sighed, "I have got to get equipped. I wasn't planning to mush somewhere in the winter."

"Jesus, it's awfully cold and dark, with bad storms this time of year. Where on earth would you go?"

"Alaska, I suppose. She should do well in Eagle or Circle City, and she can make her way to Nome or some other strike. Alice Mary can always get some man to do her bidding, and I can get back in five or six days. Lorelei's in Nome by the way."

"That's so far. That's what Alice Mary said too. She says she dreamed it, and that Lorelei has a woman for a lover," Mary glanced at her book and slapped it on the quilt, "and she says it's Wyatt Earp's wife!" She put her arms around her legs with her chin on her knees, "This is really strange. The way things are going I wouldn't be surprised if little Alice is some kind of witch herself. You should be careful."

He lay down next to her and stared at the curve of her cheek, "I hadn't thought of it that way, but I suppose you're right... maybe," he frowned, "I don't relish heading out in this weather. Every day is shorter than the last, and the cold's a bloody killer."

"You wanted to be a sourdough, Mr. Walton."

Joseph ran a hand up her back and unhooked her silk brassiere. Mary sat up, shrugged off the garment, rolled on her back, and he kissed a nipple. "I've sure gotten used to this," he murmured as he inhaled the perfume of her skin.

"I wish she'd talk to me as much as she does to you."

"It could drive someone mad eventually."

"A man, perhaps."

XXXI.

A TELEPHONE IN THE NEXT ROOM RATTLED GILT FLEUR DE LIS ON THE wall. There were footsteps and a burst of Greek that sounded like swearing. Joseph had his pants on and was slipping into his shirt by the time Alexander knocked on the door.

"There's—"

"Thank you Alex, it's Alice Mary."

"Of *all people, she* is the one I least want knowing this number! Why did you give it to her?"

"Lorelei did."

"What?"

Joseph hurried next door and nodded to a yawning Kate in a pink bathrobe as he put the black cone of the receiver to his ear, "Hello!" he shouted into the box as if his voice would go farther by doing so.

"Hey Joe, you don't hafta yell. Lorelei tol' me—"

"I know, I've been expecting you."

"Ain't it grand that she talks to us?"

"You don't sound very upset Alice, if this is about what I think it is."

"What? Oh yeah. Lunch at the Golden North?"

"All right."

"One hour?"

"Yes."

———

The restaurant was warm and crowded, but two miners stood and offered them one of the new booths upon spying Alice Mary, who was dressed properly in a fox fur coat. Joseph hung it on a peg. Underneath it she wore a green crinoline dress that matched her eyes, a jingling belt of nuggets, and tall black boots. A woman in a high-collared black dress who'd watched her enter scowled mightily and glanced around for someone to join her in outrage. Alice Mary stuck her tongue out, to be greeted with laughs from several men and an audible huff from the lady of proper standing. "Hell with you, bitch." She plopped on the wooden bench and grinned at Joseph, "Ah want pork chops."

"All right."

"Think Ah pleased her."

"What?"

She giggled, "She don't want to admit it, but Ah pleased her, when Ah kilt that—"

His hand flew to his lips, 'Shhhhhh!"

She giggled, "Sorry."

He leaned closer and whispered, "Why do you say that?"

Green eyes flashed in a pale doll's face, and Joseph found himself staring at her mouth. "'Cause Ah *know,* Joe. Look: she chose you, but Ah went and found her on my own whether she wanted me to or not. Ah got my own plans, and she's gonna give me a hand," she pursed her lips, "'cause Ah can make her."

"I don't know if anyone can make her do anything, and don't forget that she came to your aid of her own choosing when you were being savaged by Fred Dodge."

"Yep, and she showed me a girl can get away with it quite proper if she's got the moxie, Guv'ner," she leaned across the table, "how old is she?"

"I'm not sure. Several hundred years I believe."

"Ain't that *somethin'!*" Alice Mary closed her eyes and leaned against the polished planks with a beatific smile on her face, swinging her feet under the table.

He stared at her child's face seeming without care as her boots swished past his shins. No wonder the other whores called her Baby. He couldn't imagine some of the scoundrels he knew had been with her using that wisp of a body for their own pleasure, and he didn't want to. He didn't want to imagine her gutting that fellow with a Bowie knife, either.

"Can't imagine me doin' that, can ya?"

"That's just what I was thinking."

"Ah know," Alice Mary fished in her lead-beaded purse and produced a silver box. She snapped it open, transferred a cigarette to her lips, glanced around, struck a wooden match on the back of the booth making a scratch in the new shellac, and lit the cigarette.

Joseph frowned, "Chan wouldn't appreciate that."

"Fuck him. We got bigger fish to fry." She squinted through a cloud of smoke, "You know, you don't even seem like the one she'd pick. Ah'd expect some ravin' stallion, some kinda wild man, but she can have anybody Ah'm supposin'. Wonder why she picked you?"

"I don't know."

"Well, we outta get familiar seein' as we'll be travelin' together. Wanta see my new tattoo? It's a dragon with a heart in its mouth." Alice unbuttoned the left side of her dress, tugged on her silk brassiere, and thrust her shoulder forward to show him a tiny red dragon above a small white breast.

"Oh."

Tsu Bai appeared with two menus, ignoring both Alice Mary's breast and the smoldering cigarette in her hand, "Hello! Special today is—"

"Coffee and pork chops, and applesauce. Got applesauce?"

"Yes, yes, plenty applesauce. How 'bout you, Joe?"

"I—"

"And biscuits and butter too, and jam!"

"I'll just have pancakes and coffee please."

Tzu Bai snatched up the menus, "Coming up."

Alice Mary watched her disappear into the kitchen and took another drag on her cigarette. "Pretty, kinda, Ah never seen a Chink naked."

"She is rather pretty."

"Ever been with two girls?"

He swallowed, "Yes, um, quite recently. It's all been an experience. I was a virgin until—"

"That's *it!*"

"Please, keep your voice down."

"Sorry," she giggled, "Ah know now. She wanted a clean slate. Got you fresh from the farm Ah bet. Men always pay-up big time for a virgin. Been one fifty times already. 'Oh please, sir, not so roughly! Ah'm but a poor virgin girl from old Virgineee! It's so *big!* Ow!'" She leaned back with a grin in the booth and examined the ceiling, "Why should she be any different?"

"I never thought of it like that."

"Don't suppose you would. Betcha been havin' a time with Mary and Lily, huh? They're the ones, right?"

Joseph let out his breath and nodded, "Are you really sixteen?"

"Yep. Look a lot younger don't Ah?"

"Yes you do."

Alice Mary flicked black-painted nails at a bearded man who'd entered the restaurant and he broke a grin. Something much older and harder flashed through those green orbs hung in a pale doll's face, and Joseph was ready for them to change color like Lorelei's. "Ah wanta go to Nome."

"I don't have the time to—"

"Ah know, just get me to Eagle. Ah'll work it out."

"You really are something, Alice."

"Guess Ah am, fella. So when are we leavin'?"

"Tomorrow I suppose, if it's not storming,"

"Dashin' through the snow—" she sang in her child's voice, "whatcha doin' for Christmas?"

"Christmas? I haven't considered it."

"Ah'll probably be somebody's Christmas present. Maybe a buncha dirty 'ol lugs in a minin' camp or somethin'. They sure do throw the gold at ya for the few minutes it takes to make 'em happy. Most of 'em don't take no longer than that ya know, just... pop."

He stared out the window, "Why do you even mention it?"

"Ah don't know, Ah like Christmas. Wanta cigarette?"

"No, thank you."

"Ah like these. They cost a bunch and Ah have to have some fella buy them for me. Ain't that stupid? Ah can hardly get a beer in this fuckin' town, but when it comes to ridin' the pony Ah can't keep up with all the business they wanta give me, and the Yellalegs look the other way. 'Course, the Yellalegs see me too."

Joseph nodded. He wasn't looking forward to this at all.

"You're thinkin' it's gonna be hell, aren't ya?"

"I—"

"Maybe. Ever think 'bout goin' to Hell?"

"Of course, I guess."

"My dad's a Police Chief, and my uncle's a Baptist Preacher. Guess Ah'm goin' to Hell, Joe."

"Don't—"

"It felt so damn good to take that gink's life. He hurt other girls before ya know, just like that fuckin' Fred Dodge kilt my dear Honey

Bee," she stared out the window and swallowed, "Ah saw Lorelei come to her in a dream and she took her to a better place... and that pieceashit Donald *bragged* about hurtin' girls! He figured Ah couldn't do a damn thing and no one would care anyway. The lug never did anything with his life 'cept throw his big ol' weight around and hurt people," her eyes flashed. "Feel like Ah can fly like a bird now. That sonofabitch Emile, the Belgian mack who lives on Albert Street, Ah'd like to do the same to him. He keeps my friend Laura and her sister Hermine like goddamn slaves and lives off their money. Fuckin' pimps make girls think they're too weak to make it on their own," Alice Mary ground her teeth, "Ah *hate* men like that!" She took another drag of her cigarette, "Think Lorelei's from Hell?"

"No," he shook his head, "no, I don't."

"Then where?"

"I'd think that you would have some sense of that."

Alice Mary leaned back as a big chipped plate was placed before her by Tsu Bai. "Thanks, Suzy!" She tossed the girl a nugget from her purse with a spot of blood on it, and Tsu Bai stuck it in the pocket of her apron. Alice picked up a pork chop and tore off the end with her teeth, smirked at the woman across the room, and daintily dabbed her mouth with a napkin, "Ah think she was here first... or at least her kind was."

"So do I."

"Good. We should get along fine then," she winked. "Betcha got a dangle like a horse or somethin'."

Joseph felt the blood rise to his face and glanced around from the shelter of the booth, "You're a lot more forward than the last time we met."

"Found out lots since then. Ah'm startin' to realize Ah got my own way of doin' things. No one ever wanted me to know that, or what really *is*. Everything that ever mattered to me was bad or evil where Ah'm from. Would you believe the Fire Chief had his way with me when Ah was twelve? He's my cousin for God's sake, and a Baptist

Deacon too. Said Ah should be dead ever Ah spoke a word, and who'd believe me anyway? Know how many brothers and sisters and cousins Ah got who woulda made me look like some kinda crazy fool and be screamin' 'Repent, repent, ya Jezebel!' Ah'd be cast out just like in the Bible and them fuckers woulda gone on with their goddamn phony livin' like I weren't nothing. In fact Ah *was* cast out Ah guess, jus' took the step myself."

She stared into space and shrugged, "They'd close ranks for the good of the 'ol family name. Didn't look a day over nine or ten at the time and couldn't speak much worth listenin' to anyway and Ah was awful shy. Got pregnant at fourteen by another fella from 'ol Virginia stock who swore up and down that he'd take me away from all that shit. Ever hear 'a General Pickett?" She crushed out her cigarette in a biscuit, "Had ta take care of it myself just like everything else. Stole the money out of his saddlebag after he left me in Norfolk with some sonofabitch he got *paid* by to have a crack at me. Pieceashit! I cut that one. Went to an ol' black woman who lived over in Spotsylvania for some kinda potion or somethin' to stop it, Ah mean bein' pregnant, and stayed in her cabin a week. Got real sick and scared after she stuck this green stick with a ju ju poultice up me and Ah started bleedin' to beat the band. Goddamn, it burned like *hell!* It was—"

"Why are you telling me this?"

Alice Mary pulled her cigarette out of the defiled biscuit, chopped the end off with her knife, relit it, and squinted through the smoke, "Ain't she taught you nothin'?"

"Yes, that there is an older wisdom hidden in love that comes from selfless giving, and that life certainly isn't what I expected." He sighed, "Nothing is what I expected."

"Sounds like you been readin' fancy books, anyway. Ah'd like to learn to read. Maybe you can teach me."

"You don't call what you do love, do you?"

"No, Joe, Ah don't."

"Have you ever loved anyone?"

A flash of hurt rippled across her delicate features that made Joseph's gut clench, "Yeah, Joe," her voice dropped, "Ah love . . ."

"Who?"

"She was took from me and died chokin' on her own blood. Ah've laid awake at night thinkin' of it, thinkin' of her like that. Thought Ah was gonna die from the hurt. It nearly kilt me 'til I saw her pass," Alice Mary's delicate nose flared and she ran a hand tipped with black nails over her face, "Now I know she's somewhere better for certain and that there's hope for the likes of me too... maybe," she smiled, "and there's one more I surely do love for it."

"Who?"

"Lorelei, don't you?"

Joseph's fingers dug into the tabletop as the sound of that river rose from his very bones. It eventually diminished until those of the restaurant returned. He closed his eyes again and reached out to her, trying to touch where she dwelt in a place that was always there, yet so hard to reach without her. He bit his lip and opened his eyes.

Alice's hand closed on his, "If you can so love her and accept who she is, can't you accept me? Ah don't have centuries to find the answer, but Ah know there are things that have been hidden from us that she is the flesh and blood proof of, right *here,* right *now.* Ah been freed, just knowin' she exists. Ah'm gonna try and be what Ah oughta be anyway." She tossed hair from her eyes, "Think Ah'm a witch."

"I'm sorry for that comment about love, Alice."

Her upper lip rippled, "Heard worse."

"Do you know how she feeds?"

"What?"

"How she eats?"

"Ain't really thought about it, but does she have to? Ah mean, you never think about spirits and such eatin' at all 'less it's monstrous bad like sacrificed babies or somethin' awful... but she's much dearer than that Ah hope."

He lifted his fork and watched amber syrup roll off the sourdough flapjacks on the end of it.

"Well?"

"She lives on men's blood."

"Oh."

"Doesn't that shock you?"

Alice Mary shivered with delight, "Ah *knew* it Joe! That's just *right!*"

"You think so?"

"Yep, sure do."

"She gives back more than she takes."

"That's a good way to look at it, 'specially if she's drinkin' your blood."

"She doesn't drink," he ran a hand across his face, "she... she takes it while we're . . ."

"Figured that out, Joe. How else would a goddess eat?"

"That doesn't seem strange?"

"Nope," Alice Mary belched and blew the woman in the black dress a kiss, "Ah don't get that wild, maybe scratch ya up a little, but do you want me?"

"I really don't know, I mean... I certainly think you're attractive, I just—"

"You're one well-bred boy, real proper. We got the same tastes Ah bet," she grinned, "Ah'm awful curious 'bout you now, why she stays with you when she can have any man in the whole world."

"You can't do what she does. You're only mortal, after all."

"So?"

"Taking a life isn't child's play."

"That lug was trash, Joe, just like that fuckin' Fred Dodge. Lorelei kilt him, and you still love her."

"Shhhhh!" He glanced around, "But what about his soul?"

Her mouth grew thin, "Tol' ya, Joe, Ah'm goin' to Hell."

"Wouldn't you rather go where she's from?"

She stared out the window at a lamp bobbing across the river's ice with her chin in her palm and ran a finger around a puddle of coffee, "Yeah, we gotta find out where that is."

"I've been there... at least in part."

"Ah wanta go too. Where does she take you?"

"I'm not sure, I... it's hard to remember, to tell the truth."

Alice Mary gave him a wide-eyed stare, "Say what? You been fuckin' a goddamn Goddess... and you don't *remember?*"

"It's—"

"Ah been seein' her in dreams and remember every *bit,* fella. Damn, maybe she been wastin' time on you after all."

"It's not that; I think it's just too powerful for someone to take in all at once, and she's protecting my sanity or something. Everything changes, Alice. I hear creatures that walked the earth eons ago, and... and people who—"

"Damn! Ah want my turn! Jus' gimme a crack at her."

"I know you do."

"Betcha Ah can handle it."

"Not by the route she takes me."

"Oh? Think so? She's of the *Old Ones,* the witches who ran the world before that goddamn puffed-up *God* they shoved down my throat since Ah could walk fucked it all up. There's a way, Joe, Ah know. Ah made a blood sacrifice of that worthless pieceashit Donald... and presto, she spoke to me because Ah *made* her," Alice crushed out her cigarette again and fixed him in a green-eyed stare, "Ah'm findin' my own way, and there ain't nobody else around to show me 'cept *her,* and that's all Ah need."

"Perhaps she spoke to you simply to save you from being clapped in irons and hauled off for trial to Winnipeg or Vancouver."

"And it was damn nice'a her, don'tcha think?"

"And it shows compassion for you, don't you think?"

"Sure does, and remember what Ah just finished doin' to that big bugger Donald," she shrugged. "Tol' ya she's on my side." Alice Mary sat up straight and her eyes flashed.

"You actually are beautiful."

"Thank you."

"And you do seem to share something with her... to have some of her in you."

"You can be in me too, Joe, Ah mean if you want."

He ran a hand across his face, "We must prepare to get out of town."

"Bet it'll be fun."

Joseph stared at the girl fancying herself a witch whom Lorelei had told him to take into the unforgiving wilderness, and swallowed. It was all too strange.

XXXII.

THE ATHABASCAN MAID ESTHER WAS IN JOSEPH AND MARY'S ROOM UP-
stairs at the Orpheum upon his arrival and had lain two caribou
hide parkas and snow pants on the bed. She smiled and slipped away
as Joseph inspected the clothes that had rabbit fur sewn inside them.
The hoods were lined with rabbit fur and trimmed with wolverine
fur ruffs so that one's breath wouldn't freeze upon them. The larger
had been worn and was stained on the forearms as if the wearer had
been stoking a smoky fire. A beautiful red, black, and white pattern of
porcupine quills ran down the arms from the shoulders of each parka
with geometric designs on the larger and floral ones on the smaller.
The small one had a black bird beaded upon the breast over the wearer's heart. Joseph sat on the bed and ran a hand across them.

I'm sorry, but you'll have to speed things up!

"Christ."

*We've never discussed him. Listen: I cannot influence the thoughts of
anyone well from a distance, only when nearby. Quite honestly it takes
a great deal of my time and energy, and Inspector MacAtee is planning
to arrest Alice Mary this very night. You must leave quickly.*

"That's wonderful. How did you get Esther to bring these clothes?" I asked. *Her mother made them for her and her brother. She's rather a good match for our little friend, don't you think? You're going to get some exposure to the Tr'ondek Hwech'in along this river yourself soon and you might as well dress like them, and they're the most suited to the climate.*

"Where are we to go?"

Head downriver like two Indians to Moosehide Village. Someone there will help. You must head for the town of Fortymile and up that river into Alaska. There's a village past the Mosquito Fork where you shall be safe, and I'll meet you as soon as I can. I'm still in Nome enjoying the company of an interesting life, but it takes its own good time. Conception is... oh, never mind.

"What are you talking about?"

There was a pause, *I'm trying to live a different life from the bearers of my line and trying to become worthy of something promised us long before I came into the world. Now, you must get that girl out of Gertie's. Esther's brother is arriving with a sled, but there are Mounties coming from Fort Herchmer right this minute to arrest Alice Mary!*

"I need to take—"

Put on the clothes and go!

Joseph pulled the outerwear on over his flannel shirt and found his pack in the bottom of a closet under a pile of girls' under things after a frantic search. He grabbed a thick wool cap and pulled the parka hood over his head, then stood before the mirror examining himself in Native array.

Stop preening and go! Take the door on the alley!

Joseph headed for the back of the theater and took the stairs to an unheated prop room where he unbolted the door to the alley and stepped into the cold night wind. A Native man stood on the runners of a sled with a team of nine dogs lying in the trammeled snow before him. The dogs got to their feet upon spying Joseph, and the Indian held a mittened hand out, gestured at the sled, and disappeared.

"Now what am I to do?"

I have precious little time to tutor you. Just watching from this distance takes a lot of concentration, and I have someone here who is demanding of my attention. Assume that things will work out and it shall come to you. Alice Mary has a lot of faith in me and is far too prone to test my good will although it's rather flattering. You could learn something from her in that regard.

Joseph stood on the sled runners, and as he pulled up the snow brake, a familiar ripple of laughter tickled his spine. *The dogs are easy; trust them. Got to go.*

As the team lurched forward, Joseph slipped off, almost going down face-first into the packed snow before he came up running and got a hand on the sled. "Damn it, Lorelei... *trust them?*"

There was only the hiss of the runners as he pulled the hood low. The sled came out onto Second and the dogs turned toward Gertie's. "Haw!" came out of his mouth. The team wheeled around a dozen big McKenzie River huskies sprawled before a freight sled that rose to their feet and let out a chorus of howls.

———

Alice Mary answered the door in an oversize woolen shirt and canvas pants with a smile on her face and a Bowie knife in her belt. A money belt bulged under the shirt, and a leather suitcase bound with thick straps and brass buckles sat in the parlor. "A Injun suit," she grabbed the clothes out of Joseph's hands, "if that snooty Inspector MacAtee could see me in these. 'No bloomers, no pants, ladies don't walk like that, blah-blah! A girl like you should be in a... *insta-tution!*'" She shrieked, "Nya! Ah'd like to show that fuckin—"

"He'll grant your wish if you dawdle! He is on the way to clap you in irons this very minute!"

She closed her mouth and shrugged, "Ah figured that. Well," Alice Mary dropped the pants and threw off the shirt, revealing a child-sized red woolen union suit underneath. She slipped into the Native clothes quickly, but had to pause to examine herself in the mirror. She held up a hand, "How!" was followed by a high-pitched giggle.

"Please, let's go."

"Don't be such a scardy-cat. We're runnin' to the woods with the wolves jus' like Ah seen in a dream. Look at them Injun dogs, look in their eyes, Joe, them are *wolves,* boy. You and me—"

"Damn it, come on!" Joseph seized her hand as he snatched up the suitcase, and was startled by a jolt coming from her flesh just like when he touched Lorelei. He fought the sudden impulse to pick up Alice Mary and kiss her, shook it off, threw her suitcase on the sled, and lashed it on with rope. Alice slashed the ropes binding a sun-bleached grizzly hide with her knife, slid it back in its sheath, and slipped under the hide and canvas sled bag. Joseph nodded, "Stay under there."

Her head disappeared as they pulled away.

He examined the sled as they reached the end of Church and turned up Front. Hopefully provisions were in it for their journey wherever they were bound. As the dogs stopped for a wagon loaded with firewood, he checked up and down the street. A small crowd was in front of the Monte Carlo, where a drunk was attempting to right himself at the edge of the sidewalk after knocking another man down.

Joseph was about to call mush when he heard a very British voice shouting, "Stop!" and froze.

Three Mounties in brown overcoats with double rows of brass buttons and shiny Enfield rifles on their shoulders approached from Fort Herchmer, led by Inspector MacAtee in a bearhide coat. Their high brown boots echoed on the planks as they marched toward the corner of Queen and Front under their bear fur hats, and MacAtee's right hand emerged from his pocket sheathed in a brown gauntlet. He held it up in front of him as he commanded, "Halt!"

"Good God," Joseph hissed, "I thought Lorelei was watching out for us."

An unintelligible sound came from the grizzly hide.

"There is no public drunkenness allowed in this town! Corporal Pippin, issue this man a citation, as well as the establishment that served him until he was in such a deplorable state. Double time!"

"Yes, Sir!" The Corporal bolted for the drunk, who stood watching the approaching Mounties.

"Stinkin' Yellaleg dummies!" The man growled as he fought for balance, holding his hands up before him in boxer's stance at the approaching Constable.

"Arrest him for that disrespect!"

"Sir," Another Mountie saluted, "hadn't we be getting on with it? I mean: there's a far more dangerous criminal awaiting us at this moment, eh?"

Joseph barked "Mush!" as the Mounties were preoccupied and the team took off across Front. They cut between two warehouses, hit the riverbank, and bounced onto the ice of the Yukon skirting a froze-in coal barge heading downriver with the lights of Front Street on their right. Sounds of music came and went as doors were opened and closed on saloons and melodeons. No one bore them any mind as they sped along in the dark with the dogs loping in the tracks of other sleds between empty fishing shacks. Soon they'd passed the lights of the mission and hospital at the end of town, and Dawson City was behind them.

Alice Mary's head emerged, "Close call, huh?"

"I'm glad that I recently emptied my bladder."

"Pshaw, Joe, you got no faith."

"Faith? That's odd coming from the likes of you... and they can follow our tracks from Gertie's front door."

"She'll think a' somethin'," Alice Mary put hands out to her sides as they sped along, "This is fun!"

Joseph stared at the moonlit smokestacks of steamboats wintered-in in a slough across the river and the faint glow of kerosene lamps from a shack beside them. His stomach growled. What were they going to eat?

Quit worrying. You'll grow old before your time.

Alice Mary burst into laughter, "she's right, Joe."

"You heard that!"

"You betcha."

———

Barking dogs announced Moosehide, two rows of low-slung log cabins facing the river with a white-steepled church at one end. A frozen caribou hide hung from an empty fish rack, and light shone from the tiny windows of a few cabins as fish wheels sat encased in hoarfrost above the shore ice like little Ferris wheels ridden by fairies in the silver light of a past-full moon.

"Whoa!" The sled came to a stop before a cabin the dogs seemed to know. Joseph gazed at the hills, wishing beyond hope that Lorelei would appear to lead them. "What now?"

Yellow light spilled from the door of a cabin, and the man who'd brought the sled to the Orpheum, who'd somehow beaten them back to his village, emerged. "Hello."

"How!"

"Stop it, Alice."

"You must hurry downriver. MacAtee will be here soon."

"What are we to—"

"Here," the man handed Joseph a worn leather rifle case and a jingling bag of shells, "got this from Jack McQuesten. It's a lucky gun. If you live, bring it back." He un-slung a holster from his shoulder with a big British Webley revolver in it and a belt of cartridges and handed them to Joseph as well. "Be careful passin' Forts Constantine and Cudahy if it's manned, and don't try and cross the border on the big river. Head up the Fortymile. My cousins in Ketchumstuk will hide the girl 'til breakup."

"How far is that?"

"In American territory after Franklin, Jack Wade and Chicken. Just stay left, follow the Mosquito Fork west, and you can't miss it."

"Why are you helping us?"

The man shrugged, "She asked us. She'll repay the favor. She's a Sacred Being. Watch out for big blows and hole-up in a cabin if one starts. This moon is damn windy and Cheechakos can't find their way without the moon or the stars."

Alice jumped off the sled, "Ah ain't gonna hide in no damn Injun village all winter!"

As the man turned toward his cabin, his voice dropped two octaves, "Maybe the Han Nation don't need no whores from Outside in their villages neither, or any other Nation in this country."

Joseph held up a hand, "We apologize. Thank you." He scowled at the moonlit peaks, "Turning into a real vacation, eh Miss Alice?"

"To hell with this!"

"You started it. I'm just here helping because she made me."

"Shit. We don't even know this fella's name. How are we 'sposed to find his cousins in the middle a' fuckin' nowhere?"

"Trust her, remember?"

"Shit! Double shit!"

Joseph burst into laughter.

Alice Mary responded with a smile, "So, at least give me the pistol."

He held up the holstered pistol and ammo but didn't hand them over. "Can you use it?"

"Damn straight."

"You'll have to keep it hidden under the—"

"Come *on*, Ah'm no dummy, Joe."

He held onto the gun. "Try and be a bit more considerate. After all, I'm here because of something you did," Joseph swallowed as he considered what she *had* done. Was it wise to trust her with the gun?

"Cut it out. Ah ain't gonna hurt you," she stomped her mukluks on the snow, "sweet fuckin' Jesus."

"I thought you were a witch."

"Oh shut up," she made an exasperated grunt, "gonna give me the gun?"

Joseph handed over the pistol, eliciting her flash of teeth in the moonlight, and turned back to the Indian who'd been watching in silence. "Could you tell us just a bit more about the trail?"

"Forget it, Joe. He's leavin' it up to Lorelei."

"You need food. There's none on the sled," the man waved them toward his cabin, "come in."

"Thank you."

Wasillie was his name. He didn't volunteer the name of his wife, who watched from where she sat on a bed sewing a hide. Each time Alice Mary wasn't looking at her, the woman stared hard at the little blonde, but when Alice glanced back, her eyes dropped to her work.

Wasillie gave them a bundle wrapped in oilcloth. "Dried Caribou, smoked salmon, and blueberry pemmican. The fish on the sled is for the dogs," he began to speak, but waved it off. "Better go."

Joseph glanced at Alice Mary, "You ready?"

She scowled, "Sure, let's go." She walked outside, jumped on the sled, and slid under the stiff hides and sled bag emitting a high-pitched note of misery. "And Ah wanta drive this thing too when Ah get a chance."

Joseph said, "Mush!"

The dogs headed for the middle of the river, made their way onto the ice, and gained speed.

XXXIII.

Pale peaks loomed beneath an ivory half moon. Alice Mary studied their surroundings and asked questions he mostly couldn't answer until she burrowed under the robes and fell silent. Joseph stood on the runners watching for rough ice and open leads. At times he'd shout 'Gee!' or 'Haw!' and the dogs would dutifully wheel left or right, slowing occasionally when they hit rough going. After a while the biggest challenge was staying awake. A breeze picked up, and he found himself trying to contract inside his clothes. He flexed his stiffening hands in the leather gloves and switched to thick mittens, sipping occasionally from a flask of water kept next to his body so it wouldn't freeze.

Up ahead a jumble of logs loomed over the gunwales of a lumber scow that had lodged on a gravel bar. Joseph guided the team into the leeside, out of the wind. "Whoa!" The dogs halted beside a log and he stepped off. He took a storm lantern from the sled, lit it with a match, and dropped the glass inside its wire basket over the sputtering wick. Alice Mary groaned and burrowed deeper under the robes as he rummaged for food. The dogs yipped as he levered one of four bundles, taking most of the sled out from under her and eliciting more groans from under the covers. He untied the rope holding it. Even in the cold a strong odor issued forth as he opened the oilcloth. Within was a mass of dried chum salmon packed in rows. The dogs barked and closed in on the sled with ropes of saliva rolling from their mouths that froze into ice and rattled across the river's surface as they fell from their faces amongst the tangling lines.

"Whoa, hold on, damn it!" Joseph grabbed the harness of the lead dog and dragged the team away from the sled. He tied the dog to the scow so they were spaced out again and reached for an armload of fish.

Whoa is right! Only two fish for each dog. You'll use up their rations and make them ill besides. They'll eat until they're too full to run, and that shall be the end of your journey... and you must boot the left rear foot of the right wheel dog, the brown one. You should have noticed she's starting to limp. They're good friends, and you must treat them properly, as well as them being your ticket to freedom of course.

"Oh," Joseph looked around, though he knew he'd find nothing, "thank you."

You're welcome.

The lead dog leapt up and licked his face, and Joseph sat down hard on the ice. As he pushed the dog away the dog's eyes flashed blood red, then sparkled with blue like sunlight upon the ocean. They shimmered with green like the iridescent quetzal feathers women wore on hats. The dog sat on his haunches with a big open-mouthed dog smile on his face. *Didn't recognize me, did you?*

"Lorelei."

Only for these few moments. I'm keeping an eye out for you two as I promised. It also helps to have a good nose.

Joseph wiped his face with a mitt. "You're good with animals."

Alice Mary was right about wolves. These dogs are the closest of all to wolves, you know.

"So what are we to do now?" He peered into the dog's eyes searching for his lover and fought a silly grin at the very thought.

The Mounted Police have telegraphed Fort Constantine to be on the lookout. They don't know about you yet, so you can pass at a distance and they'll probably not even stop you if she's under the robes. You could give it a try I suppose.

"A try... does that mean you're not sure we'll make it?"

I'm not omnipotent.

"Oh, great!"

There's no camping gear on the sled, by the way.

"What?"

Wasillie packed it on his other sled.

"What?"

It was very decent of him to say yes. I wasn't forcing him. Besides, you can't handle two sleds and he needs his other one. He can spare the fish, but he's going caribou hunting and it's enough of a hardship to give you this one. He's not wealthy and I must certainly compensate him twice over for the kindness. Joseph felt one of those quaking sighs coming on before the air began to tremble. *Things have a cost, and this is all a bother. I'll guide you to cabins but you must learn to drive the dogs on your own, which shouldn't be hard since you had some experience in the mountains coming over from Skagway. So far I've been stepping in but I'm rather busy. Anyway you have enough to sleep in with these robes if you two stay close.*

"Why are you doing this?"

Doing what?

"You know what! Sending me on this journey! Forcing me together with—"

"Who the hell are you talkin' to?"

Joseph growled, "Who the hell do you think?"

"Looks like you're talkin' to a dog, Joe."

He threw his hands in the air. "You said to believe in her, remember?"

"Oh," Alice Mary crawled off the sled and cracked her back. "Damn cold." She walked to the lead dog and knelt before him, "Hey, so you in there, Lorelei?" The dog's eyes flashed and Alice Mary nodded. "See, Joe, we got the best help in the world."

"Let's get going," he tossed her a strip of dried salmon, "try some of that."

Alice Mary turned it over in her mitten, examining it like some kind of insect, "Well," she put the fish in her parka and pointed at the lead dog, "she's gone." The dog's eyes had returned to one blue and one brown, it being their normal state of affairs, and his eager face was fixed on the salmon Joseph had set out of the team's reach at Lorelei's admonition. Joseph gave each dog two and they set to it instantly.

"Said to get 'em water soon."

"Where?"

"Overflow up ahead. Said to watch our footing and don't fall in. Says she fell in and died Halloween night, and got pulled out stiff as a board on All Saint's morning."

"Say what?"

"That's what she said, Joe."

"Then... we've been talking to a shade?"

"Nope, some Injun boy warmed her up real good."

"Oh," Joseph stared at the bluffs.

"Let's go. Ah'm plumb starvin' for some real food," Alice Mary jumped on the sled, "bet somebody's gonna feed us good soon."

He reached into the bag and handed her some pemmican. "For someone who just came into this you sure trust her."

"You should too. Hell, she saved you from pickin' at frozen dirt in a dark hole all winter and livin' on hardtack and beans like one a' them poor moles fartin' in the diggin's and workin' for wages. Look at all the fun you've had: women and champagne, good clothes, smokin' opium at parties with the high-tone poobahs, wakin' up 'tween two dance hall girls after workin' your dangle," she cocked her head, "ever think 'bout beddin' Kate?"

"Um, I—"

"Betcha did."

"Actually, I've thought about bedding every comely woman I've met since Lorelei took me in."

"That's natural. She just brought it out in ya."

"I suppose. Let's get moving."

"You know," she hopped on the sled as Joseph commanded the dogs to mush, "I almost never get any real pleasure with a fella. Jus hafta watch 'em squeezin' their eyes shut and groanin' like the devil when they do their stuff. It gets kinda borin'." She shrugged, "They don't even notice no-how."

Joseph stared straight ahead, avoiding her eyes as they gained speed.

"Did feel it sometime, what with fellas that really seemed to care and wasn't too old either. With a couple a' mean ones too. Felt kinda funny enjoyin' it with them bastards. Girls are different though. Honey Bee loved me like the dickens, and we both..." She sighed. "Guess when you been raped real young you kinda lose your taste for it less it's somethin' awful special."

"That is awful."

"You really got no idea what Ah'm talkin' 'bout."

He stared over the top of her head at the bobbing tails of the team. "I think I know what a woman feels more than most, thanks to Lorelei. Perhaps it's her gift, but I prefer to think of it as something from my own character that's emerged."

"Sure ya do, that's what men wanta think so they can keep struttin' 'round like a banty rooster. She says you and me are gonna have'ta have a go at it you know."

"Oh I suppose."

George MacAtee tugged a ball of ice off his mustache and it came free with several hairs in it. "Ow." He scowled in the glare off the river's ice. Here he was headed out after some teenage miscreant when Assistant Commissioner Wood was arriving for inspection. George had formed an excellent relationship with Sam Steele, Major General of the North-West Mounted Police, while Steele had been in charge of the Territory, and although George knew Commissioner Walsh well, the new man Wood was an unknown and he'd been looking forward to a formal introduction that might profit his career. Now he would miss Wood's visit entirely unless he apprehended that little whore swiftly.

At first he'd listened to Three-Way Annie's story of how little Alice Mary, the one the other girls called Baby, had killed that big man alone with disbelief, until Annie had shown him the holes in the wall of the crib she'd taken over from Alice. MacAtee had measured the width of the knife's blade and had Louis Pare, the best surgeon in the Territory, examine the wounds in the remains of Donald Johnson. Pare was an acknowledged expert in postmortems, and had rushed to the task after fetching his instruments from his bags upon arriving from Tagish. He said one in a piece of vertebrae was a perfect match, which was enough evidence for a warrant given the stories of Annie and other whores who had listened to Alice Mary throwing her knife into walls accompanied by lunatic shouts of rage. Annie told him how Alice Mary had spoken of "Gutting some sonofabitch," and of an even stranger tale, of a female ghost tearing a man's heart out. Alice Mary said the man was Fred Dodge.

Obviously the girl was criminally deranged. It was a shame. In the matter of what God had given her, she was quite lovely although she was known to be a foul-mouthed little tart. Still, she looked to be not much more than a child herself.

Who is helping her?

George's hand went to the butt of his revolver. Certainly the girl wasn't running a sled down the Yukon River by her lonesome, and whoever was with her might be a tussle. No matter, the Mounties always got their man eventually, or woman, or girl in this case. It must be some customer she'd tricked into taking her to his claim with promises of her favors. Not a dumb move that.

George was still smarting from the trip to Skagway. The scoundrel Soapy Smith was blessedly dead, but the town was an utter hellhole in comparison to the Canadian side. Dressing as civilians so as not to disturb the semblance of local authority had been a slap in the face, and George had been surprised that some of the men actually liked it. Going *undercover,* as they preferred to call it.

George was proud of his uniform and the authority that went with it. It was despicable that the Americans couldn't police their territory better. Blackguards, thugs, and desperados abounded across the border in Alaska and were constantly arriving to stir up the American miners on this side with talk of oppressive taxes and even secession from the Crown. It was the natural expression of not having a moral government with a real Monarch after all: a real Queen to look up to. Edward would have quite a pair of shoes to fill after assuming the Throne.

Perish the thought of her passing! He checked himself, said a quick prayer for the health of Victoria, and wished the young Prince well also. The thought of having a negative attitude toward the Crown or any member of the Royal Family wasn't within the space George allowed himself... the place he lived.

He straightened his back and thrust his chin into the frigid wind. There would be no murderers uncaught on the watch of George Duncan MacAtee. Such was his vow.

XXXIV.

L ATE THAT NIGHT, JOSEPH NOTICED A BROKEN LOG PALISADE AND A GATE
yawning on a snow-covered expanse with log buildings visible
within. He pulled off the river, fighting to keep his eyes open. He'd
nearly lost his perch on the runners twice. There was no thrill to this
journey, only exhaustion from holding on and watching the dogs. His
face ached and felt frozen, and he wished he could grow a real beard.

The huskies pulled onto the untrammeled snow of the compound
beside a sagging hitching post, and Joseph staggered off the sled. Alice
Mary was sleeping. He went to the door of the biggest building and
peered inside. Faint moonlight shone through windows and between
skewed logs, reflecting off shards of glass amongst dark wads of sod
fallen from the roof onto a long mess table. Snow had drifted across
the floor that was crisscrossed with the tracks of fox and wolverine.
He returned to the sled, lit the storm lantern, and turned toward the
smaller cabins. One was in much better shape and appeared as if people
used it for laying up on their journeys. There was glass in the tiny single
window, a bunk, a cast iron stove, and a welcome pile of wood in a
box beside it.

He decided to start a fire before waking Alice Mary, but had to open the cabin door when smoke began to back up in the pipe. He walked outside coughing and banged on the pipe to loosen whatever was blocking the draft. A mushroom of sparks erupted as a bird's nest burst into flames.

"Hey! What the hell!"

"Have a nice nap?"

"Is it warm in there?"

"Not very and rather smoky. I'd recommend it over sleeping altogether in the out-of-doors however."

"Shit!" Alice Mary sprang off the sled and hustled into the cabin emitting high-pitched shrieks of misery.

"Might as well bring those robes. They're all we have to sleep in."

"Will you get 'em? Ah'm *freezin'!*"

Joseph yanked their sleeping gear off the sled, brought it in, and dumped it on the bed in a stiff pile.

Alice Mary hunched over the stove looking small. Joseph put more kindling and a few sticks in and shut the iron door on the blaze. She turned as he went out. "What are you doin'?"

"Taking care of the dogs, remember?"

"Oh, yeah."

He lingered after he'd fed the team and checked the feet of each dog, who curled up with noses buried in their tails as soon as they had fish in their bellies. The sounds of Alice Mary stoking the stove came from the cabin. The stars were hard and bright in the thin air, and the aurora was a green bow in the north. He brushed snow off a chopping block next to a snow-covered pile of wood and sat down.

In the west a dark band blocked the stars: bad weather coming. Joseph picked at ice on his upper lip and glanced at the cabin. Slipping under those robes with little Alice Mary wasn't enticing.

Oh? She's quite a beauty Joseph.

"She's a whore and a killer, Lorelei."

I've been called the same. In fact I am.

"But... you're far more than that."

As is she. She's a bright if uneducated girl who only acts tough to hide the fear that twists her heart for those who are cruel beyond understanding. She needs you tonight although she won't admit it.

Joseph stared at the cabin. "What shall become of her?"

What shall become of the both of you?

"I should very much like to know that. Any clues or riddles, my Goddess?"

There was a soft popping in the chill air, and he knew she was gone. Wolves broke into song in the spruce-dark hills above the old post, and two of the huskies raised their heads with ears pricked. The rest lay unmoving, too tired to care. He headed for the cabin.

Alice Mary had hung her outerwear on a peg by the stove and sat wrapped in a red Hudson's Bay blanket rubbing small hands over the meager heat. Her hair was a golden halo in the lantern light, with her upturned nose in sharp profile against the dark logs. Green eyes watched him from a young girl's face that looked afraid. Joseph remembered what Lorelei had said, and a smile crept across his lips. It was wonderful to have such insights into a woman's soul given at times by a genuine Goddess.

"What the fuck are you laughin' at?"

"What? Oh, no, I'm not laughing."

"You look like it."

Joseph sat on the bunk beside her as there was nowhere else. "You must have come to think very little of men."

"Why?"

"Well, as you said, you see them at their... in their—"

"At their worst?"

"Well, yes."

"Not all, Joe. Tol' ya that. Some fellas are at their best in a bed. You oughta know. They can drop their guard Ah guess, and be honest for a while." She grinned, having regained the initiative as soon as he'd ventured his thoughts, "Anyway what kinda work is there for me? A girl who people always called pretty but nothin' else, who ain't got no formal education, who is too small for hard work, and who knows so little 'bout a trade? Somebody who got broke in too young for jus' what Ah'm doin' now?" She stood up, almost fell into the stove, and cursed.

"Many comely young women find a husband who—"

"Fuck that!" Alice kicked a block of wood on the floor. "Ow," she grabbed her foot. "Ow! My toes!"

He let out his breath. *Fuck* wasn't in common parlance where he'd come from, and was only used by the rough crowd and wanton women of Dawson in small doses, but it made up more of Alice Mary's vocabulary than anybody he'd ever known. "Don't injure yourself. We might have to walk."

She laughed through gritted teeth. "Ah don't know *what* Ah want, Joe! Ah jus' wanta be different from the things in this fuckin' world other people say are all there *is* for me! There's gotta be somethin' else!"

"You want to be rich."

She looked him up and down, then exhaled loudly. "Everybody wants that... but what do you do with it? Ah mean besides not havin' to suck the half-limp willy of some drunk miner who's old enough to be my goddamn granddad?" She glared, "And what do ya do when you're rich? Does that make you better, or wiser, or happier with yourself? Ever wake up next to somebody and you're so goddamn alone you could die? You know why so many girls stay in this business after they're rich, Joe?"

"I—"

"It's all they know. The parties, the excitement, even some fella you started to like callin' you a dirty little whore after you seen him cry like a baby and tell you his fuckin' life story, and he's had his damn dick in you, and left seed that could sprout if you didn't take care. You laugh, 'Ha-ha,' and they laugh back, and you tell 'em how much they make you feel good, and everybody acts like friends again until you get them the hell outta there," she brushed hair from her face, "Ah don't really feel like it, but if you should care to have me now Ah guess you may."

"I don't either. Besides, I really don't want anybody who doesn't want me also."

"Boy, Lorelei sure spoiled you. 'Course you ain't built up a head a'steam goin' without yet. Try a year out in the bush Joe, or even the next few days. Then we'll see."

"I really wouldn't want to be with someone who didn't want me also."

"Then you ain't like every other fella in the goddamn world. Just wait a couple'a days, you'll be pesterin' me right and left. 'Specially after what you been used to with Mary and Lily. Betcha a sack a'gold."

"I don't know."

"Ah do," she yawned. "Got any water?"

"No."

"Let's melt snow in that tub."

"Good idea." Joseph grabbed the tin washtub hanging from the wall, put on his parka and mukluks, and went outside.

Alice Mary lay on the bed staring at the wisps of roots coming through the rafters and closed her eyes. She let out her breath, and with an effort that made her body clench, pushed out into the vast night demanding that Lorelei see her.

Damn.

"Gotcha!"

A quaking sigh trembled on the air. *You do. We are very close, little sister.*

"Ah know Ah'm a witch."

Perhaps you are.

"If they catch me, Ah would suffer bein' burned at the stake rather than abandon my love o' you." There was silence, and Alice Mary sat up and glanced around as if Lorelei were just over her shoulder. "Lorelei?"

Very well then . . .

———

Her chin pressed against her chest as she stared at the ragged holes that pikes and the heavy ball of a fusel musket had made in her pale flesh. The pile of dry leaves and birch branches around her bare legs was bright with her blood and her long black hair was soaked in it, drawing red lines across the branches as she moved. The sun burned her, yet she welcomed it with a hunger that had ruled her kind for thirty thousand years and called out to it with every corpuscle of her being. She felt the eyes of men upon her bloody breasts, and their mindless lust even now for this ravaged form.

"Striga! Vala! Witch!" voices called as people jostled for a better view of her suffering.

She caught a man's stare in her gaze and fixed him like a hare in the talons of a bird. The priest in his miter cap and robes gasped and tried to make the sign of the cross, but she wouldn't allow him, pinning his arms at his sides to exult in his fear. Air rattled her torn lung and pink bubbles sprouted from the holes in her chest, yet her soul was still strong. If she had time she could heal; she would live. The flames were to assure that she wouldn't.

A tide of weakness rushed through her, she let him go and the priest cried out, pushing away through the crowd where she stood tied to the trunk of a laurel tree.

Her gaze wandered to her lover's head spitted on a pike. The lips she'd kissed were blackened in death, and the eyes that had sparkled with joyful visions born of love were dull and thick with mortal decay.

That gun was so fast. She'd roused Marcelle from his slumber when the angry red flair of a mob awoke her from her dreams thinking they had time to flee, but men with guns had waited upon a hill beyond the town's gate. Only one ball had found her but it was enough. She'd lain as if dead from the impact, listening to her lover's pleading, then his screams as his bowels were torn from his body with scythes and pitchforks to the shouts of villagers. She gazed at Marcelle's mouth, frozen in that last scream.

I shall never know my child. That pain was more than the sharp steel that had torn her insides, or the mad hatred of her attackers. *She shall not be born!*

She lifted her head and cried out to the sky.

People stepped back as if from the bite of a lash and made the sign of the cross. A mother covered the eyes of her child. The girl pushed her hand away.

A torch landed at her feet and she watched dry leaves curl as twigs caught fire. Flames scorched her calves and began to lick at her thighs. Her multicolored eyes darted about the crowd as her flesh began to blister and sear. The girl who'd pushed her mother's hand away clasped work-roughened hands before her chest, staring back at her with love and grief. She seemed dwarfed in the darkness of the mob: a single white flower rising from a forest of fear.

The dying daughter of Lilith reached out like a mother taking a babe in her arms. She was at the end of her journey to lay down a burden she had borne for thirty thousand years of memory and six hundred in this ever youthful form. Her heart opened like the cone of a burning pine, and she spread her seed.

Thunder rolled across the town. The girl's eyes grew huge as *knowing* awoke within her, followed by great pain. The burning woman's eyes were blue and green and sparkled with the living color of blood, a river of blood that ran hot and unbroken from the place whence they both had come. Those eyes looked through her own into a future the girl could *see.* The child cried out and collapsed on the stones of the square.

———

Joseph pushed the door open with his boot while balancing the tub of snow in his hands, but a sharp shriek made him drop it on the floor with a crash. Alice Mary lay on the bed with her back arched like a bow, quaking as if lightening had struck her. Her shoulders and feet were barely touching the bed as the breath rattled out of her chest in the throes of a seizure.

"My God!" He threw arms around her, but she bucked like a mad thing and tore at his face with black nails. His blood speckled her fair skin in the yellow light of the kerosene lamp, and he jerked away and wiped his cheeks. *"Alice Mary!"*

Air ground out of her chest and tapered to a whimper. Tears coursed down her cheeks as she stared at the ceiling. Joseph let out a moan of his own and wrapped arms around her again. His face slid in tears and blood against her smooth cheek.

"Oh!"

"Alice Mary! What... what happened?"

She squeezed him hard until the air left his lungs. Alice Mary pushed away, sat up, and brushed hair from eyes twice their size before lifting a tear-streaked face to his. "She *touched me* Joe! Damn... but Ah surely did *ask* for it." She put a palm to his cheeks, "Did Ah do that?"

"I, yes," Joseph wiped his face with the back of a hand, and for no reason he could name began to cry.

XXXV.

CORPORAL PIPPIN RUBBED FROST FROM HIS EYELASHES AND SALUTED smartly, "Someone was here not two hours ago, Inspector."

George MacAtee stroked his mustache as he examined the trammeled snow. The two sets of tracks were obviously those of a man and a smaller person, either a youth or a woman. It would be wonderful to know which, but he felt a certainty. "Speedy little strumpet."

"What? Oh, yes Sir. Do you think it's them?"

"Who else? And why not stop at a roadhouse if they wanted to rest rather than old Fort Reliance? This place isn't exactly a hot toddy and a warm bed after all."

"There are Natives who prefer solitude and miners with gold who—"

George put a boot on a chopping block where the snow had been dusted away by someone sitting on it and stared downriver. "They've gone back onto the ice and the wind is picking up. Their tracks shall be hard to find if things get worse." He examined the darkening sky in the west, "But they shall stay on the river."

"That they shall, I'd wager," Constable Jones nodded, "that front will be upon us before noon, Sir."

"Indeed. The Post at Constantine has been notified by telegraph to be on the lookout for any two on a sled. They should wrap this up by afternoon if we don't catch them first."

"That would be a relief."

"I couldn't agree with you more, Corporal. However, I would prefer we apprehend them ourselves. Make sure your weapons are ready. She may well have some black-hearted scoundrel armed to the teeth and ready to fight for her. These base women do such things to foolish men with galling regularity."

Corporal Pippin drew his big Webley from its holster, broke open the action at the top, and rotated the cylinder in the frigid breeze. He checked each .455 cartridge to make sure it wasn't jammed and snapped the gun shut with a dull click. The others checked the actions of their weapons also, as gun oil had a bothersome tendency to gum up in the subarctic.

When all was in order, MacAtee lit his pipe and they headed onto the ice following sled tracks on the wind-polished surface. The sun was moving farther south each day, and was at their backs as they headed northwest. It would be difficult for someone up ahead to see them in the glare of late morning, and George anticipated apprehending the culprits around each turn and returning by midnight this very eve. He took a puff of the Cavendish tobacco he'd obtained for next to nothing from Maggie Elder, who like many women used her tobacco store in Grand Forks as an adjunct to prostitution. Maggie had good reason to keep in his good graces and always could be depended on to come up with something worth smoking. Actually George wouldn't have bothered her even if he'd had to buy it. Of course, if she'd been better-looking he might have partaken of her favors occasionally as many a Mountie did with the prettier working girls. Such a relationship was something no woman of the night in the Klondike would ever dream of divulging unless she was half-mad. The NWMP would have the strumpet in the coldest cell at the post and bound for Outside before she could grab her hat. Men would be men after all, but to impugn the reputation of a servant of the Crown was something even the basest whore knew not to attempt. It was a slap in the face no man would tolerate, let alone the effect it would have on his family, church, or fiancé, God forbid. There were unwritten rules after all, and such things had always been the way of the world and always would be.

Wrong, George.

"Wha . . ?" George inhaled smoke and broke into coughing, lost his balance, and grabbed at the sled.

Corporal Pippin glanced over his shoulder, but returned to his team upon seeing the expression upon his superior's face.

George shook his head, cleared his throat, spat, and swore under his breath. That voice was clear as a bell, a bell whose tolling awoke memories of opening night at the Orpheum and of eyes he'd sworn he could never forget. Strange thoughts roiled up inside him, fought to surface, and slid back under an opaque ocean with a wink and a grin. He saw a pale face for an instant, with full lips spread in a scornful smile. *Damn,* someone was *laughing* at him! Some woman . . .

Indeed.

"Where are you, demon!"

Oh come on. Do you call your most elevating moments with a woman demonic, truly? I've seen them, love.

"*Who* is speaking to me!"

My, such an air of command. Have you read Ozymandias?

"Of course, I went to Eton, damn it! Shelly was—" George froze at the realization he was talking to *voices,* and an icy serpent wandered up his spine. *Am I falling into madness?* The pipe fell from his mouth, and he grabbed at it as it bounced off the birch frame of the sled. It rattled on the ice, bounced again, and landed under the runners with a pop.

"Damnation! Whoa!" He stood on the snow brake, almost tipping the sled before the dogs came to a halt fifty feet on. George ran toward the shards of his favorite meerschaum bowl and picked up a piece with the carved face of a bearded Teutonic warrior. The nose was broken and bushy eyebrows jutted over sockets stuffed with ice. He cursed and hurled the piece across the river.

"What happened, Sir?"

"Ah . . .just growing too complacent while mushing, Corporal. My fault entirely."

"Shame about that pipe."

"Damn straight." George muttered as he walked to his sled.

———

Joseph squinted against the glare and listened to the hissing of the runners. Alice Mary was sitting up, staring at the bluffs across the river. She was different this morning, devoid of the harlot's banter, swearing, and smug comments he'd come to expect. The scratches on his cheeks stung in the cold, and he wiped a mitten across his face while watching smoke drifting from a lone cabin in the hills.

"Sorry 'bout that."

"What?"

"The scratches, you were rubbin' 'em."

"How did you know?"

"Felt it Joe, like lotsa things... like them nine wolves up there by that patch a' trees."

Joseph glanced up at the bluffs and saw silhouettes against the hard blue sky. He turned south and shaded his eyes from the glare. In the west the sky was the color of steel. "That cold front is almost here."

"You believe me, right?"

"Why not? You've been walking in Lorelei's country and I hardly know a thimble-full of it myself."

"Folks would say we're both crazy Ah 'spose."

He laughed, "I certainly never planned this. I'd still like to find gold next summer, but now I'm not sure I could live out here and not go crazy dreaming of Lorelei. I wonder what Mary's about?"

"Thinkin' 'bout killin' Jack Finley. With you and Lorelei gone he's pesterin' her like hell again."

"Well I hope she doesn't. I've had quite enough trouble with girls killing people."

"She won't, it ain't her way," Alice Mary yawned. "They're behind us."

He glanced over his shoulder.

"Not that close, Joe."

Joseph sighed and chewed a chapped lip. "Well, at least she's keeping one of us posted." Getting Lorelei's information secondhand was rather a pain. He much preferred to be conversing with her himself.

"She's up there in that pack'a wolves right now," Alice Mary pointed, "lookin' outta the leader, a great big black male. Guess she likes the boys. He's got golden eyes and a lovely stripe'a silver down his back. Damn, but he's big."

As Joseph studied the silhouettes on the bluff, something in him reached out to them as naturally as reaching with his hands and he begged her to speak to him. "We'll have to go right past Fortymile, either way."

"It shouldn't be that hard for her. She'll jus' make 'em see somebody else, don'tcha think?"

"Good bet. It wouldn't be that hard I suppose."

"No, not for her."

They rode in silence as the huge ravens of the north patrolled the river. Two bald eagles perched in a snag over an open lead gave them a yellow-eyed stare as they skirted a coal barge run aground in the fall. Chunks of coal were frozen in the ice where someone had dropped them from a sled while carrying the windfall to their cabin.

"You know you an' me are never gonna be the same, Joe?"

"Yes. I only wonder if she's going to let us remember all this. She hides the memory of herself away with most of those she's touched you know."

"The *men,* Joe. Women can keep secrets. It's necessary to our kind."

"You sound like someone much older."

Alice Mary glanced over her shoulder with a peaceful expression on her doll's face, "Ah am today."

"Where did she take you?"

"To... to one of her ancestors, or cousins anyway. Ah don't even know her name but she died before she could bear a daughter. You know they gotta have a daughter to carry on. Must take a hell of a long time for her kind to have a baby."

"I wonder why?"

"Ah guess they gotta learn a hell of a lot more than we do." Alice Mary made a little laugh that wasn't bitter or cynical, but that of a young girl, "We sure must look like silly little things to her, jus' fussin' and fuckin' and fightin' and breedin' all the time."

"I'd say sex is rather central to her existence."

"Yep," she turned to look for the wolves, but they were gone.

A small river opened on the right, and they skirted the thin ice around a lead where the two waters met and hugged the opposite shore. She had to get out of the sled where the ice was pushed into ridges by the pressure of the current, and they rocked the sled over the uneven surface as the dogs found the best route.

"I wonder what all the bright stuff is when I'm with her making love," Joseph said as he pushed the sled's crossbar.

"What?"

"I remember *some* things, Alice, and there are these... filaments that one sees. They seem to be full of light, but for the life of me I cannot focus on them. It's just so hard to describe."

She tugged on the front of the sled coming off a ridge just as the dogs pulled it free, sat down hard, and there was a cracking sound.

"Whoa!" Joseph threw up his hands, slid toward her, and grabbed her mitten.

Alice Mary got carefully to her feet and let out her breath. "What's a... filament?"

"Like a thread, but something that seems alive of its own accord in this case. I've noticed them every time my eyes are closed when we make love."

"Ah wanta make love to her."

"I, uh, gathered that."

"You think Ah could?"

"How should I know?"

"Ah mean Ah *know* Ah could. Ah just wonder if she'll ever let me."

He shrugged, "She's done quite a bit for you anyway."

"Yep."

The distant sounds of barking echoed off the bluffs upriver, and Joseph glanced over his shoulder. "I think we should be getting on our way!"

"Shit, let's move!"

They began to run alongside the sled, and she jumped in when they hit the smoother surface. Joseph got back on the runners.

"Maybe they're gonna catch us! Ah tol' her Ah'd suffer the death of a witch." She gulped air, "Maybe she's takin' me up on it!"

"People don't believe in witches anymore and even if they did they wouldn't burn them. Murderers are another matter however." He yanked his gaze from behind to watch their path, "They have the gallows for that."

"What about Injuns? They believe in such, don't they?"

"I don't think they'd consider a woman in that condition evil at all. Remember what Wasillie said? He called her a Sacred Being."

"Let's go see some Indians then!"

"That sounds like a good idea! Mush!"

The dogs picked up the pace as they rounded a bend and the ice smoothed. Ahead on the right was a low-slung cabin with its peeled logs a deep umber color in the afternoon sun, and in front was a tall pole with a Union Jack hanging limp in the still air.

"Oh damn."

The words had hardly left Joseph's mouth when he noticed a sled coming downriver. The barrel of a rifle was cradled in the arm of the driver, and it glittered in the sun before the sun was gone as the storm front in the west blotted it out. The Union Jack began to lift and flutter from its pole, and the approaching team let out a chorus of yips and barks that were answered by their own team. Alice Mary opened the rifle case and slid the gun toward Joseph. She fumbled under the robes for the revolver.

Cold fear percolated through him. Were they to be apprehended to be carried off like common criminals or caught in gunplay that would leave someone injured or dead? *Is she going to shoot?*

The sled was nearly upon them and they could see the broad face of the Indian driving it. He grinned and held up a hand as his team came to a halt, "Good to see you! Don't worry folks, she came to me in a dream."

"Oh," they said.

"Hurry up." He motioned toward the cabin with its flag snapping in the stiffening breeze.

They followed with eyes wide and wary. When they reached the cabin the Indian directed them to take their team around back, and they tied them between a smokehouse and a row of fish racks. Joseph hurriedly fed the dogs. The Indian had tied his team out front and he led them inside. He shook their hands. "I'm Stick Sam, Special Constable Stick Sam. Ma's Stick Indian and Pa's Han. I guide for the Mounties."

"Oh."

"Been waiting for you. Gotta be real careful. Don't want to lose this job. She promised me a girl from the Raven Clan. I'm Wolf Clan. Hell, I'd help her anyway. It ain't every day you meet a Sacred Being after all."

"No, um, not at all."

Stick Sam's broad smile bobbed under a battered beaver hat, "Okey-dokey, you two stay put." He opened the door on a gust of snowflakes and walked outside.

Alice Mary laughed, "That's what Ah call service!" She turned to examine the room. Fox, marten, bear, and wolverine furs covered the walls and hung from the rafters. She made a complete circle and sat down in a bent willow rocking chair beside a cast iron stove. Alice kicked off her mukluks, wiggled her toes, and balanced the big Webley pistol on her lap in her small hands.

"Alice, would you put that away?"

"Why?"

"If you trust her as much as you say, you won't need it."

"So? Ah like it."

"You're much too inclined to violence."

"Do Ah scare ya?"

Joseph let out his breath. "Somewhat. Not for my own safety mind you, but for that of others. After all you have killed a man and I can't forget that."

"Wonder what that Stick Sam's gonna do?"

"I suppose he'll meet whoever is after us and send them on their way with a story, I hope."

"They must be awful close." Alice Mary stepped to the small window and peered out on the Yukon River, "Guess we ain't so fast, huh?"

"Ho!" George held up a gloved hand, and his men approaching the Indian did the same. He recognized the man. It was Stick Sam, one of the Special Constables recruited from the First Nations. They'd proven invaluable in the last few years, being intimate with the country and tough as nails when things needed to get done. Dozens of miscreants had been rounded up with their help, including two scoundrels who were awaiting hanging in Dawson City this very moment.

"Stick Sam, jolly good to see you!" As George stepped off the sled, his legs spread on the slick ice and he fought for balance. The dry flakes were making the surface as slick as if it were wet and would make travel faster until it began to pile up, but any tracks left by teams would be hidden also. He brushed snowflakes off his eyebrows and extended a hand.

"Inspector MacAtee," Sam shook, "Long time."

"We are after a young woman on a sled, more properly a girl. She's a slightly built blonde who is most likely in the company of some miscreant, and is wanted for a most awful murder in Dawson City."

Sam whistled, "I'd sure notice that. Ain't seen no woman, just a guy on a sled with a black beard 'bout a hour ago with his son sleepin' under some robes. Looked plenty mean though. I stop him to check on what he's doin', and he says he's goin' to Belle Isle and up to his claim on American Creek. Kid didn't wake up. He says the boy got typhoid and they're gonna see a doctor in Fortymile. Didn't get too close. Saw yellow hair though, awful long for a boy."

"Sir, that's got to be them!"

"Indeed, and they're headed for Eagle City. They're calling it that instead of Belle Isle now, Sam. Be sure and use the proper designation from here on out so as not to confuse travelers."

The two younger Constables gazed longingly at the cabin. George could see them lounging by the stove if he dared stop and he cleared his throat, "Let us be gone. We have the chance to catch them before Twelvemile and you men will be in for commendations if we do." He turned to Sam, "Good work Constable. Your powers of observation are admirable. Keep an eye out for anything else suspicious."

Sam saluted, "You betcha."

George returned the gesture as he stepped back onto his sled and waved. "Mush!"

Sam waved back and glanced up. "I await my bride from the blood-line of Chiefs," he whispered under his breath, "as beautiful as a spring dawn."

Soft laughter rippled on the breeze. *And I keep my word, love.*

Stick Sam began a chuckle that grew into a laugh as he headed to his cabin.

XXXVI.

JOSEPH'S HEAD JERKED UP. HE SAW A SMILE ON SAM'S FACE AND RETURNED to nodding in the rocking chair beside the stove. Alice Mary was asleep on the bed.

"Gotta get goin'," Sam walked to the stove, lifted a burner, and put a cast iron saucepan over it, "wanta eat?"

"Yes," Alice Mary sprang up. "Thank you!"

"No bother," Sam stuck a spoon in the pan, "Stew'll heat up quick. Made it last night." He put a tall smoke-blackened coffee pot on another burner and a box of pilot bread from the cupboard on the table.

Alice Mary sat at the table and lifted one of the big flat crackers from the box. "Got any jelly?"

"Lotsa marmalade. Got orange, grapefruit, and lemon curd."

"Yum."

Sam put three jars on the table, wiped a spoon with a rag, threw it down, and turned back to the stew.

Joseph sat across from Alice, who grinned as she handed him a disk of pilot bread with lemon curd smeared on it.

Sam stirred the stew. "You guys don't have no idea where you are, do ya?"

"No, not really."

"People die easy out here. I coulda caught you before Fort Reliance even though you had Wasillie's team. I grew up across the river in Nuklako."

"We're lucky I suppose."

"Damn lucky, 'course you got *her*." Sam put two bowls down and ladled stew into them. Alice Mary sniffed it warily. "Curry powder. Kinda different, huh? Betcha never had moose curry before."

"It's food," Joseph took a spoonful and nodded. "Thank you."

"You're welcome."

Alice Mary lifted some to her lips and a disappointed expression crossed her face. She sighed loudly and spread orange marmalade on another piece of pilot bread. Sam shrugged and poured her another cup of coffee. "Got any sugar and cream?"

"Sure," Sam took a small sack of granulated sugar from a cabinet and put an unopened can of condensed milk on the table. Alice Mary poured sugar into her cup, then took the big Bowie knife from her belt and stabbed two holes in the can. "Nice knife," Stick Sam nodded, "good and sharp."

"Kilt a fella with it couple'a days ago but it's clean. You should 'a seen the look on his god-awful face." She wiped stew from her spoon and used it to stir her coffee, "Ever make love to a killer, Sam?"

Sam ran thick fingers across a wind-burned face and pinched his nose. His mouth opened, but nothing came out. He shook his head, "Nope."

She smirked, "Funny how a fella so big can have such a itty-bitty pecker. No wonder he was so goddamn mean, what with that poor little thing for a dangle."

Sam stared at the ceiling.

"Alice..."

"Sorry. You know, they say if you love a witch, your soul will never go to heaven."

Sam stared at the floor, "Indian Nations don't got no witches, just wise women with powers."

Alice Mary grinned, "Ah like that Sam, a lot."

"I wish you'd stop talking about witches all the time Alice."

"Why, Joe? After bein' a lover o' Lorelei Ah'd think you'd accept somethin' simple as a witch."

"She's not a witch, she's—"

"A *Goddess* Joe. Can't you see that's what she *is?* A goddamn Goddess on earth right here in the fuckin' flesh. She's the reason witches *are,* she's the livin' proof for us all. Hell, she's ours, and nobody else's, and girls gotta know."

"She speaks real good Hwech'in, an' Stick, an' Chinook, an' Ahtna, an' Tanacross, an' Gwich'in too, that's for sure. She took my spirit flyin' over this country like a eagle and showed me the girl she chose for me in Ketchumstuk Village." Sam's fingers wrapped around the little bundle hanging from a thong around his neck and he glanced at the rafters, "She's a Sacred Being, is all I know."

Alice Mary nodded, "She was in a wolf on our way here."

"And in our lead dog before that."

"Aiee! I'm *Wolf Clan!* I would like to have just one chance in this life to see from the eyes of a wolf like the great seers of my tribe!" Sam stomped a foot on the floor, "Goddamn."

"Maybe she'll let ya."

Sam stood up, "Hope she does Miss, but we can't delay all day. You two ready?"

"Where we goin'?"

"I told the Mounties that a big man with a black beard and a little yellow-haired person hidin' under robes was on a sled headed for Belle Isle, I mean Eagle, so they're goin' there. We're behind 'em now and we can go up the Fortymile. We gotta watch out for American whiskey men near the border though. They come across at night to sneak past the Mounties and I track 'em for the bounty and the Queen. We head up to this village—"

Joseph sighed and stood up, "I guess we're going to Ketchumstuk."

Alice Mary stood, "I want a bath."

"No baths 'til Franklin at least."

"How long is that?"

"A day up the Fortymile past the border, maybe two if the weather's bad."

"Then I'll take a bath now."

"Miss, we don't have—"

She strode to the metal tub in the back of the cabin, and when it was apparent they were going to wait for her to bathe, Sam helped her heat water. Alice Mary hung a blanket for a curtain across the corner of the cabin with the tub, but when the tub was steaming, she stepped out of her clothes in full view before stepping behind it. Sam stared as Joseph rummaged for something else to eat.

———

The short day was half done and it was snowing by the time they got going. Sam gazed into the air and muttered.

"She'll come up with somethin' Sam," Alice Mary said brightly as she hopped on the sled. Her clean golden hair was brushed back in a barrette of caribou leather beaded with a big black bird of porcupine quills and fastened with a polished needle of red mammoth ivory from the Klondike hills.

The dogs were dark silhouettes in the dusk. Joseph didn't hear Sam shout mush as his team took off downriver, and they followed with snowflakes tickling their cheeks. Darkness fell with only the light of a shrouded moon through clouds. They occasionally skirted patches of jumble ice, changing sides as Stick Sam moved away from an open channel with only the diffused glow of the moon filtering through snow. They swung out to avoid the lights of cabins on their right where the Twelvemile River emptied into the Yukon. The barking of dogs was muffled by snow, and they sped on with Alice Mary huddled under the robes in a white heap.

Long hours later Sam slowed and Joseph's team nearly ran up on them. "Whoa!" Sam shouted. "Fortymile's on the left. We got to stay in the middle 'case the ice's rough where the rivers meet. Fort Constantine's on the right after we turn upriver so we gotta be quiet."

Alice Mary brushed snow off her head and stretched, "Any good-time girls workin' Fortymile?"

"Used to be plenty, but all of the lookers are in Dawson now. Ain't nobody there who could hold a candle to you, anyway."

Fortymile sprawled on a wide tongue of gravel at the mouth of the river by the same name. The yellow glare of kerosene lamps shone dimly from a row of one and two-story log buildings that fronted the river behind the shapes of small vessels froze-in for the winter, and a single sternwheeler sat locked in ice at a dock. They made an arc around the half-empty town and headed up the Fortymile River. On the shore to their right, the dim outlines of a stockade and the lighted windows of log blockhouses shone through falling snow.

"The dogs don't even bark," Alice Mary whispered.

"I wonder how she does it?"

"Who knows? Maybe she'll tell us someday."

"What are you going to do when we get there?"

"Ah don't know. Ah was goin' to Nome where the strikes are and Ah wanta meet Sadie Earp, but maybe there's somethin' else she's got planned for me. Who knows?"

Ahead, Sam stopped and waved frantically with a hand to his lips.

"It's all right," She whispered. "We got Lorelei—"

Joseph squeezed her shoulder. She fell silent and ducked under the sled bag.

A sled was coming down the middle of the Fortymile, and their dogs strained toward the other team, growling under their breath and yipping softly. As it stopped, a tall figure stepped off with the unmistakable shape of a rifle cradled in his arms. Sam stepped off his sled and walked toward the driver, who appeared to be around Joseph and Alice Mary's age, with his hands to his sides.

"What do you think's happenin'?"

"I don't know, Alice."

Sam returned and the other sled resumed its journey, skirting Fortymile and hugging the middle of the river just as they had. "My cousin Pete Pingo. He's headin' to Dawson with furs." Sam shook his head. "Hope he don't lose it all. He don't drink, but he sure does like pretty girls."

"Why is he staying away from town?"

"Don't like bein' bothered. Them Mounties will take a tenth of his uncle's gold for taxes and he'll never see it again, and maybe give him grief for even havin' it," Sam's voice rose, "and it's from our land, and he lives on the American side too."

"Oh."

"Says whiskey men are all over upriver. They wanted to trade with him, so he tol' them he didn't have anything 'cept fish and asked for some whiskey on a promise. Best way to make them lose interest real quick."

"How did you know he wasn't one of them?"

Sam's teeth flashed in the moonlight as he slid a pistol from his parka, "Didn't. Lucky he didn't see our little friend here though. He'd wanta talk her up for certain."

They resumed their journey. The ice of the Fortymile was rougher than the Yukon's as the smaller channel had a swifter current, and they had to get off to manhandle the sleds over ridges and around weak spots regularly. It was exhausting, and the prospect of no warm place to sleep dampened Joseph and Alice Mary's spirits swiftly.

307

After an eon, Sam led them up a trail into a break in the hills where they came across an ancient snow-covered fence of birch limbs and followed it. "Drift fence. It was here when my granddad was a kid. Han people used to drive the Fortymile caribou herd up this valley for killin' and a big feed. They'd smoke the meat for winter, women would pick berries, and people would have a big get-together. Lotsa babies come a' that. Long time since anybody used it and some white guy built a cabin up here."

"What about him?"

"He had a still and the fella tried to shoot me when I come callin', so I had to put him in jail for the Mounties... and the hospital."

"Oh."

They trudged behind Sam through deepening snow following moose tracks up a frozen vale. Alice Mary bemoaned the peace of a warm bed as they followed a mining flume. Sam was their taskmaster now, and they were in his hands even more than Lorelei's. They came to a dark cabin, where Sam tied his team and lit a storm lantern. Joseph stumbled off the other sled, lit a lantern, and began the painful task of caring for the dogs. Alice Mary groaned.

Joseph managed a chuckle, "Not the bright lights and high jinks of Dawson, eh?"

"Shut the fuck up!" She muttered something foul under her breath.

"Don't be so grouchy."

"Dawson ain't all high jinks and laughs, fella! Getting' stalked like a rabbit, beaten, raped, and buggered ain't no fuckin' *high jinks!* Wish you knew what it's like to have some damn drunk stick it up your arse!" A wet growl rumbled her chest, "Not that you'd give a hot damn 'bout the likes a me, if'n Lorelei hadn't woke ya!"

Joseph held the wire basket of the lantern before him and swallowed, "I'm sorry, Alice."

She bit her lip and sighed, "No... Ah'm sorry, Joe. You didn't deserve that." She slapped her face with cold mittens and gasped. "Wonder if there's some way to heat water in that fuckin' hut."

"I'll check as soon as I take care of the dogs."

"Thank you."

A gout of smoke mushroomed from the stovepipe as she staggered into the cabin.

—⁓—

The rich scent of moose wafted on the frigid air as the familiar sounds and smells of her family surrounded her. The tracks of the cow they were following were deep and close together. The moose was weakening. Soon they would feast on her soft insides, tearing mouthfuls of living flesh full of sweet-tasting, life-making blood from her body. The scent of the moose was tickling her nose, filling her mind like a rushing river as the thrill of the coming feast rose within her and cold snow tickled her swollen tits. She was the strongest daughter of the pack, just as the father of her pups was undisputed leader. It was the way of things that they would bring the next generation into the future. The cow moose's life would assure so, nurturing the pups within her as it carried them through near-endless nights into spring. The moose's life was theirs: the Feast of Life itself.

The cow staggered along a birch barrier into an open vale as eight wolves spread to flank her and keep her from fleeing the little valley. On the far side squatted a flat-sided lodge of logs like a beaver's built upon land, where the two-legged creatures who'd multiplied greatly during the bitch wolf's life could be found. This one had the smell of smoke and dogs and the strong scent of two-leggeds.

The she-wolf froze as movement came from her left. The pack lifted their noses to taste the frigid air, and the hair along their spines rose. Two-leggeds were moving toward the lodge from that direction, stepping clumsily in the snow as they muttered noisily. There was the alien clicking sound that she knew came before the awful bark of their fire-things, sounding as if the bones of her skull were grinding between her ears.

Her big black mate let out a snort of disgust and wheeled away from the men who had come between them and their moose. Dogs began to growl on the other side of the cabin making noise and rude comments, and the young cow moose stumbled toward the river away from the men and stalking wolves to perhaps bear her own child in the distant spring.

—✳—

Alice Mary's eyes flew open. She sat up in the dark with a gasp, and her hand closed on the ivory hilt of her knife. She held it in front of her and fumbled for the big Webley pistol.

Where are they?

She found the storm lantern and matches and lit the wick with trembling fingers before she tossed a frayed Hudson's Bay blanket over her shoulders. *It was real!* She'd been a *wolf,* watching this very place! "Wake up!" Her voice was a thin shriek.

Joseph and Sam sat up on the floor. Joseph rubbed his eyes. "Wha . . ?"

Dogs barked before the door exploded inward as the wooden bolt split with the force of a blow from a booted foot, and cold air billowed into the cabin around a huge form with a double-barreled shotgun cradled in his ungloved hands. His upper lip curled, exposing tobacco-yellowed teeth over a thick brown beard. "Stick Sam! And a couple'a kids!"

Sam began a reflexive move toward his rifle, but stopped as the shotgun came around.

"You crazy, Injun?"

Sam held up his hands, "No."

The man made a barking laugh, "Too fuckin' bad!"

310

Two more men as scruffy and well-armed as the first appeared and shoved the door shut behind them over tracked-in snow. The short red-haired one spied Alice Mary and leered, and his heavyset companion did the same. She backed up on the bunk against the log wall, pulling the red blanket tighter around narrow shoulders.

A white rush shot up Joseph's spine as *Lorelei!* burst from his brain into space. There was silence.

The big man with the shotgun swung the barrel toward the center post of the cabin and back at Joseph. The twin black holes were dark sockets in the skull face of death. "All right! Hurry the fuck up! Kid, you get on that side, Sam, you get on the other!"

The two young men bound Joseph and Stick Sam to the post with a rope as cold and stiff as steel. When they pulled the slack out, it felt like an iron bar wrapping around them.

"Ow!"

"Shadup!" A boulder of a fist landed on Joseph's cheekbone, and his head snapped back into the post with a flash of sparks.

"You can't get away with this," Stick Sam said in a calm voice.

"Oh yeah?" The red-haired one said, "What if we dynamite that cliff up there when we're done and leave your filthy brown arse under ten tons 'a rock, Injun?" He spat and made a gravelly laugh.

"No need to do that, we—"

The big one growled, "Shut up! My brother wouldn't be at Fort Herchmer right now waitin' for a one-way trip to some clink in Seattle if it weren't for your hound sniffin' nose and Injun bush smarts!"

"They'll try him in Juneau, Dan."

"Shut up!" Saliva flew from the big man's mouth as he drove a fist into Sam's middle, and Sam doubled up with a croak.

Alice Mary was still on the bed. The men had ignored her since the ripple of lust she'd engendered, obviously expecting her to wait for their further ministrations after they'd finished with Joseph and Sam. She tossed hair from her eyes as the big Webley revolver rose out of the red Hudson's Bay blanket and held it in both small hands as the blanket slid off thin white shoulders. She was elfin in proportion to the gun. "Hey! Fuckers!"

The stocky blond one began to shout, but it was drowned out by the boom of the pistol as it flew up in Alice Mary's hands from recoil. She brought it back down to bear on the two still standing as blood spurted in an arc from the body that lay twitching upon the floor.

"Jesus God!" The big man sprang to the left, and the red-haired youth went to the right, away from the post where Joseph and Stick Sam were tied.

Alice Mary swung the pistol toward the big one as his hands closed on the barrel of his shotgun. As he brought it around, a heavy bullet caught him in the face. His woolen cap jumped at the back, spewing hair, blood and brains on the log wall. The cabin shook as he hit the floor. The redhead had reached his rifle and was bringing it up with a grunt of fear. There was another boom. The young man howled, folded up, and dropped to his knees eyes wide. He coughed, and a pink cloud blossomed from his face as he looked at the hole in his stomach. He raised his eyes to her, and Alice Mary's mouth twisted as she lowered the pistol. The rifle barrel wobbled and came back toward her.

"Shoot him again!" Sam yelled.

She did, and the boy let out a long sigh that ended when all the air in his lungs was expelled as he collapsed on his side.

Alice Mary pulled the blanket around her. She blinked and stood up, clutching the blanket with one hand and pointing the big gun at the bodies on the floor with the other. She blinked again. Her eyes were round as a cat's: two emeralds in a doll's face. She rocked the big man's body with a bare foot adorned with black toenails, put the gun down, and picked up her knife. Alice Mary didn't bother to untie the ropes binding Joseph and Sam, but slashed them in one motion.

Sam stood and rubbed his wrists, "Damn-damn-damn!"

"Alice... she's in you!"

"No Joe, that was me."

Sam held out a hand, "Give me the gun."

Alice Mary scooped the pistol off the bed with white smoke still rolling from the barrel. Sam's eyes were on it as it came up, and his broad face was a mask as she handed it over butt first. "Saved ya, Sam."

"I know." He knelt before the red-haired youth, "They're all dead."

"Yep."

Joseph looked from one to the other and ran hands through his hair, "What shall we do now?"

"You two must go on alone. I can't leave these lugs here. Gotta say I tracked them and they came back to get me while I was sleepin'. Nobody will believe a girl did this anyway."

Alice Mary kissed his cheek, "Guess you're a hero, Stick Sam."

"When must we leave?"

Sam touched his cheek with a fingertip and squatted on his haunches. "Now, you can make Steel Creek and the border by noon."

She sighed, "Oh for shit's sake. How 'bout we get some sleep Sam? Put 'em outside, there's some wolves out there that Ah owe a favor to."

Sam shook his head, "I'm not thinkin' 'bout them. What if the Mounties catch up with us? Then we're done for."

"Thought y'all could stay away from 'em."

"For all we know these lugs had a detachment after 'em. That's Big Dan McCain, one of the worst outlaws in either territory. They say he killed two men at Lake Bennett in '98 and one at Cassiar before that. The blond one's his brother. Don't know who the red one is."

"Michael O'Halloran," Alice Mary said.

"How do you know that?"

"He was a customer."

Sam grunted and stared at the rafters. "You two must get to Ketchumstuk pronto. You can make Steel Creek and the border in a few hours."

"What the hell's in Ketchumstuk anyway?"

"It's Han and Tannacross people, my relatives. No one will tell of you. She's made sure of it, and there's a girl that... never mind."

Alice Mary laughed, "Bet she's a looker too."

Joseph let out his breath, "I'm going back to Dawson after Alice has been delivered."

"Ah wanta go to Nome, not some damn Injun village... no offence, Sam." Alice Mary knelt beside the red-haired youth, brushed the hair from his staring eyes, and said something under her breath before closing them with her fingers. She went to Big Dan McCain and stuck her hand in his coat, "Bet he's got some loot. Fella like this wouldn't trust his partners with all his good stuff on the sled. Boy, his eyes are real empty. Wonder where you go when you get your brains blowed out like that."

Sam shook his head, "He could only go to Hell."

Joseph looked up, "I thought your people didn't believe in Hell."

"The missionaries brought Hell with them when they came, for people like that."

"Makes sense Ah guess," Alice Mary pulled a lumpy poke from his coat, put it on the table, and wiped her hands. With a flash of her blade, she slashed the thong tying it and dumped the contents. There were several large nuggets, coins, and two fine golden rings with what looked like a good-sized diamond in one of them.

"Do you think it's right to take their money?"

"Are you *kiddin'* Joe? They were gonna kill you! 'Course they were gonna keep me 'round for a while 'til they had their fun. Besides, you think that gold's come by honest?"

"Comin' from someone with your job—"

She turned a blistering stare on Sam, "Ah give more than measure for measure, Mister. It's an honest trade and Ah never robbed a fella, although some said so who were so in their cups they couldn't find their peckers if they wasn't nailed on. And that is really quite *rude* after all!"

"Sorry."

"Good. Ah'd like to try drivin' the dogs this go-round. Ah'm pretty sick a' sittin' on my arse in that goddamn sled, and you can catch up on your sleep Joe."

"How will we know where to go?"

"We'll know."

Joseph and Sam carried the bodies of the two smaller men out and placed them under the eaves. It took all three to carry Big Dan. His head lolled backward as they lifted his arms, dropping pink pieces of brain and skull from the hole in his hat. The hat filled, began to swell like a ripe fruit, and fell in the snow with a plop.

Joseph gagged.

Sam was stone-faced.

Alice Mary smiled.

XXXVII.

ALICE MARY STOOD ON THE RUNNERS BUMPING ONTO THE ICE OF THE Fortymile while watching green curtains of fire dance across the stars. In her mind she took the name Alice Mary Wright, crumpled it up like a tattered piece of paper, and tossed it into the night. She had to find a new name, one for a warrior. A chorus of wolves erupted from the hills in shrill agreement, and she grinned.

Joseph sat with a dour expression and the sled bag under his arms. She burst into trilling laughter, and he scowled. "What is it?"

"Ah will pay for what Ah did Joe. Ah *know...* but Ah don't care! Don't give a damn!" She stuck her tongue out at the fat moon as if tasting a disk of sweet cream. Joseph began to tense as the dogs ran on without her attention, and she laughed again. "Have some faith, fella."

"So far we've only gotten deeper into terrible trouble."

"Yep, and Ah'm the one's gotta pay, not you. We're always the ones who give our blood and hold our tongues while men pound their chests and brag of their deeds. At least now Ah've paid four brutal dastards back in their own tender," she exhaled, "so far. Ah gotta find me a new name."

You really are something, little sister.

"Ah *am!*" She grinned at the sky, "Ah don't have a thousand years to get it right, Lorelei, not even a hundred."

No, Lorelei's sigh buffeted the two on the sled with brief warmth, *you are a flame in my heart that is all the more precious in the moment when it grows brightest, for indeed, your time is short.*

"That's all right with me. Just let me make those sonsabitches see a bit of who Ah am 'fore Ah go. Let me make my mark... and if it's gotta be in blood, so be it."

Joseph glanced around for Lorelei even though he knew she was miles away. "We hear you. Seeing as I don't know the next time, tell me please: why did you have her kill those three instead of capturing them?"

That was her doing. I wasn't even paying attention until a fire flared in her heart like the sun rising in the east, at least from where I am at the moment, and by then it was too far gone to do much about. Besides, they were going to kill you just as she said and I must say she did quite well.

"What are you about?"

I've been with a lover.

"That's no surprise."

Alice Mary laughed, "And she is beautiful, but when will you take me?"

There was only the sound of the dogs and the runners hissing on the snow as the two youths waited, straining their senses for that voice from beyond their world.

You're a mystery to me Alice Mary: someone I cannot see clearly or guess the future of. I cannot even shroud myself from your dreams, which can be rather maddening. Something in your nature is strong enough to keep me from divining your path, as you have powerful forebears in your lineage. Do you remember she who died at the stake?

"Of course! How the hell could I forget?"

Like all Liliots, we daughters of Lilith are descended from an older time before an upstart God made the world you live in. She died without an inheritor... without someone to carry her blood into the future.

"But, Lorelei... she *gave* somethin' to that girl, I know it."

And that girl is within you, distilled by centuries and generations in your own blood. Her name was Angelique and she was your ancestor. I fear her awakening in you might well be a bit early, but she seems to be rising up whether I think it wise or not. This world is far from ready unless I'm happily mistaken, and I should very much like to see you have your own children to carry on toward that day, which means you must live and prosper. Your children and their children's children might well be needed to carry the gift you hold within you back to the light on that day, a day I pray for and that my dreams can barely touch. You're not of a class that can go far without engendering resentment and hatred in this world. You'd most likely die or be incarcerated should you follow the path of war and you sorely need an education. There's so much in the world that you could grab hold of if you knew it was there... and you must stay out of situations like in the Empire Hotel for that matter. No more stalking the stalkers... and you must never go back to prostitution.

"Boy, that's a passel a'stuff. Ah guess. Anyway, Ah'm done with the name Alice Mary."

Lorelei's chuckle tickled both their spines. *And what do you prefer: Esmeralda... Morgana... Circe?*

"Ah don't know two of them names, but how 'bout Valerie?"

I see a girl warrior from a tale told on the lap of your grandmother. There was a time in the forests of Europe when our Priestesses sent young women out to fight beside their men that they might earn the right to bear his child. You'd eat up such stories if you could read them and might even learn to tell new ones. I would love that, but would you really want to be that tall?

"Ah would adore it!"

A laugh cascaded like a freshet of water from heaven-touching peaks, to disappear in the aurora amongst the stars.

Joseph sighed, "When will I see you again?"

Eventually. I want you to bed Alice Mary first. After all... she has slain your enemies for you.

A rush of embarrassment began to color Joseph's cheeks. He swiped at his face.

Or Valerie, whichever you prefer.

———

Dawn turned the peaks pink under a blue sky, and ravens followed them as they ascended the river, circling and calling in their hollow voices through the still air. She grinned at the escort of big black birds and assured Joseph she wasn't tired as they mushed past miners' cabins, flumes, and snow-covered heaps of gravel beside silent dredges. He burrowed under the hides and slept.

The cough and rattle of a donkey engine greeted Alice Mary as they rounded a bend. Smoke and steam rose from an operation to their right, where fires were being used to thaw the frozen ground, and a man waved from atop a pile of boards next to a small mill. She shook Joseph awake, "We're in Alaska!"

"What," he sat up, "how do you know?"

"The flag," she pointed to an American flag hanging from a pole before a large cabin.

"Oh."

"Boy, that was easy. Thought there'd be some soldiers or somethin'."

"They said there isn't much authority on this side. How did you get past the Mounties?"

"Didn't see none, and I guess everybody thought Ah was a boy in this big ol' furry hat."

"Thank God," Joseph wiped ice from his lip, "This must be Steel Creek."

"Guess so. We can mush on while it's light. Hope there's a roadhouse with good eats. I'm gonna buy us a room with some of that whiskey man's gold."

"I could use that."

"Lorelei's orders. You and me are 'sposed to get familiar whether we like it or not."

He took over by midday, and she slept on the sled. Later that afternoon the dogs turned on their own toward a cluster of buildings to the right and passed a jumble of flumes and rocker boxes up a beaten trail toward cabins glowing ruddy-red in the low sun of the south. Dogs howled at their approach.

Joseph pulled onto the packed snow of a small compound in whose center sat a rambling log structure of two stories festooned with antlers. A sign over an arctic entry of whipsawed boards read **BONANZA BAR ROADHOUSE**, and below that, *Ole Austed, PROPRIETOR*. Several teams were tied in the yard before a row of doghouses surrounded by frozen droppings. The chorus of yapping rose in volume as he stepped off the sled to tend the team.

She crawled out from under the bag, got stiffly to her feet, and cracked her back. "Fuckin' palace!"

"Not bad for these parts."

"Hope they got a private room an' a tub."

"Perhaps you should keep that hat on and act like my brother or something."

"No Joe, they're gonna hear me and Ah'm too small and girly lookin' for that. We'll say we're eloping' from my dad who's a Baptist preacher, and he sicked the Yellaleg Mounties on us for bein' in love, and he's gonna shoot you, whup the tar outta me, and send me south to marry some rich fella three times my age. That way we can get the ol' gink to hide us for sure. With a name like that he's gotta be Lutheran, so you tell him you are too and we're hopin' to get hitched by a Lutheran preacher in Eagle or Circle City. Make sure you tell him we're gettin' *married* though, got it?"

"Jesus, when did you think that up?"

"Jus' did."

The door opened on a tall robust man in his mid-fifties with unkempt blond hair, six inches of graying beard, and pale blue eyes that widened at the sight of a girl. "Uf da, a voman! Let the boy tend the dogs, you come in, young lady!"

Alice Mary took off the wolf fur hat and let down her hair as the big Norwegian grinned like crazy. The man bowed and offered her the smoky insides of his establishment with a wave of a callused hand. Joseph hurriedly tied the dogs and followed, blinking as his eyes adjusted to the light. Alice Mary stood talking to Ole in the center of the room. Several men were seated around a long table before a big stone hearth with cups of coffee, tea, glasses of whiskey, and bottles of beer under heavy rafters hewn by broadax. The upright posts of the roadhouse were spruce trunks selected for their big round burls, and were polished to an umber sheen. Ole offered her the only store-bought chair in the place.

The men all stood, and the lone member of the First Nations in the room had taken off his ragged hat and held it before his chest, his dark eyes bulging at the sight of the young blonde.

"Thank you, sir." Alice Mary curtsied and sat in the chair. It squeaked as it settled on the rough floor.

The men didn't seem to notice Joseph at all and continued to stare at her. There was the sound of sappy spruce popping in the handmade stove as someone added more to the coals within. Someone cleared his throat.

"Welcome," Ole finally said, "and what in God's name are you doin' out here, at this time of year?"

"We're lookin' for a Preacher," Alice Mary spoke up, "to join us in holy matrimony. My Ma's dead, and my father is a Baptist Preacher recently come with me from Norfolk Virginia. He is in a perfect rage that Ah should marry a Lutheran like Joseph here, although he is of good character and we have waited to consummate our union until we can conese... consecrate our vows, when we can be wed by a man of the Cloth. We fled in the night to brave winter's bitter blows for love, and to find a Lutheran Priest to seal our sacred union before the eyes a' God."

"Ja?"

"Yes sir," Joseph spoke up, "we are on our way to Eagle City at this very moment to find one."

"Uf da!" Ole's blue eyes lit up under pale eyebrows, "The Lord's a wonderful and loving God I'm thinkin'. We got a Lutheran man of the Cloth right here!"

Alice Mary's mouth fell open.

"Reverend Ost, I want you to meet... what's yer names?"

"Joseph Aaron Walton sir, of Cottage Grove, in Oregon."

"Al... *Valerie,* Valerie Mary Wright, of Spotsylvania County, Virginia."

"Yahoo!" A burley fellow with a grey beard held his whiskey glass in the air. "A damn wedding! The Lord brought ya here to get hitched, even if it ain't a proper Catholic one!"

"It'll do, Pat."

A little white-haired man had been watching in silence from the end of the table. He now rose, cleared his throat, and the rest fell silent. "Are you two ready to live a Godly life? To cleave to one another come what may in the trials of marriage and the labors therefore, to suffer the trials and tribulations of honest labor and tithing to the church, and with the blessings of God, to bear children in the service and knowledge of the Lord?"

Joseph and Alice Mary glanced at each other and swallowed. She squeezed his hand, and they sighed in unison before breaking into a spasm of giggling.

"Kids, meet Father Harald Ost, the only Lutheran Pastor for two hundred miles at least. He's a Missionary all the way from Uppsala Sweden, and he can do the job you betcha."

Reverend Ost examined the two teens and put a wrinkled hand to his chin. "Ja, but you are awfully young. I don't know if I should do this without a parent's blessing. After all, your father is a man of the Cloth."

"Nonsense!" Pat boomed, "A strappin' couple already united by Cupid's arrows needs your blessin', Father! When's the last time you saw a white woman of such looks wasn't a dancin' girl in Dawson City or a common whore in these parts anyway?"

"Ja, Harald, how many times can you tie the knot between such as these? Sure beats burying somebody. It's a happy thing it is."

"Damn straight!"

"Please, Pat, this isn't Eagle. Watch yer language in my roadhouse."

"Yer pardon, Ole."

Father Ost studied the two youths, stared for a long moment into their eyes, and nodded, "Ja, all right."

The young Gwich'in Indian produced a fiddle and laid into a boisterous Celtic skirl, unleashing a roar from the assembled miners that shook the rafters.

The two rings from the poke of Big Dan McCain were in Joseph's pocket when Father Ost asked for them. They went on his and Alice Mary's, *Valerie's* fingers, and were a perfect fit. When Reverend Ost said Joseph might kiss the bride, Valerie Alice Mary Wright Walton held him at arm's length for a moment. The room held its breath, before she seized him with a passion that produced a gasp in the roadhouse.

As the celebration was getting started, Ole disappeared up the split log stairs. He soon reappeared, and with great solemnity announced that they might use his private chambers for the evening. There was a chorus of cheers accompanied by the low rumble of noises men make when considering the fortune of one who will take the favors of a comely woman, somewhat like the keening from the throats of dogs mellowed by their humanity but amplified by the alcohol. Valerie took Joseph's hand, curtsied to Reverend Ost, bestowed a kiss upon his cheek, and led Joseph upstairs.

The walls of the room were covered with pegs holding woolen and canvas clothing. Guns hung from slings, and the rafters were laden with traps, Native spirit masks, handmade snowshoes, and skis. The room smelled of dust, fish, and mildew.

Valerie began to take off her clothes. "Ain't nothin' we ain't done before, Mr. Walton." She stepped out of the caribou outerwear to peel off the woolen shirt and pants, and stood in red rumpled oversize longjohns looking young and small. She unbuttoned the front of the union suit and slid it down around her ankles to stand naked. She had the bones of a bird, small breasts, and a thin swatch of pale pubic hair beneath a flat stomach and tiny waist. "Brrrrr!" Valerie Alice Mary clutched at herself. With her breasts covered by her arms, she looked almost like a very young boy but for one missing part and a doll's face. "Gonna take them clothes off, Mr. Walton?"

Joseph exhaled, "All right, Alice Mary."

"Ain't my name no more Joe. It's Valerie please, Mrs. Valerie Walton."

"We're not really married."

"Why not?"

"Because your name isn't Valerie."

"Is *too!*" her eyes moistened, "Women change their names all the time. It's our way. Valerie Mary Wright Walton's my name now so you had better get used to it, and if we ain't married then Ah'm gonna go on to Nome and to hell with you." She turned away from him with a choking sound, put her hand to her mouth, and stared at the wall.

"I'm sorry, I... I've never been married before."

"Then Ah forgive you." She stuck her chin out and watched him undress. When he'd stepped out of his longjohns, she whistled. "Damn, Lorelei knows how to pick 'em."

Joseph blinked. "I think she picked me for something else besides."

"What?"

"Remember? I was a virgin, and full of dreams." He sat on the bed beside her, "Valerie, I do like the name."

"Good, 'cause you better get used to it." She put a hand to his chin and turned his face to hers. "Tol' you that Ah ain't never been happy with a man. Had a bushel of 'em," she gazed down his stomach, "but none of 'em ever were what was 'sposed to be, Ah guess."

"You got a rough start."

"Yeah, and it's been a tad rough since." She rose to her knees and pulled him against her, and he stiffened against her belly, "Guess she thinks you're 'sposed to do somethin' 'bout that. Ah mean she sure put us here, that's for sure." She hugged him tentatively as her breath rolled across his throat and pressed her face against his. "Guess Ah'll have to spend the rest of my life dealin' with the souls of them guys I kilt."

"What do you mean?"

"Ah owe even their souls *somethin'*, just like she's gotta deal with those she's kilt. Lorelei can't get off that easy. Ah bet she carries something of 'em with her, and Ah gotta do the same. A soul is a soul, don'tcha think?"

"I... guess so."

"That one red-haired fella, the—"

"The one you called Michael?"

"Yeah, him, like Ah said he was a customer. He came by my crib one night with a pocket fulla money and Ah could tell he stole it but that weren't my business. Said he wanted to be like his daddy who was Captain of a revenue brig on the ocean but that he weren't no good and he knew it. He got used by bad relations like me somethin' awful and cried when he tol' me 'bout it. He said we was just like each other and

Ah kinda had to agree. We worked up a sweat, and he spent the whole night and woke up cryin'. Ah had ta buck him up in the mornin' and even remind him to fetch his pistol he left hangin' on the wall. He left sayin' he loved me and how he was gonna be a better person. Heard that a'fore," she stared at the ceiling, "and the next time Ah see him he's gonna rape and kill me jus' to look tough for his chums." She sighed, "Joe... Ah saw his *soul,* Ah saw it *leave.* We was lookin' each other in the eye when I shot him, and he—" she shook her head. "Fuck that. Ain't the way to spend a wedding night."

She held him tighter, her mouth an inch away and her hands on his cheeks. She stared into his eyes, and slowly, her lips touched his.

Joseph sighed, "God."

She grinned, "No Joe, *Goddess.*"

Laughter echoed in the room as they closed their eyes, and light danced around them in filaments that spiraled into endless distances more felt than seen. It went on with a roar of voices, voices too beautiful to exist anywhere but in this eternal space, this place with no name that was more familiar than their own faces.

Darkness enfolded them as they clung to one another. She was the trunk of a tree whose roots were a billion fingers in the heaving earth. He was the son who had risen to manhood to give himself upon an altar in a feast of blood that the Sun might be born anew each day, and the thunder of their hearts echoed across the sky like a crimson drum.

They were motes in a maelstrom floating in a great warm sea and the sea was them. They were strings some utterly loving being played: an instrument of angels. Lorelei's laughter was all around them: a knowing parent laughing at the steps of a child. An overwhelming gratitude was the only thing left to them as they emptied themselves out, to be filled with her grace.

Joseph pulled a strand of hair from his mouth and rose on his elbows.

Green eyes stared back from the tear-streaked face of an angel over the mouth he'd kiss forever. "So," She fell back on the bed, *"That's* what it's all about."

XXXVIII.

L OUD POUNDING RESOUNDED THROUGHOUT THE ROADHOUSE.
Joseph groaned as he slid an arm out from under Valerie while marveling at her lightness. He felt a swelling in his chest as he gazed at her bathed in a shaft of morning light coming through the tiny window of precious double-pane glass, like a golden being from a time when Lorelei's kin danced upon the earth. He ran fingers down the hollow of her back, put his face to her, and inhaled the bouquet of her skin.

Someone stomped up the stairs, and the heavy door flew open with a bang. A man stood there wearing a long woolen coat with two rows of polished brass buttons and a bear fur hat upon his head. His sandy mustache sparkled with frost just melting into droplets of water that made him look as if his pronounced nose was running.

Joseph's eyes fell to the big bore Winchester rifle pointed directly at his hairless chest. "Hey!" He threw his hands up as two more Mounties crowded into the room. He recognized the tall one now. He'd met him at the Orpheum, the night of the opening, "Inspector MacAtee."

"Get up and away from the girl, son."

Valerie sat with the blanket held to her neck, brushing pale strands of hair from her face.

"Alice Mary Wright, I am arresting you in the name of Her Majesty Queen Victoria for the heinous murder of Donald Johnson in the Empire Hotel on Queen Street, in Dawson City, Yukon Territory, on the day of November seventh, in the year of our Lord Eighteen-hundred and ninety-nine—"

"Shit fella, don'tcha ever gotta breathe?" She slid out from under the blanket to stand naked before the Mounties, and George's voice trailed off, "And my name is Valerie, Valerie Walton, sir."

The three servants of the Queen stared as Inspector MacAtee's high forehead reddened. "Put something on her!"

Corporal Pippin whipped the blanket off the bed and threw it over her shoulders, eliciting another "Hey!" from Joseph, who was also naked.

George MacAtee un-cocked his rifle with a loud sigh and rested the butt on the floor. "Your claim to another name changes nothing. You are going back to Dawson City to stand trial."

Joseph shook his head, "This is America! You can't—"

"We have full authority to pursue miscreants across the border. Judge Wickersham is extremely grateful in that regard, and we allow whatever goes for authority on this side to do the same on the territory of the Crown should our own authorities not be present." George scowled, "Would that more Yanks had some sense of order over here anyway."

"Can we get dressed?"

"Please do, but do not endeavor to make any false moves, as we have orders to apprehend you no matter what, which includes shooting you should the need arise."

"Christ, I'm not going to—" Joseph glanced at Valerie as a sudden vision of her producing her knife or pistol and having at the three

Mounties came to him. She saw the look on his face and her cheeks bulged at his thought. *"Don't!"* he mouthed.

She smiled, "You Yellalegs never seem to stick up for a girl when some lug's hurtin' her, only after she's butchered or dead. Guess it makes your job pretty easy while you're takin' money from the workin' girls and enjoyin' their favors ta boot. Like to see you get beaten and raped by the likes of Donald Johnson or Fred Dodge. Ah'd like to see it in the Monte Carlo or the Palace, on a fancy stage. That'd be entertainin'."

George's eyebrows knotted, "And what exactly became of Mr. Dodge, Miss Wright?"

"It's Walton. Damned if Ah know."

"We shall see."

"Okey-dokey Inspector, if you really wanta know: a Goddess seized him by the scruff a' the neck like a piddlin' puppy and took him up top'a King Solomon's Dome, where she tore his bloody heart out and threw it across Grand Forks all the way to the Yukon River."

"You are a cruelly deluded girl, Alice Mary, and at such tender years."

"Valerie."

"As you wish, Valerie, now you shall get dressed."

"It's Mrs. Walton. By the way, the Mare sends her regards, Inspector MacAtee."

George Duncan MacAtee snorted and stared out the tiny frosted window as they were manacled and led downstairs.

Ole was standing in the common room with a bemused look on his weather-burned face, chewing on the stem of a red mammoth ivory pipe that had been out for some time now. Two Constables were at the foot of the stairs with guns ready and got out of Inspector MacAtee's way as he descended. Ole took the pipe from his mouth and pinched his nose, "Goddamn... a *murderess.*"

Valerie lifted shackled hands to her lips and blew him a kiss. "Thank you so much for the hospitality Ole. We made damn good use of it."

The post at Fort Constantine had been awaiting Inspector MacA-tee's triumphant return, and clean-cut, square-jawed men appeared from well-built buildings of four-sided logs to get a look at the girl who had gutted a big man with a knife.

As they were led to separate cells, Joseph burst from the hands of the men holding his arms and sprang toward Valerie, who slipped out of the grip of the Constable holding her like an eel from the belly of a river. They pressed together for an instant before being roughly seized and dragged away. Her eyes were bright as emeralds, and her girlish laughter echoed off the fort's log walls, "Ah love you!" She broke a glorious smile before disappearing around a building with a big man on each of her arms and a chain rattling between her wrists.

He was led to a room with a barred window, a sheet iron stove in the middle, a stained canvas cot, two blankets, a bottle of water, and a chamber pot. The Constable produced a brass key and removed his manacles, shaking his head as he did, "I pity ye boy, to get hooked up with a wee murtherin' whore such as that. Do ye know what she did?"

"What?"

"Kilt a man with that big knife, gutted him she did. 'Twas a big man, and strong too. Seen the mess she made with me own eyes. Yer lucky ye didn't get the same." The man pulled at his ruddy mustache, looked Joseph up and down, and showed tobacco-stained teeth, "Did ye get a good whack at the little strumpet while ye was at it?"

Joseph felt a jolt in his shoulders and fought an impulse to strike the man.

The Constable stepped back and swung the manacles on their chain like a club, "Damn, yer in love with the little whore." He shook his head, "Ye are. I pity ye boy." The heavy iron-bound door closed, accompanied by the grating of the key in the lock.

Joseph lay on the cot and stared at the well-sawed beams overhead. He closed his eyes and his brow furrowed in concentration, "Lorelei!" burst from his lips.

There was silence.

The Appaloosa had the smell horses get with they warm to the pace, blending with the scent of camas lilies in spring sun and the smell of mud as the mare stepped high in the marshy meadow. The green slough sparkled and trembled under the wings of mallards as they rose in a cloud from the water, and the air snapped and crackled with the drone of big blue dragonflies.

The sun beat on his skin as he rode toward the beaver pond where he'd shot his first deer. He again felt gnats crawling on his bloody arms as he tried to make a quick job of gutting the young buck and the strange mixture of triumph and remorse that had blossomed in taking the deer's life.

Joseph reached the island of dry ground between the slough and the river where an ancient maple tree spread leaves as big as his chest. The mare snorted and pulled at a tuft of grass growing between the roots. He dismounted, walked to a gnarled root whose knee made a comfortable seat, and sat in the dappled shade. Joseph closed his eyes and opened them at the sound of splashing.

Valerie stood naked in the pond. Joseph leapt up with a gasp.

She had blood on her throat. Blood sparkled in sunlight as it ran down her thigh. She cupped her hands and began to wash it away. Her face was alight with unfathomable innocence as her reflection danced like a white flame in the green water.

He stepped into the water. Warm mud squeezed between his toes as Valerie fell into his embrace. Her mouth was so soft, her skin so hot and smooth. The smell of her was sweeter than any flower that had ever opened to the world: a perfect scent—the scent of Lorelei. Lorelei's laughter came from Valerie's throat. Her eyes were bottomless pools as she kissed him again.

Lorelei's breath caressed his cheek with the scent of flowers. *Help her remember. You shall find your own redemption.*

I am her daughter, Valerie's voice echoed within him with that of Lorelei, *I am the blade that cuts the knot of the heart.*

They sunk to their knees as great blue dragonflies droned overhead.

XXXIX.

"I MUST SEE HIM THIS VERY MOMENT!" MARY POUNDED ON THE DESKTOP with a balled fist careful not to chip her nails, and for emphasis let out a grunt of frustration.

The Constable behind the desk ran a hand across a well-trimmed beard and glanced about for support. As they were alone in the office, he found none and scowled, forced to deal with this strange and angry girl himself. "Mademoiselle, please, he is—"

"I shall retain a Barrister! He has friends! Have you heard of Klondike Kate? Alexander Pantages? Swiftwater Bill Gates? Arizona Charlie Meadows?"

"No, but I have jus' arrived from Regina. Perhaps you should come back when Inspector MacAtee is in, or—"

"Damn you, you miserable frog!"

"What on earth is the racket?" George MacAtee stood in a nimbus of icy air from an open door on Fort Herchmer's parade ground. Six horses stood behind him with clouds of breath wreathing their heads and the men mounted on them. He closed the door on the military formation, removed his gauntlets, and turned to Mary. "Madame, what is your purpose here, might I ask?"

"I have come to see Joseph Walton. He was only taking that girl Alice Mary to Eagle City because he was enamored of her. He's a considerate person and somewhat of a romantic, and she promised gold besides. He had no knowledge of—"

"That is not his story, young lady."

Mary glanced from Inspector MacAtee to the Constable and tried to produce a quick tear. "May I *please* see him?"

"I suppose I could arrange that. Of course I must have a female employee of the garrison search your person first. Do you object?"

"No sir, thank you."

"Very well. Follow me," George turned toward the door, but stopped, and Mary almost ran into him, "and I want an apology to Philippe this instant."

"I am truly sorry, Philippe; I am under great strain. My womanly humors have gotten the best of me, I fear."

"No bother Mademoiselle. I hope your friend gets a speedy trial. Perhaps he'll only do a few years. Good day."

Mary was led into the stockade where prisoners were housed from across the territory after being searched by a matron in a high-collar black dress from the Post hospital. She followed a burly Constable with muttonchop sideburns between two rows of iron doors and down a narrow corridor with a row of dim electric bulbs on the ceiling. Two rough hands appeared from a tiny window in a door to the right, and one reached out between the bars.

"That'll be enough a'that!" The guard shouted and swung a short billy club at the hand.

There was a howl of pain, and the hand disappeared.

Mary glanced at dark eyes peering from another cell and averted her face. Joseph's cell was beyond that.

"A visitor, Mr. Walton!" The Constable cheerfully announced as he opened the door with a key from a ring on his belt, and his other hand on his club.

Joseph stood before a narrow bunk with his hair unkempt and a dusting of stubble on his chin, "Mary!"

They embraced.

"No fraternizin' of a carnal nature!"

They parted, holding hands.

Mary kissed him, "How are you?"

"You two, I said—"

"I'm fine Mary, I mean... considering the circumstances," Joseph glanced at the guard, "might you leave us alone for a moment, please?"

"Only if I have your word you shant be pawin' at one another in my absence."

"On our honor, sir. We need only speak about Mr. Walton's future."

The Constable glanced from one to the other before he grunted and shut the door. There was the sound of the key in the lock.

Mary grabbed his hand, "What on earth happened, really?"

"Valerie, I mean Alice Mary, I... do you remember how Lorelei told me to get her out of Dawson? She spoke to Alice Mary just as she did to us and said we must be together, which I didn't understand at the time, but that Alice Mary was a special case who'd found her of her own accord. After Lorelei killed Fred Dodge, she was stalking her in her dreams... and she *found* her, Mary. It gave her the courage to go after that lug who was after her even though the fellow was a bear of a man. Anyway we left Dawson and were led to this Indian who helped us, but whiskey men almost killed us near the border, and—"

"What... who?"

"Alice Mary, the girl from the cribs, who—"

"No, Joe, who was she speaking to?"

"Lorelei."

"Lorelei? Who are you talking about?"

He stared into Mary's eyes with her mouth half-open as she waited for an answer. Joseph fought an urge to kiss her and blinked, "Lorelei, Mary, the one who brought us together, the Goddess who—"

"Oh, you speak poetically, of a muse perhaps. But we must sit down and figure out what to say about your leaving town with that murderous little whore, Joe. I know you love sporting with girls and I can't begrudge you that, but you are in a real pickle at the moment and we must deal with getting you out of here. Now—"

"You don't... remember her?"

"I remember Lulu and Leah and Lily Joe, but not any Lorelei. It's a nice enough name though. Is she another goodtime girl, or from one of the theaters?"

"Oh dear God!" Joseph sat on the bunk with his face in his hands.

"Why did you leave with little Alice anyway? Did you really know she killed that Johnson or Johnston fellow or whoever he was? I hope you didn't. You're smarter than to get mixed up with something like that."

"What about Fred Dodge? Do you remember Fred Dodge?"

"The fellow who disappeared? Of course. I remember that awful story Alice Mary told at Halloween about him disappearing from her crib. Everyone knows she's unhinged, and we can use that in your defense. It doesn't matter if you were her paramour as long as you didn't know all that she was about. She's a sporting girl after all. In fact it will help if we say that she had you under the spell of her charms, although I can't see how you'd give up sleeping with me and Lily for *that.* Lily can't believe it either. I hope you didn't catch something. Do you think she killed Fred Dodge too?"

"Lorelei did," He glanced at the barred window, "and you remember nothing."

"What? Excuse me, sir, but my memory is excellent. I can tell you what clothes you were wearing the day we met, or what you ate the first time we dined together, or what you said upon our first tryst in the Empire Hotel, or—"

"God!" Joseph turned to the wall and slammed his forehead against the bricks. "Ow!" He put a hand to his face.

"What in heaven's name are you doing?"

He turned to her with a red welt on his brow and a look of misery.

Mary put a hand to her mouth, "Are... you all right?"

"I just, I didn't expect this."

"No one expects life to take such turns. We must simply deal with it. Kismet."

"Huh?"

"You know: fate."

Joseph shook his head, "I must discover why Lorelei has taken your memory away." His hand went to the nugget earring dangling from her right ear. Its diamond sparkled even in the low light of the cell. "Where did you get this?"

"You gave them to me after winning at faro in the Palace the day after we met. Did you think I didn't remember?"

"We found it on top of King Solomon's Dome, Mary, along with the mortal remains of Fred Dodge that were left there by Lorelei."

Mary took a step backward and her eyes darted to the door, "Joe, you're scaring me now, honestly. I'll do all I can to help you, but I really must leave now."

He took a step toward her.

Mary gasped, "Please, Joe, try and get a grip on yourself for the authorities. Alex is hiring a lawyer. Kate put him up to it, and he'll be here soon." She knocked on the door behind her without taking her eyes off Joseph and was through it before the guard had it half-open.

Joseph's breath ground out as if his chest were being crushed by a great weight. "Why have you brought us to this?" he demanded of a shaft of light falling across the floor. There was only the rattle of horse tack and the sounds of men drilling in the yard beyond.

———

"On his lonesome, George," Sergeant Fitzgerald held a hand before the breast of his red coat and the other up before him, "shot all three of those bandits dead on the Fortymile. We could use a man like him fighting the bloody Boers in South Africa. We should recruit him."

George pulled at his mustache, "They're Yanks, aren't they?"

"Yes. Big Dan McCain has been a thorn in the Crown's side since ninety-six. That Stick Sam is a bloody hero in my book."

"Frank, this can't get to the American side."

"The man deserves a medal."

"He shall get one, but we'll have a ceremony inside the walls of this fort without civilian participation, and we shall not notify the American authorities."

"What about the families of those men?"

George snorted, "The word 'men' doesn't even apply. Those were the basest thieves and blackguards, and their families are most likely unwashed trash in some hollow to the south or the huts and hedgerows of Ireland. They can rest in unmarked graves, and the world shall be the better for it."

"That's not quite decent, George."

"Damn!" George sprang up from his chair, *"Decent?* We've got outlaws and Yanks boozing and gambling and whoring and murdering all over this bloody territory, and not two hundred men in an area *ten times* that of England! *Decent?* Let them be swallowed up by the earth, and their names never spoken again!"

Sergeant Fitzgerald leaned back in his chair, wiped his hands on his blue striped pants, and a grin grew on his face, "Absolutely appropriate from that perspective I must admit. Your reading of the classics is put to good use too. Now, good chap, I'd suggest you calm down."

George broke a smile himself, "Your pardon Frank, I seem to have lost control of my emotions." He sat down behind his desk.

"Wholly understandable, anyway Stick Sam is an asset we should be proud of. He's getting married, you know. We should send something."

"Didn't know that."

"Got himself a real beauty of a squaw, the daughter of a Chief from a village past Chicken in the Fortymile country. Can't begin to guess how he did it. He's no young buck and doesn't have a pot to piss in by a white man's standards. They're probably related or something for all I know. Their ways aren't easy to understand for our kind. Perhaps we can have an Anglican Father perform the ceremony. Give him a nice honor guard here or at Constantine, some gold, and perhaps even a promotion."

"The Priest and honor guard are a good idea Frank, even the gold, but there's no promotion for a Special Constable. That's an honorary position in itself. He's a Native you know."

"Oh, right." Frank put his boots up on his desk and took a pipe from his breast pocket, "Any of that Cavendish left?"

"Certainly," George tossed Frank his beaded Gwich'in tobacco pouch.

Frank filled the bowl of his briar pipe with a pinch of aromatic tobacco, lit it with a big blue-headed match, and puffed contentedly, "So, what's the story on this little whore?"

"She's a killer, mentally askew as far as I can ascertain. I still can't reckon how she took on that fellow, but they say the truly mad have the strength of ten."

"Must be something in a bed I'd wager."

George leaned back in his chair, momentarily taken aback by the comment. He rubbed his nose and sighed, "She's but a slip of a girl too, yet she doesn't even deny killing him. Says she's proud of it."

"Really?"

He nodded, "Say's she had no choice, and that we wouldn't have done a damn thing until after he'd killed her anyway. I suppose she's right as far as that goes."

"Hard row to hoe."

"Come again?"

"Being a whore, I suppose."

George stared out at the parade ground as they smoked in the afternoon sun slanting through windows from the south. The days were fading fast, and the brief golden light was a balm that set them both to savoring the moment. An eagle cruised along the river and landed on one of the overburdened telephone poles along Front.

George sighed, stood, and reached for his favorite parka, a wolverine-trimmed caribou one with a band of beadwork around the bottom, and another down the shoulders and arms in the red, white, and blue colors of the British flag. He'd traded an old trapdoor Springfield to a Gwich'in for it and had taken delivery after the man's wife had finished several weeks of labor. He only wore it when he was in the Bush or wasn't representing the NWMP on public occasions however.

"Where are you off to?"

"To question the Perpetrator."

———

She was housed in a room at the rear of the hospital. Common drunks and whores were kept in a less secure area, but there were no cells for women of such a dangerous bent. An iron safe at the back of the room held the payroll for the Territorial bureaucracy and the detachment, and the room was secured accordingly. A cot had been set up along with a washbasin and a chamber pot.

George knocked before he had the guard open the door, and then stood for a moment while his eyes adjusted to the light. Alice Mary was on the floor with her legs crossed, clad in a drab cotton dress. She was barefoot, and her eyes were closed. "Ahem." She ignored him. "Excuse me." She didn't move an inch.

George glanced at the Constable, who shrugged. "Hain't made a peep all day. Didn't eat nothin' neither."

"Shut the door."

The Constable saluted and pulled the door shut.

George walked around the girl. Her elfin face looked as still and peaceful as a doll's, and there was a thin gold chain around her neck. He should have a matron remove that in the event she might try to strangle herself. He found his teeth in his lower lip and absently pulled at his mustache.

"The Mare sends her regards."

"Whatever are you talking about?"

"Why do you pretend you're so different? Even now you wonder 'bout me, how such a young toy for men's pleasure could do such bloody and awful deeds. Only chance says Ah weren't one a' the girls you bedded yourself, George. Me and the Mare are friends, you know."

"And such is the way it has always been in the world that we both know exists without these walls." He sat on the cot and put his hands together, "You could actually be hanged, Alice Mary, and I truly would be loath to see that."

"Valerie."

"Very well, Valerie. You might end up in an institution for the criminally insane if you cooperate. There is an excellent one in Montreal for women employing the newest techniques from Europe to excellent results. It is usually for women of the better classes, but I would do my *utmost* to find you a bed," he gazed into unblinking emerald eyes and sighed, "you are such a young—"

"Thing? A young thing?"

He clasped his hands and leaned toward her, "What is the source of this anger and violence?"

"Why would you care, Mr. Yellalegs?"

"I truly want to know. I've been exposed to a great deal of the baser deeds of men in the last twenty-five years, Alice Mary, um... Valerie, but I have never seen a man so butchered as that one at the Empire Hotel. My God... you drove that knife clean through him!" George put hands on his knees, took three measured breaths, and went on, "You look so fragile, so young, I—"

"And it brings out both the father in you and the lust in your loins, don't it? Pretty confusin', huh?"

"What?"

"The feelin's ain't always separate. Just ask my goddamn family."

"I... cannot comprehend such a thing."

"The Goddess knows them both. She's the one who does, who never forgets... and she knows me."

"Why do you persist in this double-talk?"

"Ain't double-talk, George, she's watchin' us as we speak."

He scowled and rose from the cot, "Then call upon her and have her spirit you away to some fine place where such madness rules supreme, and you may dance and sing to your heart's content. Where fountains spout wine and winters never come... and debts need not be paid!"

"She bides her time."

"And a Goddess's schedule isn't our own. Perhaps you'll be done for by the time she gets around to you."

"Perhaps," she grinned. "That Stick Sam sure is a hero."

"He is—" George sat back down and leaned toward her, "what do you mean? What have you heard of him?"

Her eyes seemed to grow larger until he was forced to blink the vision away. "She spoke to you as you pursued us when you were on your sled, and she tol' me 'bout your pipe bustin too. Believe me, George, she's watchin' us both."

George wiped trembling hands on his yellow-striped pants and made for the door.

XL.

Kate adjusted the tin tiara with seven candles and studied herself in the mirror. She struck a pose, spread her arms, straightened the headpiece, eyed herself again, and sighed, "It's just too *cheap* looking!"

"Not onstage Kitty. When the candles are burning, the flames are all they'll notice. The lights will be out and you'll have the presence of a goddess. It will grab them I promise you."

She turned to Alex, "Do you really think so, or are you simply being nice?"

"I'd wager the Orpheum. Why so ill at ease about such a tiny thing? They devour everything you do anyway."

Kate smiled, "I am so glad we took the leap and opened this place. I should place more faith in your judgment, Alex. Do you have a cigarette?"

"Certainly, my love." He produced a golden box from his breast pocket, being one of the few men in Dawson who preferred cigarettes to cigars. Alex had a tobacconist on York Street making them for him three times a week. It wasn't the cigarettes themselves but the short time it took to smoke them. Alex was a very busy man, and he was tired of leaving barely smoked cigars everywhere to be grabbed up by any transient who chanced to see them. It was a terrible waste of money. He handed a cigarette to Kate and lit it with a match he struck on the stove.

"Thank you," she took a drag and squinted at herself in the mirror through the smoke.

There was a knock on the door.

"Who is it?"

"It's Mary, I must talk to you!" Kate opened the door. Mary stood blinking with eyes on the verge of tears as Kate took the tin tiara off and took her hand. "What's that thing?"

"It's for Christmas Eve. I'm going to light candles on it and sing a song Eddie Doland's writing for the occasion."

"Oh," Mary eyed the cigarette in Alex's hand, and he gave her one. After he lit it, she resumed her dour expression.

"Whatever is the matter?"

"It's Joseph."

"You've seen him?"

"Yes, and he is worse-off than I'd feared."

"How do you mean?"

"He claims someone named Lorelei put him up to fleeing with little Alice Mary from the cribs after she killed that man in the Empire Hotel."

"Who did you say?"

"Someone named Lorelei. He's adamant about it."

Alex put a hand to his chin, "Lorelei, Lorelei... the name is familiar somehow."

"A Germanic siren that dwelt upon an island in the Rhine, she would lure sailors to her shores with her beautiful voice, to be dashed against the rocks and drown."

Mary shook her head, "You sure know a lot of stuff, Kate." She glanced about for somewhere to flick the ash, and Alex placed a bronze ashtray next to a chair where she sat down, "Joe claims that this... *Goddess* introduced us, if you can believe that. I met him at the Empire Hotel when he was looking for work for Christ's sake. He says this mysterious creature killed Fred Dodge too, and that he and I found the fellow's remains on King Solomon's Dome for that matter, and that this earring... oh, I don't know *what* this fucking earring has to do with anything! He is raving, Kate, utterly raving!"

"Well," Alex said, "we can use madness as a defense then."

Kate stared out the window at a lantern bobbing across the river's ice. "I remember that story Alice Mary told us on Halloween, how Fred Dodge disappeared from her crib just as he was about to do her harm. But, how could such a tiny thing kill that beast of a man that we chased out of here?"

Alex shrugged, "How did she gut Donald Johnson? Who knows? No one could believe that, but MacAtee and Surgeon Pare say they have the evidence, and now she's admitted it."

Kate took Mary's hand, "Does Joseph say he has personal knowledge of the murder of Mr. Johnson?"

"No... not that I know of."

"Well then, let him go on about goddesses and the like. He didn't know she was a killer. Obviously he just fell for her in a bed. He's but seventeen, and if that's a crime we're all guilty."

"How true, my lovely companion." Alex ran a hand through his hair, patted it back down, and wiped it on a towel, "That little whore is mad indeed, but sometimes the mad are frighteningly close to the truth. The ancients used such girls at Delphi as oracles, and history turned on their words."

"What do you mean?"

"When you sent me to warn her at Gertie's, she knew things about my own life that happened long ago and far away. She wasn't even born then. The girl has a strange touch, I'll vouch for that. There is something almost supernatural about her... something quite frightening actually."

"Lorelei," Kate muttered, "I swear that name rings a bell, if I could only recall where."

"Well," Mary said, "you're right about madness as a defense, but if Joe didn't know why bother? They should just let him go then."

Kate sprang up, "You're right! Let's go and get him!" She bounced on her feet and beamed, "We'll get Charlie Meadows and Swiftwater Bill and Eddie Doland, and we'll all go down to the fort and demand his release! Unless they have *proof* that he knew Alice Mary was a killer, they must let him go!"

"Yes!" Mary put a hand to her mouth, "I hope he isn't dangerous."

———

"You're a lucky fool, son." A voice echoed from the hallway.

Joseph rolled off the cot as a key ground in the lock. He'd been lying for a very long time with eyes closed trying to still his thoughts. First he would focus on Valerie, then Lorelei, then Valerie again. For his efforts he'd acquired nothing more than a headache. "What do you want?" he said as the door swung open.

"Me?" The guard growled, "I'd like nothin' more than to tan yer hide for bein' such a foolish little sonofabitch, traipsin' off with a damn murderin' whore in the middle a' fuckin' winter. But those that has the say, says yer walkin'."

"What?"

"Get yer arse up a'for somebody changes his mind, *I'd* say."

He was given his parka and gloves, and led across a dark parade ground past a brooding howitzer on hard rubber wheels toward a lighted office where Charlie Meadows was visible as he towered over several people. The red hair of Klondike Kate glowed under the bright electric lights, and a grin spread Joseph's cheeks in the frigid air.

Lily was the first to spot him. "Joe!" She threw open the door and sprang into his arms in a cloud of perfume, giggled, and squeezed his butt, "Are you crazy now? What the hell have you been doin', runnin' around the wilderness with Alice Mary? Jeez, is the little strumpet *that* good?"

"Lily!" Charlie levered her arm off Joseph's neck, "Not here. Don't talk about nothin' yet."

"Oh," Lily strove to look ashamed for the briefest instant before she turned back to Joseph with a grin, "well, Mary may think you're stark ravin' mad, but you look good enough to eat to me."

"I do not, Lily!"

"Well, Mary, you said—"

"Ahem!" Inspector MacAtee appeared in the doorway, and with a curt wave motioned them into order. Everyone dutifully fell silent and crowded around his desk.

George chewed on the stem of a new meerschaum pipe carved in the head of a Viking and sat down behind his desk as Joseph stood before it. Klondike Kate, Alexander Pantages, Swiftwater Bill Gates, Arizona Charlie Meadows, Gussie, Grace, and Nell Lamore, Mary, Lily, and Eddie Doland stood behind him. "You are to be released on the condition you remain within the boundaries of Dawson City until the investigation is finished into the murder of Donald Johnson and your testimony is taken before a court of law in the trial of Alice Mary Wright, on—"

"Valerie, sir, it's Valerie Mary Wright Walton now."

Mary's eyes widened, *"What?"*

Joseph thrust his chin out, "I married her properly before a Lutheran Priest at Bonanza Bar, on the Fortymile River in Alaska."

"Shit!"

"Please, Mr. Meadows, there shall be no profanity in this office."

"Damn!"

"You, sir, are treading on thin ice!"

"Your pardon, Guv'ner, I just can't believe this pup would go off and—"

"Joseph Aaron Walton, do you understand the terms of your release and promise to adhere to them?"

"What... what about Valerie?"

"Alice Mary Wright is a murderess, and I suggest you disregard that mockery of a wedding under false circumstances and get on with your life, and I hope all present shall never again mention it outside the confines of this room. You were obviously under the diabolical influence of this sad, deranged, and pitiful girl. I rather empathize with your predicament son. There aren't many lovely girls in these parts, and she does lay claim to that in spite of her profession. You're young and obviously prone to being swept away by such things on the often perilous road to manhood," George leaned back in his chair, "well," he pulled at his mustache, "the business at hand is concluded. You may go, if you agree to the terms of your release, Mr. Walton."

Joseph hesitated as the others began to shuffle about. He cleared his throat, "I appreciate your doing this Inspector MacAtee and will keep to the terms of my release, so help me God, but I must see Valerie once before I leave, please."

George relit his pipe, leaned back, and studied Joseph through a cloud of smoke, "You're making it harder for the both of you, son."

"Perhaps for me, but she needs to know someone cares, Inspector. What kind of man would I be to deny her that?"

George MacAtee stared at Joseph and ran a hand across his chin, "Very well but only for five minutes, and your friends will have to wait here."

"There's a bottle of champagne chillin' at the Palace Joe; don't take too long."

"I shall make sure that he doesn't Mr. Meadows."

———

George led him across the parade ground to the room where Valerie was imprisoned. "She speaks of goddesses and demons, and will not eat."

"She awaits me."

"Don't do anything foolish son. You're free now. You're but a strapping lad of seventeen, and I'd truly hate to see you foul up the rest of your life for such as she."

"Don't worry, Inspector MacAtee."

Valerie's eyes were welded to his as the door opened. She moved toward him, but stopped a pace away and held out her hands as George left the room and shut the door. Joseph stared into her eyes and swallowed. Her hands were warm and he felt a surge of energy: an inkling of that rush of light made flesh running through them in a glorious river that he'd only begun to know. Something rolled down his cheek.

"Don't worry Joe, all's as it should be."

"You may be hanged."

"Rather be burned. Ah seen it happen to somebody better than me already."

"She brought us to this. I can only wonder why."

"She was doin' me a favor. Couldn't stand to see a girl so abused, and Ah found her again 'cause Ah *had* to, but it was my own doin', and Ah got no regrets."

"She's taken away the memory of her from everyone but we two. They don't even know she exists."

"Boy... *that's* a good trick. Wish Ah coulda done that 'bout a million times already."

"Have you spoken to her?"

"You mean has she spoke to me. Nope, it's like she just up and made herself scarce as magnolia trees on that ridge up there where Honey Bee's sleepin' for eternity." She kissed him, and they stood rocking in each other's arms. He stroked her hair as their breathing merged. "But Ah been dreamin' like never before in my life Joe, dreamin' of a world where we can be free. Ah seen things that make me happy, that will make me strong when the hard times come, even if the Yellalegs kill me."

Joseph kissed her brow, "I know why she chose me now."

"Why?"

"For you."

The sound of a key in the lock announced the return of Inspector MacAtee, and he stepped into the room eying his prisoner with something akin to gentleness.

"I wonder what she had in mind for us?"

Valerie chuckled, "You know, we gotta be one god-awful bother to her."

He choked on a laugh and wiped his eyes, "What shall become of you?"

"Whatever it is, Ah'm glad Ah got this chance to know so many things that were there all the time. You know, you're only the second love Ah ever have had."

There was a cough from George, but Joseph ignored him. The truth of what she said was so clear that nothing else mattered. "There must be a reason for all this... there *has* to be!"

"Remember the gratitude we felt together at Bonanza Bar, and in our dreams? We were sharin' that whilst we was locked apart like dogs in a kennel, but we was together in spirit... *together*, Joe. The... what do you call it? The—"

"Grace!"

"Yes!"

"Yes, yes, my love!"

"Only love remains. After all else is dead and done, love goes on. She showed us that. Everythin' else is but a dream anyway. Don't forget that no matter what."

"Never!"

XLI.

"SONSABITCHES GOT LITTLE ALICE ALL LOCKED UP," LULU MUMBLED AS she poured brandy into a dirty glass. She spilled some on her bare leg and wiped it with a pillow.

Jack rubbed reddened eyes and groaned, "Say what?"

"Alice Mary, the one the other girls call Baby. She's but a little thing from the cribs that wouldn't hurt a fly, and she nearly got killed by Fred Dodge, and now they're chargin' her with killin' this great big ol' lug at the Empire Hotel."

"Who is?"

"The Yellaleg *Mounties,* ya dummy!"

"Hey, now . . ."

"Oh pshaw, I'm sorry, darlin'," Lulu laughed and jumped on the bed, spilling more brandy. "Ever have Pisco from Chile?" It's like this stuff but stronger. Got it in Frisco and it'll knock ya for a loop, Pisco from Frisco."

Jack tugged a bit of lint from his mustache and grinned, *"Piss?* What in 'ell would I be drinkin' piss for?"

She punched his shoulder, *"Pisco,* ya big lug, it's from Chile. My husband said he'd buy me a barrel of it when we went to Frisco."

"Husband?"

"Oh... that was then, this is now. Mel MacDonald from Hunker Creek, I gave him my hand for a year for my weight in gold."

"Well, you oughta be set up fine then."

"Yep, 'cept I lost most of it on the wheels at the Monte Carlo after the sonofabitch went and pissed me off and I whacked him with a fry pan. He can cook his own goddamn bacon... and fuck his eggs! Swiftwater Bill still gives me free drinks sometimes though."

"Pisco'ed ya off, eh?"

"Ha!" Lulu planted a sloppy kiss on his lips, "Yer a stallion, Jack. Ready for another go-round?"

Jack grinned again as her hand slid up his thigh. He'd been on a tear for a week, and somehow had wound up with Lulu, "Like me digs? I might have room for ya upstairs if you're thinkin' 'bout stayin' round."

Lulu lowered the shoulder of her black teddy slip to expose her right breast with the tattoo of a devil and pitchfork, and thrust it in his face with a giggle. Jack squeezed it appreciatively.

———

George examined himself in the mirror, tugged a sleeve of his red coat down, and brushed the gold braid on a black cuff. He adjusted his dress hat and placed it even more squarely upon his head. The man gazing back at him from the glass had the trim build of someone much younger, though the lines in his weather-hardened face betrayed his age to anyone who cared to examine him for more than a moment. Not that the Mare would care. He was taking Edie to the Orpheum to see a new show by a troupe of players arriving from White Horse who'd been stranded there by the river freezing and had recently arrived after it had set up properly for winter travel.

Edie was good company, her profession included, and George could count on the night ending in a bed at the Fairview Hotel in a room he'd rented from Belinda Mullroney, who could be trusted to keep such things under her hat. He was very much looking forward to it, especially after the trip to capture that murdering little whore.

The person gazing back at him gave him a look he didn't much like. George swore and went to the window to gaze out at a dark sky. The aurora was aflame above the pale swath of Moosehide Slide. It reminded him of footlights shining through cigar smoke, illuminating the silhouette of some great dark form upon a monstrous stage: something moving that he couldn't quite see. George shook away the image. *Where do such thoughts come from?*

A feeling of things beyond his touch that he could never hope to know, let alone control, brought on a deep melancholy. A growl ground its way up his throat as if he wanted to spit something out. He didn't even know where his mind was drifting... or why.

Soft laughter rippled through him like a summer breeze, and he was filled for a moment with a wonderful feeling of familiarity... of *rightness.* George rubbed his eyes.

"Damn!" He grabbed his parka and headed across the parade ground for the room at the back of the hospital.

———————

She didn't seem the least surprised at his visit, although he couldn't see her expression. She'd unscrewed the single bulb and was only a dark form with her eyes showing in the dimness. George envisioned her outlined against the night sky with curtains of light dancing behind her and a black void beyond.

"Excuse me."

"Had men slip into a room like that before, George. Wish you knew what it's like to get raped."

"I'm not—"

"Ah know. Sit down."

He sat on the cot, an arm's distance away.

"You came 'cause you heard her laugh, 'cause she's touched you before, and your heart ain't bad."

"Who... who was that?"

"You met her. She just won't let you remember. She can't afford to all o' the time," Valerie yawned. "You can get in a passel a' shit just bein' here in this room with me this time a' night. Guess you got more balls than Ah gave you credit for, Inspector Yellalegs."

He began to rise, "I really should not be here."

A small hand grabbed his shoulder and sat him back down with a grip that ground the bones together, and he gasped.

"Think we oughta talk."

"Very well... Valerie."

"Thanks. That's my name now. You understand why Ah kilt that fella, don'tcha?"

"I... perhaps."

"He was every sonofabitch who every hurt me, from my very own uncle right up through that goddamn Fred Dodge, but more than that, Ah learned that Ah could fight back."

"You did quite a job of it I must say."

"Us goodtime girls don't see a lot a' good times George. Sex is some-thin' you fellas gotta have, but when a girl gives it to you, most often you treat her like a dirty rag," Valerie seemed to grow larger until her silhouette in the darkened room began to dwarf him, "let alone give a girl room to enjoy herself."

He inhaled and cleared his throat.

"The Mare, there's somebody you like 'cause she don't give you back the like too easy, 'least not for money. You can fuck her, but you can't touch who she is. No way. And she's big and strong. You like the way she takes over in a bed, don'tcha?"

"You're remarkably strong for your size, Valerie. My shoulder is sore this instant."

"Ah could handle you like you wouldn't believe, but you're never gonna know that. But my real strong is different. Ah got a precious gift from somebody when Ah saw things those who came before me suffered. Ah saw their strength and it's made me stronger. And we're made to have babies after all. That hurts powerful bad they say."

"I must say I'm not happy about taking you to trial. It's not a pleasant prospect for me whatsoever, but I shall do my utmost to see that you are not hanged, and that you are given some chance to have a better life in the future, even if it is at a more advanced age."

"Thanks George, Ah'm never gonna get there anyway."

———

Lulu stood in the splendid bathroom above Jack's saloon holding a kerosene lamp over an open poke and let out a squeal of delight. Jack was way gone from a week of hard drinking and plenty else, and he hadn't even noticed when she'd found it under his bed. He must have left it after he'd gone down to the basement and his safe. She'd checked twice and it hadn't been there earlier. Simple habit had made her look one more time after he'd passed out on the bed. She could use a bath, but wasn't going to take the time here. Nigger Jim Daughtery had a safe at the Pavilion and wouldn't ask where she got it for a share of the loot.

She cut down Eighth to Queen and headed for Jim's place, but as she approached the plank fence running around the Segregated District, she saw Mollie Fewclothes and Three-Way Annie stepping out onto Fourth. "Hey, girls!" Lulu bounced the fat poke in her palm.

Mollie grinned, "What's for Lulu, got some other gink gonna pay you your weight in gold for a piece a' tail?"

"She's gained enough weight since then she don't need no Chinee chain mail shirt this time, Mollie."

"I was jus' about to buy you girls some champagne with this here gold, Annie. You should watch your big mouth, girl."

Mollie threw an arm around Lulu's waist, "Hey, Lulu, you know we're friends."

Lulu chuckled, "A girl needs all the friends she can get."

Annie snorted, "Got too many friends, all I need is money."

"With the way you take 'em two at a time, you oughta be rich."

"Naw, she gives 'em both half-price."

"Fuck you, Mollie."

The girls exploded in laughter.

Lulu bought two magnums of Moet champagne and a bottle of Beefeater Gin at the Westminster, and they headed for Mollie's new rooms above a dentist's on Front. She had recently moved out of the District, but was planning on spending the rest of the winter keeping both her crib and the apartment.

Lulu walked around the parlor room and gazed out the bay window at the waterfront as a low sun in the south shone through telephone lines throwing its last light on the wall in crimson bars. She whistled, "How didya find this place?"

"Doc Horton likes me, and I signed a contract with him for the room 'for he changed his mind."

"He likes what you do, anyway."

"Yeah... but don't he know he can get in dutch with the Yellalegs?"

"Got family in Ottawa, and say's he's related to Sam Steele himself somehow. Nobody'll make no noise as long as I keep a lid on it." Mollie sat on the couch, "Beats the hell outta the District, that's for sure."

"Damn," Lulu plopped down on the couch beside her and produced a silver tube with a screw cap from between her breasts. She rotated it in her fingers and tapped it loudly on the table, "Want some cocaine?"

"Sure! Where didya get that?"

"Jack Finley's."

"Oh."

Lulu unscrewed the cap, took a framed oval picture of Mollie's mother down from the wall, and tapped a pile on the glass, "Snort it right in yer nose," she said, and began to crush the powder into finer grains with the ivory butt of a .32 Colt revolver she produced from her purse.

"Don't break the glass."

"Don't worry," Lulu rolled a big blue Canadian bill she'd taken from Jack's wallet into a tube, "I lost the teeny little silver spoon, but this is better." She held it out to Mollie, "Have some."

"Just snort it up the tube?"

"Uh-huh. I been doin' it with Jack for three days now. You get a lot more with this than a little ol' spoon and it sure makes work easy too."

"I bet."

'Hurry up, Mollie!"

"Hol' your horses, Annie," Mollie snorted a line of cocaine off the glass, put hands to her face, and immediately began to sneeze.

"*Watch it!*" Lulu seized the picture just as Annie was about to snort some, and Mollie sneezed violently blowing a bit of stray powder off the table, "Whew," Lulu gasped, "saved it!" She handed the picture back to Annie and popped the cork on a magnum of champagne.

Two hours later they were finishing the gin and singing snatches of bawdy songs from the dance halls. Annie was bragging about a fellow she'd met from Eldorado who claimed he was going to marry her and take her to Spokane. Mollie was talking about opening a place in Nome and buying a house on Nob Hill in Frisco. Lulu stared out the window, lost to the world.

"Hey, Lulu, wanta go find a highroller at the Palace?"

Annie snorted, "Are you crazy Mollie? You can't go in there. The Mounties will have us scrubbin' their drawers at Fort Herchmer if we're caught in some high-tone theater."

"Hell with them! I got weighed in gold from Mel McDonald six weeks ago in that place."

"That was before you whacked him on the head and took off with his loot and put in a stint on the Line when it ran out. Everybody in town knows that, hon. Once you work the Line you ain't goin' back to no fancy-dancy theaters. Think the Yellalegs don't know you was playin' with them ginks' peters just like the rest a' us?"

"Yeah Lulu, you're a whore for shore."

"Shut up, Annie. Never took it like you did, in the—"

"Lotsa room you got to talk. You ain't no better than the rest a' us Lulu. Hell, if I had the money Mel give ya I'd be long gone from this place and livin' like Lady Stanford on Nob Hill."

"Shut up Mollie."

"You shut up, Lulu!"

"Ya bitch!"

Lulu sprang across the table with her hands reaching for Mollie's throat. Mollie shrieked and stepped back as Lulu's fingers caught in the dark curls of her hair. "Ow!" Mollie bellowed as a wad of it came free in Lulu's hand.

"Hey! You two stop it!"

"Ya bitch!" Mollie punched Lulu in the stomach, and her other hand pushed Lulu's face back with a finger poking Lulu's right eye. Lulu bit her finger, Mollie screamed, and the two of them parted panting. Mollie clutched her hand spewing threats and curses, bared her teeth, and showed Lulu a bloody middle finger in a gesture of contempt.

"Goddamn pieceashit!" Lulu spat. She swept up the kerosene lamp on the credenza against the wall and threw it.

Mollie yelped and sprang out of the way. The lamp flew past her to shatter against the papered wall, and a pool of kerosene ignited as it spread across the floor. Yellow flames licked up the wainscoting in an instant.

"Oh no!" Three-Way Annie howled, and ran out the door and down the stairs. Two fires had been started by goodtime girls in Dawson already and had burned down great swaths of town. She wasn't going to be around for this one.

XLII.

THE ACTORS ON THE STAGE BELOW FLITTED LIKE FIGURES ON A PLANE OF smoky glass: transparent beings from another world without substance between him and all he knew... and all he loved.

"Wasn't that clever, Joseph?"

"What?"

"It's Oscar Wilde. There are so many double entendres he weaves into the dialogue. I do so miss such little diversions. The English are so sophisticated. It's brilliant."

He stood, "I'm sorry Kate, I can't concentrate at the moment." Joseph felt Mary's hand on his own and squeezed it reflexively.

"Where are you going?"

"Just down to the water closet."

"All right... Joe?"

"What?"

"You're all right, aren't you?"

"Certainly," Joseph descended the stairs and took his coat from the adolescent girl who used to sell waffles. He handed her a small nugget, passed the bar of the Orpheum nodding at several people who seemed to know him, and stepped onto the porch. The sky was clear and moonless black. The air was very cold and stars burned like ragged blazing holes torn in the vault of night, hardly twinkling through the thin air of the north.

"What am I supposed to do?" he demanded of a night devoid of the lights that had become his friend in solitude. Their shimmering dance across the sky reminded him of feelings he could not give name to, feelings that came only with Lorelei... and Valerie. The lights were gone as if they too had been but figments of his imagination. "No!" He spat on the frozen street. *Damn it, Lorelei is real! Valerie was destined to be my lover and it's real!*

A shout from down the street broke into his funk, followed by a woman's scream. A red glow from the second-story windows of a building down Front brought him back to the present as the word being shouted and passed from voice to voice, over and over, broke into his reverie: *Fire!*

He stepped into the street to get a better view of the conflagration bringing people out into the frozen night. A loud clanging arose, and Joseph turned to see a team of horses pulling a wagon with a steam engine mounted upon it manned by several men who were all shouting at once. The fire appeared to have started above a dentist's office at the corner of Church and Front, and a breeze from the northwest was spreading it to other buildings. It had crossed Church and was working its way toward warehouses along the Klondike River. The scaffolding of the Presbyterian Church under reconstruction from the last fire was being draped by parishioners with blankets soaked in water that froze as soon as they were laid in place, and they began to steam as the flames approached.

Mounties were streaming from the gates of Fort Herchmer toward the massive Commissioner's Residence where smoke was coming from the roof as voices rose in alarm all around him. "Not again!" someone roared. There was a dull boom as something in the dentist's office exploded, and a pillar of red smoke full of sparks twisted toward the sky showering glowing embers across the roof of the Commissioner's Residence and the Mountie post.

"Get the hoses! Get the hoses!"

Several men appeared from the direction of Harper Street with a roll of flat canvas hose on a wagon and began to pull it onto the river ice. Two men were throwing wood in the boiler of a donkey engine mounted on a sled, and another was chopping furiously in the bobbing light of storm lanterns at a hole in the ice that had been frozen over for some time, as those whose job it was to maintain the holes for fire-fighting in the event of another conflagration had been in the saloons.

"Give us a hand!" someone yelled.

Joseph pulled on his gloves and sprang to help, fumbling with the six-inch canvas hose as they snaked it toward the hole and secured it to an iron pump on the engine with a brass fitting. Another hose was attached to the other end of the pump, and the engine began to turn over as steam formed in the boiler.

He took the axe from the hands of the first man who'd been chipping at the ice, who was now bent over with his hands on his knees. It was Bill Gates. Since his heroics at Five Finger Rapids that had earned him the moniker Swiftwater two summers before, the company of dance hall girls and a diet of champagne, whiskey, opium and cigars hadn't done much for his stamina it seemed.

Joseph jumped into the hole to get closer to the mark, praying he wouldn't fall through when it broke, and took a swing. Others called encouragement as he hacked away in the waxing light that made the surface of the river a weird tableau of red.

"Here, damn it!" A miner shouted and held up an iron bar used for moving rocks in the diggings.

Joseph nodded and climbed out of the hole. The man jumped in and began savagely stabbing at the bottom. Joseph wiped his face as sweat froze on the end of his nose.

Another man appeared with dynamite, set it in the bottom, threw ice on top, stomped it tight, and clambered out of the hole. He lit the fuse, and there was a WHUMP as water geysered in a million droplets that became crystals of ice and sparkled in a glittering cascade in the red light of the flames.

"Wa-hoo!" a voice from the saloons shouted.

The donkey engine was chugging, and the conical brass end of the hose was inserted into the hole.

Joseph glanced back toward town and gasped. The flames had spread down Front and up Church, where more buildings were being draped in blankets doused in water that froze on the instant in an attempt to protect the dry and fragile edifices beneath.

The hose filled, and ten men pulled it toward the fire as an arc of water began to sputter from the end. There was a cheer as the front of the Commissioner's house was splattered under the direction of the Mounties before the hose coughed and the flow slowed. There were curses as it stopped completely.

"She's froze!" a man yelled, and ran to the hose and kicked it, "Ow!" He hopped on one foot. Where the man's boot had connected with the hose, it had split open to reveal a solid cylinder of ice. Flames were beginning to rise behind the walls of Fort Herchmer.

"Valerie!" Joseph burst into a sprint across the river ice and almost collided with two men hustling down the bank. He dodged one, sprang past the other, reached the surface of Front Street on all fours, and rose to his feet.

Mounties and civilians were running to and fro through the gate of the fort with axes, buckets of sand, and blankets. Cries for water rose above the crackling sound of flames as they feasted on tinder-dry wood. The hospital was being emptied, and a man was being led out with eyes bandaged and hands held out before him by two women in high-collar black dresses. One of them glanced at Joseph and shook her head. "They're all out!"

Joseph ignored her and ran through the door. Thick smoke hung at head height. He coughed, dropped to the floor, and his fingers touched hot wood as he moved in a crouch through the smoky darkness.

A woman behind him screamed, "Out, everybody out! Don't go in there!"

Joseph felt his way. His eyes stung. His throat ached. His chest felt like hot iron filings were filling it. He found the steel door at the end of the hall where the safe and Valerie were kept and seized the handle. It was locked, and he gave it a fierce heave. The room was sealed tight, and he pounded on the door. "Valerie!" There was no sound.

Joseph laid his face against the door with his head spinning from lack of air. He dropped back to the floor and inhaled the cleaner air drifting across it. The smoke was thickening as flames roared above and behind him.

There was a loud groan overhead and a popping sound before a burning roof beam accompanied by shards of boards crashed through the smoke to land in an explosion of sparks on the floor behind him. Joseph sprang back against the door.

"Joe!" A faint voice came from beyond it.

"Valerie!"

"Ah take it back! Ah don't wanta be burned!"

He took a breath, stood up, and seized the handle of the door again. It was hot. He hissed, closed his throbbing hands around it, yanked, and yanked again. He coughed violently as smoke poured into his lungs.

"Get outside!"

"No! I will never leave you!"

"Get a axe and go for the window!"

"Wha... you're right!"

He dropped to his knees and scuttled across the floor around a burning pile of debris. More flaming wood fell from the floor above as Joseph staggered onto the parade ground retching. He rubbed stinging eyes and almost walked into a cannon squatting in the snow. A man dressed in a silk vest and pinstriped shirt with arm garters passed by with an axe in one hand and a bucket of sand in the other. "Give me that axe!"

The man stuttered, "Wha . . ?"

Joseph seized the axe from his hand and ran around the building screaming at the top of his lungs. A row of barred windows greeted him, and his head swung from one end to the other. Smoke poured from the ones on his right. "Valerie!"

Glass exploded from a narrow window to his left, and two small hands appeared from between the bars. "Here!"

"Stand back! Get away from the window!"

The hands disappeared.

He swung at the base of the window, and a painful tremor ran up his arms as the axe bounced back with a clang. The bars were set in a strip of iron placed across the sill, for just such an occasion as someone trying to break in. "Damn!"

"Joe! The smoke is awful!"

"Lay on the floor!" He swung at the log wall, and the blade stuck. He put his foot against the log and tugged with a scream of frustration. The axe came free, and he ran back to the front of the building.

The upstairs was burning like a torch with smoke pouring from the first-floor doors and windows. It wouldn't be minutes before the room holding the girl he'd come to love with his all became her flaming tomb. She could be dying already. Joseph let out a howl and sprang into the hospital with the axe over his head.

He stumbled through a boiling caldron, leapt over flaming debris, and swung the axe by instinct as he approached the door at the place where the hinges met the wall. It sunk deep with a sound lost in the roar of the fire and he worked at the heavy hinge, twisting with all his might. His lungs were searing in his chest. Joseph pulled the axe free and swung again. He screamed from the pain and dropped to his knees. Blackness and heat were seizing him, trying to enter his every pore through his clothes with maniacal joy like a burning demon. It felt as if his hair were burning off his head to leave a blistered and blazing skull that would explode at any moment.

A scalding wave of air crashed over him as he was swept from the floor and flung into the night. Soft lips touched his, and sweet, clean air poured into his lungs. His very cells blazed with another kind of fire as beautiful voices filled a skull that had been about to burst. He'd been carried from the inferno in the arms of an angel.

Save Valerie! he cried out in a voice more real than mouths could ever form as his fingers clutched at skin like a silken raiment underlain with steel. He stared into eyes that were huge and the color of the fire itself: a deep and glowing red with the blood that had ruled Nations. A tent of hair hung all around him accompanied by the scent of flowers.

Lorelei glanced at the hospital and brushed hair from her face, "I am not looking forward to this!"

Joseph lay on the frozen parade ground as his soul opened to the sky like a flower. Tears of gratitude froze as they reached his ears and throat, forming crystals of ice. Lorelei stood above him in the light of the flames, naked and beautiful. The glow from her skin was brighter than the fire itself, bathing her in an aura as if the lights of the north had entered her and illuminated her from within. A smile flashed across her face, and she disappeared into the burning hospital.

The building gave out a groan as the roof beam broke and the upstairs began to sag as it fell into the floor below. A cloud of sparks spread across Joseph on a wall of hot air, and he let out a yelp and began to roll away from the wave of heat as a flailing body landed across him. He tumbled with Valerie in a tangled pile of limbs, gasping and coughing. Joseph rose to his knees and seized her in his arms. She moaned and hugged him as huge sobs wracked her chest. He kissed her trembling mouth, pressing his face against a throat smelling of smoke and sweat and tears that froze as they fell. He ran his hand through damp hair and held her head, staring over the top of it at the flaming pile of the hospital.

"Lorelei!"

Valerie shook like a leaf in his arms, and let out a wail. "She's in there Joe! She's dead!"

XLIII.

JOSEPH AND VALERIE STUMBLED ONTO GERTIE'S PORCH SHIVERING AND wrapped in smoky blankets. They'd hardly recognized it, as the house was draped in frozen bedspreads hung in protection against the fire. The roof of the Commissioner's Residence still steamed nearby, and Gertie's place looked downright morbid sheathed in ice and misshapen from the covering, but a light was on. Joseph pounded on the door, and the glass in the little window rattled. The red silk curtain finally pulled back, the Mare's face filled the glass, and the door flew open.

Edith Neal seized both of them by the shoulders and dragged them inside with enough force to throw Valerie across the room. Joseph tripped over her and went sprawling as Edie slammed the door behind them. "Nice to see you kids. Have yourselves a grand time on the Fortymile?"

"Jesus Edie, you didn't have to—"

"Oh yes I *did*. Anybody see you?"

"No," Valerie answered, "The fuckin' Yellalegs left me in that place to burn."

Joseph swiped at his sooty face, "I think they forgot in the ruckus. MacAtee wouldn't let you die like that. I bet he's pretty shook up about it right this minute."

Valerie sniffed and wiped her face, "Good!"

The Mare placed three teacups on the kitchen table, poured black English tea from a blue ceramic pot, and placed sliced lemons, sugar, and cream next to them, "She said you'd be comin'."

"Who?"

"Lorelei. Who else?"

"You *spoke* to her?"

"Sure honey, we're friends."

Joseph's mouth fell open, and Valerie made a high-pitched giggle. He shook his head, "Thank God somebody still remembers her besides us two!"

"Some girls can keep their traps shut. Besides, if she ever tried to take my memory away, I'd kick her sleek white supernatural arse all the way to Nome."

"How would you know?"

Edie grinned, "Good question, and like all good questions it's one that can't be answered without a lot of consideration." She sipped her tea, "You two are supposed to leave here pronto by the way, while they think you're dead."

"They do?"

"Sure. She was locked up in a room that's smoldering ashes, and you were last seen runnin' in there with an axe in your hands screamin' like a crazy man right before the whole kit and caboodle came down in flames."

"How did—"

Valerie seized his arm, "See, Joe, Ah tol' you she was watchin' out for us!"

Joseph sat on the couch with the cup in unsteady hands, "I need a moment to get my bearings." He leaned back against the white knitted coverlet and his hair made a smudge, "Jesus, there's so much I don't know: how this all happened... what was meant to be. We can't be more than a little burr that got under her saddle somehow. I guess she felt she had to take care of us because she's just that way, but what about her? She ran into that burning building and never came out." He blinked away something and put down the cup, "Is she dead?"

"Hope to God not," Edie muttered. "We need all the girls like her Providence can muster and she says she's the last. Anyway she told me you'd be comin' so I bet she had something figured out. We'll just have to go along with her instructions and get you set to travel."

Valerie stared into the distance with a dirty face and drained her tea

"You two need a bath. Alice Mary knows where the tub is."

"It's Valerie, Edie."

"Sure dear, whatever."

———

Jack's reddened eyes roved about the room seeking the solace of a drink. His head was splitting. "Just sleep," he lifted a warm bottle of beer to cracked lips. A terrible thirst was constricting his throat as if two rough hands were choking the life from him. A thud in his chest was followed by a sudden sharp pain, "Me 'eart!" He sat up and coughed, finished the beer in one gulp, and let the bottle roll onto the floor. Jack fell back with a moan to stare at the ceiling and rubbed his eyes. A chuckle rippled tobacco-stained lips, "King o' the Klondike!" he proclaimed to the beams overhead.

People had said he wouldn't get enough business at the base of the hill where he'd built his digs after the business district had filled up, and now their joints had burned. The fire had stopped two blocks up from the river, and had taken a nice big bite out of the saloons, hotels, and showhouses there. The ground was well-froze, and it would be a while before most of his competition could get back in action. Meanwhile Jack was sitting on a big pile of Irish whiskey and Chilean brandy in the basement, all nine breweries in town were unscathed, and he had plenty of special stuff besides. The smell of smoke was a tonic to his blood-clotted nostrils.

"Business 'll be rippin' tonight!"

He ought to get bathed, dressed, and go down to greet some of the newly displaced. People would be wandering in to console themselves over a drink, and to talk about the fire while he commiserated and showed sympathy by offering them a free one. Opportunity abounded. Jack coughed and shook his head. *Two damn tired.* It had been a hell of a run and he had to get some sleep. His heart felt like a player piano with too many holes punched in the roll.

A seductive scent mixed with the smell of smoke wafted into his half-plugged nose, and he glanced around. "Lovely." A vision of fresh clover in a spring meadow came to him, and the barely remembered flash of a girl's perfume the first time his father had taken him to Dublin, mixed with the smell of peat fires under a fat harvest moon.

"That memory's as pretty as a poem, Jack. It's more than I expected of you."

He sat up with a start, searching for the source of that utterly feminine voice.

A dark form stood in the hall with two eyes glowing like copper coins in the yellow lamplight fixing him like a hare in the gaze of an owl. The creature that stood before him was a mass of blackened and burned flesh with her skull visible where white cheekbones protruded from the seared skin of a face that had been beautiful. Even now it had a grace to it, like a sculpture half-begun or half-destroyed. The shining hair that had wreathed her form was gone, burned off completely. White teeth shone in a death's grin through the remnants of full lips that were now paper-thin shards of dying flesh. She groaned and lifted the blackened claw of a hand to them. "Not my usual appearance." The creature let out a rattling sigh, and her voice softened, "I'm in great pain, Jack, and I'm going to need your help."

"Daemon!" He sprang back against the headboard, and it banged like a gun against the log wall as visions of darkness and barrow mounds hiding the angry shades of witches and warlocks of ancient times filled him. He saw tall stone in a foggy meadow under a harvest moon and heard the screams of tortured souls. Jack's heart rose into his throat as those blood–red eyes gazed upon him. He slapped himself, and blood flew from his ravaged nose, "Jesus, Mary and Joseph, wake up, Jack!"

Musical laughter came from the being that tottered on fleshless feet before him, "You're quite awake."

"What *are* you!"

"They can't hold a candle to ya, lass," Jack's own voice came from the thing that stood before him, who drew closer as she spoke his own words, "Sweet Jesus, you and I are the perfect partners for this."

"Lorelei!"

I have returned your memory of me. It's only fair that you should know me, at least as best as you can."

"A witch of Satan you are!"

"No I'm not, but I don't have time to explain things. I'm growing weaker by the moment and I don't have the luxury of indulging your curiosity for a lesson that's wasted on your selfish soul... and it's not like you'll be around to use it anyway," a sigh rattled her singed lips, "It's time for you to do your part."

"Wha—"

She threw him on the bed and ripped off his pants. A piece of her tore off in a blackened strip on the point of his nugget-studded belt buckle as she did, and it tumbled through the air with his trousers like a strip of smoked salmon from a summer's catch. The smell of smoke was overpowering as she rose above him with eyes the color of blood and mounted him as he quaked like a leaf in a gale. Jack's chest constricted in a rush of terror, and he made a pitiful cry as he attempted to utter a prayer that fell from his mouth in a torrent of babbling.

Part of her was truly sorry as well as self-conscious at her appearance. She shook it off and, returning to the task at hand, commanded him to produce an erection. Lorelei forced it deep inside her, past the seared skin of her thighs, past the hungry lips of her womanhood no longer pink and sweet but blackened and dry. She let out an enormous sigh as she took without reservation every drugged, drunken, and polluted drop of Jack's life and mortal essence. He vibrated like a bell and became translucent, exposing every layer and sheath of muscle, every organ glowing in its juices as the beating of his heart became a raging drum. The sound of that sea of souls became a roar as it swallowed him with something far greater, something even Jack belonged to as Lorelei took his life that she might keep her own.

She released the empty husk and sank to her knees. New skin stung as it rubbed against the Turkish carpet. She bent over trying not to vomit. Her head swam. Lorelei put trembling fingers to her face and felt the tender young flesh upon it. She ran them up her cheeks, across fresh little ears, and over her head. Downy new hair greeted her hesitant fingers: soft, short hair like that of a baby that would swiftly grow longer. "God!"

Jack's soul cried like a cornered cat as it kicked and wailed in the vastness of her own. His petty character would fade quickly, as it contained nothing lasting, and Jack would disappear like a drop of water returning to the sea. Lorelei cracked her back to make room for knitting nerves as her senses returned. She must devour at least one more man to regain her corporate being. It was the only way.

She went to the mirror, where a red-skinned being stared back with eyes the color of blood, and willed them into their bright blue-green until only tiny flecks of vermillion betrayed the spirit within. Lorelei leaned toward the glass and touched the skin of an again lovely face. She examined her hands and flexed graceful fingers. Now that she had come out of the shock of the burning with one poor meal, she was starving. Each and every cell of her cried out for sustenance that she might become fully herself again, and the drugs and alcohol in Jack just made it worse. She sighed and ran hands through her hair once more. It had reached her ears.

She didn't look half-bad with short hair. Some earrings would set it off, at least when her skin was a nice white again, but by then it would be long of course. She took a deep breath and cracked her neck.

Well. One more worthless sonofabitch was on the agenda for the unexpected fulfillment of his life tonight, someone who hadn't gotten too drunk hopefully, some handsome and healthy yet cruel and selfish man that Dawson wouldn't miss in the morning. There were plenty to choose from. She took a deep breath and went into the night.

Valerie heated water for a bath, poured in something from a tall crystal decanter that made bubbles, and they slipped into the tub to scrub off the smoke and soot. Afterward she drained the tub and refilled it with hot water and lavender salts, and they lay with arms around each other staring into space. Joseph kissed her ear.

She lit a ceramic pipe, and he shook his head when she offered it. "Nope, the high life of Dawson isn't for me anymore."

Valerie let out a last cloud from her lungs and tossed the pipe in the water where it hissed, broke in two pieces, and disappeared, "You're right, that's done, and Ah'm not ever gonna work the cribs again long as Ah live either 'cause she tol' me never again. Hell... I'm married now. So what do we do, and where do we go?"

"I don't know; we're not rich. Could you fancy Oregon?"

"Sure, but you're right, Joe, we ain't got a dime now." She put her hands behind her head and stared at the ceiling, "Ah wonder where Lorelei is."

He stroked her throat. "I wish I knew."

A sob trembled under his hand as it welled from her chest and her eyes filled with tears. "Said Ah'd take the burnin' Joe, and she took it for me. What if she's really dead? Then there'll be no more of her kind forever and ever and what will become a' things? She can't be dead; Ah don't deserve to live *that* much. Jesus Christ, she's a angel or a Goddess or somethin' from a place we can only touch in dreams, and Ah'm only a little whore from Virginia... least so far," she swallowed, "but she let me see where I'm *really* from." Another sob boiled up her throat, and she punched the water. It splashed across the floor accompanied by a grunt of misery, "She didn't have'ta *die* for me!"

Joseph stared at the window. No stars were visible as a frozen blanket blocked the view of night. A lump rose in his throat, and when he spoke his voice was a croak, "I pray to God she isn't dead. She's the very last of her kind after all. It would be the end of an entire age that people never even knew existed."

She wiped her eyes, "Ain't that strange, that we should pray to God for her?"

"No Valerie, not at all."

The stovepipe in the parlor ticked and soughed as its heat flowed into the night. They lay in silence with their hearts seeking the sky as the aurora danced unseen above them.

"Ah love her so much, Joe!"

"So do I."

"Why did she even save us?"

"I guess she loved us just as much."

She burst back into sobs, and he stroked her wet hair as she quaked in his arms. Joseph breathed her in, closed his eyes, and let her sorrow fill him knowing it was the gift of Lorelei that he could.

"You two gotta hustle!" Edie yanked Valerie out of the tub, threw a towel around her, and sat her on a stool. She cut her hair and dyed it red, then darkened Joseph's with something foul from another bottle while admonishing him to keep it out of his eyes. Afterwards Edie made them coffee and waffles, and they sat at the kitchen table in the hours before a late dawn discussing the journey to Skagway and boarding a steamer south.

"MacAtee will be siftin' those ashes with a rocker box come morning if he ain't already, lookin' for your bones. He don't give up easily, especially when his own charges disappear in a puff a' smoke, so we gotta get your arses up and out of here while the gettin's good," Valerie fingered her shorn locks and Edie slapped her hand, "Let it dry!"

"But, what happens when he don't find any bones, Edie?"

Edith smiled, "What makes you think he won't?"

"Huh?"

She changed the subject, "The train's runnin' again, so you just gotta get to White Horse somehow. I've got enough money for your passage, and some besides." She went to the other room and returned with two large pokes.

Valerie held a hand up, "You can't do that."

"Pshaw, what goes around comes around."

They stood at the sound of the back door as someone stepped into the house and stomped snow off their boots. Valerie slipped into the parlor and reappeared with her little chromed revolver.

Gertie appeared, saw Joseph, blinked, stared at Valerie, and blinked again as the diamond between her upper teeth flashed, "Not too shabby for a redhead, Alice Mary. I need a strong fella like Joe here to help me get this big 'ol box somebody left on my porch into the house before somebody sees it." They followed her to the door, where a stout birch box sat on the top step. "I've got plenty of admirers, but the note says this is for you. It even has Alice Mary's new name. It's Valerie, right?" Gertie pointed to a slip of paper tacked to the box.

Valerie nodded.

Joseph snatched up the paper and glanced down the alley at smoke rising from the remnants of a building across Church Street as the aurora spread its glory over Mooschide Slide. He took a deep breath of the cold air, closed his eyes, and called out to her with all his being.

"Joe?"

"Oh, yes," he grabbed the rope handles, gave a heave, and set it back down. "Damn, that's heavy!"

"Here," Edie took the other end, and they lugged it into the house.

Joseph read the note. When he finished he sighed and smiled at Valerie, "She's alive."

"What's it say?"

"You'll have a long time to learn how to read it yourself. I'll make sure of it."

Valerie tugged at the latch of the box and threw back the lid. Sacks of nuggets, flakes, and dust glowed in the light of the lamps, and she hefted one with a grunt. "Hey Edie, Gertie, guess you're gettin' some of our loot instead. What goes around, ya know!"

"Damn," Gertie said.

Valerie's eyes glistened.

There was a knock on the door. They hesitated for a moment before everyone rushed to open it.

Wasillie stepped off the porch and pointed to a waiting sled and team, "Just White Horse this time. Please send it back with my cousin Pete. He will meet you." He began to say something else, but shook his head and stalked off down the alley.

Joseph took the hand of his bride, "You ready?"

"You know it."

The Oregon Mare chuckled, "I wonder if we'll remember any of this at all. I wouldn't let a soul if I was dealin' her hand."

"Hope we do," Joseph gazed at Valerie, "she said my redemption was helping you remember. It would be a shame if we forgot now."

Valerie shrugged, "If'n we deserve to." She tossed a nugget toward the ceiling and caught it, "That's only fair I guess."

Joseph let out his breath, "It is, isn't it?"

THE END

THE AUTHOR HAS TRAVELED SINCE A TEEN AND HITCHHIKED AROUND THE west coast of North America at seventeen. He left San Francisco State College at twenty-two, where he was the only undergrad in the graduate writing department to journey to South Dakota as the student of an Oglala Lakota medicine man. He fled with the medicine man's abused girlfriend, ranged from the Canadian Rockies to Mexico, attended the University of Oregon's journalism department, the University of Alaska, and has lived in Alaska and the Pacific Northwest since. He's a founder of the Alaska Writers Guild, has worked with the American Indian Movement during the occupation of Alcatraz, has fished, logged, built log cabins in the wilderness of the northwest and Alaska, and has rescued a dozen sex slaves in Alaska since the times of the pipeline boom. He has known corrupt cops and politicians, upright madams and honorable criminals, spent a dark winter under a pall of volcanic ash keeping fifteen starving moose alive and looked down the muzzle blast of a pistol. He loves the haunted old towns of the west, from the Barbary Coast to the dirt streets of Dawson City Yukon Territory where the history of America changed and where the footprints of a goddess are easy to find, and often finds the ghosts he encounters there better company than newcomers. With proper coaxing, they occasionally speak to him.

www.ingramcontent.com/pod-product-compliance
Lightning Source LLC
Chambersburg PA
CBHW020934020726
47495CB00002B/497